The
Covenant

Also by Jeff Crook

The Sleeping and the Dead

The
Covenant

A JACKIE LYONS MYSTERY

Jeff Crook

Minotaur Books
New York

This is a work of fiction. All of the characters, organizations, and events portrayed in this novel are either products of the author's imagination or are used fictitiously.

THE COVENANT. Copyright © 2015 by Jeff Crook. All rights reserved. Printed in the United States of America. For information, address St. Martin's Press, 175 Fifth Avenue, New York, N.Y. 10010.

www.minotaurbooks.com

Library of Congress Cataloging-in-Publication Data

Names: Crook, Jeff.
Title: The covenant : a mystery / Jeff Crook.
Description: First edition. | New York : Minotaur Books, 2016. |
    Series: Jackie Lyons mystery ; 2
Identifiers: LCCN 2015037862 | ISBN 9781250000293 (hardcover) |
    ISBN 9781250031426 (ebook)
Subjects: LCSH: Women detectives—Tennessee—Memphis—
    Fiction. | Women mediums—Fiction. | Murder—Investigation—
    Fiction. | Paranormal fiction. | BISAC: FICTION / Mystery &
    Detective / Police Procedural. | FICTION / Mystery &
    Detective / Women Sleuths. | GSAFD: Mystery fiction.
Classification: LCC PS3553.R5463 C66 2016 | DDC 813/.54—dc23
LC record available at http://lccn.loc.gov/2015037862

ISBN 978-1-250-00029-3 (hardcover)
ISBN 978-1-250-03142-6 (e-book)

Our books may be purchased in bulk for promotional, educational, or business use. Please contact your local bookseller or the Macmillan Corporate and Premium Sales Department at (800) 221-7945, extension 5442, or by e-mail at MacmillanSpecialMarkets@macmillan.com.

First Edition: January 2016

10 9 8 7 6 5 4 3 2 1

Thou camest in, said they, as a
stranger, was it to be a judge?
—GENESIS **19:9**

In all her intercourse with
society, however, there was
nothing that made her feel as if
she belonged to it . . . She stood
apart from mortal interests, yet
close beside them, like a ghost
that revisits the familiar fireside,
and can no longer make itself
seen or felt.
—NATHANIEL HAWTHORNE,
THE SCARLET LETTER

The
Covenant

1

I WAS PARKED IN FRONT OF THE liquor store at the corner of Poplar and Highland, about to stick a fat envelope in a mailbox in the hope that my photos of the dead and their uniformed attendants might earn me a fat government check. I wrapped every corner of the package in three layers of tape to keep the postal inspectors from steaming it open. I hoped to score some real money from the pedigreed jokers who decided what was and wasn't art, the kind of money that could make a real difference in the train wreck of my life, not the nickel-and-dime stuff I usually got from the police and the insurance companies for my photographs of accident victims and overdoses.

Since I had nothing else to depend on, hope seemed a good plan, but I might as well have spent the postage on a lottery ticket. Who was I, after all? Just some aging nobody with a car with no air-conditioning and a broken taillight, too dry to summon enough spit to lick her stamps. I had a disk drive full of photos of the faces of the dead, and a few who had left their faces on the road, and all that work had got me exactly nowhere, living in a by-the-hour motel on the outskirts of Memphis. If you could even call it living, chasing ambulance sirens, waiting for the phone call that would be the difference between ramen noodles or nothing to eat at all. I'd been off the smack for over a year now and I was still waiting for my life to turn around.

I opened the mailbox and dropped my package inside. When I returned to my car, I found a woman crawling into the passenger window. I shouted and she backed out waving a steak knife that she had probably lifted from a restaurant back when she had enough money to steal from restaurants.

"Gimme," she shouted. She might have been my age, probably a lot younger—the meth had aged her like a broken time machine. She looked like she needed a hit in the worst way. She was about to shake apart. I noticed a couple of kids, two girls, peeking out from behind a van parked in the gas station parking lot on the corner.

"Are those your kids?" I asked. That threw her for a second. She wasn't used to robbing people at knifepoint. She probably never did anything worse than lifting purses out of grocery carts and open car windows at the convenience store. She glanced back at her kids, then at the closed liquor store, then at the traffic passing not twenty feet away. It was like she only at that moment realized she was trying to rob somebody in broad daylight on a Sunday morning.

"Gimme your purse, bitch!"

I could have taken the knife away from her and dented the rusting hood of my car with her face, but that was the last thing she needed and the last thing I wanted. By this point, she was just looking for a good enough reason to run away. So I gave her one.

"I ain't got a purse," I said as I reached behind my back. "But I got a gun."

She took my advice and lit out, shouting for her babies to run. I got in my car and closed the open glove compartment. It was empty anyway.

As I pulled out onto Highland, my phone started to ring. The name that popped up on the display seemed familiar, though I couldn't remember why. I almost didn't answer it, but I needed a job more than I needed not to answer a wrong number.

"Jackie?" Her voice sounded familiar, too. "Jackie Lyons?"

"Yeah," I said blankly.

"I was afraid your number had changed, it's been so long since we talked," she said. "How have you been?"

"Fine." I still didn't know who she was.

She seemed to sense it. "You probably don't remember me. This is Jenny. Jenny Loftin."

I said, "Yeah," again, because her name meant almost nothing to me. I knew a Jenny once, for less than an hour, and I never learned her last name.

"You found my cell phone and returned it to me," she said. "I was Ashley's friend."

"I forgot I gave you my number." It was the only thing I could think to say to her at the moment. Ashley St. Michael was a photographer, and I had bought her camera from her husband, James. They were both dead now, murdered by the same man four years apart. I had met Jenny when I found her cell phone, unaware that she and Ashley had been friends long before I met either of them.

"I saw you on the news," she said. "It must have been awful, what you went through."

"It was pretty bad." She didn't need to hear my sea stories, so I didn't go into detail, but the same lunatic who killed Ashley and James had very nearly greased me over some pictures I took of him without his permission. I managed to punch his ticket first, but not before he put me in the hospital and all over the local news for a week or two.

"But you're OK now?" she asked.

"I'm doing OK." The physical wounds had healed, but in my nightmares I wasn't nearly so tough as I liked to pretend.

"I think about you sometimes, but I just never had a reason to call before."

I don't know why she was apologizing. I hadn't thought of her at all. I had forgotten her completely.

"Are you still a photographer?" I allowed that I was still in the business and tried not to let her hear the hope in my voice.

"The pastor of our church needs somebody to take some pictures. I was wondering if you could meet him here at my house this afternoon, if you're not too busy."

"I think I can fit you into my schedule," I said.

2

JENNY TOLD ME HER PASTOR was planning to renovate an antebellum home and he wanted it photographed in its current ruined state. The house would be the parsonage for the church they were building on the adjacent land.

Jenny lived on Plantation Lane at the end of a forested cul-de-sac in Stirling Estates—a wealthy gated community in Malvern, Tennessee, fifteen interstate miles and two worlds away from Memphis. I had just enough gas to get there and back, so I drove out Sunday afternoon, feathering the pedal and coasting down hills. It was April, jacket weather, still cool in the morning, though today it had warmed up enough to feel like June. Patches of buttercups lined the highway and the trees were budding and blooming like adolescents in love. I drove with my windows down just to smell the honeysuckle.

As I pulled up to the gate, the elderly gentleman in the Bavarian guard shack didn't like the look of my papers, but my name was on his list so he raised his barber pole and let me through.

Apparently Sunday was Dressage Day at Stirling Estates.

People in top hats and split-tail coats sat atop fifty-thousand-dollar horses that pranced along the verge, skipped rope, mixed martinis, and maybe solved calculus equations, while grounds-keepers followed in golf carts to shovel up the turds. Most of the estates had barns, and pastures surrounded by miles of white, three-rail fence, or vast green expanses of front lawn for artillery practice. There were two golf courses, because one is never enough, which had hosted pro golf tournaments in the past, a lake big enough to ski and sail, tennis and squash courts, and a clubhouse with a world-renowned restaurant that only served residents. It was the sort of place where you didn't need a membership sticker on the bumper of your car. Everybody I passed knew I didn't belong. I left them in my mirror worriedly reaching for their phones.

I could smell money all over this job, megachurch money, slobs of it. I didn't have all the proper photographic equipment, but I had to make my pitch. Maybe there'd be enough to outfit myself like a professional photographer.

One section of property at the north end of the lake had never been developed—forty acres of old timber and brambles hiding the ruins of the plantation house that had given the Stirling community its name. All those putting-green lawns I passed on the way had once been cotton fields, back in the day when this was still boondocks and Memphis was a two-day buggy ride away. Then the railroad came through and turned the old tavern and Chickasaw trading post into Malvern—a market town of considerable though brief prosperity, until it was burned to the ground by the zealous torchbearers of Northern aggression. A historical marker near the gate declared

Stirling Plantation the approximate location where General Sherman might have very nearly almost been captured, according to local legend.

Where Plantation Lane ended, a two-track dirt trail continued across a weedy field, dipping down and to the right to enter the woods. On the left, the ground rose up to the levee that created the lake. This street was lined with the newest houses of Stirling Estates—huge, modern monstrosities with more bathrooms than common sense. The lots were considerably smaller than the older sections of the community; these barely had room for a pony. The houses were clean and blank and dimensionless, like photographs from a glossy real estate magazine, especially with all the For Sale signs in the front yards. Times were hard, even for the pearl-wearing set.

Jenny's house was the last house on the left. It was smaller and considerably older than the other houses on her street, a heap of blood-colored brick, wooden shutters painted coffee-black, and a green front door. Hedges twenty feet high bordered a deer park lawn shaded by hundred-year-old pecan trees. As I parked on the street, I didn't see any other cars, but there was a man walking in my direction across the levee. He seemed to be waving at me, so I killed the engine.

Three girls were jumping rope in Jenny's driveway, wearing polished Mary Jane shoes and red, blue and yellow Sunday jumpers from church. As I collected my camera gear from the trunk, they sang a rope-jumping song:

Wire, briar, limber lock.
Three old geese in a flock.

One flew east, one flew west,
one flew over the cuckoo's nest.

The girls were so lively and pretty in their primary school colors, with the spring flowers in manicured beds as backdrop, I knelt in the street and uncapped my lens to take their picture. I'd heard the song before, maybe in elementary school, which was the last time I skipped anybody's rope. The rhyme was part of something longer, but I couldn't remember the words.

The oldest dropped her rope and walked toward me. "What are you doing?"

"I'm a photographer," I said as I snapped her photo.

"If you want to take my picture, you have to pay me."

If she hadn't been so serious, I might have laughed. She was maybe eleven, but already nearly as tall as me and nearly all of it leg. With her cheekbones and jade-green anime eyes, she might already be doing modeling work for *Elle* magazine. She wore a pair of diamond earrings that cost more than my car. I tried to make a joke to cut the tension. "So this is how kids earn money these days. Whatever happened to lemonade stands?"

"The homeowners' covenant doesn't allow lemonade stands," she stated as though it were the most obvious thing in the world. The other two girls looked eight or nine and more interested in getting back to their rope jumping than interrogating me. "Or unescorted visitors," the girl added with a pretty sneer.

I reminded myself that she was only eleven, even if she was as big as me, and that her mother would call the cops if I ruined all those expensive orthodontics. I smiled and asked, "So how long have you been modeling?"

That melted her icy little heart. "Almost four years!" She made it sound like a lifetime.

"I bet you make a lot of money."

"Not really. I haven't done anything national yet. Just local photographers."

"I'm a local photographer," I said.

"But you're a girl!"

"Lots of photographers are women."

"I've only ever worked with men."

Of course she had. "So what's the going rate for one picture?" I wasn't really negotiating with her. I just wanted to see what she'd say.

"Depends."

"On what?"

"On what you want it for."

"Just something for my portfolio."

"Oh, I've done lots of portfolio stuff. How about twenty bucks?" I guess I was getting the family discount.

I patted my pockets. "Gee, I think I left my checkbook in my Ferrari. I'm actually here to meet a preacher named Deacon Falgoust. Do you know if that's him?" I pointed at the man walking toward us along the levee.

She glanced in that direction and said, "Is what him?" I barely heard her. Something was wrong with the guy. He was staggering around and shielding his head with his arms as though being dive-bombed by birds from a Hitchcock movie.

After a few steps he stumbled and went down, then popped up again, took another drunken step and pitched over the lake side of the levee.

I handed my camera to the girl.

The slope was steeper than it looked from the road but I climbed it faster than I thought I could. By the time I reached the top of the levee I had dialed 911 on my phone, but the operator hadn't answered. I found the man lying facedown in the water just at the edge of the rocks. My old Coast Guard training kicked in and I jumped feet-first into the lake. The water looked shallow but it was over my head, and at first I couldn't move from the shock of the cold. All I could do was watch the cloud of bubbles rise in the murky black around me. He was silhouetted against the surface above me, his glazed eyes staring out of a blank, bloated face.

I felt stone under my shoes, pushed off and came up beside him. I rolled him over, even though there was no point in trying to save him.

He'd been in the water for a couple of hours, at least—long enough to ice him down to the temperature of a dead fish.

3

IT WAS A QUIET, peaceful place to contemplate a drowned man. I waited, shivering in the sunshine while water dripped from the ends of my hair. Three geese passed overhead, quietly honking to one another. They flew so low, I could hear the whoosh of their wings. One split away and disappeared over the woods; the other two crossed the lake, chasing their reflections across the glassy water. The cops took such a long time, I wondered if my call to 911 had even gone through. I couldn't find my cell phone. I didn't know if I had dropped it before or after jumping in the lake.

Finally, a Malvern City squad car pulled up at the end of the street. The officer hadn't even turned on his flashers. I waved him over and he climbed the levee, swimming with his arms through the tall grass. He was short, dark, with crew-cut hair and a neck like the hump of a bull. His uniform was so tight over his bulges, if he took a deep breath it might peel off him in rolls, like old wallpaper. When he reached the top, it was few seconds before he saw the body in the water.

I grabbed him before he could strip off his utility belt and dive in. "He's been dead for hours," I said. Then I had to sit down or I'd shake the long sticks out of me.

He asked what happened and, stupidly, I told him everything. Maybe I was still in shock. I said I'd come to meet a preacher about a photography job, that I saw him fall into the lake, and that I'd jumped in the water to save him but it was too late. Toward the end I could barely get the words out. I couldn't stop shaking and the cold only seemed to be getting worse, creeping into my bones. He called it in on his radio, then ran back to his patrol car. While he got something out of the trunk, I listed to the sirens coming from every direction— police, fire, ambulance. The officer returned with a blanket and wrapped it around my shoulders. I looked at his name tag and said, "Thanks, Officer Lorio."

He made his way down the rocks to the body. It was a man about my age, full head of hair starting to gray, body trim and fit, the dark tan of a man who had worked outdoors for many years. Cut down in the prime of life. He was wearing a light jacket, pale green golf shirt, khakis, hiking boots. "What was he doing before he fell in?" Officer Lorio asked.

"Having some kind of fit."

"Can you identify him?"

I shook my head. "I was here to meet a preacher named Deacon Falgoust. I've never seen him before, but I guess that's him."

"This isn't your preacher. I know this man. His name's Sam Loftin."

I remembered that Jenny's name was Loftin and wondered

if this day could get any worse. I didn't have to wonder for very long.

I noticed a woman walking toward us from the direction of Jenny's house. She had a couple of kids in tow. Even though I hadn't seen her in years, even though she was still a hundred yards away, I recognized her. Every third or fourth step, she had to stop herself from breaking into a run.

"Here comes his wife," I said. Lorio nodded heavily and climbed up the bank.

When Jenny saw him, she started to scream. Her screams blended with the wailing of the first fire truck. He managed to wrestle her back to the house before her kids saw their daddy in the water. Eight or nine volunteer firemen trudged up the hill, dragging their boots through the weeds, bearing medical kits and a stretcher and God knows what-all, already sweating under their helmets. They looked tired and bored, as firemen usually do, even when the world is burning down around them.

By this time, the Fayette County sheriff's department had also arrived. Nobody seemed to know what to do first. The firemen wanted to save somebody but there was nobody to save. The deputies wanted to arrest somebody. I was the only one available for either service, so while one fireman strapped an oxygen mask to my face, checked my pulse and gazed deeply into my eyes, a deputy asked me what I had seen.

I had recovered enough from the shock of events to realize I couldn't tell them I'd seen a man who'd been dead for several hours waving at me barely twenty minutes ago. But that left me in a hell of a spot. Anything I said from this point forward was going to make it look like I was hiding something.

So I played sick. I fell into the fireman's arms, babbling nonsense and shivering. They strapped me on a stretcher and took me to the ambulance, grateful, I think, for something to do. They stuck needles in my arms and hung bags of fluids over my head. It was a wonder they could find a vein. I lay in the warm, antiseptic ambience of the quietly humming ambulance and listened to the beeping of my heart signal, trying to think of some way to explain what I had seen without coming off crazy or guilty or both. Eventually the shaking stopped. Eventually. Officer Lorio climbed into the back of the ambulance and I knew they weren't taking me to the hospital.

He didn't have his cuffs in his hand, so they weren't ready to arrest me just yet. After checking with the medics, he asked me to follow him to the MCC. "What's that?" I asked.

"Mobile Command Center."

The fire trucks were still there, idling alongside the idling firemen, but now a half-dozen black Suburbans lined the other side of the street. One was a K-9 unit—I could barely see the German shepherd inside, panting against the tinted windows. A seventh Suburban was parked on the levee, a county coroner emblem decorating its driver's door and its rear door open to accept its charge of flesh. Ten or twelve deputies loitered around it, keeping the curious onlookers at bay. A chopper circled overhead—at first, I thought it was a news chopper, until I noticed the black-and-gold colors of the Fayette County sheriff's department.

The Mobile Command Center was a luxury motor home

about eight blocks long. Officer Lorio led me across the street to it, where a granite-faced footman in paramilitary black uncoiled the tattooed pythons of his arms and opened the armored door. Seventy-degree air poured out, smelling of new carpets, expensive electronics, and English Leather. The uniformed rack of meat sitting behind the mahogany desk was Sheriff Roy Stegall.

Roy Stegall had been elected despite his lack of law-enforcement experience, but in his own estimation that didn't make him any less of a Law Man. Born in McNairy County, he fancied himself a modern-day Buford Pusser.

"Close the door," he said without looking up from his laptop. A flat-screen television on his desk played some cable news program with the sound muted. The bank of monitors on the wall behind him showed front, rear, and side views from the top of the MCC, as well as a live feed from the helicopter camera. A cell-phone earpiece hung like an apostrophe from the cauliflower pasted to the side of his enormous head.

I sat in a leather chair while he finished pecking at his computer. Lorio stood at ease in the corner, fingers laced behind his back, his eyes nowhere. Finally, Stegall closed his laptop and pushed it to the side. "Sorry about that," he said to Lorio. "Mickelson's due in town this evening. You know how it is." Senator Mickelson was Tennessee's senior United States senator, but it wasn't election season.

"Now, about this witness," Sheriff Stegall said. He picked a notepad from the jumble of papers on his desk. Lorio came to life like somebody had flipped his switch. He removed a pen and notepad from his pocket and waited. "What's her name?"

"Jackie Lyons," I said.

Stegall looked at me as though he didn't care for what he saw. "Address?"

"Deertick Motel. Room 102."

"Deertick? Where's that?"

"Highway 70," I said.

"I think she means the Detrick Motel," Lorio suggested.

"That's the one," I said.

"No permanent address then?"

"Times are hard," I said.

"Are you on food stamps, Mrs. Lyons?"

"I don't see what that has to do with anything."

"I was just wondering if my tax dollars were buying all your expensive toys."

"Toys?"

He flipped through a folder on his desk. I guess it was my dossier, because he read out of it. "Camera, laptop. Says here you had a cell phone but you lost it in the lake. You also have a car. Times don't sound too hard if you have a car." He closed the folder. "This country is getting sick of supporting moochers like you. One of these days the tit will run dry."

I shrugged against the cables of nervous tension tightening across my back. "I work out of my car. I sell my car and I can't work, then I really will be on welfare."

"What about your cell phone?"

"I don't work if people can't call me."

"And were you working today?"

I told him how I was supposed to meet a preacher about a job. "Strange place to meet a preacher," he chuckled. "Maybe it was a *blow* job. You're not a hooker, are you, Mrs. Lyons?" When I didn't answer, he said, "Don't worry, I won't bust you."

"Especially if I give comps, huh? I bet you got a nice bed in the back of this thing—tinted windows, soundproof walls, the whole shebang."

Instead of getting mad, he smiled and folded his hands on the desk. He was going to humor me now, feed me enough rope to hoist myself by my own petard. "So you're here to meet a preacher about a job. What kind of job are we talking about?"

"Photography."

"Professional photographer, huh? I just paid a fortune for my daughter's wedding pictures. Her photographer drives a bigger car than I do, but here you can hardly afford a decent place to live. Maybe you should think about another line of work."

"Are you hiring? I know how to shoot radar and write tickets."

"That's funny as hell. You almost made me laugh."

"It's what I live for, Sheriff," I said.

"So, you work out of your car and you're a photographer." He said it almost like he didn't believe me. "Where's your camera? Did you lose that in the lake, too?"

"I gave it to that girl, the one that looks like an *Elle* model."

Lorio flipped back several pages in his notes. "Mercedes LaGrance."

"What made you give her your camera and run off like that?" Stegall asked me.

My only choice now was to brass it out and hope for the best. "I thought I saw somebody fall in the lake."

"People fall in the lake every day. Nobody calls 911."

"The guy looked like he was having some kind of fit. I thought he might drown. Of course, I could have been mistaken."

Stegall nodded and leaned back in his chair. "We all make mistakes. But that's the problem. You didn't make a mistake. Somebody really had fallen in the lake and drowned. Only not when you say he did. How do you explain that?"

"Maybe he had a stroke."

"That's not what I mean and you know it."

"All I can tell you is what I saw," I said. "I can't explain how I saw it."

Stegall closed his notebook and put his shoes up on the desk. They were cheap, black leather, so shiny they looked like plastic, remnants of an old wad of gum stuck to one heel. "The coroner believes the deceased had been in the water for several hours. Officer Lorio said you mentioned this fact, yourself, when he arrived on the scene. You claim you saw the deceased fall in the water, yet this girl . . ."

"Mercedes LaGrance," Lorio filled in the blank.

". . . says she didn't see anybody on the levee at the time."

All I could do was shrug.

"That can only mean you had prior knowledge . . ."

"Just one problem, Sheriff. I wasn't there when he drowned. If you want to know what time I arrived, ask the old man at the gate."

"I intend to do that," he said.

"Good." I crossed my arms and waited.

"Meanwhile, I'll hold you as a material witness until we can get this straightened out." Stegall nodded to Lorio, who removed the handcuffs from his belt and asked me to stand.

While he cuffed me, Stegall came out from behind his desk. "I hope you understand, this is just procedure. Senator Mickelson has a house at Stirling Estates. Until we can be absolutely sure what happened, we're forced to treat this as a possible threat to national security. No doubt it will all be straightened out in the morning and you can go on your way."

"Yeah, it's just one night in jail." I twisted my wrists in the cuffs—Lorio hadn't put them on too tight. "No biggie."

"I'm glad you understand our situation," Stegall said. His smile said he didn't give a rat's ass if I understood or not. "Of course, you'll be staying with us in the county lockup. Our jail is much nicer than the one in town. Probably a whole lot nicer than that roach motel you live in."

"I can hardly wait to get there."

Lorio led me to the door and opened it. "Just one last thing, Mrs. Lyons." Stegall stuck his thumbs in his belt and leaned back against his desk. "The EMT said he had a lot of trouble finding a good vein due to all the tracks in your arm."

"Yeah?"

"I've ordered a search of your vehicle. Just thought you'd like to know."

As he held my elbow to help me down the first step, Lorio whispered, "Sorry." Then he handed me over to one of Stegall's goons.

4

IT WAS NEARLY MIDNIGHT when they finished booking me. I used my one phone call to leave a message with Preston Park's answering service and went to bed in a cell with three cots, a sink, a toilet and half a roll of John Wayne. About two in the morning, they brought in a pair of women. One was a meth addict who spent the first hour throwing up in the toilet and the rest of the night organizing the lines on her pillow. The second was a hooker who stared at me like I was a work of art. Finally, she asked, "Didn't you arrest me once?"

"Probably." I turned my face to the gray concrete wall. Back in the day, I'd been a vice cop in the Memphis Police Department. I wondered for about ten seconds if she would shiv me, then I fell asleep. Me and the bedbugs had a lovely four-hour gonk.

When the officer of the day banged on the door, my cellmates were already awake. "Let me just get my things," I said when he called my name.

"Hey," the hooker said from her bunk. I looked up while the officer handcuffed me. "You Jackie Lyons?"

"Yeah," I answered.

"You had a visitor last night, asked for you by name."

"Did I?"

"Some old lady. Stood right there, said not to wake you."

"That was nice of her."

"Come on." The officer pulled me into the hall. "Don't listen to that tweaker," he said as we walked away. "We don't let people back here, especially after visiting hours."

"That's OK," I said. "I don't know any old ladies."

He delivered me unto the offices of Sheriff Stegall. Preston Park stood up from the leather chair in front of Stegall's desk. "Jesus, she's still in cuffs." Preston was an old friend of mine as well as my occasional employer. He paid me to photograph the auto accidents and nursing home patients that made up the bulk of his law practice, but he would sometimes go slumming in criminal law and take on hopeless cases like me.

At a nod from the sheriff, the jailer unlocked me and bowed out. Preston led me to his chair. "Are you OK?" I nodded that I was.

Stegall's office desk was even bigger than the one in his motor home. Green felt and pockets at the corners and you'd have a decent pool table. Windows to either side framed an antique bookcase that climbed to the ceiling, left wall checkerboarded with photographs of sheriffs past, with little brass plaques telling their terms of office and noting which ones died in the line of duty. One had heroically eaten a German shell in World War II.

A half-dozen biographies and books on military history bookended a library of photographs of Sheriff Stegall shaking hands with nearly every politician within three hundred miles, plus a couple of dead presidents. The top shelf was reserved for his model collection. I spotted an A-6 Intruder and an A-7 Corsair, along with an aerial photo of an aircraft carrier and some kind of shadow box containing a gaudy jumble of ribbons and medals.

"Sheriff Stegall, was it really necessary to parade my client through the entire building in prison clothes and cuffs?" Preston asked. He was polite, but there was a professional edge to his voice that sometimes intimidated even me. "I was told that she had been released."

Stegall wasn't the least bit impressed. "She's still being processed out." He ran a hand over the smooth white knob of his head, then set his fists on the desk in front of him, fingers laced together. A new wedding band had barely begun to leave an impression in his ring finger, but on the other hand he wore a heavy ring of old, worn-looking gold with a black stone in the center. "May I ask your client a question before she goes?"

Preston looked at me and I shrugged. "Go on."

"Refresh my memory. How did you happen to find the body?"

I sighed. I would never be able to explain to him or anyone else that I had seen the last moments of this man's life played out like a movie, or how, for as long as I could remember, I'd been seeing things like this, ghosts, spirits of the dead. Not all the time and not everywhere. Sometimes I'd go months without seeing them. It had been over a year since I tried to hide my friends behind a snow-white curtain of heroin. Whenever I started seeing ghosts again, it was usually a sign that my life was about to fall apart.

And here I'd just got it back together.

"I thought I saw somebody fall in the lake." I shrugged and flexed my hands. I could still feel the band of cold where the cuffs had bit into my wrists. "Obviously, I didn't see anything. It must have been a coincidence."

"That would be an incredible coincidence."

"You know my client had nothing to do with this man's death," Preston interrupted.

"Her story about meeting a preacher for a photography job checks out. The pastor called yesterday to vouch for her. And as it so happens, due to circumstances I'm not at liberty to reveal, the coroner has ruled the drowning a suicide." He unlaced his fingers and tapped his ring on the desk.

I tried not to laugh out loud. What I had seen yesterday afternoon on the levee was no suicide. The man was in some kind of distress, but he hadn't walked into the water and drowned himself. The coroner's ruling was a joke.

Stegall continued, "We've also verified with the guard when Mrs. Lyons arrived on the property."

"Miss," I corrected.

"However, I still have questions about her involvement in this."

"What kind of questions?" Preston asked.

Stegall tapped his ring several times on the desk, giving himself time to think. It was obvious he didn't like questions that didn't have easy answers. He much preferred his answers lined up in neat little rows that he could tick off before clocking out at five every day. He shuffled some of the papers on his desk to see if he could find his answers there.

"Why exactly did you jump in the water?"

"I was trying to save him."

"He'd been in the water for hours. You said so yourself."

"I didn't know that until I was in the water with him."

"Sam—that is, the deceased, Samuel Loftin, was a big man. You're not exactly built for dragging grown men out of lakes."

That was true enough. I was five-three and still had the body of a heroin junkie. Always being hungry will do that to you. "I've had some training," I said.

"YMCA swim lessons?"

"Coast Guard. Rescue diver school."

"So you were a spar in the knee-deep navy," Stegall sneered. "I'm an Annapolis grad, twenty years flying off carriers."

"I never took you for a Navy man," I said to the anchor-faced ring-knocker. I pointed to his toys and the box of fluff on the shelf. "I thought maybe you picked those up at a garage sale."

"Jackie." Preston warned, then inserted himself between us. Stegall had gone scarlet to the point of his head. "If you have no intention of charging my client, may we go?"

I'll give Sheriff Stegall this much. He could screw it down tight. He didn't answer. He just shooed us away, like flies trying to land on his pie.

5

IT TOOK A MERE two and half hours for them to locate my camera in the property cage. Someone had filed it in their office without bagging it as evidence first. When they finally returned it to me, the photo I had taken of the three girls skipping rope had been erased.

Preston drove me to the impound lot to retrieve my car. We found it sitting under some pine trees in a pasture of junked and seized cars. Its rear seat was lying on the ground beside the door panels, the dashboard dismantled, front seats slashed to ribbons with the springs showing through. "At least they didn't cut up the tires," Preston said.

While he helped me stuff the seat into the back, I had a few choice words about Sheriff Stegall and his methods. Preston said, "A little town like Malvern, they do whatever they want. I could sue for damages to your vehicle, but most likely he'll be fishing buddies with the judge." He closed the door and stood back to examine my POS. "I doubt you could get more than a couple hundred, even if we won."

We shoved the dashboard in the trunk, but it stuck out the

back too far to close. The front seats were hopeless and I didn't have the money to get them reupholstered. "What you need is a new car."

"Yeah." I sat in a patch of sunlight to rest and warm up. "Let me call my broker."

"Can I buy you some lunch?" he asked.

I shook my head no. They hadn't fed me that morning and the last thing I'd eaten was a couple of bites of horse dick at the jail the night before. Not that I wasn't used to going without food. I wasn't particularly hungry. And it wasn't the lack of sleep, something I was also used to doing without.

I could still feel the cold of that lake, all the way down to my bones. When I closed my eyes, I could see him floating above me, his arm gently waving. I should have known before I jumped in the lake that what I saw fall in the water was no living, breathing human being. God knows I'd had enough experience. But it had been so long since I saw one of my special friends, I think he caught me by surprise.

"Preston," I said. Why was I about to tell him this? I already knew what he would say, but I couldn't help myself. Preston was one of the few people in the world I could talk to. He was always honest with me. He knew my history, both legal and mental. I'd first met him after I was fired from my job with the Memphis Police Department. I wanted to sue for wrongful dismissal. Preston had advised me that my dismissal had not been wrongful.

"I don't think Sam Loftin killed himself," I said.

He looked at me over the top of his sunglasses. He was the gentlest man I never wanted to get on the wrong side of.

"I saw him go in the water."

"Yes?" he sighed.

"He was having some kind of fit. Maybe a stroke."

He leaned against my car and stared up into the pines. There was no wind and the air beneath the trees was heavy with the smell of dead brown needles.

"Why would the coroner try to cover this up?"

"Do I need to remind you that this is none of your business?" Preston asked.

"It never is."

"Jackie, you know I don't think of you as just another client, or even as an employee," he said, still staring up into the trees. "It's my job to make trouble go away, but your trouble never pays, except with more trouble. Trouble follows you like a dog."

I resented the reminder that I was a perennial liberty risk, but I needed Preston more than he needed me. "I don't know where I'd be without you."

"Still in jail." He helped me to my feet. I tried the ignition and my car started on the first crank. For once.

Preston leaned into the window. "Your problem is, if trouble doesn't find you, you go looking for it. And if you keep looking for it around here, you'll find so much I may not be able to get you out of it."

"Bastards took my car radio," I said. It didn't even work, but the fact they took it pissed me off more than anything had all day.

————

I wanted to call the preacher, but I had lost my cell phone at the lake, so I drove back to my room at the Deertick Motel. The cockroaches met me at the door like dogs. Everything was pretty much as I had left it. The mildew stains might have grown a bit.

The room actually had a working telephone. It was padlocked to a chain that was bolted to a heavy staple set in the wall. The handset was likewise chained to the body of the phone. You had to sit on the floor with your head about three inches away from the keypad. I called the preacher to try to salvage that photography job. Another week with no work and I'd be living in my car.

A giant answered on the third ring. Even through the phone I could feel the booming power of his voice. "God bless you for calling, this is Deacon Falgoust." He pronounced it "Fall-goo."

"Jackie Lyons. I'm sorry I missed our meeting yesterday."

"Yes, I know. Isn't it terrible?" He didn't have the exaggerated "Missippi guvnah" voice of your typical Southern Baptist preacher. I couldn't place his accent at all. "If it weren't bad enough already, they put you in jail, and after you tried to save that man. I asked Sheriff Stegall, is this how we reward our heroes? By arresting them?"

"They let me out this morning. Thanks for vouching for me."

"Being as how I was late for our rendezvous, it was the least I could do."

After we finished apologizing to one another, I asked if there was any way I could see the house today. "Actually, I was hoping you would call," he said. "I'm sorry to ask you to return to this house of grief, but it's the only place I have to meet with you, and Jenny doesn't mind. If you could be here around four-thirty, I would be much obliged to you."

That gave me enough time to scarf down a sandwich from the convenience store, followed by a short nap in which I dreamed I was drowning in a burning house.

6

A FTER A QUICK SHOWER and a change of clothes, I was passing the German gatehouse and returning to the scene of the crime. As much as I needed the money, I was starting to dread seeing Jenny Loftin again. I wasn't ready for her questions, her grief, her kids, any of it. I just wanted the job. I parked on the street in front of the house, looked up at the levee where everything had happened. For the hundredth time, I pictured it in my mind, watched him wave, stumble and fall, then go headfirst into the lake. It didn't make sense.

There were no cars parked in the drive and it looked like no one was home, but I rang the bell anyway. It didn't take them long to answer. The man who opened the door was dressed like an undertaker in a suit nearly as black as his hair. He was forty-ish and handsome in a hard way, his long arms making him look taller than he really was. His smile pushed up the soft wrinkled corners of his eyes. "Hello Mrs. Lyons, I'm Deacon Falgoust."

"Miss."

When we shook, his hand felt almost fleshless. It was all bone and sinew and calluses, its strength born of something other than muscle. "I'm glad you could come," he said. "Won't you follow me?"

The house was velvety quiet and dark, shades drawn. The hall led away from the door toward the back of the house, past an empty dining room on the left, half bath under the stairs on the right. I noticed that the back of the preacher's neck above his collar was creased and sunburned. "I'm looking forward to seeing the place. How far away is it?" I asked as he led me into the spacious living room.

Before he could answer, I was enveloped in arms. "Thank you for trying to save my Sam," Jenny whispered in my ear. I nodded and said something about being sorry. I didn't know what else to say to her. She hugged me like her oldest and dearest friend. I tried to return an affection I did not feel or deserve. I had only met her once, for a few minutes at a bar, half a lifetime ago. Why she remembered me, why she cared enough to try to help me, I didn't know.

She introduced me to her children—a boy and a girl. I'd seen the daughter, Cassie, yesterday, jumping rope. She was tiny for her eleven years and looked more like eight or nine, small-boned and pretty like her mother, with big brown eyes that stared holes through you. The boy was barely old enough to walk and would grow up with few if any memories of his father. His name was Eli. Dressed in his little black suit with a red choo-choo engine tie, he held on to the hem of his mother's dress and shook my hand very gravely.

Jenny hadn't changed much since the last time I saw her, still the same girlishly pretty face and too-sharp nose, but she bore the pale, worn, faraway look you see in the eyes of tornado victims. Her lips trembled as she smiled and held me at arm's length to look me over. "I'm so glad you're here."

Another woman creeped into the room behind her. She looked younger than Jenny by several years and nothing like a sister, a tall, leggy brunette, dressed like everyone else (except me) in black, but hers fit her better. She didn't need to wear heels, but she wore them anyway. She'd been in the bathroom, trying to hide her swollen dewdrop eyes and perfect little red nose under a layer of expensive powder. The only thing not gorgeous about her was her weak, thin-boned chin, but the rest more than made up for it. She slipped her hand behind the preacher's elbow and clung to him like a tree in a flood. Jenny introduced her as a friend of the family—Holly Vardry.

I said, "I'm ready to see the house whenever you are."

"Meemaw's house?" Holly's eyes widened a little too dramatically, and she gripped his arm tighter than ever as she pressed her svelte body against him.

"Mrs. Lyons is going to photograph it," he said as he shrugged himself free of her. It bothered me that we hadn't even negotiated the job yet, but I decided to let that ride for now. No doubt, he could afford my services. "We can go now if you like."

I said I would like that very much. I could see the questions in Jenny's eyes, questions she would find a way to ask if I hung around for very long. The preacher started for the door and I followed him.

"Can I go with y'all?" Holly asked, but she didn't wait for an answer. As soon as we were outside, she dodged around me and sank her claws into the preacher's arm again.

"I hate Meemaw's old place," Holly said as we crossed the wide, shaded lawn.

"If you hate it so much, why'd you come?"

She wrinkled her nose for an answer, but I had no idea what that meant. Just before he slipped on his shades, the preacher's glance told me he was wondering the same thing.

The sun was warm on our backs as we crossed the field below the levee, headed toward the woods. Tiny green grasshoppers rose up on papery wings and buzzed away in long arcs. We walked between the twin corrugated tracks left by some bull-dozer ages ago. Holly had a difficult time of it in her heels, so she kicked them off and left her shoes lying in the weeds. I thought about going back and picking them up. They probably cost more than my weekly rent.

As we entered the woods, the air seemed to lift and draw away, as though we'd climbed to a different altitude. Long ranks of trunks, brown and gray with lichen, towered away into numinous green clouds of foliage overhead. Wild grape vines as thick as my leg swung in long curves from branch to branch.

A footpath wound its way through the undergrowth, crossed a dry creek by way of a single log and began to rise up. Dozens of other paths split off from it at irregular intervals—deer trails, the preacher called them, but all I saw was a few old beer cans hiding under the leaves.

Eventually, a green mound loomed up through the woods ahead of us, like a lost pyramid in a Mayan jungle. We were almost standing on its steps before I realized it was a house, an

entire antebellum ruin blanketed by decades of kudzu. Dusty
vines with large, three-lobed leaves wrapped around the trunks
of the columns and spread along the walls like ivy, even growing over the roof. A bit of crumbling brick chimney poked up
from one end of the viny mound.

"Kudzu can grow up to a foot a day," Deacon said. "All the
windows were bricked up years ago to keep it out of the house."
Even the fanlight above the door had been bricked over. A
path of somewhat newer boards had been laid across the rotting porch, otherwise we'd have had to swing like Tarzan to
get inside.

"You want to restore this?" I asked while he unlocked the
padlock that secured the door. "How long has it been since anybody lived here?"

"A little over a year." He opened the door and clicked on a
flashlight he had brought with him. "Mrs. Ruth's son finally
convinced her to move into a nursing home."

"Kidnapped, you mean," Holly said.

"Mrs. Ruth?"

"Ruth Vardry is Holly's Meemaw. She owns this house, the
woods, and all the land hereabouts."

While the exterior was a ruin, the inside of the house was
merely a wreck. The main entrance staircase had fallen against
the interior wall, and chunks of plaster, some bigger than me,
littered the floor. A length of chain and a bit of frayed, cloth-
covered wire dangled from a brass fixture overhead, the last
remnant of what had probably been a crystal chandelier.

Deacon kicked a bucket that stood in the middle of the hall,
shloshing a little murky water onto the floor. In some places,

the floorboards had been ripped up to reveal the bare gray earth below. "One good thing about the kudzu, it mostly keeps the rain out. Mostly." He pushed open a door that had swollen shut in its frame. "Once the vines are cleared away, our first priority is rebuilding the roof."

There was a strangely familiar smell about the place, and not just of rotting wood and crumbling masonry. It was a barn-like odor, only wilder, like the cave of a bear. I'd smelled it before, somewhere, maybe way back in the lizard part of my brain. "Before she moved to the nursing home, Mrs. Ruth used to share this house with a pack of feral cats. There must have been twenty living in here with her."

We found a partially dismantled fireplace in a rear room of the house, its ancient bricks scattered across the floor. "It looks like you've already started your work," I said to the preacher.

"This was done long ago." He picked up a brick and turned it over. His hands were hard as horn, the hands of a bricklayer or a carpenter, not a preacher. "Old Gus Stirling believed his father had hidden gold or silver in the chimney to keep it from the Yankees. The usual family story, you know. Mrs. Ruth refused to let anyone clean this up."

"Meemaw is crazy," Holly elaborated unnecessarily.

I photographed the fireplace. Holly hobbled barefoot across the broken bricks to pose beside it. "I used to be a model," she said. I wondered if everybody around here was in that line of work.

"It will cost a fortune to rebuild this place," I said.

"Money is no concern. The Lord has provided," he answered, not without a touch of pride. "And I will direct the restoration myself."

He carried his brick into the next room, which he said had been a dining room. He pointed out a door which led to an exterior kitchen. The door stood open, but the path outside was so overgrown as to be nearly impassable.

"Even after we clear away the kudzu, the windows will have to remain bricked up for a while. I've ordered some stained-glass windows brought from an old church that was damaged by Hurricane Katrina, but it will be several months before they can be delivered."

Next, he pointed out the walls. They were the color of old ivory, stained brown in places by seeping moisture, with a seafoam-blue paint flaking from the woodwork. As the beam of his flashlight played over the surface, I could just make out the ghosts of old landscapes and people, houses and Greek temples, horses and dogs, blue like ancient tattoos on pale, mummified skin. "This is Zuber wallpaper, from France. As you can see, the images are nearly lost. I'm hoping you can pull these out with your photos, so they can be re-created by an artist I know."

If anybody could work that kind of photographic magic, it was my pal Deiter Marks. He owned a small camera shop that was so exclusive, it was hardly ever open. He was usually too busy building photography equipment for NASA and the Pentagon to serve ordinary customers. I snapped a few pictures to give him something to start with.

"It's gonna be a lot of work, turning this place around," I said. "You'd do better to tear it down and start over."

He shrugged. "That's not an option, so we're rebuilding it.

Before I was called to the service of the Lord, I restored homes in Louisiana. I learned construction from my father. He rebuilt hundreds of homes after Camille wiped out the Gulf Coast."

"Deacon is a man of many talents," Holly mooned. "He was a soldier in Iraq—the first time, not this last time." Deacon frowned and walked away from her, but she followed him, wagging her tail. Her desperation was a thing to behold.

"Most of the wood in here is chestnut, which can't be replaced. I want to preserve as much of it as possible," Deacon said as he pointed out the cornices above the doors. "The American chestnut tree was wiped out by blight in the 1930s and 40s. It has never recovered, and so much that was built with it has already been lost."

He dropped his brick with a hollow thump on the floor. The sound was echoed by a loud bang upstairs. "Jesus!" Holly shrieked under her breath. "God, I hate this place. It gives me the creeps!"

When I first set eyes on the dilapidated ruin, I was certain I would find a congress of ghosts inside. But since crossing the threshold, I hadn't seen the first wisp, not even a shadow of movement in the corner of my eye. This was perhaps the strangest thing about the place—its deep and abiding emptiness. Now it seemed we weren't so alone after all.

A creaking noise, like footsteps, moved slowly overhead. Holly's fingers tightened around a loose fold of Deacon's jacket, pulling it taut as a drum.

We followed the noise into the next interior room. Deacon's flashlight beam crawled along the crumbling plaster of the coffered ceiling, revealing the laths beneath, and in some places tiny glowing eyes staring back. "Once the cats are gone, it doesn't take long for the rats to move in," he said.

The footsteps passed over us. Deacon pointed his beam at a narrow door in the opposite corner of the room. "That door leads to the servants' stair," he said. Soon the stair steps behind the door began to creak, one at a time, with deliberate slowness. Holly shrank behind the preacher, doubled her death grip on his jacket, and buried her face in his back.

"There's nothing to fear here," Deacon said, though I noticed the beam of his light wavering ever so slightly as it dropped to the gilded doorknob, which was, at that moment, turning.

The door burst open and a dark figure leaped into the room. Holly screamed and I snapped its picture. At the flash from my camera, he recoiled, swearing obscenely.

"God dammit Nathan!" Holly shrieked.

Our intruder burst into outrageous, puerile laughter. "You should have seen your faces!" With the same long body lines and straight, dark hair, you could see he and Holly were brother and sister. His face was stronger, with a narrow, proud nose and deep-set eyes beneath dark brows. The dust and sweat stains on his white button-down shirt made me think he'd been crawling around in the attic. He collapsed with laughter, his hands on the dusty knees of his trousers.

"You're such a juvenile shit," Holly said, then to me, "This is my stupid brother, Nathan. He's retarded."

"I'm not retarded!" He glared at Holly.

"Are, too."

"Holly's the slow one in the family," he said to me. "I dropped her on her head when she was a baby. On purpose."

I believed him.

"Y'all were so scared! I thought you were going to pee yourself. You were scared, too, Deacon."

"You got me, Nathan," the preacher chuckled.

Nathan's eyes dropped to the camera around my neck, then traveled down the length of my body, taking me in with a hungry glance. "You about blinded me with that flash."

"Sorry."

"What kind of Canon is that?" He reached for it, as though he expected me to give it over. I shook his hand instead. Too surprised to pull away, he cleared his throat and said, "I'm a photographer. Not a professional, of course. I have a real job and a business to run."

"Is that so?"

"Nathan is a popsicle man," Holly snickered.

"My company, Happy Time Frozen Treets, has a fleet of twelve vans," the brave young entrepreneur boasted. "I don't drive one, of course. I have an office."

"Daddy bought it for him."

"At least when I was your age, I wasn't still living at home." He turned back to me. "My camera's a Nikon D3X digital SLR with 24.5 megapixels. I bet your Canon isn't as good."

"It's several years old," I said.

"What are y'all doing in Meemaw's house?"

"This house will soon belong to the church, Nathan." Deacon introduced us, but this time we didn't shake hands. "Jackie is doing the photography for the restoration." Although he still hadn't officially offered me the job, I was starting to consider upping my fee, especially if the Lord had been so generous.

"I'm free all this week. I could start shooting tomorrow."

He shook his head. "There's a lot to do before you can begin," he said. "We should run power to the house. It hasn't had electricity since the ice storm knocked the lines down in 1993. And it'll be three weeks before we can clear the brush around the house and bring in a cherrypicker."

"What do you need with a cherrypicker?"

"Do you want to hang off the roof to photograph the cornices and architraves?"

I saw his point. "I could start inside the house while you do all that." I really needed that money right away.

"But I won't be here. I have to leave for New Orleans after Sam's funeral. I'm already supposed to be down there. We're closing on a house that will be dismantled and used for the restoration of this place. I'll be home in Louisiana for two weeks maybe."

"I could let her in, show her around, keep an eye on things," Nathan offered. Although I desperately needed the money, I didn't care to spend any time alone in the house with him. I figured I'd be too busy batting him away to take any pictures. Handsome as he was, something about him put me off. It wasn't just his adolescent behavior or the way he stared at my tits.

"I need to be with Mrs. Lyons to show her what I want photographed," Deacon said as he led us back to the front door. I don't know who was more disappointed—me or Nathan. He sulked along behind us, kicking bits of plaster at his sister.

"Where in Louisiana?" I asked the preacher.

"My church used to be in New Orleans, but my mother's family lives in Opelousas—the Trapagniers of Opelousas." They sounded like a trapeze act.

Once we were outside on the porch, Deacon padlocked the door. "Well, Jackie Lyons. What do you think?"

"You haven't made me an offer yet."

"I'm willing to pay professional rates, in exchange for which you will supply me with copies of the photographs. The originals remain yours, of course. You can use them or sell them to other people, if you can find somebody to buy them."

"I'll do it," I said. I'd have to pick up a tripod and some lighting, but I was pretty sure Deiter would loan me the equipment I needed. That wasn't the problem. "I just wish there were some way we could start right away."

"There's plenty of time to make the pictures after I return," he said. Then he looked at me in an odd way. His eyes had a strange light to them that I'd never noticed before, an intensity that was almost disconcerting. "If you're in need of money . . ." he started to say.

"I just want the work." I'd lived most of my life off the charity of men, and it had got me into more trouble than it was worth. I was through being a leech.

Well, mostly through.

"I can respect that," he said, but his eyes lingered on me, as though he were seeing for the first time the holes in my jeans and in my arms. I thought he might change his mind, but he only nodded and returned the key to his pants pocket. "It's getting late. We should head back."

We walked down through the twilight woods in single file, Deacon leading, Nathan dangling from my hip pocket. "I don't usually go for older women but your body is amazing," he grunted in my ear, his breath smelling like cinnamon Certs.

"Not so amazing with the lights on."

"Bullshit, lady. You're hot."

"Thanks." I tried not to make it sound like I meant it. "The years have not been kind."

"You should let me be the judge."

"If I ever need a jury, I'll let you know."

Clouds had moved in while we explored the house, and it was getting dark quicker than we expected. We hadn't gone far before we heard kids playing in the woods ahead of us. They were running and shouting all along the paths that crisscrossed the forest. A couple of times, I saw a whirl of color or a flash of long blond or red hair. Somewhere ahead of us, two girls were singing the jump-rope song I'd heard the day before. I wondered if they were jumping rope in the woods.

Suddenly, I heard the song repeated behind me, in a soft, dreamy voice. It was Holly, and she chanted it all the way through:

> Wire, briar, limber lock.
> Three old geese in a flock.
> One flew east, one flew west,
> One flew over the cuckoo's nest,
> Up on yonder gallows hill,
> Where my father's bones do dwell.
> He had jewels, he had rings.

He had many pretty things.
He had a hammer with two balls.
He had a cat with nine claws.
Whip Jack! Lick Tom!
Blow the bellows, old mon!
Saddle the horse and beat the drums,
Tell me when the Yankee comes.
Sit and sing, by the spring.
Clap, clang, clattery, cling.
Hintlery, mintlery, cutlery, corn,
Apple seed and whipple thorn.
Screw a dishcloth up his snout.
Turn him over and shove him out.

She finished with an embarrassed smile. "That's the way we used to sing it."

I was finally able to remember where I'd heard the chant before. "Where I grew up, that was a counting song. Like eeny-meeny-miney-moe." The words were a little different—our version didn't have a Yankee or a father with bones on gallows hill, but it was essentially the same.

The kids had stopped singing by the time we crossed the log bridge over the dry creek. We were almost to the edge of the woods before they started up again, but they sounded miles away now. We hadn't passed them on the footpath. We stopped to listen, but their voices drifted into silence, swallowed by the vastness of the woods.

"I saw a Bigfoot in there once," Nathan said in a soft voice.

"God, you are such a liar!" Holly snarled.

7

THE DAY BRIGHTENED considerably once we were out from under the trees, and the westering sun, coming out from behind the clouds, was almost hot on our faces as we crossed the field. Our feet kicked up a cloud of dust that seemed unusual for that time of year. It hadn't rained in a couple of weeks.

Jenny greeted us at the road, posed by her mailbox in her black dress dotted with small white flowers and a little round black cap with a half veil covering her face. She had just taken a bundle of letters from the box. Cassie and Eli were sitting on the grass beneath the trees, the boy pushing a toy truck around and the girl pretending to play with a doll. Nathan crossed the lawn, knelt beside Eli and helped him make truck noises. He grabbed Cassie and rubbed her head with his knuckles.

Jenny invited us in to dinner. "There's just so much food, we can't possibly eat it all," she said. "Everybody has been so good." Part of me wanted to say I had to get back, but I had nothing to get back to—an empty motel room without even a fridge to keep a cold beer. I had spent too many hungry nights to turn down a free meal, no matter what it cost.

Also, I wanted to get another look at the place where Sam Loftin drowned. I don't know what I hoped to find—maybe whatever the coroner was trying to hide. As we crossed the lawn, Cassie followed just behind me, and once we were inside she sat next to me on the couch. Nathan pushed in beside her and tried to make her giggle by squeezing her knees. She looked like she wanted to crawl into my lap and cry. I got up to explore the house.

Jenny cut me off in the hall by the grandfather clock, her eyes swimming with questions I couldn't answer. I edged into the half bath and closed the door, turned on the faucet and let it run while I sat on the toilet and tried to talk myself out of bailing on these people with their soul-sucking grief. Their money kept calling me back.

As I turned off the faucet and dried my hands, I heard Jenny and Deacon in the kitchen. "She can help you. You will need her strength."

"But I can't afford it now, Deacon."

"And I told you before, I can help you with that, too."

"I don't want charity. I can't. I just have to trust in God. He'll find a way."

"God helps those who help themselves," Deacon said.

Holly met me in the hall with a plastic cup of pale wine. I took it and left through the back door.

Jenny had a swimming pool between the house and the lake. It was shaped like the print of a shoe, with a diving board at the heel and a waterfall at the toe end, fan palms in pots and a hollow concrete tiki statue that they used as a chiminea. Beyond the pool, a path led down to the lake, where a dock and boathouse stood over their reflections in the water. One side of the yard sloped steeply uphill, and an iron gate let out to a small orchard of plum trees with dark purple leaves and pale pink flowers that glowed in the gathering dusk. A path climbed up between the trees until it reached the levee.

I found Officer Lorio standing on a limestone boulder at the water's edge and turning something over in his hands. At first I didn't recognize him, because he wasn't wearing his uniform. He was dressed in a white T-shirt, jeans, cowboy boots and a hat. The wind had come up and was blowing toward us, bringing the smell of frying fish.

He seemed surprised to see me, so I explained my visit. "That preacher again," he mused. "Did you finally meet him?"

"Just got back from the house. Mrs. Loftin has invited me to dinner."

"Jenny's a good woman," he said, almost to himself. "She doesn't deserve any of this. God knows she's been through enough already."

He was standing above the spot where I'd found Sam Loftin facedown in the water. I glanced back toward the street, but didn't see a car parked there. "Do you live around here?"

He snorted and shook his head. "Not on my salary. I couldn't even afford one of the golf lots." He explained that a golf lot was a piece of undeveloped land that the community sold to people who didn't live at Stirling. The lots were scattered around the borders and too small to build a house on; people bought them because ownership gave them access to the clubhouse, the golf courses and other amenities. It was like the membership fee of a country club, except it could be taxed as property by the county.

"Where's your car?" I asked.

"I parked on the other side of the lake and walked across the levee." He turned and climbed up the rocks. "I remembered you said Sam was coming from that direction when you saw him. I was hoping maybe he dropped something."

I took a sip of wine and swirled it around in my mouth, remembering that I didn't like wine. Lorio was taking me at my word about what I had seen, even though I couldn't have actually seen Sam Loftin walking anywhere. "Did you find anything?"

"Just this. I think it belongs to you." It was my cell phone. "It was down there by the water's edge between two rocks."

I thanked him. "How did you find it?"

"It was ringing."

I checked the last call received. It was from my mother. She had phoned a dozen times since this morning. Her normal routine was to phone me every other Sunday, never on a weekday, except when she found some nice gentleman from her church who was about my age and had just gotten a divorce and was available if I wanted to meet him and settle down, preferably back home in Pocahontas—the small town in Arkansas where I grew up and where she and my father still lived together in nominal matrimony.

"I'm sorry about what happened to you yesterday." Lorio pulled up a tuft of dry grass and shook the loose, dry dirt from its roots. "It's hard to believe it's only been one day."

"Y'all were friends?"

He took a deep breath and nodded without looking at me. "Sam called me from the office. He was working yesterday morning."

"On a Sunday?"

"Sam worked all the time. He wanted to meet after my shift ended. We were gonna watch the Cardinals game at his house. That's why I was the first one at the scene—I was already in the neighborhood. Then, when I saw you standing here, I just knew . . ." He took his hat off and and wiped his forehead with the back of his arm.

"What did you know?" I asked him.

"That Sam had killed himself."

"Why would you think that?"

"Yesterday . . ." he began, then sighed and pressed his hat on his head. "Sam's oldest daughter, Reece, drowned herself at this same spot, five years ago yesterday."

8

WE ALL SAT DOWN TO A dining table practically groaning with food: Jenny and her kids, Deacon, Holly, Nathan, Officer Lorio and me. My seat was at the end of the table, opposite Deacon. A large picture window to my left provided a view of the pool and boathouse. The preacher thanked the Lord for the bounty provided by Jenny's neighbors at this, her time of need, amen. Jenny passed around a box of cold fried chicken bought at a local convenience store.

"Doris Dye brought the Jell-O salad," Holly said.

"I wouldn't eat it," Nathan muttered with his mouth full. "It's probably poisoned."

"There is good in all of us. Even Mrs. Dye," Deacon said as he took the plastic container and passed it to Jenny.

"Doris is our neighbor next door," Jenny explained. "She calls the police on us almost every weekend, accusing us of hosting loud parties at all hours of the night." She still spoke about *us* and *our* as though her husband were still alive.

Holly passed me a bowl of peas. "Doris is crazy. Daddy's got her number blocked on his cell phone."

Jenny explained, "Holly's father is Luther Vardry. He's the president of the homeowners' association."

"Pastor Luther Vardry?" I asked.

"You've heard of him?"

Luther Vardry was pastor of one of the largest Baptist churches in the state of Tennessee. They used to broadcast his Sunday-morning church services on local television, back when I was married and still went to church every other month or so.

"Of course, Daddy's unofficially retired now," Holly said. "He doesn't preach anymore, but he still does his *Benedictions* commercials on the radio." *Benedictions* were these trite little one-minute sermonettes, basically infomercials that Stirling Baptist Church bought on all the top radio stations in Memphis. He was a gentle, soft-spoken man who reminded us that we may all be God's children but only the Baptists were getting into heaven.

I ate as much as I could stomach and remain ambulatory. Holly had already finished her bird's portion and gone off to sniff some diet powder up her nose, but Deacon and Nathan were just getting their second wind. I pushed my plate away and set my wadded napkin beside it. "Are you sure you got enough to eat?" Jenny asked. I noticed she mostly just shifted the peas and mashed potatoes around on her plate without tasting any of it. "There's enough to feed an army. If somebody doesn't eat it all, I'm going to have to throw it away."

"I'm stuffed." It wasn't a lie. A half a sandwich would last me all day.

"Jackie has agreed to shoot my photographs for me," Deacon announced.

"I'm so glad!"

"I'm just happy you were able to recommend her."

Jenny smiled and touched my hand across the table. "I believe these things happen for a reason. There's a connection between us. God keeps bringing us together for a reason." I smiled back as sincerely as I could manage, which wasn't much, but she didn't seem to notice. Whatever God had in mind for the two of us, He hadn't bothered to pencil it into my calendar.

I stood and pushed the chair back from the table. "I was hoping we'd have a chance to talk before you left," Jenny said.

"Just callin' my mom." I held up my cell phone as proof of my intentions.

"OK. But you need to eat some dessert when you're done. I hope you'll take some of this home."

French doors in the dining room opened onto a deck big enough to hold a square dance. The deck had two levels that hugged the rear angles of the house, with the higher level overlooking the lake. I found a hot tub in one corner, glowing and bubbling like a witch's cauldron. The last light of sunset was still bright on the lake. The levee was dark and empty, not even a ghost of a ghost. I lit a cigarette and blew the smoke at the sky.

I hadn't really intended to call my mother. I only wanted a chance to get away from everyone trying desperately to be brave in the face of death. I almost would have preferred some

obnoxious display of grief to all this onward Christian soldier-
ing and bold stiffening of the upper lip. But while I was sitting
on the edge of the hot tub, Mom called me. I stubbed out my
cigarette in a potted plant so I wouldn't have to lie to her when
she asked me if I was smoking.

I was surprised to hear my father's voice on the line. He
never phoned me. He never phoned anybody. He always had
Mom do it, then stood beside her and told her what to say.

"Jacqueline, you need to come home."

"Dad?"

"Tonight. Right now."

I didn't ask why. I already knew why. I could hear it in his
voice. He never called me Jacqueline. "I've been trying to reach
you since yesterday. There's money waiting for you at Western
Union. Use it to fill your gas tank."

I didn't bother saying goodbye to anyone. I just jumped the
deck rail, circled around to the driveway and hopped in my car.
As I pulled away from the house, I looked back and saw Jenny
standing at her front door, as still as a pillar of salt.

9

*She could no longer borrow from
the future to ease her present
grief.*
—NATHANIEL HAWTHORNE,
THE SCARLET LETTER

ONE OF THE FIRST THINGS I had to do was buy a
decent dress. My father wore the same black suit that he
only wore to funerals. He'd bought it several years ago, when
it seemed like every other week someone he knew was dying.
"I've had a lot of good use out of this suit," Dad said as we rode
in the limo behind the hearse. "As you get older, it's a good idea
to invest in a decent suit of clothes appropriate for the occasion. And when it's my time, you can bury me in it."

They buried my mother next to my brother in Pastor Corner, a small, cedar-fringed garden in the oldest part of the

Masonic Cemetery in Pocahontas, Arkansas. Somebody at the funeral said, "Lucy will be happy now," and I thought, yes, she would be. I didn't believe there was a heaven where she and Sean could finally be together again, but no doubt as the arterial bubble in her brain ruptured and the fearful darkness closed over her head, she probably consoled herself with that thought—*Soon I'll see him*. My little brother had died too young, and not once since the day of his murder had I seen my mother truly, completely happy. Sean had been her baby.

There were only two empty plots remaining in the corner where they buried some of the first pilgrims to settle in Pocahontas. Dad and I were all that was left of the old family name of Pastor, which was really Pasteur. Lyons was my married name, though I was no longer married. I don't know why I kept my ex-husband's name. Maybe I didn't want to go back to being a Pastor. That name didn't belong to me anymore. I didn't know why I couldn't just give myself a new name without having to marry into it. But it wasn't worth dealing with the courts and the Social Security Administration. Even if I changed my name, I'd still be Jackie Lyons. Jackie Pastor had passed away a long time ago.

The funeral was held at the church where Mom and Dad were married. I hadn't sat in those pews in over twenty years. Some of the faces were new, but the church hadn't changed at all, except that everyone was a stranger to me, even those I should have remembered.

None stranger than my father. He took it all in perfect stride, a picture of Southern gentility, dressed like a don in his black suit with the black armband and the white carnation in his buttonhole. The only sign of grief he showed was when we were waiting for the service to start. He leaned over and whispered, "It wasn't supposed to be like this."

"Like what?"

"Your mother going first." As the first song began, he added, "We had it all planned out," and winked at me with a tear in his eye. Just one. That's all he had for her.

When I was ten years old, I had sat in this same church pew looking at my grandfather's shark fin of a nose sticking up from his open casket. I was too short to see anything else of him. A few years later, my brother's casket sat in the same spot, but it was closed. Both funeral services were pretty much the same as this one. The same songs, the same litany, the same praises and exhortations to celebrate a life lived well in the service of God Almighty whose wisdom is never-ending and whose ways are as mysterious as the stars and the sea. Only the names changed, meaningless names, one funeral blending into another as the years between shrank into nothingness.

Yet there was some subtle difference to my mother's funeral that I couldn't nail down. It started to bother me even before the final amen. At first I thought they had shortened the service. I remembered it being much longer, but back then I was just a kid, when ten minutes seemed a lifetime. Still, something was missing.

I couldn't let it go.

We sat at the dining room table because all the furniture in the living room was crowded with people, most of them women dressed in funereal black, perched on the arms of couches and chairs like crows. The church organist, old Mrs. Passwater, sat at the table next to me and sketched with her finger on its undusted surface the recent history of deaths and divorces in Pocahontas. The Passwaters were another of those indigenous town families like the Pastors, older than the oldest houses, older even than the trees that dropped dead limbs on their roofs when it stormed. Mrs. Passwater had played the organ at my parents' wedding, and she'd played it at my mother's funeral. Old Mr. Passwater was killed in Sicily during the war, fighting for General Patton. He had never been old, but that's what we called him. Mrs. Passwater still had the general's letter where he said her husband was a hero and a patriot, writing:

The meek and pious have a place,
And necessary are,
But valor pales their puny rays,
As does the sun a star.

Every Sunday service before Memorial Day, she read these lines to live by. She had never remarried, keeping the memory of her hero husband Corporal John Passwater foremost in her heart.

It turned out that most of the women fussing over my father were either widowed or divorced. They took it in relays to bring food from the kitchen or freshen his drink any time his ice looked like melting. Sometimes they even brought me a nibble. I watched my father wolf down a bowl of peach cobbler as though he hadn't eaten in weeks. As soon as it was empty, the bowl was replaced by a slice of apple pie. I said, "This is less a funeral than a holiday."

"It's a celebration of your mother's life." He sucked a bourbon toddy down to the ice and set the empty glass on the table. It was immediately whisked away, hey presto, like magic. "She would have wanted it this way. Besides, there's no sense in wasting good pie. Or good bourbon, thank you, Melanie." This was to the redhead who brought him a new drink.

"That's pretty near her real color, too," Mrs. Passwater whispered.

I couldn't help noticing the difference between this house and Jenny's. Two small towns, two untimely deaths, yet this one really was a celebration, as contrived as that always sounded, while Jenny's was . . . what? Here, there were people constantly in and out of the house, kids playing in the yard, men on the porch smoking and drinking, widows in the kitchen conducting cold-war evolutions against each other as they plotted angles on my father. At Jenny's, her neighbors had dropped off green-bean casserole and buckets of fried chicken, but none had stayed to comfort her. Her kids had no friends their own age to play with (Nathan didn't count) and help them forget their grief, even for a little while.

My mother seemed too young to have died of a stroke, but when I mentioned this, Mrs. Passwater said, "Your grandfather, Dr. Pastor, was your mother's age when he died, and his was a stroke, too." I had always thought of my grandfather as ancient, only slightly younger than the hill upon which he perished. In my mind he was this frightful old dentist, with smelly breath and clean fingers, who still haunted the upper precincts of the house and used to wake me in the night with his ghostly pocket watch ticking in my ear. My mother was still the young woman who used to dress me up in pretty things and send me out to play, only to discover me naked and swinging like Jane in the neighbor's trees.

Neither of them had aged in my memory; one remained dreadfully old, the other strangely youthful, and I supposed they would always be that way now.

Eventually the house poured our visitors out in drips and drabbles and left my father and me alone, truly alone. We sat at the dining room table. There was a bottle between us now, and a bucket of ice, and a world of silence. He wouldn't look at me, but his lip got stiffer with every drink.

Finally, he pulled off his black armband and tossed it on the table. He stood up and walked to the den with the graceful stagger of a gentlemanly drunk, one hand ready to catch himself against the nearest wall and prevent his drink from spilling.

"This is where I found her," he said, pointing to a place on the rug by the television. "She got up sometime during the night. I thought she had gone to use the bathroom. When she didn't return, I looked for her."

He stood over the spot, absently caressing it with his socked foot. "I don't know why she came downstairs. Maybe she wasn't feeling well and didn't want to bother me. When I found her, she was still breathing, but the light had gone from her eyes. She didn't see me, didn't hear me. It was already too late."

He brushed against the door and caught himself on the doorknob. "But that's not what's bothering you," he said.

"It doesn't feel like she's gone," I said.

He staggered back to the table and slid into his chair. "I know what you mean."

Did he? I had been seeing her ever since we got home from the cemetery. She'd be in the kitchen or the den or somewhere, but when I looked, it was another woman or the edge of the china cabinet or the shadow of a drape. I wasn't seeing her ghost so much as my own memories of her. It was like we'd gone to somebody else's funeral. She should have been there beside us, playing the gracious hostess, a role she had mastered ages ago. Her absence was an aching hollow.

"Everything just feels unfinished, somehow," I said.

"What if we finish this bottle?" He held it up to the light. It was about half full. "Would it be finished then?"

"Maybe."

He made us fresh toddies and we clinked glasses. My old man could mix a damn good cocktail, but I had a difficult time enjoying it. I heard her walking around upstairs. Or maybe it was my grandfather. Dad didn't seem to notice. We had never talked about my special friends. Considering all that had happened over the last few days, and how their sudden reappearance always seemed to presage my life falling apart, I figured it was about time I told him.

"What time did you say Mom passed?"

"I didn't say. I'm not sure what time it was. After midnight, I think. I left the hospital around five in the morning."

"I was in jail." He looked a little surprised as he sipped his drink. "There were two other women in my cell. Sometime during the night, an elderly woman came to the door and asked for me. My cellmates said she told them not to wake me."

He glanced at me over the rim of the glass, his eyebrows wrinkling his forehead. "You think it was your mother?"

"The jail doesn't allow visitors at night."

I couldn't read his eyes. He blinked once, then drained his glass. He set it down with a shrug. "Maybe it was her."

It was my turn to look a little surprised.

He smiled. "Jacqueline, it's just like you to think you're the only person in the world who ever saw a ghost."

"Have you seen Mom?"

I think I hoped he had, but he shook his head no. "Now, your grandfather is a different matter. He's still hanging around."

"You know about him?"

He chuckled at my surprise, then waved his hand vaguely at the ceiling. "You can still smell him sometimes. He had a distinctive smell, something you never forget."

"Like coffee and cigarettes," I said.

"And hair tonic and wool and body odor. Your grandfather only bathed on Saturdays."

"Sean and I tried to tell you." A light shone suddenly in the window. A car had pulled into the driveway. Dad leaned back in his chair and parted the curtain to see who it was. "But you didn't believe us."

"You were just kids, scared to death. What was I supposed to say? *Yes, your grandfather's ghost lives in the attic, now go back to bed*?"

He walked to the door, opened it, stepped outside and closed it behind him. I finished my drink and left the glass on the table while I fetched a slice of chess pie from the fridge. When

I returned, Dad was still outside. I peeped through the curtains and saw him talking to the redhead from the funeral. I sat down and ate the slice of pie, then made another drink. While I was pouring, the car backed out of the driveway. Dad waited until it was gone before he returned.

He didn't tell me about his visitor and I didn't ask. He just said, "Did you make your old man one of those?" So I made him a toddy and got another slice of pie from the fridge and watched him eat it.

"So who picked out Mom's dress?" They had buried her in a hideous black fringed thing with tiny white flowers, sequins, and pearl snap buttons, something she'd have never worn while she was alive.

"Deedee Mills took care of everything for me."

"I wish they had done a better job with her face." I don't know why I was bringing this up. I knew I sounded like some grumpy old maiden aunt complaining about the fecklessness of the mortician. I don't know why I wanted my mother to look like the woman I knew instead of some wax effigy poured by someone working from a bad photograph.

I liked the way they did things back in my grandfather's day. People used to keep their dead at home until it was time to bury them, instead of sending them off to be powdered and puffed up with facial prosthetics by medical school dropouts. Because when you lived with the dead taking up the dining room table or the parlor or the bed, with the smell of them getting a little riper every hour, you got used to the idea they were dead and after a few days of having them around, you were finally ready to put them in the ground. Glad to put them in the ground, glad to be rid of them so you could move on. Because they were only meat, and rotting meat at that, and the funeral was a release from grief, a thing to be welcomed, realized, and got through and put behind you, rather than dreaded and avoided. Because the funeral is just the beginning of grief, and because we tidied it up and perfumed and preserved it, people could go on pretending their loved ones weren't dead for a couple more days, until the day we laid her in the ground and pushed the dirt in the hole, and stood a rock up over her and carved into it her name, a couple of ultimately meaningless dates, and maybe a lie or two, until even the names and dates and lies were erased, until even the meaning of the rock itself was forgotten and it was pulled up and used as a doorstop and the field was plowed over and planted, until some day someone decided to put a highway through and they unearthed her bones with a backhoe and called in some college professor to bend over her with his patient brush and his dentist tools and pronounce, *Here lies a woman.*

So the grief started out stunted and deformed and pretended and only realized at the end, when they filled in the hole. That's why you see those little crosses and wreaths all up and down the highway—people can't let go of the dead because we create the illusion of burying them alive, or if not alive, then not entirely dead either. You end up suffering your grief alone with nothing but the memory of that lifelike body lying in the cold airless dark all alone, listening to the descending convocation of politic worms.

Maybe that's why I hated my father so much at that moment. He was moving on, eating his pie and drinking his bourbon and already thinking about tomorrow's redhead. Maybe he could do that because he had a chance to say goodbye to her, while I had avoided her telephone calls and slept through her last attempt to reach out to me. Who was I to judge the dryness of his wrinkled face? Where were my own tears?

"Didn't she know I was staying the night?" I asked Dad.

"Who?"

"That redhead from the funeral."

The bastard didn't answer. He got up and put his plate on the kitchen counter and poured his ice out in the sink. I followed him, my insides buzzing like a horsefly, itching to shoot my heart out of a cannon against the white hump of his infidelity.

"I guess there'll be no end to the pussy now," I said, spat.

He set his glass in the sink. I think I grieved him more than the passing of his wife of fifty years. I always was his favorite. At least I got to be somebody's favorite. "Do you think your mother was stupid, Jackie?" He stared out the kitchen window into the dark.

"No."

"Do you think she could be married to me all these years and not know?"

"Do you think she enjoyed living a lie, Daddy?"

"Your mother enjoyed being married to me. She accepted what came with that, the good and the bad. I can't help the way I am. I loved your mother, but I loved other women, too. Some of them very dearly. It wasn't just the sex, but that's all you could ever see. Ever since you were a little girl, you've never been able to love more than one thing or one person or one idea at a time. You're either mad in love, or you're crazy with hate. You're old enough to know by now that people are nothing if not a rat's nest of contradictions. Even the people we love."

"Yeah, I keep forgetting how complicated you are," I stabbed from hell's own heart. "How many sacrifices you made to keep your marriage together. But that's all over now. You're free to chase all the tail you want."

He passed without looking at me, shuffled wearily down the hall and climbed to the top of the stairs. He stopped with his hand gripping the wooden rail. He looked old. He had aged a hundred years before my eyes, this frail, tottering old drunk. "I'm going to bed."

I stayed downstairs, because I had to finish something, even if it was only a bottle of whiskey.

10

I WOKE ON THE PORCH SWING ABOUT eleven in the morning, my throat as dry as an old eraser, the singing of the birds in the trees like fingernails clawing the blackboard of my skull. Dad sat in a glider rocker reading the morning paper, a tray at his elbow with two glasses and a sweaty pitcher of orange juice. I grabbed an empty glass and poured it to the brim, downed about half of it before I started tasting the vodka. I surfaced long enough for a breath of air, then finished it off and wiped the crust from my lips with the back of my hand.

"Have another," Dad said, so I did.

We sat on the porch and drank a pitcher of brunch while the unseasonably warm morning turned into an unseasonably hot day. He read his paper and I read my fortune in the bumps on my tongue. We said nothing about what we said to each other the night before—actually, what I said and now regretted. He regretted nothing, except perhaps being my father. For the next few days we pretended it never happened, drank like a pair of old sailors on shore leave, sat up nights watching basketball on television. Pretending was how we got on with our lives without making them any better. I pretended to be trying to pull my life together and make something of myself, and he pretended to believe me. He wore a black armband any time he left the house or had visitors and I pretended to grieve with him, while he took his phone calls in the bedroom with the door closed and I pretended not to notice or care. If I were the suspicious kind, I might have suspected him of tumbling Mom down the stairs. But this was real life, not a movie.

In the end he paid me to go home so he could stop pretending. He was anxious to get on with his widower lifestyle. I drove back to Memphis that afternoon and cashed his check.

His money kept me from sleeping in my car a few more weeks. In the old days, which is to say about a year ago, I would have blown it on a bank of heroin taller than my head. They say it gets easier with time. They lie. It wasn't getting any easier and I was still an addict. I hadn't used in more than a year, yet I still wanted it every day, still thought about it all the time. I used to tell myself I wasn't an addict, that I could quit anytime I wanted. If you can lie to yourself, you can lie to anybody.

Speaking of liars, the preacher had told me it would be three weeks before I could start photographing his plantation house, which was about how long I calculated my dad's money would last. Three weeks stretched into six and I stretched that money until the threads were showing, adding to it whenever I could, which wasn't often. Times were hard. April and May were hot and dry, which made for fewer car accidents and fewer opportunities to make the pie higher.

I called the preacher occasionally and left messages. He

called me back less often and dropped excuses. For some reason, he never asked me why I skipped out that night at Jenny's
and I was happy enough not to offer an explanation. The house
he had planned to salvage in New Orleans was on some list
of historic homes. Never mind that it had flooded up to the
Plimsoll mark during Hurricane Katrina and sat abandoned
ever since, crack house and flophouse for every derelict and
wretch in the area. He said it was easier to get a visa to North
Korea than permits to dismantle and salvage whatever history
the house had left in it. Then there were difficulties arranging
the trucking, difficulties getting construction equipment. I
was starting to think I'd never see a dime from his collection
plate.

Preston called one Tuesday in May and sent me out to Pleasant Acres Hospice to photograph a women who had caught a
fifty-five-gallon steel drum with her face after it fell off a truck
and smashed through her windshield. They said it was a miracle she hadn't died. People have funny ideas about miracles.
Now she was a twenty-seven-year-old potted plant who spent
her days staring at whatever potted plant they planted her beside. God only knew if she had a thought in her head at all, or
if she was screaming inside all day long. Her family had already
collected on the accident. Now they were going after the nursing home for neglect. I hated working nursing homes, but I
needed the money.

Pleasant Acres wasn't very pleasant, nor was it situated on
any acres. The place was locked up like a maximum-security
prison, fences topped with razor wire, mag-locked steel doors,
and bulletproof glass around the nurses' station.

Nurse Ratched buzzed me in and met me in the lobby wearing faded paisley scrubs, white Jasco shoes and a Prozac smile. Her narrow brown eyes flicked across my camera as I told her the patient's name. She looked for my name on her clipboard.

I pointed at the video camera hanging from the ceiling above the exit. "What's with all the security? Keeping people out, or keeping them in?"

Her lips tugged themselves a wrinkle closer to her half-closed eyes and she asked, "Are you a member of the family?"

"I'm here at their request." They hadn't called ahead because they didn't want to give the staff time to clean their daughter up. They wanted pictures of the pool of piss under her bed. They wanted the jury to see the suppurating bedsores.

"You'll have to leave your camera at the front desk," the nurse said.

"I can't do that."

"We'll take very good care of it."

"I'm sure you will, but I'm here to photograph the patient."

"For what purpose?"

"Glamour magazine."

She laughed softly, like a woman hiding a coat hanger behind her back. "I need to know what kind of pictures you will be taking."

"That's not really any of your business, is it?"

"I'm afraid it is."

"Are you going to let me see her?"

"I'll have to call the family and obtain permission."

"You do that."

I sat in the corner beside a potted schefflera that had dropped most of its leaves. While I waited, a family of three and a couple of doctor-looking men in white coats were buzzed in without being questioned. I stepped outside and spotted a security video camera above the door. They had seen me coming from the parking lot and were ready for me. Next time, I'd make sure to hide my camera in a backpack instead of wearing it around my neck.

I gave her about five minutes to call the family; then I hit the buzzer. When no one answered, I leaned on it until they did. Nurse Ratched came through the door like a horse out of a gate. "Please stop that!"

"What did the family say?"

"I'm afraid I was unable to reach them. I left a message. If you'd like to wait . . ."

I handed her the letter Preston had given me.

"What's this?"

"A demand, giving me permission to enter the facility and photograph the patient."

"Our lawyer will have to look at this."

"Fine."

"I'm afraid he's not here."

"Of course he isn't."

"You can wait here while I call him."

"I'll do that."

I pretended to sit, but as soon as she opened the door I bolted in behind her.

Their lawyers had trained her well, because she didn't lay a hand on me as I slipped by her. "Ma'am! You can't come in here," she said as she waved to a couple of big orderlies standing at the end of the hall, probably the guys they called in to wrestle with the paraplegics when they wouldn't take their pills. "You have to wait in the waiting area."

"Thanks. I'll find the patient while you call your lawyer."

The nurse ran off to fetch somebody important enough to ignore my letter. The orderlies started down the hall like a couple of bulls that had just spotted a Spaniard with a red neckerchief. I picked a hall at random, then cut through a laundry closet to try to lose them. The place was miles and miles of identical halls, identically carpeted and wallpapered. Apparently they let the more harmless inmates wander unsupervised, because I passed a couple of barely animate corpses gaping at the ten-dollar landscape paintings hanging between every cell.

I didn't know where to look. All the doors had numbers instead of names, and I was moving pretty fast to keep ahead of the orderlies. In the next hall, I met a finely dressed old woman sitting bolt upright in one of the hall chairs. With her pearls and her white gloves and her little black hat, she looked like she was ready to head out for a night on the town, about sixty years ago. She stopped me as I passed.

"Have you seen my brother? He promised to take me to the party."

I fought the urge to pull away from her. Her hand on my arm was as light as a spider. I wondered how many years she had been waiting in this hall for a brother who was mostly likely dead. I said, "He just called. He's on his way."

"Oh good. Thank you so much. He said he'd meet me here."

She settled back in her chair and folded her hands in her lap, prepared to wait until the crack of doom.

I heard shouting at the end of the hall, so I dove through a pair of double doors on the right. The change was abrupt, from soft lines and soothing colors to harsh metal and cold hospital tiles. The floor was beige and shined as though recently mopped. It reminded me of the killing room at the dog pound, designed for easy clean up. Two naked bodies lay on gurneys—two old women as small as children, as alike in their naked anonymity as twins. Somebody had parked them here and gone to lunch. Next to them stood a shrink-wrapped case of industrial kitchen-sized cans of lima beans, and beside that a pallet of bags of rice and a cart of soiled linens. I figured Preston would want to see this, so I started snapping pictures.

The next door I opened brought me to the hall where they piled the human wreckage before it headed out to the loading dock. The smell hit me like a garbage truck. I choked down a full bore of gorge and continued snapping the shutter at everything I saw. There was an old lady bent almost double upon herself by osteoporosis, gazing and mumbling into her own crotch. An elderly pantless gentleman pushed himself slowly along by his only foot—the other leg ended in a raw, naked stump just above the ankle. There were people picking at bleeding sores, moaning or mumbling or softly weeping or just sitting, gape-mouthed, blank-eyed, staring into the horror or the nothingness that had blasted their minds.

Suddenly, I was thankful Mom died the way she did—suddenly, with little or no warning, in her own home surrounded by everything she knew and loved, instead of spending

months or years lost in a fog of cold piss and hopeless dementia.

As I moved slowly along the corridor shooting pictures, an
eight-foot tree of an orderly caught me from behind, spun me
around and yanked the camera from my neck hard enough to
break the strap. I felt my head dislodge and fall against his
chest, which he seemed to enjoy because he kept it there,
trapped in the crook of his rough arm.

He twisted my elbow up around my ear and rooster-marched
me back into the carpeted areas of the nursing home. "You keep
dragging me around like this, you're liable to scuff my shoes,"
I said. I was wearing sandals.

"Can't let you run around like that."

"Afraid I'll trip over a corpse?"

"Something like that." He had to stop and get his bearings
for a moment. I was beginning to suspect they had built it like
a maze to keep people from finding their way out.

"Maybe you should have left a trail of breadcrumbs."

He said, "What?" Then started off, still swinging me along
by one arm.

"If you put me down, I promise not to run away."

"I don't mind," he said. "You're not heavy at all."

When we reached the nurses' station, the warden was just
buzzing somebody in. The orderly handed Nurse Ratched my
camera, then pushed me into a chair. He stood beside me,
one hand on my shoulder, crushing me like an empty can.

The nurse was all smiles again, smiles that didn't touch her
eyes, smiles that she wore like a name tag pinned to her face. I
wondered if she took them off at night and kept them in a jew-

elry box on the dresser. "As you are employed by a lawyer, I'm sure you'll understand that we can't let people wander the halls unescorted. It's a liability issue."

"Nobody's escorting him," I said, nodding at the man who had just entered. He glanced at me, then stopped, almost as surprised as I was. He was my lost preacher, Deacon Falgoust. I didn't even know he was back in town.

He was dressed in the same black suit I'd seen him in at Sam Loftin's wake, same black shoes, same tie. The only thing different about him was the raggedy, dog-eared Bible in his hand. "Is there a problem?" he asked.

"No problem," I said. "These nice people are just trying to keep me from doing my job." The orderly's fingers tightened painfully on my shoulder. I shifted in the chair until my heel was crushing his pinky toe. He gritted his teeth and escalated our silent game of Uncle.

"You trespassed into the facility," Nurse Ratched said.

"You were illegally denying me access. I have permission to be here."

"I'm afraid you don't."

"You saw the letter. It was signed by the family."

"There's no need for all this," the preacher said to the nurse. "Mrs. Lyons is a friend of mine."

"Miss," I corrected.

"In fact, I asked her to meet me here. She is my guest."

Whatever it was she really wanted to say remained safely behind Nurse Ratched's smile. She swallowed it with some difficulty, then cleared her throat. "Well, then, I suppose . . ."

I shrugged off the orderly's paw and stood up, shifting all

my weight onto his toe for a second before stepping off. "That was fun," he said. "I should take you dancing."

"So glad you could come," Deacon said as he took my hand. "I'm sure this was all just a misunderstanding."

"Yeah, that's what it was," I said. "I was just looking for my friend here."

Nurse Ratched settled herself into a chair behind the nurses' station. "Perfectly understandable." Her face had resumed its usual catatonic composure. "But we do have our little rules to follow to keep the lawyers happy."

"Naturally. What about my camera?"

"As the reverend's guest, you are free to visit whomever you like. But you'll have to leave your camera with me until I have permission for you to take photographs on the premises." She locked it in a drawer under the desk. "It will be safe here until you return."

Before I could answer, the preacher pulled me down one of the few halls I hadn't got around to exploring.

11

FIRST THING I NOTICED was the change in light. Gone were the fluorescent bulbs, replaced by lamps on tables in the interior hallways, giving off a warm yellow glow. The exterior halls had windows, and gardens outside the windows, and gardeners in the gardens mowing the lawn and bending over nasturtiums and buttercups. This was the cruise ship deck of the nursing home.

The residents we met in the halls were, for the most part, not so wrecked and thrown upon the shore as the ones I'd seen elsewhere. Dr. Dementia made his daily rounds here as well, punctually and without fail, but his patients were better situated, with nicer furniture and smiling nurses to change their diapers. The pernicious stink of piss was gone, replaced by a wholesome smell, like bacon, with just a touch of rolls warming in an oven, which we soon tracked down to the dining room, where the old ladies dozed over their pudding while a concert piano in the corner played a rondoletto all by itself.

We passed a group of old men who had gathered in a small sitting area, reading their papers or sleeping beneath them. One or two called out to the preacher, lifting their trembling hands in passing. He blessed them with his Bible, drawing crosses in the air. "I come around a couple of times a week to hold services in the chapel," he explained.

"You lied for me back there, preacher."

"Call me Deacon."

"What's your church say about lying, Deacon?"

"It's no sin to lie to the devil," he said. We turned a corner and nearly ran over a couple of elderly women, one pushing the other's chair, both dressed in cashmere lounge robes and fuzzy slippers. They batted their eyes at the preacher and giggled when he told them how the Lord seemed to have blessed them with eternal youth. The one in the chair straightened her robe where it had fallen open in her excitement.

"I didn't know you were back in town."

"I only got in this morning. I came here to see Mrs. Ruth— Ruth Vardry—do you remember her?"

"Sure. The crazy cat lady who lived in the woods. So this is where they stuck her."

"Mrs. Ruth is well taken care of here."

"Have you seen the rest of the place?"

"Many times." He stopped in front of a closed door. A white hand towel was draped across the doorknob, as though the occupant didn't want to be disturbed in the midst of fornicating.

"Since you're back, does that mean I can finally start working?"

"Whenever you like."

"You got everything straightened out in New Orleans?"

"By the grace of God, yes."

Deacon softly knocked on the door. A woman's voice answered almost immediately. "Come in." He took the towel from the knob and opened the door.

"I thought you had forgotten about me," she said as we entered. The room beyond was as dark as dusk, with faint rose-colored light sifting through a red curtain hung over a far door. The room itself was spacious and no warmer than the belly of a Philistine idol. A single long silhouette lounged on the shadow of a divan, but my first impression was that the room was full of people.

She pulled the jeweled chain on a Tiffany lamp. The dim light chased away the shadows and the shades—four and twenty ghostly blackbirds, a dim regiment of men who faded into the patterns in the wallpaper and were no more. The preacher didn't notice them, but that didn't surprise me. What surprised me is that Ruth did. A sad smile passed across her face; then she turned her bright, dark eyes upon me.

"Preacher, you didn't tell me you were bringing someone," she pouted.

I could see where Holly and Nathan got their looks. For a woman in her eighties, Ruth Vardry was still a striking figure. She wore a long gown of red satin. Her straight, smooth hair was still almost completely black, and not that fake boot-polish black you see on some old women. Hers spilled like a fall of water over the arm of the divan. Her face was long and narrow, with large wide-set eyes of a disconcerting color that never seemed quite the same each time you looked at her. Her nose was as straight and sharp as the blade of stiletto. Her worst feature was her mouth, which was slightly pinched, but perhaps that was due to the oxygen tube pressing her proud upper lip.

Framed photos hung on every wall and stood on tables and bookshelves all around the room—glamour shots of Ruth going back decades, some even to World War II and maybe earlier. In the later color photographs, she was even more beautiful than in her younger, Hollywood pictures. She had a face to launch a thousand ships, a beauty to bring an empire to ruin. I wondered how a veritable Roxana had been born from such quintessential clodhopper stock.

She noticed me admiring her pictures. "Do you like them?"

Deacon said, "Jackie is a photographer. She's going to take the pictures of your house before we start the restoration."

"Are you, now? Well. Take a look at this, then." She stretched her long arm over the back of the divan and took a framed photo from the piano against the wall. In it, she wore a tight, short-skirted Little Bo Peep outfit and was holding a crook between her legs while she cuddled a lamb. "That was taken by Irving Klaw," she said.

"Didn't he shoot the Bettie Page photos?"

"Some of them." She seemed pleased that I had heard of him.

I set the photo on the coffee table and crossed the room to the largest portrait. It was a full-length deal, nearly as tall as me. In it, Ruth couldn't have been more than sixteen, though you'd have lost money guessing her age in any decade, from what I could tell. She wore a dark dress that clung like spiderwebs to her slim, straight body. She was turned away from the camera, her hair flowing down her bare back almost to her hips. The logo in the corner said MGM. "You didn't look like the typical pinup girl, Mrs. Vardry."

"I wasn't. But not every man has typical tastes."

"Were you in movies?" I asked.

"None that you've ever seen. They didn't show my pictures on *The Late Late Show*." She laughed, then coughed, covering her mouth with a thin hand while she wheezed and gasped.

Deacon reached down beside the divan and checked the valve on her oxygen tank. When she had recovered, she tugged at the tube beneath her nose. With surprising tenderness, Deacon knelt and tightened the strap that held it to her face. "I hate that I have to wear this thing," she said.

"It's for your own good, Mrs. Ruth."

"I just feel so damned helpless. I've never been so helpless in all my life." Despite her protestations, she obviously enjoyed being ministered to by the handsome preacher from Louisiana. She groped him with her eyes. He cupped her face in his hands and she leaned forward and moistened her lips with her tongue, but he only adjusted the tube to best feed oxygen to her starving lungs.

"If I was ten years younger . . ." she breathed.

"I'd be *foutre*," he said as he stood.

"I don't know what that means, but I like the way you say it." She leaned back on the divan and looked at me as though I had just appeared. "So you're a photographer," she said.

"Yes, ma'am."

"Dear God, I'm not a ma'am. Call me Ruth, please."

"Yes, Mrs. Ruth," I said, copying the preacher.

"Have you seen my house?"

"I've been through it once."

"How does it look to you?"

"Pretty run-down. I've lived in worse."

"Did you see anything there that interested you?" I wasn't exactly sure what she meant, whether she had caught my look of surprise upon entering her room and finding it full of ghosts, or if she was talking about something, or someone, else.

"It must have been a beautiful place, once," I said.

"Maybe, but not in my lifetime," she sighed.

"But it will be again, when I'm done with it," Deacon said. He told Mrs. Ruth about the house in New Orleans he'd salvaged. "We got two entire levels of wood flooring that stayed above the flood, and a flatbed loaded with trim and doors and windows, every bit of it chestnut."

Ruth's eyes glowed as he described how he would return the old ruin to its former glory. "I hope I am spared long enough to see it the way you see it, Deacon," she sighed when he was done. "To tell you the truth, I would like to see it now. Just one more time."

"Now Mrs. Ruth," he said.

"You could take me." She plucked at the sleeve of his jacket, clinging to him just like I'd seen her granddaughter do the day of the wake. "Luther wouldn't have to know."

"You know that's not possible." He gently untangled himself and folded her hands across her breast. She lay back and closed her eyes, her chest rising and falling in tiny, rapid pants. Even with the oxygen, it was all she could do to get her breath.

Her eyes still closed, she said, "Jackie Lyons."

"Yes ma . . . Ruth?"

"I want to see the pictures."

Deacon cranked up her oxygen, then rested his big, sun-burned hand on her forehead, feeling for a temperature. "I will pay you," she added.

He knelt at her side and, with his hand still covering her eyes, bowed his head and began to pray. I tried not to listen, but it wasn't like any prayer I'd ever heard in my mother's church. No craven cowering or appeals to the Almighty to work His grand magic on this worthless flesh—it was more like a conversation between three people, one of whom I was not presently privileged to see or hear. Maybe they could hear Him, or maybe it was just the soft, melodic sound of Deacon's voice, or maybe it was the oxygen hissing from the tank, but Ruth's breathing gradually evened out.

When the preacher had said amen and stood, Ruth opened her eyes. There were no tears quivering, no peace bringing heal-ing sleep, only bitterness, the helpless anger of a strong woman betrayed by an old age she didn't feel in her heart. "It was my house. I was supposed to die there, but they took me away and locked me up in this place. I want to see it again. You will help me do that, Jackie Lyons."

It wasn't a request, but I answered, "Yes ma'am," because I couldn't call her Ruth any more than I could call my mother Lucy.

12

But look at these lonely houses,
each in its own fields, filled for
the most part with poor ignorant
folk who know little of the law.
Think of the deeds of hellish
cruelty, the hidden wickedness
which may go on, year in, year
out, in such places, and none
the wiser.
— SIR ARTHUR CONAN
DOYLE, "THE ADVENTURE OF
THE COPPER BEECHES"

I RETRIEVED MY CAMERA from the front desk and left
without getting any photographs of Preston's client. He
was going to have to file a court order before Nurse Ratched

would let me see what was hidden in her chamber of horrors. She had made sure to delete all the photos from the camera's memory. I wondered how much they paid her to be so thorough. Not nearly enough, I guessed by her faded scrubs and worn-out shoes. She was only too happy to do it for free, anyway.

Deacon agreed that I could start shooting that afternoon, so I stopped by Deiter's to pick up the equipment I'd need. Deiter Marks's camera shop was tucked away in a nondescript converted residence on a small street just off Memphis's busiest retail corridor. Most of the time his place wasn't even open, and he didn't bother posting his hours on the door.

He was best known as one-half of Grant-Marks Paranormal Investigations. In his spare time, he and a few of his closest lunatics liked to hang around abandoned mental hospitals and Civil War battlefields trying to record the voices of the dead. Deiter was one of the few people in the world I'd told about my ability to see ghosts. He once admitted to being intensely jealous. In all his years hanging out in cemeteries, he'd never seen the first spirit. Graveyards, I told him, were usually empty.

Deiter met me at the door wearing a pair of paisley pajama bottoms and a quilted housecoat he had stolen from somebody's grandmother, one pocket of which was stuffed with oatmeal cream pies, the other with empty plastic wrappers. He was just finishing a pie as he opened the door. He wiped his hands on his hay-colored beard and welcomed me inside.

I told him why I'd come and he quickly set about dragging things from the pack rat's nest that filled the front of his camera shop. He laid at my feet a tripod, lights, light stands, reflective screens—everything I needed to complete the photo shoot. None of it was new and some of it was held together with duct tape, but it was easily a thousand dollars' worth of photographic equipment.

"I'll pay you after I get paid," I said.

He pushed one of his flippers at me and rolled his eyes. "You do me a favor taking this junk out of here. I'm up to my eyes, I can hardly move." He seemed to move around the place just fine, despite his bulk and the clutter stacked to the ceiling. He could put his hand on exactly what he wanted almost with his eyes closed. My expensive little pile hadn't made a visible dent in his hoard.

"Speaking of," I said as I dug a CD out of my back pocket. "See what you can do with these."

"What's this?"

"Photos of some old, faded wallpaper that's supposed to be really rare."

"Zuber?"

"Something like that."

"I've only ever seen reproductions." He tucked the disk into the waistband of his pajamas. "I'll do my best, but you really should have used infrared."

Deiter helped me load the case with all my equipment in the trunk. The morning was growing hot, hard beams of sunlight dropping through the trees, and Deiter was dripping by the time we finished, big dark stains under his pits. I offered him a smoke, but he waved it away in favor of another oatmeal cream pie. He folded the whole thing into his mouth and tucked the empty plastic wrapper in the other pocket of his housecoat. "Those things are bad for you," he said of my cigarette.

I shrugged and blew a cloud of smoke at the clouds. The sky was a perfect shade of blue, blotted with fluffy white clouds in perfect symmetry, as though painted by some obsessive-compulsive deity.

"So where's this big job?" he asked.

I told him about the preacher's plan to restore Mrs. Ruth's antebellum home. I knew he'd be interested, but his face grew grim when I mentioned the name of the place. He shook his head and folded another pie into the hole in his beard. "That place is bad. Have you seen it already?" I said that I had. "And you didn't notice anything . . . anyone . . . you know what I mean?"

"I thought I would." I took another drag, remembering my first view of the place. Stirling Plantation should have been a neon-lit Vegas for creatures that went bump in the night. I had expected to find it as crowded as a casino. "There was nothing there. Nothing dead, anyway."

"That's damn strange," he said, shaking his head again.

"Why?"

"It has a black history. Some bad shit happened there a long time ago."

"What kind of shit?"

"I don't know. I'm not a historian."

"Well," I said in a cloud of smoke, "maybe it was so long ago the house has forgotten."

He leaned close, his breath sweet-smelling, like cake. "Some guys I know—a rival group of paranormal investigators—went out there last year after the owner, what's her name?"

"Ruth Vardry."

". . . moved out. They didn't have permission, but they wanted to see if the stories were true, took a shitload of video equipment to try to film it. They thought they'd make a movie and sell it for a million bocks. Two weeks later I heard they quit, closed down their website. Two sold their house and moved to Montana."

I laughed, crushed the cigarette under my heel. "Are you trying to scare me, Deiter?" I climbed in my car.

He closed the door and bent down beside the window, his man-boobs hanging out of his housecoat. "I'm focking serious, Jackie. Be careful out there. It's a long way from Memphis."

I started the car. "I will be."

Deacon met me that afternoon in front of Jenny's house. I hadn't seen her since the night I snuck away, and I dreaded running into her again. Her house looked abandoned, nobody parked in the driveway or peeking through the curtains as I pulled up.

Deacon was wearing mirrored aviator sunglasses, his shirt stuck to his chest and little trickles of moisture ran down the back of his neck, soaking his collar. The meadow beyond was like an open oven door. A mirage of heat rose off the levee rocks, but thankfully no ghosts.

"Is it always this hot in May around here?" he asked as I killed the engine.

"Sometimes. Can you help me with this?" I opened the trunk.

"For a minute I mistook I was back home in Louisiana."
He grabbed one end of the heavy case and lifted it out, hoisted
it onto his shoulder as though it were a basket of bread and
started off.

He led the way down into the woods, picking out the path
through the brambles, which seemed to have doubled in size
in the month since I last passed this way. Unseen creatures skit-
tered through the undergrowth at our approach. As we crossed
the dry creek by the log bridge, I asked, "Is this where the lake
runs out?"

He stood balanced on the log with the heavy case on his
shoulder, pointing away into the woods. "The big lake is up
yonder ways. The spillway comes out on the other side of the
hill. This creek is from a smaller pond away there in the woods,
called Spring Lake, fed by artesian springs. If you go a hundred yards up the creek, you'll find a boulder with a hollow
place worn out of the stone where slaves used to wash their
clothes."

We hadn't gone far up the next hill when we started to hear
the angry droning of chainsaws and grumbling of heavy en-
gines. Deacon stopped again and set my case on the ground.
He took a handkerchief from his pocket and toweled the back
of his neck.

"Here's the old scuppernong arbor." He walked toward a
small but densely overgrown thicket of vines. "My workers
found it this morning. It's original to the house, planted before
the Civil War. They were about to chop it down when I stopped
them." Old muscadine covered in furry black bark, arched over to
form a leafy cave against the hillside. I noticed something

hanging just inside the entrance, something that moved as we drew near.

"There's a big damn bat in there," I said.

"That's not a bat, he is *un rat de bois*—rat of the woods. Jackie Lyons, meet my guard possum, Paul. At night, he comes up to the house and wanders around the rooms." Deacon stepped under the arbor and reached up to stroke the creature. It was hanging by its tail from a vine. At Deacon's touch, it opened its mouth and yawned, a nightmare of teeth.

"The Opossum Paul?" I asked.

"Do you think God will strike me dead?" He scratched the prehistoric monster between its ears. "He's his own little dude."

We continued up the hill, and it wasn't long before I began to smell diesel smoke. The undergrowth suddenly gave way and the forest opened out on either side of the path. Before us rose the house, stripped of its kudzu mantle, lying naked and gray beneath the sun like a Greek ruin. A dozen men were busy tearing off the roof and jettisoning the rotted lumber over the side. More men were clearing undergrowth with chainsaws and sling blades, women and kids dragging briars up out of the woods to throw into the scoop of a bulldozer that sat idling on the slope of the hill. A pillar of gray smoke rose into the sky behind the house, somewhere beyond the trees.

"As soon as we get all this cleared out, we'll run new water, sewer, and gas lines up to the house." Deacon set my case on the ground beside what appeared to be an old brick-paved drive or loop. The bricks were green with moss and nearly buried in the deep loam.

"Who are all these people?" I asked. There were dozens, and

everywhere I turned I saw more. Several had noticed our arrival and raised their hands in greeting. Some dropped their work and headed our way.

Deacon spread his arms as though to embrace them all. "These are my saints, the congregation of my church. Most of them were scattered by the hurricane, but after Mrs. Ruth deeded us this property, I sent out word and they came. See how much we have already accomplished, with the Lord's help?"

The whole hillside had been transformed. It was already starting to look like a place where somebody could live—if you knocked down the house first. Without its veil of kudzu you could see just how close it was to collapsing upon itself.

We continued up the hill, now surrounded by a swarm of Deacon's saints, all crying his name in an apparent ecstasy of joy. Two took my camera case and carried it along. I counted half a dozen different languages in the first five minutes, a veritable Babel of Creole-speaking Cajuns, Asians, Mexicans, Jamaicans and Haitians.

A tottering old Vietnamese man came out of the house and called Deacon over to the porch. They huddled together and Deacon read something from the worn red-letter edition of the King James Bible that was always in his hand or his back pocket. Next, the children gathered, dangling from his arms like parrots. Now the women came and shyly took his hands and drew him away to where they were steaming tamales and boiling crawfish over open fires. They had set up a weird, circuslike encampment on the edge of the woods, rusting campers and tattered pop-ups and pickup trucks with camper shells, scores of dogs and chickens, goats staked out and bleating like tiger bait, and more half-naked children than anyone could count. They surrounded Deacon, dancing, clapping, kissing his hands and singing. He walked among them, his arms lifted as though riding a human wave.

I looked around until I found several Coleman coolers under a folding table. Deacon finally worked himself free of his followers and found me digging through the slushy ice. "Do you want a cold drink?" he asked.

I shook icy water from my hand. "Just wondering where you keep the Kool-Aid."

13

GRADERS AND BULLDOZERS scraped the earth beyond Deacon's circus camp, leveling the hills and preparing a place where, in a few days, they would begin pouring the concrete foundations for his church. With a stick, he scratched out the plan in the dust for me: sanctuary, entrances, baptistcry, offices, fellowship hall, food pantry, job-training school. I was anxious to start work in the house. Before he had a chance to give me the grand tour, I was rescued by the arrival of a flatbed truck bringing in another backhoe. Deacon hurried away to show them where to off-load.

I found my camera equipment next to a truck camper sitting up on concrete blocks. I squatted in the shade, lit a cigarette, watched the workers clearing the forest around the house. One in particular caught my eye. He was a young man, short and wiry, deeply sunburned across the back of his neck, dressed in dirty coveralls and yellow safety vest, a black cap that had nearly turned yellow with dust pulled down low over his eyes. The faded logo on his cap said GMPI. I watched him cross and recross the ground, like a man plowing a field with invisible mules, occasionally pausing to spray a line of orange paint on the dirt.

I finished my smoke, stamped it out. He wasn't using the normal electronic detection equipment for locating buried pipes and electrical lines. Instead, he carried a pair of thin brass divining rods in his fists, walking along with them held in front of his chest. Wherever his rods would cross, he'd stop, shift them to one hand and spray an orange arrow on the dirt with a sort of paint can on the end of a stick. Then he'd continue on, holding the rods loose so they could swing free in his hands.

His row brought him directly to me. He removed his cap and wiped the sweat from his face with a red bandanna as big as a pillowcase. "I wish I had known it was you there, Jackie," he said without even looking at me. I'd known Trey for several years, but you couldn't really call us friends. In addition to being the call-before-you-dig man, he worked with Deiter at Grant-Marks Paranormal Investigations, using his dowsing rods to detect ectoplasmic residues and buried cables. Despite my own unique abilities in this sphere, Trey and I were not kindred spirits. Something about me jammed his frequencies. He tucked his handkerchief away and looked back along the line he'd just finished spraying, probably wondering if he needed to check it again owing to my psychic interference.

"I didn't think the house had water or gas," I said.

"They's a big gas pipeline runs across this property." He scrubbed his lips with the back of his hand and shoved his hat back on his head, revealing a stark, white forehead above the sunburn of his face. A couple of days' worth of faint, blond stubble speckled his cheeks. "You working construction now?" he asked.

"Photography. I'm shooting the house."

"You been inside it yet?"

"Once."

"Nice place, huh?"

Deacon returned from overseeing the unloading of the backhoe. "Everything OK?" he asked my friend.

Trey spit past me, a black gob that cratered the dust next to one of his orange lines. He wiped his mouth and took up his dowsing rods. "I want to show y'all somethin'. Foller me, 'bout five paces back, if you don't mind." He started toward the house. After a moment's hesitation, we followed like a pair of dutiful wives. We entered the woods and Trey angled toward a thicket that Deacon's workers hadn't begun to clear. As he slowed, his dowsing rods swung together in front of his chest.

Deacon pulled his sunglasses from his face and pinched the bridge of his nose between his thumb and forefinger. "Please don't tell me the pipeline runs down here. The plans didn't show anything in this area."

"Pipeline's back yonder. This here is a tunnel," Trey said.

Deacon opened his eyes and blinked. "A tunnel?"

"Rods don't lie, man." Trey spit again and scuffed it into the dirt with the toe of his boot. "Leads from the house off into the woods there. That's how I know it's a tunnel. Ain't no gas, water, or sewer lines into that house, and the electricity used to come in on a pole. Only thing it could be is a tunnel."

I wondered if Trey's employers knew he was using hillbilly magic to guarantee the safety of that gas pipeline. Deacon must have been thinking the same thing. "I thought you usually used some kind of machine to detect buried pipes."

"Got a Dynatel back in the truck. Already tried it. Won't work on this hill." He clicked the rods together. "I figured something was interfering, so I got out my rods. First thing I found was water. It's all up under here."

Trey shifted his chew around in his jaw, his eyes wandering all over the house and the trees surrounding it. "Sometimes these old houses have their well down in the cellar. When this house was built, they probably still had trouble with Indians. I bet if you tore the walls down to the original timbers, you'd find loopholes for shooting."

Deacon's face lit up at the thought of all that history, buried and hidden for who knew how many years. He slid his sunglasses back on to his nose to free his hands for talking. "The house was built in 1858. Legend says it was a dead end on the underground railroad. Escaped slaves would crawl into the cellar through ventilation holes in the back. But those who made it here never got any farther north. The strongest were disfigured and resold into slavery, the old murdered, but the women and children just disappeared."

"Seriously?" I asked.

Deacon shrugged. "That's the family legend. You know how legends are. Infant mortality was extremely high, and women died all the time while giving birth. In that time, families would lose two or three children before the age of ten. For slaves it was even higher. Men would go through two, three, sometimes four wives."

"It ain't never a good idea to build a house over a well." Trey was still stuck on whatever was bothering him about the house. "Sometimes a well can be a kind of gate into the spirit world, or hell, whatever you want to call it."

Deacon said, "I've been all over this house a hundred times and I've never seen any sign of a tunnel or a well."

"Preacher, they is things about this house you won't see if you go over it a thousand times, not unless you got eyes to see them. I can find hidden things with my dowsing rods. And Jackie here can see them with her nekkid eyes."

I couldn't tell what Deacon was thinking behind his sunglasses, couldn't see if he was looking at me or had even heard what Trey had said. I hoped not. It would only remind him about that day on the levee. But he was looking at something quite far away.

Trey cleared his throat and said, "Well, them lines ain't gonna paint theyselves."

Deacon smiled and shook his hand. "Thank you for your help. I'll only keep you from your work another moment. A minute ago, you said the first thing you found was water. Then you found the tunnel. What else did you find?"

Trey shifted uncomfortably, his small hand gripped tightly in Deacon's paw. "I can't say for sure," he mumbled.

"What can you say for sure?"

Trey started to spit, then thought better of it. He shifted his wad of tobacco to his other cheek. "I'll tell you this, preacher. I wouldn't walk them woods after dark, not for any money."

Deacon nodded, released him and strolled off in the other direction, smiling and mumbling to himself. "I shall fear no evil, for thou art with me. Thy rod and thy staff, they comfortest me." Soon he was pulled in a hundred directions by his people, all demanding his attention. Trey hurried back to his work, vanishing into the crowd without a backward glance at me.

It seemed everybody was looking for something they couldn't find. I wondered if I could find someone to help me move my equipment into the house.

14

I SET UP MY LIGHTS AND TRIPOD in the foyer. The tiny old Vietnamese man I'd seen earlier helped me string a power cord into the house from the circus camp. I shot everything, every inch of wall as high as eye level, with closer studies of any bit of trim or ornamentation I could find. Dust sifted down the whole time, workers moved in and out of my frame as though I wasn't there, shifting furniture, bringing in lumber and stacking it along the walls, forcing me to pause, move, set up again and repeat the same shots. I must have worked three hours just covering two walls and not once did I see the preacher.

When I started, I hadn't the first clue what I was supposed to be doing. After those first three hours, I didn't feel much smarter, but at least I had some shots to show for my time and maybe get a little bit of an advance on my pay.

It must have been siesta time, because they had stopped working on the roof. I only noticed because the blizzard of dust had changed to more of a flurry, with occasional sleets of loose plaster. I shook the rubble from my shoulders and continued to shoot. Other than the clicking of the camera's shutter, the silence went on and on, and I found myself stopping more and more often to listen to it.

I had put Deiter's earlier warning and Trey's half-spoken fears from my mind. Very little about the dead could frighten me anymore. I'd been seeing what you would call ghosts for most of my life. I hadn't always dealt with them very well—in fact, they'd nearly killed me more than once. Not directly. Just their being there, visible, but only to me. It wasn't everybody who could maintain being in both worlds at the same time, having to keep a sane face while you're questioning some john about what happened to his hooker, listening to his lies while she's standing there the whole time, bleeding on the rug, looking at her own brains slipping down the wall.

My special friends had cost me my job, my marriage, any semblance of a normal life. I had tried to drive them out of my head by filling my veins with smack. I knew I wasn't the only haunted ex-junkie in this crazy old world, but that didn't make me feel any better. Plenty of people in my boat had eaten bullets or walked off a pier in an effort to make the voices and the visions stop. The only thing that kept me from hanging myself in a closet was the thought of hanging there forever, waiting like a spooky house decoration for the next confused little girl who had been born with a caul on her head to come along and open the door to my hell and join me there.

I stopped shooting to listen, waiting for the rap of hammers, the endless chatter of the workers, the throb and rumble of their machines. There was nothing. I'd never felt more alone in my life. A house this old should have been choked with ghosts. It was as though something had driven them out. Driven them out and taken their place.

When in Rome, I thought. A siesta sounded like a good idea. I shut down the lights, capped my lens, and stepped outside. The *fitz* of a beer bottle opening spun me around. Deacon sat in a dining room chair on the porch, leaning back against the wall like a gunslinger in an old Western. He held a dripping bottle of Abita beer out to me, an unopened one in his other hand.

I accepted his offering and sat on the step, my legs crossed in front of me. "I don't usually drink before five," I lied as I took a swig.

Deacon opened his bottle and held it up to a shaft of sunlight filtering through a hole in the roof. "I usually don't drink after five, so we're even."

I lit up and let the smoke drain out of me in a long slow sigh. It was like I'd been holding my breath for an hour. Sweat dripped from my hair into my eyes, dangled from the tip of my nose. The heat of the day had crept into the house while I worked and wrapped its woolly arms around me and clamped its thick, musty-smelling fingers over my mouth. Now a delicious bit of breeze fanned across the porch. I took another drag and felt my lungs ache from lack of abuse.

"It's a hot one," Deacon said. I allowed that it could be considered warm for a day in May. He tasted his beer and set it on the porch beside his chair. I got the crazy idea that he didn't really drink at all. I sucked mine down in about three swallows and rolled the empty bottle against my knee.

"This kind of heat reminds me of Kuwait." He pushed his

chair away from the wall and sat with his hands on his knees, leaning forward, the big aviator sunglasses resting on his nose so that I couldn't see his eyes at all.

"So it's true what Holly said. That you were in the military before you started this preaching dodge."

"Go Army. First Armored Division. Desert Storm. You strike me as ex-military yourself. Squid?"

"Coast Guard."

"Must have been hell."

"I could tell you stories," I laughed. I spent the war aboard the *Cape Hazardous* protecting Maryland crab boats from Saddam's Atlantic fleet.

"We were one of the first across the border at the beginning of the invasion. Them Iraqi boys had had the fight bombed out of them and started giving up as soon as they saw our tanks. My unit didn't fire a shot in anger. I remember, it was about the fourteenth hour, we jumped this group of Republican Guards coming out of their fortifications and running toward us with their hands in the air. They didn't have any weapons, but it was making the captain nervous so he told me to put a shot over their heads to make them sit down. I don't know what happened. Maybe I misjudged the distance. Or maybe it was God directed my hand, because I killed one of those men, shot him with the fifty right between the eyes from maybe a half mile out. I couldn't have made that shot if I tried. His head just disappeared. I'll never forget that."

"It's not something you forget," I offered.

"I don't blame myself. It was an accident. We were at war

and I was following orders, and on top of all that, I suspect the Good Lord guided my hand for a purpose He has yet to reveal to me. I can but trust that one day I will know His divine plan."

I stubbed my cigarette out on the bottom of my shoe and flicked the butt into the trash pile in front of the house. People were starting to appear from the circus camp, yawning and scratching as they made their way back to their dropped tools.

Deacon turned his head to watch them go by. From that angle, I could see just the hint of a smile, his eyes crinkling up behind his sunglasses. "The VA doctor says I got PTSD."

"I take it you don't agree?"

He laughed a little and shrugged. "I got no nightmares, no hallucinations. Jesus freed me from my demons and I'm at peace. But I can't forget that soldier."

Why this confession? What did he hope to gain? Certainly not absolution, nor even much camaraderie. I got the impression he'd spent a lot of time in musty church basements unburdening his soul to groups of perfect strangers. Maybe that was where he'd picked up this preaching gig—I'd seen it happen before, people trading dope for Jesus, one addiction for another.

"That soldier haunts me. Sometimes when I preach, he's sitting right there in the front pew. He's got no head, but it's him. He goes everywhere I go. I can't get away."

A couple of Deacon's workers passed, said hello and hollah, and went up the scaffolding like squirrels. I didn't respond to Deacon's confession, just sat there rolling the empty beer bottle between my palms. Pretty soon a rotted piece of roofing sailed down and landed with a crash on the garbage pile.

"We'd better get out of the line of fire," Deacon said.

We retreated into the house. I turned on my camera lights and moved them to the next section of wall. The electrical cord had gotten itself wedged between a couple of loose floorboards. Deacon helped me pry it loose. "Anything like that ever happen to you?" he asked.

"Happens all the time with these long cords."

"That's not what I meant."

I tried to play it cool. Lying to myself made it easier. I was good at it. I had lots of practice. I just shrugged and snapped a picture.

"You can see the dead, can't you?"

I shot a couple of photos of the wall. Somewhere behind the house an air compressor cranked up. A man appeared in the rear doorway, pushing a wheelbarrow full of old bricks. He crossed the room and exited through the front door. "What makes you think that?"

"I think you know."

I nodded and silently cursed Trey for an idiot. It wasn't really his fault, even though he'd dropped that bomb about me being able to see hidden things with my nekkid eyes. It had been too much to hope Deacon had forgotten about my little prodigy on the levee.

"I'd rather not talk about it."

"I can well understand your reluctance. I rarely tell anyone about my soldier. Most people don't understand, so we hide it in our hearts, afraid and ashamed." He took his little black

Bible out of his back pocket and began shifting through the soft pages. "But there's nothing to be ashamed of. The Apostle Paul wrote in his first epistle to the Corinthians, the manifestation of the Holy Spirit is given to each accordingly, for to one is given words of wisdom, to another words of knowledge, to another great faith, to another the gift of healing, to another prophecy, and to another the *discerning of spirits*."

"You think this is some kind of gift?"

He put his hand on my arm, gently cupping the elbow, as though about to help me across a busy street. "I have counseled others who are haunted by the dead, Jackie Lyons. Most of them, like you, believe it to be a curse rather than the gift it truly is."

I extracted my elbow from his hand.

"But it shows that the Lord favors you above all others! And if it can bring some comfort to Jenny Loftin, and perhaps a measure of justice to her family, would that not make it a gift?"

"Justice?"

"You know as well as I do, but for very different reasons, that Sam Loftin didn't kill himself."

I just shrugged. Maybe I did know. Or maybe I didn't have a clue. I reminded myself, this was none of my business. It certainly wasn't any of Deacon's business what I knew or didn't know.

"For the last year, I have counseled Sam and Jenny. In some ways I know them better than they know themselves. Sam loved his daughter Reece and still grieved for her, but he had living children that he loved equally, and he was devoted to Jenny. He wouldn't take himself from them."

"Did he have life insurance?"

Deacon nodded. "And the insurance company won't pay if it's suicide."

So that was why they needed me—to help complete the profile of a man who had no intention of killing himself, to dangle before Jenny Loftin a strand of hope, however thin, that her husband's death was anything but suicide.

But in all my years photographing the dead—for the police, for insurance companies, for lawyers—I'd seen plenty of suicides that didn't make sense. The act itself contradicts all logic and reason. So what if they bought plane tickets they would never use, or called to complain about a credit card charge, hung up the phone, and shot themselves in the head? Something snapped inside. People who had everything to live for, but just couldn't go on carrying all that hidden grief or buried pain or whatever it was that made them kick over the chair.

The only reason I didn't believe Sam Loftin had killed himself was because of what I had seen on the levee. But that made all the difference in the world. My "gift" wouldn't win Jenny Loftin that insurance money. Life insurance agents were funny that way.

I said, "I don't know what you want from me."

"I just wish you would talk to her. When you ran out the night of Sam's wake, she said you'd be back. She said you promised to go to Sam's funeral."

"I had another funeral to go to."

"I'm sorry. What it someone close?" He asked like he didn't believe me.

"My mother."

For once, he looked shocked. "I'm so sorry. I didn't know."

"It's OK. We weren't that close." This wasn't a lie, but I don't know why I said it. A month had passed and still I had the feeling that something had been left unfinished. It wasn't that I hadn't had a chance to say goodbye to her. I didn't know what was bothering me.

"You should let Jenny know about your mother. She'll understand. And I think if you tell her what you really saw that day on the levee, she'll understand that, too."

People always say that if you have never seen war, you can never really understand what it's like. It's the same way with the dead. Deacon had seen war, and he said he had seen the dead, but I didn't know whether to believe him. How would he like it if I tried to tell him how to feel about the war? "Do you really want Jenny to spend the rest of her life staring out that window, waiting for her dead husband to appear? How would you like to watch your wife drown over and over and over?"

"I didn't think of it that way."

"Most people think I'm crazy when I tell them I see these things."

"I believe you."

"Why? Because you see spooks, too? Because your guilty conscience fills your pews with the manifestations of your PTSD? Tell you what, preacher. Let me know next time you see him and I'll tell you if he's real."

"I will do that."

"When I do, maybe you can tell me why God's plan included you blowing an innocent man's head clean off. Because nobody asked that soldier if he wanted to be your final exam in Theology 101."

"Why are you so angry all the time, Jackie Lyons?"

"Preacher, you don't know jack about me."

"I would like to, though. I wish you would tell me."

"There's nothing to tell. Now can I get back to my work? I got rent to pay."

Why was I so angry? Because sometimes I felt like Deacon's dead Iraqi—an object lesson in someone else's life, with no other purpose than to get my head blown off to teach some holy fraud I didn't even know a lesson I'd never be privileged to learn.

15

I WORKED ALONE UNTIL almost dark. I knew it was
time to quit when the nail guns stopped spitting. A couple of old Mexican women were waiting for me on the porch.
One handed me an envelope full of money. I didn't count it in
front of her. The other gave me a flashlight.

I thanked them and they left me alone on the porch. The
beer Deacon had been drinking earlier still sat by the steps,
nearly full. It was warm as spit but I drank it anyway, washing
the dirt dobber nests out of my throat. The sun was going down
quickly, the earth giving up its heat in a moist fume that smelled
like rotting leaves and chainsaw smoke. I counted the money
in the envelope by the light of the flashlight. Ten pictures of
Andy Jackson so crisp and new they stuck together like refrigerator magnets.

I walked down through the woods, following the trail back
to where I'd parked my car in front of Jenny's house. I hoped
I wouldn't run into her there. When I got there, the only
thing waiting for me was a tow notice from the neighborhood

security guard taped to the driver's-side window. Jenny's house looked dark and empty, the house beside it brightly lit with a picturesque little old lady peeping through one curtain in an upper window. I guessed she was the one who called security.

I lit a cigarette and leaned against the hood of my car, watched some geese cross the purple velvet of the sky headed for the lake, the whoosh of their wings sounding close enough to touch, and thought about that day when I'd stood almost in this exact spot and watched a replay of the moment of a man's death. I wondered if there were some way it could be conjured up like an instant replay, so that a person could review it from eighteen different angles to determine if the man was dead before he went in the water or if someone put him there.

I dropped my butt and got in my car, started the engine and clicked on the headlights. They shone across the field to the edge of the woods, where a little girl stood just under the trees. She was dressed in a little pink and white Cotton Carnival dress, all petticoats and bows with ribbons in her hair. She didn't look like any of the kids at Deacon's camp. She was too clean, too Caucasian, but maybe I had missed her in the crowd. There were a lot of people in that camp and I couldn't have seen them all. I was afraid she had followed me.

I stepped out of my car. She half turned and edged back into the woods as though about to run away. "Hey kid!" I shouted, and started toward her, but she only retreated deeper into the woods. I walked faster, pushing through the tall, dry grass, trying not to break an ankle in the tractor ruts.

For a moment I lost sight of her behind a blackberry thicket.

By the time I had cleared it, she was gone, replaced by a black figure like a dog, hunched over. It didn't so much move as merge into the shadows beneath the trees, as though the darkness had opened up like a door and it had slipped in with the alien grace of an octopus, headfirst, drawing its long, thin tentacle limbs behind it. I felt myself go cold inside, a drowned-at-the-bottom-of-the-lake cold.

I looked back at the house and the little old lady peering out her window. She was either watching me through a tele-scope now, or drinking from a bottle of hooch. I doubted she was drinking hooch. If she had, I might have knocked on her door and asked for a swallow.

Then a little girl screamed and I was running. The head-lights of my car cast my shadow huge before me against the wall of trees. I entered the woods, passing through the same dark door the creature had entered moments before.

The path seemed different than before. It twisted and turned in unfamiliar ways. I knew I should have crossed the log bridge at some point, but it never appeared. I shone the flashlight up the path and back the way I had come. With a shriek, the little girl crossed through the beam of my light about thirty yards away. Something large and dark coursed behind her, close on her shiny Little Bo Peep heels.

I dove off the trail into the underbrush, limbs whipping at my face, thorns ripping my flesh like mad weasels, chasing something. I didn't know what it was. I don't know what I would have done had I caught it. All I had for a weapon was a cheap plastic flashlight.

I saw them maybe twice more before I lost them completely.

They didn't so much escape or leave me behind as simply cease to be, as though they had never been there at all. Which they hadn't. I should have recognized the little girl in her period dress and odd nocturnal behavior. She had probably died before I was even born. It had been several years since I let one trick me that way, not since my days as a vice cop for the Memphis Police Department, back before I traded my badge for a heroin spoon.

Deacon's flashlight started to piss out on me as I headed back, but I had no idea which path would return me to my car before it ran out of gas. I knew the woods were bordered east and west by the highway and the lake, north and south by Stirling Estates. This wasn't darkest Africa. If I started walking, sooner or later I had to reach the border of something resembling civilization.

I hadn't gone very far before I stubbed my toe against an old piece of headstone leaning against a tree. Its outline was rough and the letters almost illiterate, crude as though scratched into the stone with a hammer and nail, not the fine chiseling of a professional monument carver.

Hyer lies Bob Wharton
Ded of Plursy
Janerary 7, 1932

I found another headstone sprouting from the other side of the tree. A group of cedars had nearly overgrown a small plot surrounded by a rusting iron fence. Everywhere the wavering beam of my flashlight fell, I saw another leaning, vine-draped headstone half buried in leaves. I realized I had stumbled into the middle of an old cemetery in the middle of the night.

And I wasn't the only one there.

I saw a woman floating slowly among the graves. From behind, she looked about the same age as my mother, her gray hair piled up under an old-fashioned hat, and a long black dress with an enormous bustle and puffy sleeves that ended in lace cuffs. Her shawl was a net of spiderwebs drawn across her shoulders. I was starting to understand why Trey said you couldn't pay him to walk through these woods at night.

I followed her until she entered a large stone crypt with the name "Stirling" inscribed above the severe bronze door. A tall black cedar leaned against one corner of the tomb, carpeting the ground with reddish-brown needles.

The door, mossy green with verdigris, stood partially open, as was the rusting iron gate beyond it. Another gate at the back of the crypt also stood open. Old caskets lined the walls; one or two had tumbled to the floor and cracked open, loosing scraps of faded silky rags, a scattering of dusty bones and a long spill of wispy gray hair. The nooks and corners were properly draped like a movie set with shrouds of cobwebs. The only thing missing from the milieu, other than my ghostly companion, was a rat crouched atop the cracked lid of a sarcophagus.

Beyond the second gate a stair led down into the earth. While I stood there wondering if this was the same tunnel Trey had found with his dowsing rods, the gate behind me swung shut with a shrieking clang of metal.

This was hilarious. Somebody was trying way too hard to scare me. The gate had no doubt been blown shut by some tornadic gust of wind supplied by props. The same wind had also locked it and rusted it shut. It looked like it hadn't been opened in a hundred years. I didn't bother shouting for help. The flashlight batteries were fading fast. I didn't relish the idea of spending the night in this hotel, so I started down the stairs, hoping to find another way out.

Instead, I found myself in a narrow, coffin-shaped arch of brick supported every ten feet by crude columns. I picked up an old kerosene lantern lying on the floor just at the foot of the stairs, and a moth fluttered out and struck me in the eye. Probably the same thing had happened to whoever had dropped the lantern in the first place, because that's what I did. It clanged on the bricks loud enough to wake the dead.

Having nothing better to do, I shook a little more light out of my dying flashlight and started down the tunnel. I hoped it would end in some forgotten basement in the house. After about fifty yards, the roof grew furry with roots, pushing the bricks loose in places and causing the ceiling to sag alarmingly. Broken bricks littered the floor, surrounded by little piles of pale dry dirt.

The tunnel ended at a brick wall, as good as nowhere at all. At that moment, my flashlight finally gave up its weak ghost and joined the heavenly torches triumphant. I tried clicking the button a couple hundred times, with the usual results.

The air was no stuffier than you would expect, being buried alive, but I quickly began to resent it. I could have gone back but I didn't especially want to walk that tunnel in complete darkness, feeling the weight of the earth pressing down on the air, each breath smaller than the last until you're not breathing at all. Buried alive, wryly biting back a histrionic scream. Buried alive!

In any case, the tunnel only led back to the crypt and its locked gate. I took my lighter out of my pocket and lit the flame, but there was no point standing there broiling my thumb just to look at a dusty brick wall.

I could have called for help, except my phone was receiving about as much signal as if I'd been at the North Pole. Whatever it was that jammed Trey's frequencies was also jamming mine. I pushed every button on the phone anyway. After listening to my own heart pound in my ears for a couple of hours, I started seeing lights and hearing voices. The lights were like fireflies, floating down the tunnel toward me from the direction of the crypt, six or seven tiny dots fading and growing brighter and fading again though never disappearing altogether. If they were fireflies, I couldn't see their wings when they flew close, nor feel the touch of their tiny feet when one landed on my outstretched hand.

The voices were indistinct at first, everywhere and nowhere, but gradually I was able to sift a word from the mumble, enough to realize they were speaking Spanish. I laughed at the horribleness of the pun and said aloud, "Spanish firefly."

"Odio este lugar," it answered. (I hate this place.)

Spanish ghosts, I thought. Two voices, both male. Maybe the ghosts of Hernando de Soto's soldiers.

"Creo que la caja de fusibles está aquí." (I think the fuse box is over here.)

Or maybe not. Conquistadores searched for lost cities of gold, not fuse boxes. They sounded like they were just on the other side of the brick wall.

"*¿Está rota la linterna?*" (Is the flashlight broken?)

"*¡Mear sobre esta linterna!*" (Piss on this flashlight!)

"*Que brille la luz aquí.*" (Shine the light here.)

Almost close enough to touch. I cupped my hands to the wall and shouted into the bricks, "Hola, amigos!"

"*María madre de Jesucristo!*"

"*¿Ha dicho algo?*" (Did you say something?)

"*Yo no dijé nada.*" (I didn't say anything.)

"Hola, hombres! I'm over here." I beat my flashlight against the wall until the cheap plastic case cracked in half and spilled its discount batteries on the floor.

"*¡Es un fantasma!*" (It is a ghost!)

"*Vamonos!*"

As I listened to their feet pounding up some stairs, I was starting to understand what it must be like to go through eternity invisible, only to have the one person who really can see you run away in terror. And I was starting to wonder if there had been a transition for me. Maybe I had fallen off the log bridge and my body was lying back there in the woods with a broken neck. What if they were right? What if I was *un fantasma*?

I put my hand against the brick wall, assuring myself of its cold reality. This was no satin-lined coffin. I counted the rows of bricks as high as I could reach. The lightning bugs drifted past me and landed by my hand.

Then a male voice spoke with authority, startlingly close, almost in the tunnel beside me: "In the name of the Lord God

Almighty, I command you to reveal yourself." A curious request, I thought. Your usual exorcist would have commanded
me to begone, depart, go back to the darkness or walk into the
light. Not being one to argue with the Lord, I answered.

"Jackie?" Deacon said, surprised for the second time this
day.

"I'm here!" I picked up one of the flashlight batteries and
beat it against the wall. It didn't make much noise, but it was
better than trying to chew my way through the bricks.

"Bring me a sledgehammer and a crowbar!" he shouted to
his workers.

16

Deacon felt compelled to walk me back to my car. My explanation of how I got lost in the woods wouldn't have convinced a civil jury I was competent to cross a parking lot without a Boy Scout holding my hand. "You were lucky your friend the dowser told me about that tunnel," he said as he led the way. He wasn't even using a flashlight to pick out the trail. The woods seemed to open a few feet before him and close a few feet behind me. "I sent two masons into the basement to look for it. We never would have found the entrance if you hadn't been banging on the wall."

"I'm surprised Mrs. Ruth never told you about it." He held my hand as we crossed the log bridge over the dry creek.

"Maybe she didn't know."

We arrived back on the block a little before eleven. It had taken longer than I thought to dig me out. "My battery's probably dead. I'm going to need a tow truck."

"Looks like a tow truck has already been here," Deacon said.

———————

"That'll be Doris Dye," Jenny answered as she poured three glasses of wine. I washed my hands in the bathroom under the stairs. We had found her still awake with a book in her hand when Deacon knocked on her door.

She handed me a glass as I exited the bathroom. "That's the lady I saw at the window?"

"Our neighbor. She probably called security as soon as you ran off."

"Mrs. Dye takes it upon herself to keep out all the riffraff," Deacon said from the den.

"She thinks we're riffraff, too," Jenny said. I followed her into the den, where Deacon was stretched out with his wineglass balanced on his stomach and his fingers laced behind his head. The television was on with the volume down, some preacher with a cheap felt banner hanging behind his head, proclaiming his church's intent to conquer the world for Christ.

"It's past your bedtime, Deacon," Jenny said.

He yawned and nodded but didn't move from the couch.

"There's no point in walking back through the woods in the dark. We have plenty of room for you here." She turned to me and smiled. "For both of you, of course."

I would almost rather have spent the night back in the crypt than risk having a quiet heart-to-heart chat with Jenny about her dead husband's ghost. "That's really nice of you, but I should be going. If I could just borrow a phone book . . ."

"You'll never get a cab out here this time of night," Deacon yawned.

I considered asking him for a ride, but his truck was at the circus camp and he appeared to be settling in for the night on Jenny's couch. Neither could I ask her to take me home—her kids were asleep upstairs. Jenny grinned at my look of helpless resignation and said to Deacon, "You can sleep in the downstairs guest bedroom . . ."

"I'll be fine here on the sofa." He waved at the preacher on the television. "This old Bible-thumper is about to put me to sleep."

"Suit yourself, but the kids wake up at six to watch cartoons."

He rolled off the couch without spilling his wine. "Good night, ladies." He went to his appointed chamber and closed the door.

Jenny led me upstairs, to a room at the far end of the hall. "Here's the bathroom, if you want to take a shower."

"I could use one."

She opened the opposite door. "And this was Reece's room." The pink comforter fringed with lace looked like it had been ironed on the bed. I didn't ask Jenny why she wanted me to sleep here. I didn't have to ask. Her eyes wandered the room, desperately searching for ghosts.

She opened a dresser drawer still filled with carefully folded panties and bras and little polka-dot pajama tops. "I don't think any of these will fit you, but I can lend you a pair of mine," she said.

"I usually sleep commando," I said.

"My son, Eli . . ."

"I'll lock the door."

"I'll just get you a towel, then." She disappeared down the hall. I walked to the window and pulled back the pink curtains. The lake was visible beyond the tops of some trees, with the levee angling off to the right. From this height, I could see the lights from one of the larger houses across the lake shining off the wet rocks and rippling on the surface of the water where Reece Loftin had drowned herself, and where Sam Loftin's ghostly body floated facedown for a few slow heartbeats, then vanished into the black depths.

It was nice to take a shower where you didn't have to put a quarter in the meter to get hot water, even if I did have to step around toy boats and plastic army men to turn on the tap. I shampooed the brick dust and grave soil from my hair, the water red as blood running down the drain, then sat on the toilet to dry off. A small plaque hung on the wall above the toilet—a Dolphin Award for Best Swimmer in Class, awarded to Reece Loftin by the Stirling Baptist Church Summer Day Camp.

I brushed my teeth with a new toothbrush I found still in its box in a drawer, and while I was brushing, Jenny absconded with my dirty clothes, leaving me with nothing but a towel to wrap around my bare bodkin. At least the kids were asleep.

When I returned to Reece's bedroom, I found a framed photograph lying on the floor by her desk. It was a picture of a girls' softball team. I assumed she was one of the girls, though I couldn't tell which was her. "Fayette County Champions" was written on the photo, along with the date and a long string of letters, DLGOXOXOX. In the Coast Guard, we had DILLIGAF—does it look like I give a fuck?

This one meant, Daddy's Little Girl. Hugs and Kisses.

While I was looking at it, Cassie said behind me, "What are you thinking about?"

"I was just . . ." I started to say, but the doorway was empty. The hall outside was empty, too. I walked down to Cassie's room. She was asleep in her bed, one arm thrown over her face. I returned to the bedroom and closed the door behind me.

There was a bare nail in the wall above the computer, so I hung the picture from it, locked the door, dropped my towel and climbed into bed.

Two hours later, I was still lying there. I always had trouble sleeping in a new bed. The last person who had slept in this bed had been dead five years, and yet her room looked the same as the day she died, a museum of grief. Her clothes were still in the closets and drawers, her pictures cut out of teen magazines still pinned to the walls.

I slid out of bed and looked through one of her closets until I found a white terry cloth bathrobe. To my surprise, it fit. As I snuck downstairs, the house was silent and dark, except for the kitchen, where the refrigerator hummed and the light over the stove threw out its lonely yellow circle on the tile floor. I filled a glass with water from the dispenser in the fridge door and drank it standing at the sink, looking out the window at the pool. I refilled my glass and strolled out to the edge of the pool, lit a cigarette and stood looking down at the water glowing from the light at the bottom. I wondered how much it cost to run that light all night long.

The wind blowing across the lake seemed to clear out the last of the cobwebs from the crypt. I finally felt sleepy enough to try bed again. As I walked along the edge of the pool, the green glow shining up through the water threw wavering lines across the back of the house. I saw my own wraithlike reflection in the glass door, cut off at the hips and floating legless toward me. As I opened the door, a shadow fluttered across the surface of the pool, momentarily darkening the patio. I turned, but there was no one there, no one in the pool, no one anywhere.

17

I WOKE WITH THE IMPRESSION that somebody was whispering my name. It was still dark outside. I rolled over and looked at the clock radio on the dresser—3:32 in the morning and I felt like I hadn't slept at all.

I lay in that strange bed in the dark with the frilly edges of the sheets tucked under my chin, smelling the unfamiliar, vaguely mildewy smell of a bed that hadn't been slept in for ages. I looked at the dark rectangles of the *Teen Beat* posters above my head without actually being able to see what they portrayed. I tried to remember who was in the photos, their faces if not their names. The only one I could identify was the softball team photo over the computer, the one that had fallen earlier and was missing from its nail once again. I sat up.

Someone knocked softly three times on the door.

I waited to see if they were real. They knocked again, softly. Maybe it was the knocking that had woke me. I rolled out of bed and wrapped myself in a robe, opened the door and was surprised to find Deacon standing there. I recognized him by his size and his whispered voice. "Did I wake you?"

"Isn't that why you were knocking on my door?"

"I thought I would find you already awake." He scuffed the carpet with his shoe and shrugged. He was fully dressed in his black suit and tie, sunglasses resting on the top of his wavy black hair.

I stepped back to allow him into the room. He reluctantly entered. "Why's that?" I asked.

"I had a dream."

I closed the door behind him and flicked on the light. He turned around and stood in the middle of the room, hands clasped behind his back, feet spread in a military at-ease posture, but his eyes were frozen to the ceiling. I sat on the bed and pulled the pillows into my lap.

"I was walking naked in a splendid garden, so beautiful," he began in his preacher voice, drawing out each word as though tasting it. For once, he didn't have his Bible in his hand, and he looked naked without it. "It pained my heart to know that such beauty could not last. I was happy, but I was also alone. As I walked along the bank of a river, an angel appeared before me clothed in flame. The angel said, follow me, and he led me out of the garden to the edge of a burning desert."

Deacon dropped his eyes and looked at me and I felt his gaze go right through me, like a pin through a bug. I knew then the true power of the magnetism that drew people to him. I felt the full extent of that strange attraction, yet at the same time I was repelled by it, because I knew it for the illusion that it was. I'd seen too many magic tricks to be fooled, but even as I rejected it, I felt it buzzing inside me, like stepping on an exposed wire.

"I saw you, Jackie, wandering in the desert, also naked and alone."

"I've never heard that one before," I said. Men were all the same, and preachers were the worst of the breed. He'd done nothing more original than trying to put the make on me in a dead girl's bedroom. He wasn't done yet, either.

"The angel said to me, go unto this woman, for the Spirit of the Lord is with her."

"So you came up here to see how I compared to your dream?"

"You were dying, Jackie Lyons," he said, ignoring my gibe. "I saw you fall and went to you. There was a demon inside you, eating you from the inside out." He knelt beside the bed, took my hand and turned my arm over to expose the old needle scars lacing my skin.

"You noticed those earlier," I said as I pulled my hand from his grasp. "It's a good trick. No doubt any other junkie would already have lain back and opened her legs to Christ, but you can't guilt me with your Come-to-Jesus, preacher. I've been guilted by the best in the business—my mother." Somehow it felt blasphemous to mention her in such context, but at the same time, deeply satisfying. Maybe I was getting my demon on.

Deacon seemed to like it, too, because he smiled.

"I woke up from the dream knowing that the Lord had commanded me to see you," he said. "So *I* should be asking *you* why I'm here."

"It was your dream, not mine." I stood up and walked to the window, feeling his eyes follow my every step. I looked down at the levee, but there was no sign of Sam's ghost. Even the dead must sleep, especially at this time of night.

The clock radio caught my eye again, but this time I saw its reflection in the mirror on the closet door. It read 5E:E.

When they're that obvious, you just have to go along or they never let you rest. I slid back the closet door. Reece's shoes were neatly lined up along the left wall, her clothes, jackets and coats still hanging from the rod, though they were all pushed to the right. The missing softball team photo leaned against the back wall beside a large pink pig that somebody had won knocking over milk bottles at the county fair. Maybe with her pitching arm.

As I leaned into the closet and picked up the photo, my arm brushed the pig. It toppled over, revealing the outline of a small door in the back of the closet. It was about two feet tall and made to blend into the wall in such a way that you had to know it was there to see it.

Deacon touched my shoulder. "What is it?" I shifted to the side so he could see. He dropped to one knee and pushed the door with the palm of his brown hand. It opened without a sound and let out a warm, dusty breath of air.

"It's just an attic crawl space. Probably gives access to the furnace." He nodded at the photo in my hand. "What's that?"

"It's a photo of Reece's softball team."

He took it and pointed her out to me. "She was such a beautiful child," he said. Reece had long, straight blond hair that framed a narrow, handsome face, the kind of wholesome, thirteen-year-old American doll loved by major cable television networks that catered inane sitcoms to voracious teen audiences.

"More lovely even than her mother, though she has her father's nose." Sam Loftin was her coach, smiling in the back row with his hand on Reece's shoulder. I hadn't recognized him because he wasn't dead yet.

I didn't tell Deacon that this was the second time tonight I'd found this photo off its nail. Nor did I try to explain how it fell across a room and into a closed closet. He didn't need that kind of encouragement. Next thing he'd be telling me Reece was trying to speak to me from beyond the veil and I didn't need him or anybody else telling me my business. I grabbed his phone, shone its lighted face into the attic crawl space and onto the dark, bulky object tucked between two joists, partially hidden beneath a fold of insulation.

I pulled out a small, dusty hardshell suitcase covered with tweedy gray fabric and brown leather straps. It still had a bag-check tag attached to it with a destination of MEM. Deacon stood behind me as I set it on the bed and opened it. It was full of loose cash, mostly twenties and hundreds.

Any other situation and I would have assumed this was drug money, but I couldn't see Jenny dealing. "That's a lot of money," Deacon whispered, a worried look on his face. Just my luck. The first time in my life I stumble across unguarded riches and I've got a preacher attached to my hip.

There was a heavy brown envelope tucked into the suitcase lid pocket. I opened it and dumped its contents on top of the money—a cache of photos of Reece, printed on regular copier paper. In the photos, she looked to be anywhere from ten to fourteen years old, the photos shot at different times in different places, some of which I recognized—the log bridge in the woods, Jenny's pool and boathouse, the levee, the bed of a truck parked in front of Jenny's house. Other places I didn't know—a log cabin, a lake with crystal-clear water, and the front of a ski boat.

The photos themselves were disturbing. The youngest ones seemed innocent enough, but as she got older, her clothes got skimpier and her poses more suggestive. Nothing pornographic or obscene in the youngest photos, nothing you wouldn't see in teen-clothing advertising, but still wrong in this context—swimsuits and bikinis, short skirts, Catholic schoolgirl uniform, pajamas, panties. Somewhere around thirteen, she went goth, dyed her hair black, pierced her nose and her eyebrow, heavy black eyeliner and black or blue lipstick. She posed seductively, partially dressed, showing off her bottom, wet T-shirts, bare back, a translucent white bikini that might as well have not been there when it was wet. In one picture she sat in a booth at some restaurant, a strand of her long black hair hooked behind one triple-pierced ear. She wore a tight Rob Zombie T-shirt, no shoes, rings on almost every finger, some of them homemade from pieces of wire and zippers, one bare foot propped on the ratty tablecoth and her toenails painted black. A dictionary picture of teen insolence.

In another photo, she was partially submerged in the clear water of a lake, her naked torso suggesting complete nudity. Deacon whispered, "That was taken at Spring Lake in the woods." I don't know why he was whispering.

The last photo in the stack was of Reece sitting in the rain by Jenny's pool. She looked about fourteen and was completely nude, squatting with her arms wrapped around her knees. Her goth hair was growing out blond at the roots, and she had lost the makeup and piercings. Her wrists and legs bore the scars of a habitual cutter, some fresh and red, others almost too faded to see. She looked cold and her smile was forced. She was crying, but her tears could have been the rain on her face.

"Put them away," Deacon said. "That poor child. Put them away."

He was thinking what I was thinking. Reece had drowned herself because she couldn't stand the abuse any longer. "We can never tell her mother," he said.

"Jenny has a right to know."

"To know what?"

"That her husband was abusing her daughter, that she killed herself, and that five years later he killed himself. Out of grief, or guilt, or something."

"You don't know that. And if you told Jenny, it would kill her."

"What about the truth, preacher?"

"Jenny doesn't know, so it's not a lie to keep this secret. Far worse to reveal it. As Jesus said in one of his most misunderstood passages, let the dead bury their dead."

"Don't talk to me about the dead," I barked, then immediately regretted it.

But he was too preoccupied to notice. "I just can't believe Sam did this to his own daughter. I knew Sam. He loved Reece and grieved for her every day of his life. There must be another explanation."

He actually believed that, but I knew better. I knew you could never really know anybody, not your best friend, not your parents, not even the person who shared your bed every night. When Dennis Rader was sitting in the church office composing letters on the church computer, did the congregation know their deacon was describing for the edification of newspaper editors the way he bound, tortured and killed his victims? Did John Wayne Gacy's wife really know the man who stacked boys under her living room floor?

Sometimes a person with everything to live for bites the barrel of a gun because the pain they've bottled up inside hurts more than the bullet they eat. The grieving widower doesn't confess how, when the doors were closed and the lights were low, he mind-fucked his wife until she washed down a handful of barbs with a bottle of Chardonnay. No, he'll be properly mystified for the benefit of onlookers, just like everybody else, and when the funeral service is over and everybody has gone back to their beautiful lives, he'll quietly burn her suicide note in the fireplace.

I'd seen brother stab brother in front of their own mother. I'd seen children left to rot in a cage by their grandparents, grandparents left to rot in a nursing home by their children. Sometimes there just aren't rational explanations for the horrors people commit. Sometimes people really are monsters, even the people we think we know best.

18

THIS NEXT MORNING I FOUND my clothes freshly laundered and lying across the desk chair in front of the computer. It was like being back home. I dressed and checked Deacon's room, but he was already gone. I hadn't heard him leave the house and wondered if he slept. He had left my room around five that morning. We stayed up counting the money in the suitcase—$38,235. It was more cash than I had seen in one place at one time, and even Deacon, flush as his bank account was with Mrs. Ruth's largesse, seemed awed by those neat stacks of green arrayed across the bed.

On my way down to the kitchen, I looked into Jenny's bedroom. She was dressed but asleep, napping with her children tucked into the curves of her body. I poured myself a glass of milk, went to get the paper from the end of the driveway. The morning sun felt hot on my face. I sat by the pool and read the paper but there was nothing in it except the usual greed, corruption, rape and murder. After a while I noticed Jenny in the kitchen making breakfast. She waved at me through the window.

I decided to phone the guard shack to find out where they towed my car. The guard checked their log and said there hadn't been any tow-aways the previous night. Jenny brought me a piece of toast with fig jam and a cup of coffee and sat cross-legged in the chair next to me. "I see Deacon's gone already," she said. "He's always working."

I nodded without saying anything. She leaned over and lifted a plastic cover from the side of the pool to check the skimmer trap. "How long do you think it will take you to photograph Mrs. Ruth's house?"

"No idea." I folded the paper and set it aside.

"Something's wrong."

"Somebody stole my car last night."

"Oh my God!" Jenny gasped.

"I think maybe it's time you introduced me to your favorite neighbor."

Doris Dye opened her back door and greeted us with a cold, cockeyed stare, her purse dangling from her arm and her keys clutched in one arthritic claw. She was dressed for church in a coarse black dress that looked like she had made it herself, black block-heeled shoes and stark white hose too thin to hide the blue veins mapping her legs. It wasn't even Sunday and I thought maybe she was going to a funeral. She looked like the kind of woman whose social life primarily consisted of funerals.

I introduced myself by saying I was working for Deacon. "You remember Deacon?" Jenny added.

"Have you come to apologize?" the old lady asked. With her

eyes pointing in two directions, I couldn't tell who she was talking to. "Because if you have, I don't have time to listen. I was just leaving."

Jenny apologized for keeping her but I remained where I stood, blocking the path to the brown sedan parked in the detached carriage house. For her part, Doris tried to fill the doorway so I couldn't see into the kitchen behind her. "Last night," I said. "I saw you at your front window. I believe you saw me."

She allowed that she may have noticed when I ran off into the woods and left my car parked in the street with the headlights on and the car door open, and that she had, in fact, been about to call security to have it towed, but by the time she got her phone and returned to the window, somebody was already driving away. "It wasn't you," she noted with a smile. "It was dark and my eyes ain't what they used to be, but I know a black man when I see one. I just assumed he was a friend of yours." She meant that as an insult.

I thanked her for her time. She closed and locked her door. Maybe she had changed her mind about the funeral.

Back at Jenny's house, I called the police to report the theft. Officer Lorio arrived about an hour later. I hadn't seen him since the day of the wake. He looked like he had packed an extra ten pounds into his shirt, most of it muscle, plus an extra pound or two in the bags under his eyes. He seemed to think we had a fair chance of catching the car thief and suggested we head over to the Fayette County sheriff's office. "The gates are monitored by twenty-four-hour infrared video. We should be able to get an exact time when it was stolen, and hopefully a good picture, maybe match it to somebody using our new facial-recognition software."

The cops in this county had more toys than the FBI.

Lorio and I sat in a small monitoring room down the hall from the first-class jail where I'd taken lodgings my last trip through Mayberry. We passed Sheriff Stegall in the hall but he pretended to be reading something important on the back of a box of crackers. Using the department's computer, Lorio was able to tap into the DVR files of the security company that handled Stirling Estates.

"You know they ruled Sam's death a suicide?" Lorio asked during a long stretch of no activity. We watched the tape at sixteen-times speed, slowing down any time a car appeared at the gate.

I told him how Stegall had informed me, that day in his office.

"Did you believe it?" he asked.

"Not at first." After what I saw on the levee that April morning, I assumed the coroner was covering something up. Now I knew he'd killed himself. Maybe out of regret, maybe for reasons no one could understand. The only thing missing was how, and that question no longer kept me up nights. I didn't care.

"You believe it now?" Lorio asked, to which I shrugged. "But if what you saw is true . . ."

"What I saw doesn't matter. You know that."

"I know the facts of the case," he said in his best policeman's deadpan, "but I also knew Sam. I've known him since high school. I don't think he would kill himself, not anymore. He loved Reece, but he loved his other kids, too. He wouldn't leave them without a father."

Deacon had said the same thing. These people thought Sam Loftin was a saint. Even after we found that money, Deacon couldn't bring himself to think Sam killed himself. But he was right about one thing—Sam Loftin may have been a monster, but he was a dead monster. Dragging him out of his grave wouldn't make anything right. All exposing him would accomplish was more pain, like an unexploded shell left over from a meaningless war, waiting in the ground for some child to step on it.

"Something must have happened to Sam. You said that yourself. I think maybe he had a stroke or a heart attack. The coroner found a deep contusion to the back of the head, but it wasn't enough to kill him. You saw the rocks on the levee. He says Sam may have slipped and struck his head." I remembered the limestone boulders, rough and jagged, certainly capable of punching a hole in somebody's skull, but not very slippery unless wet. It hadn't rained in almost a week when Sam died. "So if he didn't kill himself, why rule it a suicide? He didn't leave a note."

"Not all suicides leave notes," I said. God knew I'd photographed enough of them. "Was he depressed?"

Lorio shrugged and paused the tape at a small white car passing through the gate. It wasn't my car. "Sam had his bad days, just like anybody else, but he was usually a pretty happy guy."

"What about his finances?" Here I was pretending to be a

cop again, asking cop questions as though there was any question about what happened. I don't know why I did it. Maybe I couldn't help myself.

"Business has been good for the last year. He worked practically all the time. He was working the day he died."

The time stamp on the video read 8 a.m. My car never passed the gate during the night. "It must still be on the property," Lorio said as he turned off the computer. The room went dark, but I could still see his round face in the lingering glow of the monitor. The bags under his eyes looked like deflated marshmallows.

"We should check Doris Dye's garage."

"You check," he said. "I like my job. I'd like to keep it."

19

LORIO DROPPED ME OFF at the end of Jenny's drive. I found everyone by the pool eating watermelon. Holly sat on the edge of the patio wall in a black bikini a little smaller than a pirate's eye patch, teaching the kids to spit watermelon seeds. Nathan swanned around, snapping photos of everybody with his camera and reminding us how expensive it was.

I brought Jenny and Deacon up to date about my car. The worst part was, I'd left my camera and computer on the front seat. "I doubt they'll still be there when they find my car," I said. "If they find it. The camera was worth more than the car, anyway."

Jenny scratched her head for a minute, then cut me a slice of watermelon. "I think Sam's old camera is up in the attic. I gave it to him when we were dating."

"No thanks," I said.

"It's a good camera."

"Thanks all the same." I'd had enough trouble out of second-hand cameras that once belonged to dead people.

Without batting an eye, Deacon said, "We'll buy you a new camera, then."

As much as I needed to hang on to this job, I shook my head no. "The camera will go to the church when you're done, of course," he added. "The thing is, I need those photos to send to the craftsmen I've hired to do the wood carvings. They're in Pennsylvania. So I can't wait until the police find your car."

That seemed like a fair deal, one I could live with. "I know where we can pick up a good camera cheap." I took a bite of watermelon, so cold and so sweet it made my teeth hurt. "I'll need a ride into Memphis."

"I'll take you," Nathan offered. Before I could say no, Jenny insisted on driving me herself.

We left Jenny's kids with Holly. Before he departed, Deacon gave me a signed blank check drawn on his church's checking account to buy the camera. All he asked for was a receipt. I'd never met people so oblivious with their money before.

As we drove up Highway 70 toward the city, Jenny questioned me about my adventures beneath the House of Usher. I played the whole affair as a minor inconvenience, with lots of comical French shrugging. I left out the part about the creature chasing the girl because I didn't want to give her the wrong impression. Jenny didn't believe I wasn't scared stiff, especially when I found myself locked in the crypt.

"I would have been terrified."

I had a feeling I already knew where this conversation was going, even before she asked, "Do you remember how we met?"

I said that I did. "I saw you for like ten minutes at that bar and then you just disappeared. Next thing I know you're all over the news for a couple of days, then nothing. But I always knew I'd see you again."

"Well, here I am," I said.

"Here you are." She pulled up in front Deiter's shop and parked. I waited for her to unlock the doors, but she just sat there, thin fingers wrapped around the steering wheel, her eyes staring at something I couldn't see. She was working herself up to ask the question she'd been waiting three months to ask.

For all her outward poise, it was clear she was barely holding herself together. It was still too soon for her to hear what I had to say, but she was reaching out to me, as if I could bring her some final message from her dead husband. I didn't have a final message. I didn't have anything that could help her, and I knew that would tear her apart.

"Officer Lorio told you what I saw."

She nodded, her eyes welling up with tears. She had the same big brown eyes as her daughter Cassie, only older, softened by smile lines in the corners. She snatched a Kleenex from a box in the center console and pressed it to her face, still nodding, violently, her back heaving.

She wanted to be torn apart.

I described the scene to her as though reading it for the court record. I didn't embellish it or read anything into it. I didn't offer any theories as to what might have happened or try to explain how I had seen her husband alive when he'd been dead for several hours at least. I described how I found Sam in the water and how I tried to rescue him. I told her just enough and no more, certainly no more than she probably already heard from Lorio.

She nodded all the way through my story, never once looking at me through the Kleenex pressed against her face.

"What I saw that afternoon wasn't your husband. I don't know what it was. It's like I told Sheriff Stegall. I can't explain it." I could be a convincing enough liar when I needed to be. They teach you that in cop school—after hours.

"Thank you," she snuffled.

"I don't know if this is any help at all."

"It is. It helps just to know." She reached across the center console and took my hand, pulled it close and pressed my knuckles to her lips. I could feel her tears hot on my skin. "You've helped me more than you can know."

She released my hand and unlocked the door.

I left her in the car to finish her cry rather than take her into the shocking rat warren that Deiter called his shop. He answered the door wearing nothing but a pair of plaid boxers and a black army beret. His teeth were still blue from the half-eaten cupcake in his hand. "It's my birthday," he said.

I pushed inside and closed the door behind me. "And I didn't get you anything."

"What do I need?" he shrugged, a comically helpless look on his face as he glanced around the room. He seemed to have everything his Teutonic heart desired.

We went into his office. It was his office because that's what he called it. It looked no different than the rest of the shop, which is to say, the dumpster behind a legitimate camera store. After I told him about my stolen car and camera, he dug out his best hand-me-down Nikon, charging me less than half of its retail value because he'd used it a couple times during his sideline paranormal investigations.

Of course, even Deiter's hand-me-downs made my equipment look like a fossil dug out of a tar pit. His camera did everything short of wiping your nose. The handbook weighed more than the camera. I filled out Deacon's check and gave it to Deiter. He dropped it on his desk without looking at it. Two seconds later, I couldn't find it again amid all the clutter.

"I'm including an infrared filter," he said as he slid a round plastic case into the camera bag. "Use this when you're shooting that Zuber wallpaper. Speaking of . . ."

He pushed a pile of dirty laundry and a matching pair of Siamese cats out of the chair behind his desk. I thought at first the cats were dead but they tumbled out of the pile eventually and stalked away, tails twitching. "I didn't know you had cats, Deiter."

"Yah, I'm keeping them for somebody who used to be a friend," he answered. "Look at this." He pulled up an image on his computer screen of the antique wallpaper I'd photographed that first day in Mrs. Ruth's house. The images, though still faint, looked as though a couple of decades of dust and cigarette smoke had been stripped away, leaving behind pale blue images of men and women in early nineteenth-century dress, hunters on horses with packs of dogs boiling about their hooves, happy cartoon slaves plowing in the fields, a grinning black Mammy bouncing a little white cherub on her hamlike knee. However, in many places huge brown stains, like the outlines of a topographical map, had nearly erased portions of the scenes, leaving fuzzy images whose shapes could only be guessed at. Deiter said, "This is the best of the bunch, and I could only do so much with what you gave me. The infrared filter should help."

"What about the other pictures?"

"Useless." He scrolled through several hazy, overexposed images filled with white bubbles of light that completely obscured whatever it was I had been trying to shoot. "Too much dust in the air. Your flash picks up nothing but blobs. Lots of people in the business call these orbs."

"What business?"

"Ghost business. Focking amateurs, they tell you these are spirits of the dead, but they're just little specks of dust reflecting off the flash."

I left that one hanging in the wind, even though I could tell he was dying to hear my ghost stories about Ruth's house. "They're taking the roof apart right now. The air is full of dust."

"You're wasting your time until they finish."

"They can't finish until I've shot my pictures."

He scratched deeply into his straw-colored beard, loosing a blizzard of crumbs down the alpine slope of his naked belly. "You need to keep the dust out of the area you're working."

"That won't be easy in a construction zone."

"You could curtain off the room with plastic sheets and duct tape, bring in some fans."

Always listen to your German engineer, if you have one handy. "I'll try that," I said, knowing I never would. The house was already a sauna without sealing myself inside a plastic bubble. They'd find my bloated corpse before the first siesta. "Burn me a copy of the best shots. Deacon will want to see them."

"Already did." He dropped a disk into the camera bag and zipped it shut. I followed him to the door, along with the pair of cats. They twined back and forth between his feet as he walked, tripping him every other step. He opened the door and they darted out, vanishing into the drought-stricken shrubbery.

"Aren't you afraid they'll get hit by a car?" I asked.

"I should be so lucky." He glanced past me at Jenny in her SUV. "You look like you're meeting a better class of people these days."

I snapped a desiccated branch from the boxwood beside the door. "You ought to water your bushes, Deiter. They're dying."

20

EVERY MORNING DEACON PICKED ME up at my motel and dropped me off back home in the evenings. He never asked if he could see my room and I never invited him in, even though sometimes I didn't particularly want to be alone. Because I was already so far behind on the job, I worked Saturdays and Sundays, but there was still so much dust in the air from the roof construction that most of my photos ended up hopelessly obscured with orbs. I had to take a dozen shots just to get one I could use.

Then the Nikon broke and Deiter spent two days repairing it. Deacon seemed to take all these setbacks in stride. He never asked to see my pictures. He expected the Devil to throw up every obstacle he could. "It's Satan's job to try to stop me, just like it's my job to push ahead and continue doing the Lord's work. I got nothing against a man trying to do his job. I respect that, even in the Devil."

While I waited for the dust to settle between shots, I explored Ruth's old mansion, poking into its corners, peering into crannies, opening doors and always finding another door to open, another room I hadn't seen before. All it meant was more work. I began to suspect the house of growing, and pretty soon I came to understand why Ruth fought so hard to keep it. I was starting to dream about the place at night—those nights that I actually slept. When I couldn't sleep, I killed cockroaches and counted the needle scars in my arms.

Sunday mornings when he picked me up outside the motel, Deacon always asked me to go to church, and every Sunday morning I declined. "I will get you one day, Jackie Lyons. And then I'll save you whether you want to be saved or not." By the third Sunday I wasn't entirely sure he was talking about my soul.

I came to relish those Sundays, with or without him. Construction shut down and the circus camp emptied out about an hour before church, leaving me utterly alone with the house. It was the best time to work, but I didn't bother working. I took excursions into the woods, more often than not getting lost for hours at a time. I rediscovered the cemetery in the woods and spent an hour walking among the gravestones. In daylight, the Stirling family vault looked about as threatening as a garden shed, and since they had broken the lock off the rusty gate in rescuing me, I had no fear of being trapped inside a second time. I found Deacon's friend, the Opossum Paul, scrabbling around in the leaves, searching for converts among the roly-poly gentiles. He poked his apostolic head out and hissed like a radiator.

Enough sunlight slanted through the cracks in the roof to read the bronze plaques fixed above the niches in the walls. The oldest vault belonged to Josiah Overton Stirling, born in 1833, died 1930. His beloved wife Beatrice and four darling children—Murray, Phillip, Mary and Claire—all died within days of each other in 1873, the same year that yellow fever nearly turned Memphis into a graveyard. Beside him lay a second beloved wife, Estella Ruth, who had no birth date but died September 1, 1898, the same day that Caesar Augustus Stirling was born. Caesar died in 2002 at the age of 104 and was interred in the imperial Roman sarcophagus in the center of the crypt, with winged Victories reposed above his bones and naked prepubescent caryatids holding up his marble deathbed.

One name seemed out of place: John Allen Vardry (1918–1942). A bronze plaque, Ruth Stirling Vardry, hung beside his, minus the date of death. When they finally laid her bones here, no more Stirlings would pass that rusty iron grate, as hers was the last and only unoccupied niche in the tomb.

In all my explorations, I never did find Spring Lake. The dry creek that Deacon said would bring me to it led instead to a shallow gully overcome with wild rose and blackberry vines. Most nights around dusk, the neighborhood children would come out and I could hear them playing in the woods until after dark. I tried to find them once or twice but never did. I didn't really expect to.

Late in the third week of my work, I could tell something was going on over in the estates—that's what Deacon's people called the area beyond the forest where the rich people lived. One Friday evening I couldn't find Deacon when it came time for my ride back to the motel. One of his parishioners said he'd gone to see Mrs. Loftin. I borrowed a flashlight and set off through the woods along the now-familiar trail. But this time I must have taken a wrong turn, because it led me out at the base of the levee near the spillway. The neighborhood children were starting up early tonight—I caught snatches of Holly's *wire-briar-limber-lock* song drifting through the trees.

I climbed to the top of the levee, stopped to light a cigarette and blow the cobwebs from my lungs. There were some big houses over there across the lake, big enough to fit two or three of Mrs. Ruth's crumbling white mansion inside and still have enough room to park a private jet. The nearest had a long wooden pier jutting halfway out into the lake. It was lit up with spotlights, and someone had built a stage at the far end and decorated the rails with enough patriotic bunting to float a barge.

Jenny's house sat dark and silent at the other end of the levee. Though it wasn't late, only one light shone in a downstairs window. I noticed then that I was near the spot where Sam Loftin had killed himself. I clicked on my flashlight and walked along the shore, shining the beam down into the water, not really looking looking for anything in particular but looking all the same. All I saw were the same limestone boulders, and the trapped and dwindling pools where a few tadpoles struggled in the mud, and one condom floated like a dead jellyfish beside a smooth, oblong cobblestone.

I got close enough to the house to see that Deacon's truck wasn't parked in Jenny's driveway. There was nothing left to do but head back, so I turned around and walked right through Sam.

I came out the other side of his ghost with an icicle banging around my ribs. He was facing back the way he had just come, from across the levee, and he wasn't waving so much as waving something away. He turned around and walked toward me and I backpedaled, not wanting to experience that level of spiritual intimacy again. He took a few steps, then his head jerked forward and he staggered, then lurched, too quick to avoid, and I felt him enter me again, and again the icy cold and now the additional blind, paralyzing, rush of terror.

He passed through me and was gone, trying to escape the death already inside him, his hands over his head like a man on fire. He dove, but there was no splash, just a profound stillness, the lake below me as black and empty as a well. The flashlight in my shaking hand was dead, its batteries as drained as the woman holding it.

I sat down and began to shake, just like that day when I dove in the lake. It was a cold that went down to my bones, a cold no blanket could warm, a cold worse that the coldest, illest heroin withdrawal on a bare steel bunk in a piss-stained jail.

Sam Loftin hadn't drowned himself and he hadn't died of a heart attack. Someone had attacked him, someone I couldn't see. I'd stood beside him and inside him, been baptized in his fear and shared the moment of his death like a conjoined twin. Never mind the record of hideous crimes I found in his suitcase in the attic, never mind that he died the same day as the daughter he was abusing, never mind how much it looked like suicide, someone had attacked Sam Loftin. I didn't know who, not yet anyway, not unless he decided to show me.

But I would find out. Somehow.

21

There are few things . . .
hidden from the man who
devotes himself earnestly and
unreservedly to the solution of a
mystery.
— NATHANIEL HAWTHORNE,
THE SCARLET LETTER

THE FOLLOWING DAY WAS a Monday. I woke up anyway, showered, brushed the hair on my teeth, and was waiting outside watching the heat rise off the asphalt when Deacon called. I noticed by the clock on my phone that he was late.

"You're late," I said.

"You don't remember last night."

"Sure I do." I barely spoke to him on the ride home, didn't

tell him about my encounter with Sam. I'd seen plenty of ghosts, but I'd never been one of them, never shared its terror at the moment of its death. Deacon had talked the entire way home, as he usually did, but I hadn't listened. "Tell me again, just for kicks."

He sighed and said, "We're not working today."

"Why not?"

"It's the Fourth of July."

"Is it really?" That would explain the big fireworks tent parked across the street from my motel.

"I'm at the nursing home picking up Mrs. Ruth. Luther Vardry is hosting the annual Independence Day Coon Supper for Senator Mickelson. Mrs. Ruth wants to be there, of course."

"Of course."

"Luther is actually letting her, probably because she won't make a donation to the senator unless she can put the check in his hands."

"Naturally." I knew he'd get to the point eventually.

"Anyway, Mrs. Ruth wants to know why you're not here."

"Tell her I wasn't invited."

"Well, you are now. We'll be at your place in about twenty minutes."

I said I was looking forward to it, even though I wasn't. Normally I would have declined such an invitation, but after last night on the levee, I was fully prepared not to be surprised by anything I found. I just hoped I'd find something.

I heard the siren of an ambulance pulling into the motel parking lot and stepped outside to see who died. The back doors of the ambulance opened and out stepped Deacon, dressed in his usual funereal black, but he had added a splash of festive color in the form of a star-spangled tie that flapped in the diesel exhaust. It took me a second to realize this was my ride to the picnic. I climbed in the back.

"I almost didn't recognize you, Jackie," Deacon said as he shut the doors. I had put on my best secondhand Liz Claiborne blouse and a pair of designer shorts I'd dug out of a donation box one night. He wasn't the first man to notice how well I cleaned up.

By her smile, Mrs. Ruth approved as well. I rode beside her gurney. She was dressed for her big scene—slinky black dress, diamond earrings, pearl necklace wrapped half a dozen times around her impossibly long neck. She had an IV drip sticking out of one well-veined hand and a tinkling glass of bourbon gripped in the other. Even with an oxygen hose nestled under nose, she still made me look like the personality girl in the middle school clique. She held my hand while we punched red lights all the way to Malvern, the ambulance weaving into oncoming traffic, bucketing over the potholes until I felt the fillings shaking out of my teeth. "Are you growing out your hair?" Ruth asked.

"I thought I might try something different," I lied. I didn't have the money to get it cut.

The driver didn't turn off the siren until we passed the guard shack at Stirling Estates. Little American flags were stuck in the ground every ten feet along the road and flags were attached to every fence post, every mailbox was wrapped in flag tape, flagpoles fifty feet high flew flags big enough to blanket a tractor-trailer down to the treads of the tires. Every yard had

at least one sign supporting the reelection of Senator Mickelson, every tree a yellow ribbon wrapped around its trunk, every minivan and Mercedes parked along the road leading to the
park sported a magnet that read, "Support Our Troops."

We pulled up in front of Luther Vardry's house to find a
Malvern policeman directing traffic. Roy Stegall's urban assault
RV idled in the driveway. Both sides of the road were lined with
people heading to the park next to Luther's house. A sign by
the gate into the park read, "Stirling Estates 23rd Annual Coon
Supper." Way back under the shade trees that lined the shore
of the lake, a catering truck from Hungry Bob's Country Bar-
B-Q and a band's trailer were parked next to Nathan's popsicle van. The long pier that I had spotted from across the lake
last night ran out from a promontory, ending in a sort of ga-
zebo where the band was setting up its instruments.

"So what's this shindig all about?" I asked.

"Don't tell me you've never heard of a coon suppei,"
Mrs. Ruth said.

The ambulance stopped and the driver got out, leaving
the engine idling. "Sure, but I think I may be a little under-
dressed for the occasion. I left my best bedsheets at home."

"It's for the benefit of Senator Mickelson." Deacon opened
the back doors. "Everybody will be here, every politician and
political smoothie within a hundred miles. Of course, we're also
invited to Luther Vardry's private picnic."

I hopped down. "So glad we don't have to mingle with the
ordinary millionaires."

He and the driver lifted Mrs. Ruth's gurney out and set it
on the ground. Nathan Vardry appeared, pushing a wheelchair

as though driving a race car, making *vroom* noises with his lips. He winked at me as Deacon and the paramedic helped Mrs. Ruth into her chair. Nathan pushed her up the driveway, making tire-squealing noises all the way up to the house.

"Nice kid," I said to Deacon. "How long has he been twelve years old?"

Luther's house was built like a temple, designed to awe the supplicant upon her approach. The house was a modest affair of eight or nine bedrooms, with ten antebellum-style columns across its Federalist front and twenty-foot doors topped by a Palladian window. It only took a moment to realize this was Mrs. Ruth's house in the woods, only built to a grander scale, a monument to the Vardrys' infinite wealth.

Deacon led me around to the back by way of a brick path bordered with bright yellow rosebushes on one side, and river cobbles as big as softballs on the other. It brought us to an iron gate guarded by one of Sheriff Stegall's goons. Though it pained him to do so, he let us through without a body-cavity search. Only another half-mile hike and we entered the deer park that was Luther Vardry's backyard. A police helicopter passed low over the house, sounding like a war flashback, while a mob of overdressed children chased its shadow across the lawn and waved as it banked out over the lake.

The path cast us up on the shores of Caligula's summer palace, with its Roman fountain of naked cherubs frolicking with dolphins and emperors, a marble obelisk carved with the Ten Commandments (even the one about coveting), a pergola not much larger than airship hangar, and concentric rings of raised rose beds surrounding a koi pond paved with polished brown river cobbles. A concrete path ran straight as a ruler down to a boathouse on the lake, where a smallish yacht bobbed in the wakes of passing jet skis. A pair of Irish wolfhounds the size of small horses came bounding around the corner of the house, nearly knocking us down in their frantic joy, then circled back and beat me to death with their tails.

22

FIRST, THERE WAS THAT BRIEF, awkward period where you enter a party and wait to be noticed. With Deacon at my side, it was briefer than usual. Luther Vardry's wife, Virginia, appeared long enough to stick a beer in my hand, then vanished smoothly into the shrubbery. Next came Holly, dressed in her high school softball uniform, slinking up behind Deacon with her tongue between her teeth. Finally, Luther appeared, gliding along on tiny, polished loafers that glinted in the sun.

Luther had a bright round face like a Russian doll and a mustache that looked like it had been drawn with eyeliner and a ruler. His mouth was very thin and shut up tight beneath his nose, even when he smiled. His slicked-back black hair showed nary a trace of gray, but it was starting to wear a little thin above the temples. I could see the family resemblance to Holly and Nathan, but they favored their grandmother more than their father, and their mother barely at all—a woman so nondescript I couldn't pick her out of the bushes, where she lurked, nibbling a Communion cracker.

"Jackie is a photographer," Deacon said as Luther took my hand.

He perked up and gave my fingers a weak squeeze. "Perhaps I should hire you to photograph my daughter's wedding."

"I ain't getting married, Daddy," Holly protested.

Luther smiled in polite embarrassment. "Justin is a fine young man. He has asked for your hand in marriage and I have given it."

"But I don't love him!" The fine young man that Holly didn't love was at that moment sitting in a chair not ten feet away, scraping dog shit off the soles of his four-hundred-dollar loafers. "You can't make me marry him," Holly said.

"Your mother and I can't take care of you forever."

"Then I'll move in with Nathan."

"Like hell, you will!" Nathan had just exited the back door, pushing his grandmother's wheelchair ahead of him. Mrs. Ruth had to fend off the door with her oxygen bottle. She looked angry enough to wrap her air hose around his neck.

Holly said to Nathan, "Why not? You got a million bedrooms in that house all by yourself."

"You know why not." He rolled his eyes at me. "Like I want my sister moving in with me."

Ruth raised her voice above the familial din. "How long do I have to wait before somebody fetches me a God-damn drink?"

"You want some punch, Mama?" Luther offered.

"Hell no I don't want any of that Baptist piss. Get me a real drink, and when you're done, take this boy and drown him in the lake."

"Now Meemaw, you know you're not supposed to drink hard liquor," Virginia rustled from the shrubs.

"Well, for God's sake, woman, give me a beer before I perish!" For a woman strapped to an oxygen tank and confined to a wheelchair, she could still shout the squirrels out of the trees.

Deacon took me around and introduced me to several other guests, who politely ignored me. My secondhand clothes didn't have the charm of their secondhand clothes, because they'd overpaid for theirs to be ironic, while mine were stolen out of necessity. How Deacon knew them all, first and last name and all their relations down to their dogs and cats, remained a mystery. He seemed to have a politician's gift for faces and facts, a font of information I hoped I could tap in the future, double entendre and all. I wasn't ready yet to tell him my new idea about Sam Loftin's death, not until I had more information and maybe a suspect or two.

Sheriff Stegall arrived to announce that Senator Mickelson would be arriving soon to deliver his Coon Supper speech. Luther took control of his mother's wheelchair and led the way. For a retired Baptist minister, he seemed pretty spry. Someone had found Ruth a floppy beach hat to keep the sun off her face.

Out of the shade of Luther's trees, the sun was murderous. It hadn't rained in weeks, but the park's grass was kept lush by frequent and expensive irrigation. As we crossed the baseball diamond, the wheels of Ruth's wheelchair roused clouds of rust-colored dust that blew toward the lake.

Holly dropped in between Deacon and me and whispered, "Isn't it amazing how Meemaw doesn't burn up in the daylight?" Deacon pushed his sunglasses onto his face, waved with the tips of his fingers and slanted away into the throng, leaving me with her.

"She never seems to get any older," Holly said, dragging the metaphor out for one more bow.

"She's a remarkable woman," I said.

"When I was little, I thought Meemaw was a vampire."

The police helicopter settled in the soccer field. Sheriff Stegall hurried over to open the door for Senator Mickelson—a tall, white-haired, smiling old nodder who had recently been considered a possible vice presidential candidate. He made a beeline for Luther and Ruth, stepping briskly in front of his security escort and waving to the corral of local reporters. After he had kissed Ruth's hand, we continued on our way. A stage had been erected near the pier.

"I almost didn't recognize you," Stegall said as he sidled up beside me. "How did you get invited to this bash?"

"Do you want to see my invitation?"

He patronized me with a smile. "What do you think of the show so far?"

"You've put on a marvelously vulgar display of power," I said.

"Senator Mickelson likes to see how we're spending his money."

"You're doing as thorough a job as any I've seen." I didn't seem to bother Stegall in the least. He rattled on, preciously proud, as though the whole affair had been created for his amusement and benefit. "The senator has a house here in Stirling Estates. He's chair of the Senate Intelligence Committee and president pro tem, fourth in line of succession. My department is so flush with Homeland Security money, I got a guy on the payroll does nothing but think of new ways to spend it."

"We all have our problems," I said.

"Speaking of problems, I made a few phone calls, did a little checking around. Seems you used to be a cop."

"I didn't know you cared."

"You should have mentioned that during our little interview."

"Why? Did you want to offer me a job?"

"No, but I might have gone a little easier on you, maybe."

"Maybe?"

He stopped and considered me with comic gravity. "Sam Loftin was a friend of mine," he said without a lick of sincerity. I almost laughed. "For a while there, I thought you had murdered him. Do you know the last time we had a murder in Malvern?" He didn't wait for me to answer. "Not once since I've been sheriff, and I've run unopposed the last two elections." We had reached the edge of the stage, which the senator had not yet mounted, he was so busy kissing flesh and pressing babies. Luther and his family were already standing serenely near the microphone, like so many cardboard cutouts against the backdrop of drought-stricken trees.

"Your mother must be proud," I said to Stegall. I think what most upset him about Sam Loftin's death was the possible damage to his record. Having it ruled a suicide kept his sheets clean.

"She is very proud. There's no crime to speak of in Malvern, not like in Memphis. The people here love me."

Mickelson finally arrived. Stegall took up his position near the stairs and settled into his best Secret Service pose. Luther Vardry stepped up to the microphone and cleared his throat. The crowd quieted down while he reminded us why we were there—to see and hear their native son. And then he launched into a long biographical narrative while the senator stuck his thumbs in his button holes and beamed like a lighthouse.

Luther finally drew the curtains on his story. "Malvern loves Bill Mickelson. By golly, all of the Seventh Congressional district loves him, even if he is still a Democrat." Mrs. Ruth rolled up beside me in her wheelchair, Deacon at the helm.

Someone in the crowd shouted, "Because he votes like a Republican!"

This earned the heckler a big laugh from the crowd. It also allowed the senator to muscle the microphone away from Luther.

Ruth said, "Listen now, preacher, and you will hear a real preacher."

"It is true that I vote more often with my Republican colleagues than with the Democrats. This has earned me the ire of many in this state, who accuse me of betraying the Democratic party." This was met with general applause and a good deal of cowboy whoops and catcalls.

"To them I say, it is not I who betrayed the party. I have not changed. If anything, it is the party who has changed and betrayed us all, by consorting with Socialists . . ."

Huzzah! said the crowd.

"And Marxists . . ." *Huzzah!*

"And tree-hugging liberals who would sell your jobs just to

protect some little bitty fish in a stream nobody has ever heard of." He had to raise his voice to be heard. "And flag-burning atheists who want to take God out of the pledge and the classroom!" It was a while before he could speak again. He didn't seem to mind.

"The people of Tennessee are good, God-fearing people. I am your representative in Washington. I have served the people of this state in one capacity or other most of my adult life—first in the state legislatures, then the House, and for the last twenty-nine years in the United States Senate. I am a Democrat, yet my Republican constituents vote for me because I have always served the people of this state. Not just the Democrats. Each and every one of you, whether you vote for me or not. If you are willing to cross party lines to vote for me and return me to office, then I am willing to cross party lines to serve you."

He launched into a recitation of his bacon list. It was obvious from the glow on the faces of those around me that many of them had directly benefited from the federal dollars Senator Mickelson shoveled into their Swiss bank accounts. Especially the man standing just behind him—Sheriff Stegall.

23

IT OCCURRED TO ME, not for the first time, that Sam Loftin had been the treasurer of this band of well-dressed thugs, and that he had died with a respectable amount of cash stowed in a suitcase behind his daughter's closet. A suitcase that also contained barely licit photos of his underage daughter. I could see how somebody might have wanted to kill him if he were skimming money from whatever graft operation the senator had set up around here. I couldn't see, as yet, how the photographs fit into it.

Senator Mickelson spoke just long enough for Mrs. Ruth to have a nice nap, but not so long as to put the rest of his audience to sleep. She woke up as the prayer meeting started to break up, and asked Deacon to take her back to Luther's house.

We hadn't gone five steps before a bookish older gentleman greeted her boisterously. He seemed about Luther's age, maybe a little younger, though considerably wider in the middle and babyishly flabby in his white guayabera shirt and Panama hat. He wore it tilted at what he probably thought a rakish angle.

"Hello Eugene," Ruth whispered tiredly. "Deacon, I believe you've met Eugene Kitchen, vice president of Luther's little community chest."

Without breaking his smile, Eugene turned his head and spat a skeet of dark brown tobacco juice through the gap in his front teeth. It arched like a meteor past me and cratered the dust. "You can't build that church, preacher. I've seen the plans you filed with the county. The entrance is on the highway."

Deacon pushed Mrs. Ruth's chair through the uneven grass. "Everything has already been approved by the county engineer."

"But that entrance will allow unregulated access to Stirling Estates," Eugene said. "That's against the covenant."

"The entrance only allows access to the church and the parsonage." He nodded to Luther Vardry and his family as they joined us. Holly tried to climb into Deacon's hip pocket, while Nathan slid his arm around my waist and nuzzled my ear. Mrs. Ruth's head nodded forward in sleep again. Deacon put a hand on her shoulder to steady her.

Eugene continued, "I've also heard you plan to use the parsonage as a halfway house or something. You can't do that without approval." He seemed to know everything people weren't allowed to do at Stirling Plantation.

"It's not a halfway house," Deacon said. "We provide counseling and employment placement for drug addicts and indigents."

"Sounds like a front for farming out illegals," Eugene snipped.

"The parsonage belongs to the church, not to me, and its uses are decided by church committee, not by me. I live there as long as my church will have me. I am a poor man. But who among us truly owns anything? Look to your own house. Do you own the bricks, the wood, the wires and pipes?"

"The bank owns more than I do." Eugene laughed until no one joined him.

Deacon's Bible had appeared in his hand, almost by magic, and as he spoke he waved it about, like a conductor's baton, while still pushing Mrs. Ruth's chair with the other hand. "Everything belongs to God. It came from God and it returns to God. Even our souls. We are but renters of our own flesh, abiding for a few years upon this earth."

"Amen," Luther said.

"But while you abide here," Eugene sneered, "you have to live by the covenant."

Ruth stirred in her chair and tugged at her oxygen tube. "God dammit Eugene, can't you give a body peace for one day?"

Eugene stepped in front of her chair, forcing Deacon to stop. "Mrs. Vardry, this church proposal violates numerous provisions in the covenant. I intend to file a stop action with the court tomorrow morning."

This lit the fire in her cold furnace. She jerked the oxygen hose from her face and nearly came up out of her chair. "I'd like to see you try. While you're at it, call your son-of-a-bitching lawyer and ask him about article thirty-six of the covenant. He will find there a clause that states my house and property exist outside the statutes of the covenant."

Ruth motioned for Deacon to steer a course around Eugene, then continued, "I insisted on article thirty-six when I deeded the remainder of my father's farm to Luther so he could develop it. If not for me, he'd still be pumping gas and hand-ing out religious pamphlets on Highway 70."

"People pump their own gas these days, Meemaw," Holly said.

"Holly, dear girl, your mouth is good for one thing and it isn't talking," Ruth said.

Luther finally decided to come to Eugene's rescue. "But Mama, the agreement also states that if you sell . . ."

"Or if I die and Nathan inherits it."

". . . the property will fall under the homeowners' covenant," Eugene finished with his thumbs stuck proudly in his trouser pockets.

"I haven't sold the property, Eugene. I have given it to the Hope Church of the Gospel Revealed. It's a charitable dona-tion, transfer of title, severed and subdivided, in perpetuity, from Stirling Estates."

"Meemaw!" Nathan wailed.

"Which means, dear boy, that you're never going to see a clod of that dirt. So you'd better start looking for a real job, unless you plan on selling popsicles the rest of your life."

"I make good money, Meemaw. I bought my own house right here."

"Because your daddy drove those people into bankruptcy and foreclosed on their home."

"Now, Mama," Luther began.

"I know all about it, Luther. I know a good many things. I still have deep connections in this community. You'd be sur-prised how much I know about what happens around here." She looked at me when she said this. I couldn't read her expression, whether she was trying to tell me something or if her gaze just happened to rest on me for the moment. She looked tired, but her wellspring of piss and venom had not yet exhausted itself. She grasped the wheels of her chair and jerked it around with surprising strength, until she was facing her son and grandson.

"It's long past time you found this boy a wife, Luther. He needs settling down. If you can't find somebody his own age, maybe you can buy him some stupid little second cousin from Virginia's family. But you'd better hurry. You're not getting any younger, Nathan."

"Neither are you, you old vampire!" Nathan howled. Holly ducked behind Deacon to hide her giggles. "I wish you would just go on and die."

"I'm tired, Luther," she sighed as she tugged the oxygen hose back to her nose. "Take me back to the house so I can rest before dinner."

Luther nodded and started to push her away. Eugene moved aside to let them pass, but then stepped in front of Deacon, his flabby chest puffed out. Even standing on his toes, he barely came up to Deacon's chin. "This ain't over, preacher. I know you tricked Mrs. Ruth into giving you that property. Luther will have her declared mentally incompetent and the title transfer voided. Luther Vardry owns this county."

Deacon smiled beatifically. "But God owns the land, and He is with the righteous."

24

L UTHER LEFT US AT THE PARK gate to take his
mother home, while Holly took to the mound to pitch for
the North Lakers against the South Lakers—apparently there
was a whole other lake in the neighborhood that I hadn't seen
yet. Though friendly, both teams sported enough former college and high school baseball and softball stars to give it a vicious edge. Holly had been a high school All-American and
led the Malvern High School Mustangs to the state champi-
onships two years in a row. She wore her old high school uniform. It was tight enough to make my eyes water.

I sat with Deacon in the stands and tried to tease a little
information out of him about the people around us, but he
seemed more interested in the outcome of the game than ex-
amining the players. To me, they all looked like potential mur-
derers, from the pitcher who beaned a runner trying to steal
second, to the catcher who spiked a woman sliding into home
and sent her to the hospital in Mrs. Ruth's ambulance. Deacon answered with grunts and shrugs, so I turned the conver-

sation to a topic nearer to his heart. "How did you get Ruth to deed you that property? It's worth millions."

"I gave Ruth something more valuable than all the land and all the riches in it," he answered. "I gave her the true, revealed Gospel, the forgotten Gospel of Jesus Christ."

I wondered if it was the kind of Gospel that involved the handling of venomous serpents to the accompaniment of dueling banjos. "How did you get to be a preacher, anyway? You don't seem the type."

"How did you get to be a photographer?"

"It's a long story."

"So's mine."

"I asked first."

He adjusted his sunglasses and settled in on the bleachers. "After Iraq, I decided I had had enough war and went AWOL for a while, until they caught me. I spent a few years as a guest at the federal hotel. When I got out, I didn't have any skills other than driving a tank, for which there are fewer opportunities than I was led to believe when I enlisted. I had a good speaking voice. I tried to get into radio but I never could make it past the first interview. Even though I wasn't a religious man, I'd been raised in the Church. I knew my Bible verses and I could do a good imitation of the old fire-and-brimstone preacher back home, good enough to make my grandmother cry.

"So I started preaching on the streets of New Orleans. At first, I shared a corner with a man who sold what he claimed was Jordan River water. I'd preach for a while and then I'd pass around a Community Coffee can, but I never did much good,

barely enough to keep from starving. So I tried working corners in the wealthier parts of town, but they'd just call the cops
and run me off. I ended up ministering to the lowest of the
low—alcoholics, drug addicts, gamblers, ex-cons—because
they seemed to be the only people who wanted or needed to
hear my message. That's where I should have stayed, but I'm a
hardheaded man. I wanted to be the next Jimmy Swaggart, but
I wasn't preaching the gospel of wealth. Mine was a different
kind of gospel."

He removed his black jacket and leaned back with his elbows on the bleachers behind him. His glasses slipped down
his sweaty nose. I didn't see how he wasn't dying under that
sun. I had been following the shadow of a light pole for ten
minutes, trying to catch a little relief.

He continued, "You see, working with those people, I had
come to a realization. You could even call it a revelation, of the
true Gospel, not the Gospel taught by the church, but the true
Gospel, the true word that swept the world and transformed it
in a generation. The Gospel of the modern church carries no
such message, it has no transformational power. It is no different than the pagan religions it replaced. In many ways, it *is* the
pagan religions it replaced, with only the names changed.

"I began to preach the new Gospel, and my preaching
brought people hope who had no hope, joy where there was
only sadness. People came to hear me, and once they heard me,
they stayed. I was doing three services a day on Sundays and
packing them to the rafters—black, white, you name it, they
were there.

"Then Katrina hit and our little Ninth Ward church was

washed away. The Lord took my church and scattered my saints. Me and my mama ended up living in a FEMA trailer for about nine months before the Lord tested me again by taking Mama. I never did find out what killed her—she started coughing up blood one morning and she was dead by dinnertime. Them FEMA bastards put her body in a plastic coffin and flew her to Atlanta and next thing I know they had burned her up and scattered her ashes, they wouldn't tell me where. They kicked me out of that trailer so I was living on the streets. But I found out Mama had a life insurance policy, so I cashed it in and moved here, rented a space for my church in an empty strip mall in North Memphis."

At the beginning of the fourth inning, Holly took the mound. Deacon paused his narrative to shout *"Hey batter batter!"* His voice drowned out the others in the crowd and seemed to carry to the farthest reaches of the park.

"Let's see if you still got the old pepper, sweetheart," Eugene shouted as he squatted behind the plate. He popped a flabby fist in his glove and people started to cheer. "Come on Holly! Let's see what you got, babe!" She kicked the dirt around with her cleats while she loosened up her throwing arm, adjusted her ball cap to shade the sun lowering behind the plate, unbuttoned the top button on her jersey to give everyone the best possible view of her tits.

While Eugene was still popping his glove and shouting, "Throw the damn ball!," she whipped an underhanded scorcher across the plate. It bounced off the top of his mitt and his nose exploded in a mist of blood. He went over backward, screaming like a peacock. The game ground to a stop while they stretchered him off the field. Her next toss was a strike that the batter never saw.

Before I could swing the conversation back to the topic of the residents of Stirling Estates, Deacon picked up the narrative of his Pilgrim's Progress. He wasn't kidding about it being a long story. I should have gone first. "You can't have a church without a congregation and my saints were scattered I knew not where, but the True Gospel was revealed in my heart and I had to minister to somebody. So I opened up my Bible and found Matthew 25: 35–36. *'I was hungry and you fed me; I was thirsty and you gave me drink; I was a stranger and you took me in. Naked, and you clothed me; I was sick, and you visited me; I was in prison, and you came to me.'* I thought, *Where can I find those who are hungry and thirsty, strangers naked and alone, sick and in prison?* I thought about it for a long time and I prayed on it, until one night I had a dream about my grandmother in her nursing home.

"So that's where my ministry took me—to the nursing homes, to minister to those in their last and in many cases worst days upon this earth, to bring them such comfort as I could and the Gospel that could set their souls free. At one home, I met a woman named Ruth Vardry. Her son had forced her out of her house so he could sell it. To spite him, she gave the house and what remained of her land to me to build my church. She gave me the money to restore her house to its former glory, so that, in her words, it can finally do some good in the world instead of causing only pain and misery.

"I didn't start ministering in the nursing homes for the money, but the money is good because of the message I bring.

It is the Good News, the lost Gospel that was buried and hidden by the bishops of the early Church. I bring people hope when they have no hope, when they are staring down their last days upon this earth and wondering what will become of them and all their works and all their sins. I bring hope and peace, and in return, they fill my cup to overflowing. Naturally, some are like Ruth—I have no illusions about her. She has bestowed such bounty upon me to keep her children and grandchildren from inheriting it."

He took a check out of his shirt pocket and showed it to me. It was made out for nine grand and assigned to his church building fund. The paper was damp with his sweat and the date was almost a month old. He was so flush he hadn't bothered depositing it.

"The man who gave me this has been in that nursing home for three years now. He can count on one hand the number of times his children have visited him. His mind is as bright as yours or mine, but his body has failed him and he is a widower. His children have all but abandoned him, but after he wrote me a check for twenty grand, they came."

There was a break in the bell of his voice, just the slightest quaver of an emotional fracture. His body was still relaxed, reclined upon the hot metal bleachers, but his jaw was clenched so he could hardly get the words past his teeth. "Oh yes, they came. And they brought their lawyer."

25

HOLLY'S NORTH LAKERS WON by three runs. They might have scored more if Nathan hadn't hit into a double play with the bases loaded in the last inning. After the game, the cotillion moved back to Luther's Roman garden.

The sun was still high and hot, but there was enough shade to survive as long as the beer didn't run out. I wandered through the dinner crowd, casually overhearing as many conversations as I could, but no one was discussing murder, just the usual racketeering, embezzlement, insider trading and corporate espionage that everyone does without thinking or even trying very hard to hide.

Through some error I had been assigned to Senator Mickelson's table, between Holly and Nathan. I tried to wrangle a seat next to Mrs. Ruth so I could mine her for gossip, but Luther and his wife had already bookended her before anyone else could get close. Senator Mickelson was seated directly across from Ruth. There was an empty spot for Jenny Loftin, but she hadn't arrived yet. The other empty seat was reserved for Eugene Kitchen, but they had taken him by helicopter to the hospital in Collierville. Eugene's seat was between Deacon and the senator, so I grabbed it, even though it upset the seating arrangement. At the far end sat Holly's fiancé Justin, and Nathan's date Annette LaGrance (the *Elle* model's mother, I later found out).

Senator Mickelson had changed into a sailor-blue jacket with chicken guts on his sleeves. He doffed his white captain's cap and handed it to Stegall as he sat down, then squeezed my knee under the table. Perhaps he thought I had been brought in for the evening's entertainment. Ruth was a picture of misery between her son and his wife. Every time Virginia Vardry tried to whisper in her ear, she swatted at her like a horse fly.

When we were all seated, Luther asked, "Has anyone heard how Eugene is doing?"

"His nose is broken, but he'll be OK," Nathan answered.

Holly sipped her wine, leaving behind a small rose petal of lipstick folded over the rim of the glass. She hadn't changed out of her uniform. She leaned across and whispered to Deacon, "I meant to hit him, just not in the face. That was his fault." She scraped a breadstick through the table butter, meticulously inserted it like a catheter into her mouth, then swiftly munched down its length until her ruby lips met her scarlet fingertips. Patting her lips with a napkin, she added, "He's always hanging around, hitting on me and drinking Daddy's liquor."

"I thought your father was Baptist," I said.

"He is."

"What were you aiming at?" Deacon asked.

"His nuts," she laughed. "First pitch. My arm was a little stiff." She performed the same perfunctory operation with a second butter-lubed breadstick, so swiftly that were it not for the minute and rapid oscillations of her munching jowls she might have been performing a carnival trick, like a sword swallower.

Ruth said, "Luther tells me you don't want to marry that boy, what's his name?"

"Justin. His name's Justin, Meemaw. He's always accusing me of cheating on him. I can't cheat on him. I don't even love him."

He sat next to her at the end of the table, quietly stabbing postholes in the butter with the broken half of a breadstick.

"You're wearing his ring," Ruth said.

Holly moved her hand to allow a shaft of sunlight to sparkle the crush of diamonds caked atop her finger. "It is a pretty ring." She squeezed Justin's arm and kissed him on the cheek.

"Only the best for my Holly," he sighed to the tablecloth.

"Oh my God, that is *not* a Coach handbag!" Holly cried.

"This old thing?" Jenny said as she sauntered up, flaunting a patchwork denim purse before us. Her shoulder-length blond hair was pushed back and held in place by an orange bandana. Her face was fresh-scrubbed and freckled, and she wore a pair of tiny, rectangular, wire-framed sunglasses perched on the ridge of her sunburned nose. Her lacy white blouse hung loose out of her jeans, and floppy beaded sandals dangled from her long toes. She flopped into her chair as though at the very end of her resources.

When the house servants announced the buffet was ready, we queued up. While the good senator stood behind me surreptitiously pressing his boner into my back, folks let us skip ahead until we were at the head of the line. He piled his plate with barbecued pork, pork ribs, barbecued chicken, fried catfish, hush puppies, baked beans, slaw, spaghetti, potato chips and fried pickles.

"Aren't you eating?" he asked. Apparently my portions were too small for him to see without his reading glasses. His breath smelled like dentures and minty-fresh death.

Arriving back at our table I found that Stegall had misappropriated my seat. I was forced to dine beside Nathan. The dinner proceeded without unnecessary effusion of sophomoric sexual innuendo for the first ten minutes or so. When Senator Mickelson leaned back and unbuttoned his trousers with a groan, it was as though the lion had staggered away from its kill and gone to lay down in the shade. Hyena laughter broke out at one of the tables. Luther's dogs were fighting underneath it, knocking people over like bowling pins.

Holly consumed barely enough to keep a goldfish alive before pushing away her plate and departing into the house to change out of her uniform. Jenny, I noticed, supped exclusively from a bottle of Chardonnay. Deacon received a phone call and was spirited away to some theological emergency. I watched to make sure he didn't follow Holly inside, hating myself for caring, but he left by the side gate.

Nearly everyone had eaten their fill, but Nathan seemed to get his second wind along with his second helping. He grunted and shoved a forkful of barbecued raccoon topped with mashed

potatoes into his mouth. He pointed at the barely polite bit of
meat still on my plate. The coon was merely symbolic, like the
bread and wine of olden times, when people knew their places
and kept to them. Everyone was expected to partake, if only in
sacramental portions. "What's the matter? Don't you like it?" he
asked.

"I'm full, thanks," I said.

"I love this shit."

Elbow on the table, I rested my chin thoughtfully on one
hand. "Did you kill it yourself?"

"Hell no. We buy the coons from some niggers I know."

"Nathan!" Luther barked.

"It's OK, Daddy. Ain't no niggers around to hear." The ca-
terers were white. No doubt they'd been selected off a picture
menu just like the chicken and ribs.

"It's ironic, don't you think?" Nathan said to me.

"What is?"

"We buy our coons . . . from the coons." His face broke
apart. He'd been saving that one all day, just waiting for someone to pull his finger. Luther straightened his tie and gazed
mournfully across the lake, perhaps noting that some shirtless,
drunken woman was riding the prow of a speeding boat, like a
figurehead of winged Victory.

I stood, collected my paper plate to throw it away.

"You didn't eat much. Aren't you hungry?" Nathan asked.

"Us girls have to watch our figures."

"Let me watch it for you. Do you work out? Your body is
amazing."

He was a broken record. He had the same five lines memorized and repeated them endlessly. I started to walk away. "Jackie," Ruth quavered. "Take me away from here."

I dropped my plate in a garbage can and pulled Ruth's chair back from the table. "Take me down to the lake," she said.

"Can I call you?" Nathan asked as I pushed his grandmother away.

"You can, but I probably won't answer."

"I'll see you around then."

"Sure. We'll probably run into each other at the cross burning."

26

I PUSHED RUTH DOWN the long path to the boathouse and out to the end of the dock. Jet skis and speedboats roared up and down the lake, dense as rush-hour traffic, towing sunburned skiers saluting each other with beers lifted in their hands. The sun was still high and bright. Ruth sat blinking in her chair and I wondered if she could see anything that passed before her.

The day had seemed to age her. She leaned wearily on the arm of her chair, her veined and knobby fingers clinging to a sweaty glass as she sucked watery bourbon through a tiny cocktail straw.

"So much has changed, Jackie," she sighed. "I can't remember how the land looked before they flooded everything, before Luther built all these damn houses. I want to see the hills and the hollows again, the old farms and pastures. It's all gone."

When I was a cop, they taught us tricks for stimulating the memory of witnesses. I needed Mrs. Ruth to tell me about the people who lived in all the damn houses her son built over her memories. The only thing I had learned today was that everybody worshiped Sam Loftin. He wasn't just the HOA treasurer. His company mowed their lawns and raked their leaves. He coached their daughters' softball teams and taught their Sunday schools. Mrs. Ruth knew Sam and she knew all the people Sam knew. Hopefully she knew who hated him, who would want to see him dead.

Even a trained observer can't recall details cold, like looking at a picture held up to the eye. That's not the way the mind works. Humans evolved remembering stories and songs; sequences of events, not moments in time. If you ask a man to describe a photograph of his wife of twenty years to a police sketch artist, the picture would come out looking like a stranger. But ask him to describe her at the supper table last night, when they fought about the woman she thought he was sleeping with, and what you get is nearly as good as a photograph.

"Close your eyes," I said.

She closed her eyes.

"Pick a time, the best time you remember, before everything changed. How old are you?"

"Fifteen." She smiled.

"It's your fifteenth birthday. What do you see?"

"I see our herd of Jersey cows. My God, I forgot we had them. They were the prettiest dairy cows you ever saw. They all had names. I can still smell their breath in the morning and the warm milk steaming in a cold pail."

"What else?"

"I see Lonnie behind his plow." She smiled and opened her eyes and there were tears on her thin cheeks.

"Who is Lonnie?"

"The first man I ever loved. He was one of our sharecroppers. He was thirty-three years old, with a wife and four kids. If ever he got a spare nickel he lost it playing dice." She looked up at me, squinting against the sun. "I know what you're thinking."

"I'm not thinking anything."

"Yes, you are. You're thinking he took advantage of me. But times were different then, and I was no child. How could I be? I was already overseeing the farm and running our store. Daddy made the finest whiskey this side of Lynchburg, distributed it across five counties and three states, managed a fleet of illegal runners, all while operating five whorehouses. But he couldn't run this farm. He wasn't a farmer. I ran it for him. That's how I met Lonnie. He was the most beautiful man I ever saw. I was a grown woman of fifteen and I knew what I wanted and how I wanted it. I knew exactly what I was doing when I lured him down to Spring Lake."

"Evening, Meemaw," Holly said as she sashayed by in her pink and purple Bendito Romanni bikini, big lemon-yellow Hollywood diva sunglasses, and pink stacked heels by Vince Camuto. She dropped a white towel at the end of the boat dock, kicked off her heels, and dove into the lake with barely any splash at all. Twenty yards out she surfaced, backstroking hard, sleek as an otter, out into the boat traffic and apparently oblivious to the danger. I waited to see her run over and chopped to pieces by the props, but she lived a charmed life. By some miracle, she reached a small rocky island and climbed out, water streaming from her black hair.

Ruth said, "They call that island Holly's Spot. Thirty years old and she still believes one good fuck will fix her life. I tried to teach her to be a heartbreaker, but she prefers to wreck herself on the shores of love."

"Mrs. Ruth, I believe you are a poet."

She handed me her bourbon glass. "I can't take credit for those words. Bobby Darin sang them to me on my forty-fifth birthday."

Holly spread herself out to sun on the rocks. The boats weren't passing so quickly now, but there were more of them, mostly full of shirtless boys and tattooed young men waving cans of beer in the air and shouting obscenities.

"Well, times are different now," Ruth said. "And at our age we have the luxury of being choosy, don't we?" In her mind, Ruth was still a young woman, as young as me, at least. Not that I was very young.

"When you're fifteen years old and in love, every moment is so desperate. You just can't see how tomorrow will ever come. I remember the first time I saw Lonnie. He was splitting wood. Lightning had hit a sweetgum tree out behind his cabin and the storm blew it down on top of his hog pen, killing two of his sows. He broke his arm trying to get the others back in their pen. To compensate him, Daddy gave Lonnie permission to cut up the tree and sell whatever firewood he didn't need. He cut that whole tree up himself, sawed it one-handed into sticks with an old lumber saw Daddy had in his barn, then split every stick of it into firewood, lifting that eight pound maul in one hand over his head as easy as you pick up a back scratcher."

She straightened up in her chair, pushing herself up on the arms. I leaned over the dock rail and looked down into the water at the minnows schooling around the wooden posts, and the green, moss-grown concrete piles beneath them.

"I was coming home, riding my Bayard, a big black horse with a white blaze on his nose. Daddy said he was too much horse for me but I loved him. I heard the fall of that ax, like the report of a rifle echoing across the meadow, regular and spaced out every minute or so. It wasn't hunting season so I turned Bayard into the lane beside Lonnie's cabin and rode around back. That's where I saw him first, with his broke arm hanging in the bib of his overalls like a sling. He lifted the ax with the other hand and swung it like a baseball pitcher with the whole of his body, and when it hit, the two pieces of wood flew apart like they had been split by a stick of dynamite, bouncing end over end across the yard. His boy would gather up the halves and set them up to be split again into quarters and then stack the quarters and stand up a new stick for his daddy to split. His wife was sitting on the porch watching him work, a baby latched on to her tit like a tick. I could see she loved him and knew she had the best man in the county but I didn't care. I wanted him. And I got him, eventually."

Obviously, she hadn't married Lonnie. "Whatever happened to him?"

"Daddy finally caught us. It was bound to happen, but we just couldn't quit each other. He beat Lonnie half to death. Lonnie had crossed the line, you see. Oh, not the difference in our ages. I told you, those were different times. Daddy was trying to shake off his reputation as an outlaw and a hoodlum and set himself up as a respectable citizen. Lonnie was a share-cropper and I was the daughter of his landlord. Daddy had every right to beat him. He had to do it. He'd have been shamed if he hadn't. But he beat him so bad, Lonnie couldn't make his crop that year and pay the share he owed. So Daddy threw them out. I never saw Lonnie again."

The sun crept toward the tops of the trees. I lit a cigarette and blew smoke at the gathering clouds. "Thank you, Jackie," Ruth said as she patted her eyes with a bit of Kleenex.

"For what?"

"For helping me remember. Lonnie's hog pen was where the softball field is now. His little shack was right down there." She nodded off to her right, at the bottom of the lake. "Me and Lonnie used to meet at night at the top of that hill." She pointed to the island where Holly lay stretched out on the rocks.

Ruth slipped a hand under her leg and pulled out a silver hip flask. "Pour me another," she said, "and one for yourself."

"All your ice is melted," I said.

"Who wants to drink watered-down whiskey anyway?" I poured half the flask into her empty tumbler, then took a sip for myself. It was strong but not unpleasant, cool in the mouth, exploding like a cherry bomb in the chest. It would have gone down better on a cold winter evening by the fire.

"I am eighty-seven years old, Jackie Lyons. We Stirlings are a long-lived people. Maybe it's something in the water around here that keeps us young. My father Gus remained virile well into his nineties. He died at the age of a hundred and two with a full head of hair as black as the day I was born. He was one-quarter Chickasaw, you know."

I'd seen his sarcophagus in the tomb in the woods. I took another sip of her whiskey and felt it erupt around my heart.

My father would love this stuff. He would love this woman, the old philanderer. He'd wreck himself upon her shores, as blindly as the drunken boys buzzing around Holly's Spot. Strangely enough, my mother would have loved Ruth, too, for very different reasons.

"Deacon mentioned to me that your mother had recently passed. I'm sorry," Ruth said, seemingly reading my mind. It felt like years since we buried her in Pastor Corner.

"Thank you," I said.

"Was she very old?

"Not so old. She died the same way as my grandfather, and about the same age."

"Well, now you know how many years you have," she said. I didn't find much comfort in that. There weren't so many years between me and my mother. "Count yourself lucky to have had a mother. I never knew mine. She died when I was very young."

I tried to picture this tragic figure of a young mother. I wanted to see her standing over Ruth, her ghost watching and waiting patiently. I wanted to see her father Gus, or old forgotten Lonnie, left for dead seventy years ago, still crawling home across the dark bottom of the lake. But Ruth was alone, utterly alone, abandoned by both the living and the dead, frail in her chair, burning away in the sun before my very eyes. There was no room in her life for anyone else. I couldn't see their ghosts, but I could almost see her fierce, enormous spirit burning up the last of her flesh. The liquor seemed to be the only thing keeping her alive.

She went on, talking sleepily between sips of her toddy. "But

I can't complain. I've lived a full life, a storybook life in many ways, a life some might envy and others would surely condemn. I was young and beautiful, and I remained young and beautiful well past the age when most women start thinking about grandchildren. I've been a movie star, an outlaw, a respectable planter, and a paid whore. I have loved and lost more men than I wish to remember."

"Mrs. Ruth, I'd like to take your picture one day."

She held out her glass and I topped it off from her flask. "Suit yourself. There's not much to look at anymore. But you'd better not wait too long."

"You're still a beautiful woman," I said.

"My body has betrayed me. Too many cigarettes, too much corn liquor. When I got my first gray hair, I knew the end was near. Now I am old and helpless with cancer. But that's not what is killing me. I am bored, Jackie, bored to death. You can't live the kind of life I've lived and be content to end your days surrounded by people so weak of mind they don't even know when they've pissed themselves."

She finished her whiskey and I downed the last of her flask in one icy, incandescent swallow. A long sleek cigarette boat roared by close enough to feel the mist of its prop spray, dragging a long, skittering ski rope across the water behind it. There was no sign of the skier.

"Can I get you anything else, Mrs. Ruth?" I asked.

"To tell the truth, I'd betray Christ to the Romans for just one puff of your cigarette. Luther won't let me have them."

I gave her one from my pack and dug a lighter from my

pocket. The cigarette resting effortlessly between her long, frail fingers gave her hand a grace it had almost forgotten. She licked her dry lips impatiently and smiled.

"Turn off my oxygen, first. I don't want to set myself on fire." I did as she asked. She pulled the oxygen hose down around her chin. "I don't really need this, you know. I just wear it because it's so damn sexy."

27

THE FIREWORKS WERE SCHEDULED to start around nine and every volunteer fire truck in the county was standing by to douse the least little spark, lest it burn down somebody's Maserati. It was getting dark and Deacon hadn't shown his face since supper. Mrs. Ruth was staying at Luther's house—they had hired a nurse to sit with her—so my transportation options were dwindling faster than the twilight. I looked around for a decent park bench to spend the night, but all I found was Luther's porch swing. That's where Jenny found me, curled up with a bottle of wine for a pillow. It was past my bedtime.

"Having fun yet?" she asked. Her glass was empty so I filled it. She sat beside me and kicked the swing into motion.

"Loads."

"This is the first time I've gone to one of these parties alone," she said. That confession hung out there like a slow curve over the plate, but I didn't swing. She played with her wineglass for a while. "I almost didn't come, but Cass and Eli wanted to see the fireworks."

They could have watched the fireworks from her house, and I didn't see her kids anywhere. Something else had brought her out.

"Have you seen Deacon lately?" she asked.

"Not since dinner."

"He's probably hiding from Holly. It's disgraceful really, the way she chases after him."

"I hadn't noticed."

"Really?" She kicked off her sandals and tucked her legs under her butt, made herself comfortable. "We should be able to see the fireworks from here."

Senator Mickelson seemed to have the same idea. He crossed the veranda and wedged himself between us on the swing.

"Jenny, my dear. So good to see you," he said. "How are you holding up?"

"Just taking it day by day, Bill." So she was on a first-name basis with the president pro tem of the Senate. This girl was full of surprises.

"Sam was a hell of a man and a good friend. I miss him."

"So do I," Jenny said. Even the good senator. I couldn't turn over a rock without finding another of Sam's closest friends. It was starting to look like the only way I would find his killer was if I moved in and became one of these people.

"It was good of Luther to invite you to his table. He tells me they're voting for a new treasurer at the next homeowners' meeting. I'm putting in a word for you." Jenny's phone rang and she answered it. The senator turned and put his hand on my knee.

"As a resident, I get a vote. And what about you, my dear? Jackie Lyons, isn't it?" Like most politicians, he had a gift for putting names with faces. "I'm sorry if I seemed forward with you earlier. Ruth just told me you are her guest. Any relation to Reed Lyons?" Not just putting names with faces. He had a detective's knack for putting names with other names. It probably served him well when it came time to pry open people's pocket books.

"My ex," I said.

"It's a small world, isn't it? Reed is one of my biggest supporters in Shelby County." He massaged my knee with his hand. The mint in his julep barely disguised the dead animal reek of his breath. All his front teeth were caps. His back teeth smelled like they were rotting in his face. "How long have you two been divorced?"

"Not long enough," I said as I lifted his hand from my knee. He nodded and stood, doffed his cap and ran a hand through his wavy hair.

"I hope I can count on your vote this November."

"Do I have any choice?"

"The Republicans always run a token candidate to keep me honest."

As he walked away, Jenny turned off her phone. "Senator Mickelson is something of a ladies' man," she whispered.

"He's quite the little sailor."

"That was Deacon," she said as she dropped her phone into her purse and stood. "He's at my house. Eli fell asleep, so he took both kids home. Holly's with him, and he asked me to please hurry home before she takes her clothes off."

"Is she drunk?"

"Holly doesn't have to get drunk to take her clothes off." She waited as though it was assumed I would join her. For some reason I resented the assumption, no matter how reasonable. Deacon was my ride home, unless I wanted to sleep in the park, and somehow I doubted Luther's rent-a-cops or Stegall's goons would let me camp out on their playground. But more than that, I had an idea of where I could rent a room on a more permanent basis. Granted, it was slightly used and the old owner was still hanging around knocking pictures off the walls, but I was used to that. At least it was clean. It was close to work, and there was a bar downstairs that never closed.

"I'm ready to go whenever you are. Where did you park?"

"I walked. It's miles around the lake by car, but it's not far on foot. Just across the levee."

It was miles by foot, too, or seemed like it—across the park littered with families sprawled on blankets waiting for the fireworks to begin, through the empty softball field and past home plate still speckled with Eugene Kitchen's nose blood. The party was still going strong under the trees, but most of the boats were off the lake.

We crossed the levee, through the high, dry grass crackling and turning to dust beneath our feet, with the lake bright and dark on one side and the forest full of distant laughing children on the other. Jenny showed me the spillway, but there wasn't any water going through. "The lake is low for this time of year. It hasn't rained in forever," she said, gazing up at the dull stars. I assumed she and Deacon had been maneuvering for weeks to bring me to this spot, but now that we were here, Jenny seemed reluctant to go any farther.

Until that moment, I never realized how difficult it must be for her, how frightening to walk toward that place where her husband died, with me walking at her side, wondering if I saw him, wondering if I was pretending not to see him. Like a child cowering under the covers while her mama pretends to check under the bed for boogie monsters. Jenny stood looking down at the spillway, biting her lip and swinging her handbag against her thigh, trying as hard as she could not to cry.

"Let's go," I said, taking her hand. She let herself be pulled into motion. And for a second I wondered, if Sam did show, would I be able to maintain awareness in her presence? Jenny was too sharp a steersman not to notice. Lucky for both of us he spared me from having to tell the sort of lies that normal people tell to comfort themselves.

"Sometimes I sense Sam," she said when we were safely past the spot. "I wake in the night and I can almost feel him lying beside me. And there are times I can still smell Reece in her room. Her head had the strangest smell, like freshly turned earth. When she was a baby, I used to hold her and just breathe."

We arrived at the house and found Holly swimming laps in Jenny's pool. She was still wearing her swimsuit. Deacon greeted us at the back door. He looked like he had been mauled. "Thank God you're here," he whispered.

Jenny laughed and helped him straighten his tie. "In the nick of time."

28

AT NINE O'CLOCK THE FIREWORKS started and we went outside by the pool to watch. Holly floated on her back at the pool's edge, barely breathing hard after her workout, a plastic cup of wine resting on her breastbone. She was too cool, too relaxed, too much like a pretty girl in a Jimmy Buffet song with nothing in the world to do, but whenever she rolled over to take a sip of wine, flames shot out of her eye sockets at Jenny and me. We'd interrupted the movie script that ended with her and Deacon naked in the pool while reflected fireworks exploded in their loins.

Cassie sat in Deacon's lap so Holly couldn't. I lay in a sunbathing chair beneath the moon, watching colorful explosions and trying to think of a way to move into Jenny's house without her knowing why. I knew I wasn't thinking clearly, but with the wine and the warm night whispering sweet nothings to my better judgment, moving in seemed like a fine idea, a glorious idea even.

Jenny liked her wine cold and kept bottles of it in a bathtub of ice by the door. I usually liked my wine out of a paper bag, provided it was whiskey and not wine, but this stuff helped cool the heat of the day's sun radiating out of my pores. I could feel the skin starting to tighten around my eyes. I hadn't spent that much time in the sun since I was a cop. Too much exposure would ruin my heroin pallor.

The wine helped me not to mind so much. The bombing seemed to last well past midnight. Holly got bored and walked to the end of Jenny's boat dock. It wasn't nearly as long as Luther's boat dock, but Holly strutted it just as insolently as she had her father's. I thought she had a boat tied off there—people seemed to use their boats like cars around here—but instead she dove in the lake.

"She'll swim home," Jenny said in answer to my surprise. "She does that sometimes."

"Must be how she keeps her figure." I could smell the smoke from the fireworks, and bits of burning paper and ash were starting to drift down, speckling the surface of the pool. Jenny covered her wine with her hand. I wandered inside to relieve myself, finished and climbed the stairs, not really going anywhere but finding myself in Reece's bedroom all the same.

It was much as I had left it, everything in its place including the photo of Reece's softball team hanging on the wall. I wondered if I could sleep here, or if I really wanted to. The bed was neatly made, the curtains folded back. I looked out the window at the reflection of the fireworks exploding in the water and the distant, tiny ripple that was Holly, far out in the dark water swimming with slow and deliberate strokes toward

Luther's house. My gaze strayed hesitantly down to the dark, overgrown levee where for the moment no ghosts walked or stumbled and fell.

I sat on the edge of the bed, wrinkling the pool-table smoothness of the bedspread, took my phone out and dialed a number I wasn't supposed to know. It rang three times before a man answered.

No hello, no how ya doin' Jackie old buddy, old pal. Just, "How the hell did you get this number?"

"Nice to hear your voice, too, Dr. Wiley," I said. Paul Wiley was the chief medical examiner for the city of Memphis. He and I had crossed swords a time or two in days of yore. He didn't like the fact that I did freelance photography of crime scenes for defense lawyer types. I didn't like the fact that he was possibly the most colossal dick in all of Memphis.

"How long's it been?" I asked.

"I'm hanging up now."

"I need a favor."

He didn't hang up. He didn't say anything, either. I think the idea of me asking for a favor must have caught him like a short hook. While he was still shaking off the cobwebs, I said, "Sam Loftin. Fayette County drowning, back in April. Local gravedigger ruled it a suicide. Know anything about it?"

He was quiet for a moment while he whetted his tongue. "Mrs. Lyons, in case it has slipped your mind, I work for the city of Memphis. If you have questions about a Fayette County suicide, I suggest you interrupt the Fayette County coroner on his Fourth of July."

"Paul," I said. "I think this guy was murdered."

"All the more reason *not to bother me!*" He hung up as viciously as you can hang up a cell phone. Guys like him missed the old days when you could slam a phone down to really get your point across. I called him back, but the line was busy. He was probably calling the IT department to get his number changed.

I reminded myself that none of this was my business. I was here to shoot some photographs, nothing more. If Wiley didn't see any need to investigate a possible murder just because it took place on the east side of the county line instead of the west, why did I? I owed Jenny and her family and their ghosts nothing. If I started digging around and turning up bones, I might only make things worse.

My life was complicated enough without inviting new complications. The last time I tried to play family doctor, I got the patient killed and damn near received the mortal chop myself, all over some ugly pictures wanted by a man with a shard of broken glass for a soul.

But I couldn't help myself. It was like my heroin addiction. No matter how long you stayed clean, that gorilla never left your back. It was always there, whispering in your ear—just once, just once. Just this once, stick your nose into somebody else's business. Never mind it might get chopped off. Just this once, you can poke around without losing yourself in it. Just this once, your own jacked-up problems won't become a part of the problem. Move in with this poor woman, find her husband's murderer, win her some insurance money, and maybe save your own soul in the process.

Such a damned liar, that gorilla.

If I moved in with Jenny, I knew I'd eventually steal that suitcase full of money hidden behind Reece's closet. Just standing here in her room, I could hear the siren song of those unguarded Benjamins, promising me a good time. Sooner or later I'd need five bucks for cigarette money and the next thing you know I'm buying furs and summering on the Isle of Capri. Money like that would change my life forever and for the better and nobody would know I'd taken it except me and Deacon and whoever put it there.

I should have slipped away, just like I did the day my mother died, slipped away and this time changed my phone number and never returned. I could have opened that window, climbed out on the roof and into the tree at the corner. I could see the route from the window. It would have been absurdly easy, so easy a child could do it, and nobody in the house would know she was gone.

Until it was too late.

By the time I returned downstairs, the patriotic aerial bombardment had ended. Cassie was in the den playing dolls with a girl in a red swimsuit. I hadn't seen this girl before, but then again I hadn't seen most of the people I'd met today. Maybe she was spending the night.

Jenny called Cassie to the kitchen as I entered. Deacon handed me a bowl and a spoon. "Did you have fun today?" Jenny asked her daughter.

"Un-hnn," she shrugged as she took her ice cream and sat at the table.

"Can you give me a ride home after this?" I asked Deacon. "My truck is at Ruth's nursing home."

Cassie looked up from her treat. "Where do you live?" she asked me.

"I live in a motel."

"Are you on vacation?"

"Not exactly," I laughed.

Jenny asked, "Which motel?"

"The Deertick. That is, the Detrick Motel on Highway 70."

"I thought it had been condemned!" Jenny said in horror.

"What's condemned, Mama? Is it going to hell?"

Deacon said to Jenny, "What if she stayed here?"

"For the night?"

"No, I mean move in." He pushed his bowl aside and turned to me. "The money you pay in rent to that motel will help Jenny, and you get to move out of that fleabag."

Jenny sat down next to him and smiled. "You could stay with us while you are working for Deacon, at least until they find your car. We have more than enough room."

"And we have a swimming pool," Cassie added.

I told myself this is what I had asked for, hoped for. This is what had to happen if I wanted to find out what happened to Sam Loftin.

I told myself one place was as good as another. I also told myself that it wasn't any of my business, but I wasn't listening to that part. This place was a damn sight better than my motel room, even if it did come with a woman whose grief was still as raw as hamburger.

———

I let them talk me into it, and Jenny seemed genuinely happy when I agreed. Deacon drove me to the motel in her van. In less than ten minutes I was packed and ready to leave the old place forever. I paused at the door to shake the cockroaches from my shoes.

I would have been happy sleeping on the couch for the two weeks it was going to take me to finish the photography job, but Jenny had already decided that I would move into Reece's room. She helped me carry my luggage upstairs. "If you need space, I can clean out these drawers," she said, opening them one by one. "I just never had the heart to go through her old clothes and throw anything away. I kept telling myself that one day Cassie could wear this stuff."

I was unpacked, moved in, and crawling into bed by one o'clock. As I lay there in the dark, the door safely locked, naked beneath pink sheets, surrounded by all the cultural detritus of a teenaged girl dead these last five years, just beginning to drift off into a dream of coffee-black nights and bacon-bright mornings, I sat up suddenly in bed. Cassie's friend in the red swimsuit hadn't joined us for ice cream. She hadn't been in the house at all.

29

In either case, there was very much the same solemnity of demeanour on the part of the spectators; as befitted a people amongst whom religion and law were almost identical, and in whose character both were so thoroughly interfused, that the mildest and severest acts of public discipline were alike made venerable and awful.
— NATHANIEL HAWTHORNE, THE SCARLET LETTER

I'D BEEN LIVING THERE ABOUT a week when it really hit the fan. Jenny was outside vacuuming the pool while the kids played in the shallow end. I watched them for a while, especially Cassie. A strong swimmer, she still avoided the deep end and kept busy herding her little brother in his arm floaties away from that side of the pool, as he seemed determined to drown himself.

It was strange living in a house with children. The noise level was startling. I'd lived on my own for so long, I was used to being the only living source of sound. I wasn't used to locking doors. I'd be in the bathtub and the door would open and it would only be Cassie, looking for her hairbrush, or Eli coming in to stand at the toilet and pee with his pants around his ankles. Being among the living on a regular basis took some getting used to. I was practically feral.

Now that Deacon's workers had finished the roof, the dust had settled considerably in Ruth's house. I took tremendous pains not to stir it up again, and everything seemed fine while I was working, but when I checked my work on the computer, most of the photos were fouled with orbs. A whole day's work and I'd end up with maybe ten usable pictures.

So there I was, sitting at the kitchen table trying to clean up some photos, using Reece's old laptop, which was newer than the one I'd lost when my car was stolen, while still learning the photo-editing software Deiter had given me. Jenny came inside to get a drink of water. She watched me work for a while and listened to me swear, which she found strangely edifying when her kids weren't within earshot. "Maybe you need to clean the lens," she suggested unhelpfully.

Eugene Kitchen knocked at the back door. He'd boated over from his house. A gauze bandage still covered his nose, like a pirate's eye patch that had slipped down. Bruises the size and color of plums surrounded both eyes. He was wearing a little white captain's hat just like the one Senator Mickelson had been wearing at the Fourth of July picnic. It might even have been the same hat. I wondered if he had picked it out of Luther's garbage.

Jenny opened the door. "How are you Eugene?"

"I still can't breathe," he said, pointing at his nose.

"I'm sure Holly didn't mean to hit you."

"Luther made her apologize." He entered the kitchen and stood just inside the threshold, his eyes scouring the room before coming to rest on me. He nodded, perhaps to me, or maybe to himself. I couldn't tell. "I'm having surgery next week."

Jenny sat at the table and tinkled the ice in her glass. "Who is your surgeon?"

"Dr. Ledbetter. You know the Ledbetters, from over on Jefferson Street?"

"I go to him for my sinuses," she said. "He's good."

"The best. Listen." He took off his cap and twisted it in his hands. "The reason I stopped by is because there is an HOA meeting at the clubhouse tonight. You should be there."

"Why?

"Well, for one thing, we're voting on a new treasurer."

"Yes, I heard. I'm not interested." Jenny said.

"I say this as a friend. It would be in your best interest to be there." He turned to me. "Both of you."

"I have nothing to say. I don't want to be the treasurer. I'm not Sam."

"Still, you should be there. I can't tell you why."

"You've been sworn to secrecy?" Jenny asked.

He nodded gravely, as though he'd signed his name in thumb-blood to an oath taken in a graveyard with Huck Finn, Injun Joe and a stray dog. He clapped his cap on his head, took his leave, and thumped down to the boat dock, where his wooden Hacker-Craft speedboat bobbed expensively.

"I wonder what that was about," I said, returning to my work.

"Sam used to say they were worse than the CIA. They made him sign a nondisclosure agreement before every closed meeting. It was ridiculous."

"Well, at least Eugene was friend enough to give you a heads-up."

Jenny said, "Eugene Kitchen has never been our friend, Jackie."

That evening, we left the kids with Holly. Jenny drove to the meeting, which was held at the clubhouse. It looked like someone had gone to Switzerland, stolen one of their ski lodges, and set it down at the edge of the lake.

Back in my rich, married days, I'd stayed in casino hotels that weren't as nice as this. The place reeked of fir and gin and the expensive sweat of golfers. The dining room advertised on the menu their star in the Michelin guide. The HOA meeting was being held in a small auditorium shaped like an amphitheater. It was the sort of place where you took freshman psych with three hundred other people. Residents were filing in as we arrived; many greeted Jenny by name and asked her about her kids and how she was holding up, to which she replied with the constancy of an answering machine, "Just taking things day by day."

Presiding over this snake pit was HOA president Luther Vardry, his associate president of vice Eugene Kitchen and Secretary Annette LaGrance, birth mother of the *Elle* model I'd taken an instant dislike to that first day. The first order of business was the vote for the treasurer. Several people spoke on behalf of this or that resident, or on their own behalf, and about five names were floated, including Jenny's. Finally, they voted, placing their ballots into a box guarded by two of Stegall's goons.

Luther sat with his little sausage fingers folded in front of him, eyes lowered as though he were half asleep in prayer, while Eugene banged his gavel on the table long after everyone was seated and quiet again. Finally he tucked his dick away and checked his notes, as if he hadn't already memorized everything he was about to say.

Eugene spoke while Annette took the minutes. "The votes will be tallied and the results announced next week. Next order of business is the posting of signs along the roadway and on light poles. This is strictly prohibited by the covenant. The only signs allowed are For Sale signs by a licensed realtor. The covenant does not allow for-sale-by-owner. This bylaw was ratified in the annual meeting in January 2006. Also, there shouldn't be any Garage Sale signs, much less garage sales. As you know, we hold a semiannual community yard sale. The second weekends in April and October are the only weekends when garage sales may be held. This also goes for the sale of

automobiles and boats. You can't park a boat in the front yard
and stick a For Sale sign on it. This isn't Memphis. We aren't a
flea market. If you have a car or boat or any other large item
you wish to sell, you know that you can place a free ad in the
monthly newsletter. The same goes for missing cat and missing
dog notices. Send me an email and a photograph and I'll broadcast it through our phone app. Everybody in the community
will see it. There's no need to trash up the place with missing
pet posters taped to every light pole."

"What about missing children?" A woman at the back stood
up and repeated her question. "It took you three days to send
out the notice when my daughter disappeared."

Eugene looked more pained that she had spoken out of order than by the accusations in her statement. Luther didn't look
at all. He was playing churches-and-steeples with his fingers.
Eugene said, "It was already all over the news, Lauren. I didn't
see the point."

"Not everybody watches the news day and night, Eugene.
Some people have to work for a living," the woman said.

"I made an honest mistake."

"You tore down her posters!" A man stood up beside her and
took her elbow. She jerked it away. He took it again, gently, and
leaned close to whisper in her ear.

"The covenant is clear . . ." Eugene started to say.

"To hell with the covenant! We're not talking about a stray
dog. Lindsey was my daughter! She disappeared!"

"Ran away," Eugene muttered. The woman froze, her chin
wagging in the air as she tried to find words for a rage that had

no words. The man at her side turned her into the aisle and guided her to the door.

Luther finally roused himself. He leaned forward, steepling his hands, his brow thoughtfully furrowed. "We've already been over this, Lauren. This is neither the time nor the place to bring it up again. Eugene is truly sorry, and as you know we've changed our policies and procedures. As soon as an alert comes in, Eugene forwards it to everyone in the community. So some good did come of that whole unfortunate incident."

"Good? Good God!" the woman shrieked as the door closed behind her. The council members shuffled their agendas and tried not to look at one another. For a few intensely uncomfortable moments, the room was as silent as a tomb.

Then it got worse.

Eugene called Jenny's name.

"Yes?"

He glanced at Luther, who shrugged, nodded and folded his hands across his waistcoat. Eugene cleared his throat. "I'm sorry to have to mention this, but our rules are clear. It has been reported to this council that Jackie Lyons . . ." Here he pointed at me, as though identifying a suspect in a Perry Mason courtroom. ". . . is renting a room from you. As you know, this is a violation of the covenant."

Jenny smiled thinly, but the hand behind her back clenched into a fist. "Jackie isn't renting. She's my guest." Someone behind us snorted.

"And I suppose y'all are just friends."

"That's right," Jenny said after a moment's pause.

Eugene stuck his thumbs behind his bracers and addressed the ceiling. "Would you say you are good friends?"

Jenny looked at me, a question on her face. I winked at her. "Yes, we have become friends," she said, winking back.

"And does Mrs. Lyons have her own bedroom?"

I came up out of my chair. Eugene had the gall to look surprised. Jenny said my name and snatched futilely at my elbow. I noticed Stegall's goons closing in on either side, but I knew I could get to him before they brought me down, unless they had Tasers. Eugene backed into the American flag and knocked it over. Somewhere a Boy Scout fainted.

The doors banged open and Deacon entered and for some reason I stopped as though I'd reached the end of my chain. He was dressed in black slacks, black silk vest over a dusky red shirt, black watered silk tie, aviator shades and black leather cowboy boots. All he needed was a cheap tin star. "Sorry I'm late."

His timely entrance saved me eleven months and twenty-nine days' participation in the Fayette County highway beautification project. "Evening," he said, tipping his invisible hat to me as he passed. Jenny glared at me, barely able to contain her glee.

While Stegall's goons rescued the flag, Eugene recovered his composure by banging his gavel on the table. "Late?" he said. "Late? You weren't invited at all, preacher. This is a homeowners' association meeting and you aren't a homeowner."

"I am here to represent the interests of Ruth Vardry on this council."

"You can't do that."

Deacon continued to the front of the room, then turned and

sat on the edge of the officers' table. "According to the HOA bylaws, Ruth Vardry maintains a permanent advisory seat on the homeowners' association council. If you want, we can look it up." He removed a piece of paper from his back pocket, unfolded it and set it in front of Luther. "This is an affidavit in which she names me as her representative. I am authorized to speak on her behalf, and I intend to do so."

Luther scanned the document and said, "Everything seems to be in order here. Fetch him a chair, Eugene."

"But Mr. President . . ."

"Be quiet, Eugene. I want to hear what Mama has to say."

When the goons had brought his chair, Deacon ignored it and walked forward to address the audience. "Thank you, Mr. President. My name is Deacon Falgoust. I am the pastor of the Hope Church of the Gospel Revealed. So you know that I am but a humble servant of our Lord and Savior, Jesus Christ.

"First let me say that I am appalled that Jenny Loftin and Jackie Lyons are being questioned in this shocking manner. When last I checked, this association was not a court of law. This is not Boston Colony and we are not the Puritans. Should we publicly shame our neighbors for minor violations of a homeowners' agreement, much less call into question their living arrangements?"

Eugene fumed and toyed with his gavel, while Luther smiled beatifically at his own hands. Annette's pen hovered above her steno pad. She had stopped writing. The minutes ticked by, un-minuted.

Deacon slipped into that peculiar booming cadence that I called his preacher voice. His rhythms were poetic, the pitch rising and falling, expressing love and disappointment in the same paternal breath. He used a sonorous Southern drawl that he could tune like a dial to suit his audience, with the occasional Cajun inflection or word thrown in to hammer home a point. "If Jesus were standing here tonight, what would He say to us about this situation? Would He say, no, you may not give shelter to a stranger or even to a friend in need? No, He would not. That's not the Jesus of the Gospels. The money changers in the temple might say that, but not Jesus.

"These are difficult economic times, scraping times, when even a family that works hard and is frugal can get into difficult straits, but when one of us is struck by disease or a death in the family, we may not be able to survive at all. Because of these hard times, we are *mal pris,* we can't find a buyer for our house, yet neither may we rent it. Would Jesus say, too bad for you, sucker? The money changers might say that, the scribes and the Pharisees in the temple might say to the poor widow with two young children, go and pauper yourself, destroy your good credit, bankrupt yourself rather than rent even a single room of your house until such time as it can be sold. But Jesus, He would not say that. Not to me and not to you, dear friends."

"The community has standards to keep. If we let people . . ." Eugene said.

Deacon interrupted, still addressing the audience, "Every year you pay your homeowners' association fees. These fees are considerable, and for some here they are unbearable. Ruth Vardry wishes to know what is being done with this money."

"Our books are open. If you want to audit them, you need only obtain a majority vote at the next annual meeting." Eugene's voice was small, like the whining of a mosquito. Deacon spoke over him.

"*Mais*, I don't need to audit the books, ladies and gentlemen. You can tell me all I need to know. Are we spending these fees for them to mow the park? To trim a little bitty strip of lawn by the road and plant a few pansies in the median? Or are we throwing it away on holiday parties for the glory of a single man, a politician some of us may or may not support?"

"We've been having these parties long before you got here, preacher," Eugene said.

"*Co faire?* Are we a community?" Deacon asked. No one in the audience answered. Some didn't want to answer and resented him for asking. Others were too afraid to answer, but looking around, I could see a few were beginning to ask the same questions. They were starting to put two and two together and seeing that it came to several million a year.

Deacon walked back to the council table and finally took his seat beside Luther. "Our neighbors are like our family. We should be using this money to help them, not to grind them down and force them into poverty and bankruptcy. Therefore, Mr. President, it is Ruth Vardry's request that the HOA set up a hardship fund with these fees, so that when your husband dies you don't lose your house, or when you get sick or lose your job and can't pay your mortgage, the bank doesn't foreclose on you before you can get back on your feet, and you aren't forced to sell that which is nearest and dearest to you just to keep body and soul together. I don't want to lose you as a neighbor. You are all, every one of you good God-fearing people, but this homeowners' association is run like the old temple. Jesus drove the money changers out of the temple and said, you have turned my father's house into a den of thieves. It's time we drove the money changers out and started helping each other, as neighbors should."

"I'm not paying . . ." Eugene started.

"*Because that,* brothers and sisters, *that* is what creates real property value. Not the color of your paint. Not the cut of your lawn. Not the cars parked in your garage. Community. When we create a community in which neighbor helps neighbor, people will want to live here, they will pay top dollar to live here, no matter how difficult the economy. If the scribes and Pharisees cannot see this, then they are blind. They do not want to lift up and ennoble their fellow man. They want to profit off their neighbor, to stand on his back, your back and my back, so that they may stand a little higher and look down at the world."

"These are serious accusations, preacher," Eugene said.

"I have made no accusations. I have named no names and pointed no fingers. But if you believe I have just described you, it is not my words that have condemned you, brother. As Jesus said, you have said it, not I."

"Oh, he's good," Jenny whispered. She wasn't the only person who thought so. Luther hid his grin behind his pudgy hand. People in the audience began to snicker.

Deacon continued, "Regarding Mrs. Lyons, she moved in with Jenny Loftin at my suggestion. I will vouch, upon my honor, that she is not paying rent."

Luther nodded and said, "And I will second the motion put forward by my mother, that a hardship fund be set aside for the

temporary relief of those in our community who find themselves in difficult circumstances. It will be considered by the
full committee Thursday next, and if approved will be put to a
vote by the entire homeowners' association at the next annual
meeting." Luther was, if nothing else, a master politician. It was
lucky for Senator Mickelson that he didn't harbor ambitions for
national office. No doubt the Republican party would bend over
backward to run him for Mickelson's seat.

"As for the matter of Mrs. Loftin, I think it has been satis-
factorily settled, unless you wish to doubt the word of an or-
dained minister, Eugene. Mrs. Lyons is a guest of Mrs. Loftin
and is welcome as long as Jenny wishes her to stay. Does anyone care to dispute this?"

No one did, not even Doris Dye.

"Then this meeting is adjourned." Luther was the first to
stand. He turned and shook Deacon's hand before Eugene
could get his gavel out.

I followed Jenny to the bar to wait for Deacon. Jenny ordered
wine. I went for the Wild Turkey with a lot of ice. "That was
interesting," I said. "Other than poor reflexes, what's Eugene's
malfunction?"

"He and Sam had issues." The bartender brought our drinks.
Jenny paid with a credit card. "Sam couldn't talk about it
because of the nondisclosure agreements, but I think it had something to do with money. Sam was the HOA treasurer."

I already knew that, but it bore repeating. Money has a way

of making enemies even among the best of friends. People have been known to kill each other over the stuff.

"At least Deacon was able to get the hardship fund started." I knew he was doing it for her sake.

Jenny snorted and shrugged. "If it ever happens. The next annual meeting isn't until January." She knew how these things worked as well as I did. Six months was plenty of time for the motion to be tabled and quietly forgotten, unless Deacon was there to keep pushing it. And if Mrs. Ruth died in the meanwhile?

"Deacon has been suggesting you move in with us for a long time. We just didn't know how to ask."

"Why would he do that? He barely knew me. You barely knew me."

She stared into her wineglass. "He said you could help us."

"I don't know how."

"I thought he meant with money. I'm not sure now what he meant. But I trust him." She turned and touched my wrist, lightly, just the tips of her fingers. Her eyes had a bit of wildness to them. "Deacon has a gift, Jackie. You must have noticed. He has a way with people. It isn't just his magnetism, though he has plenty of that."

Enough to turn a compass needle.

"There's a power working through him, a Godly power. He's so wise, sometimes it's like he can read your mind. He doesn't really, but it feels like he does. It's impossible to hide anything from him. He knows things about you that you aren't even aware of."

"He sounds like a regular Carnac the Magnificent."

"But it's impossible to get a read on him. I've known him for almost a year now, yet I hardly know him at all. He takes our burdens and makes them his own, but he doesn't share his troubles with us. He never talks about himself, about his past or his feelings or anything." I didn't tell her that Deacon had told me quite a bit about his past. Maybe all of it was lies. Or maybe not.

We moved from the bar to a table near the windows. The couple who had left the meeting early were outside on the deck. The woman was still crying as she stared out over the lake, her fingers buried up to the knuckles in the deck rail, while her husband made useless gestures of comfort. I asked Jenny, "What happened to their daughter?"

"It was after a softball game in Somerville. Lindsey told her teammates she was riding home with a friend, but nobody saw her leave. Sam wasn't coaching the team anymore or he would never have let her go off on her own."

"Did they find her?"

"No. And it's been three years. Lindsey was fourteen. She and Reece . . ." she started to say, until Deacon arrived. Jenny wrapped her arms around him. "I'm so glad you showed up when you did."

"I'm glad you called me," he said. "I would have been here sooner but I was dealing with a *possedé*." He ordered a beer from a waitress. "All that talking. *Podna*, that's thirsty work."

"You were just in time. I don't like to think what Jackie might have done to Eugene." She nudged me with her toe. "Would you really have hit him?"

"I doubt I could have caught the little bastard." I took a sip of the Turkey. The taste always reminded me of my dad—a little bastard of a different stripe. "He was ready to bolt. Speaking of, you lied for me, preacher."

The waitress brought his beer. He lifted it to his lips without drinking. "Unlike Jesus, I do not have the power to soften a man's heart." He tilted the bottle up. I watched his Adam's apple rise and fall, over and over until the bottle was empty. It took about six seconds. I'd never seen him sock one away like that.

He carefully set the empty bottle on the table and stepped back, brushed his hands down the front of his vest. "God will forgive me because my heart is true. Besides, it's no sin to lie to the devil."

30

THE NEXT MORNING I WOKE UP in a puddle of sweat. It was the hottest day of the year so far, so naturally Jenny's air conditioner broke down. She met me in the hall, fanning herself with a magazine. "I just . . ." she said, exasperated to the point of tears. "I don't know."

"I'll talk to Deacon," I said.

I found him rebuilding the porch on Ruth's house. His shirt was off, the sweat sheeting down his naked back, the blaring sun baking his skin to the color of an old penny. His back and shoulders were laced with old blue tattoos. He sported the usual Army propaganda—eagles, knives through skulls, that sort of thing—plus a couple of prison tats from that stint in the federal hotel for going AWOL. His body was tight as a coiled spring. It was the first time I'd ever seen him without his suit or at least a tie. He sat back and pushed the hair out of his eyes as I climbed the steps.

I told him about Jenny's air. "It's Friday. We won't be able to get anybody out here before Monday."

"My HVAC guy went home to Texas for the weekend, but I can take a look at it when I'm done here."

It hadn't rained since early May. A pall of dust hung low in the sky, turning the sun red as blood as it set. There didn't seem to be as many people working on the house as before, and other than the grading and leveling in the field, they hadn't started on the church. Maybe the heat was keeping them away. Or maybe they did the sensible thing and got most of their work done early in the morning while I was still in bed.

After about two hours of sweltering in the closed up house trying to take photos, I packed it in. Another wasted day. Every photo I took was obscured by orbs. If only I could shoot without the flash, but all the windows were still bricked up or boarded over.

I staggered outside and flopped down on the steps. Deacon was hammering on the porch, all alone. "I wish I could have photographed before you tore everything apart," I said.

"There are always setbacks," he said through the nails in his mouth. Deacon felt good about his work on the porch, though I could tell he was disappointed with the progress with the rest of the house.

We headed back to Jenny's. Deacon disappeared around the side of the house while I went inside, hung my camera on the hall tree. The place had heated up considerably, though it was still bearable. Jenny's house was built in the days before air-conditioning. With the windows open, you could almost live in it in the summer.

I heard Cassie playing with her dolls in the den and talking to somebody in a play voice pitched dog-whistle high. Suddenly she dropped the play voice. "No, you're not doing it right!"

I edged around the corner and found her, to my surprise, quite alone, sitting with her back to me, cross-legged on the floor in front of the fireplace, doll clothes tossed about as though a Barbie house had exploded in her lap. She turned to search for something and stopped, staring back at me.

"What's up?"

"Playing," she said.

I moved some dolls to sit on the hearth. The bricks were cool against the back of my legs. "Who were you talking to just now?"

She didn't answer at first. She stared down at the doll clothes heaped in her lap, turning a tiny plastic pink shoe around and around her pinky. Finally, she dropped the shoe and looked up at me. "My friend."

So she called them her friends, too. I had wondered that night, when I saw the girl in the red swimsuit, whether Cassie was aware of her invisible companion.

"She's gone now," she added.

"Where did she go?"

She shrugged.

"Does she live around here?"

Cassie pointed at the fireplace.

"She lives in the chimney?"

"No."

"What's her name?"

"Cassie."

"But that's your name."

"She says it was her name first."

"Is she your pretend friend?"

"No."

"She's real?"

"I don't know."

"If she's real, how can she live in the fireplace?"

"She doesn't live in the fireplace."

"Where does she live?"

Cassie didn't answer. I waited and after a while she sighed and started picking up her dolls. She wasn't going to answer.

"She must be a special friend," I said. "Is she a nice friend?"

"Sometimes."

"Is she mean?"

"Sometimes."

"Does she talk to you?"

"Sometimes."

None of my special friends talked to me. They were just there, waiting for something I could never understand. The sweat started to drip from the end of my nose.

"Does she ever tell you things?"

"I don't want to talk about this anymore." She took the few dolls she had already gathered and ran upstairs, leaving me sitting on the hearth. I looked at the fire-blackened bricks at the back of the fireplace. I could still smell the ashes of an old fire, though the ashes had been swept up months ago. No one appeared. Apparently, Cassie's friend didn't want to be my friend.

Jenny came inside from the pool, carrying Eli wrapped in a towel. Deacon was right behind her.

"It's your compressor," he said. "You'll need a new one."

"Great." Jenny set the boy on the couch and viciously rubbed his wet hair. "That's just fantastic."

31

NATHAN AND HOLLY HUNG around the pool all day Saturday because it was too hot to go inside, even to pee. Nathan wore brown swimming trunks and a turquoise Hawaiian shirt unbuttoned to the navel. He had brought his camera and spent the morning impressing me with it. "Don't you have a home somewhere?" I asked.

"This used to be my house," he said, oblivious. "I sold it to Sam and Jenny."

Holly wore a little black thing that looked painted on, or maybe it was black electrical tape. As I didn't have a swimsuit of my own, I asked Jenny to lend me one. She didn't think any of hers would fit, so I tried on one of Reece's—a white two-piece with little red dots like measles. The white blended perfectly with my junkie pallor. "I can't believe it fits," Jenny said when she saw me in it. "I should probably hate you."

I took a quick dip to cool off. When I climbed out, I noticed the suit had turned translucent. "Are you sure this belonged to Reece?" I asked Jenny as I wrapped myself in a towel. Thank God Nathan had gone on a beer run.

"It was in her drawer. Maybe it's one of Holly's. She does her laundry here sometimes." It wasn't Holly's. Now that I was wearing it and seeing my areolas and pubes through the sheer fabric, I remembered seeing the same suit in one of the peekaboo photos I'd found in Sam's suitcase.

I went inside to change and found Reece's team photo lying on the floor in front of her desktop computer. I picked it up and hung it on its nail, then locked the bedroom door to keep out any surprise visitors while I tossed the entire room. I went through her drawers looking for a compromising photo of her daddy, a diary, maybe a love letter taped to the underside of a dresser drawer. Jenny told me that she'd never had the heart to go through Reece's clothes, so I was looking at things pretty much as she'd left them the day she died. I dumped her jewelry box on the bed, but didn't find anything too expensive for a teen girl. I turned the pictures off the walls, including the team photo, felt the paper backs for loose spots, pried off the cardboard, peeled back the posters and magazine clippings that she had taped above the bed, shifted the bed and checked the box springs.

Nothing. I got the feeling somebody had already been over the place. It was too clean, too generic. Nothing personal remained—no ticket stubs, no snaps of her and her friends, no diary tucked away under her bras and panties. This wasn't a bedroom, it was a museum.

Then I thought, girls these days don't keep diaries and love letters, and their pictures are on their cell phones, but I hadn't come across a phone, either. Not the sort of thing a parent would let sit in a drawer, anyway, and she wouldn't have compromising photos on her phone, in case she lost it. I turned on her computer, but it took a while to boot up. It had probably been five years since anybody had looked at it.

While I waited, I picked out a little turquoise two-piece with a scallop shell over each boob. I looked at myself in the dresser mirror. I'd been clean for a year, clean but still living a junkie lifestyle in many ways—broken sleep, never seeing the sun, garbage for food when I could get food at all. A week of regular eating and semiregular sleeping habits couldn't erase a decade's worth of damage. I looked like the star of some sad television special, *The Little Mermaid—Where Is She Now?*

The computer finally came up and I did a quick search of the hard drive for photo files, found a few family snaps but nothing out of the ordinary. Next I checked for saved emails and documents and mostly found old homework assignments, book reports and science projects. I opened her trash bin, but it was empty; then I checked her temp file folder without turning up anything incriminating. Her internet bookmarks folder didn't lead me anywhere, either. The last place I checked was her browser history. I found her email account right away, but without a username or password, I couldn't access it. I scrolled down the list until I saw a social website that had been extremely popular five or six years ago. I clicked the link and brought up the login page. The name Piglet59 was prefilled in the user name box. The website was still in business, but I wasn't. I tried all the obvious passwords—admin, combinations of names of family members, her name, her birthday, but nothing worked.

This girl had covered her tracks better than most criminals. Either that, or someone had covered them for her.

Among the ennui-afflicted bourgeoisie of Stirling Estates, any event was an occasion for a party. As soon as people heard that Jenny's air conditioner had broken, they were lining up in the driveway bringing coolers of ice, cases of beer, boxes of wine and buckets of cheap Mexican booze. Mostly women, friends of Jenny, which suited Nathan just fine as he was too busy chasing expensive tail to pay attention to poor little me. I noticed he spent a lot of time courting Annette LaGrance, the HOA secretary, and she did little to dissuade him. By her second margarita she was sitting in his lap. Her daughter, the *Elle* model, played with Cassie and Eli in the shallow end of the pool.

I spotted an older black man sitting on an upturned bucket at the end of Jenny's pier. I hadn't seen him come in, and no one had spoken of him or seemed to notice that he was there. I wasn't sure whether he was real or not, and I didn't want to point him out, in case I was the only one who could see him. I asked Jenny to show me the boathouse.

"We don't have a boat anymore," she said as she opened the gate. I followed her down the path. "I sold it to Nathan not long after Sam died. There's nothing much to see."

The wind was rising on the lake, blowing moist and warm as a sauna. Waves slapped hollowly against the piles beneath our feet. The old man turned around on his bucket and Jenny said, "Hey, Bert." He lifted his hand in greeting but kept his eye on the fishing pole propped in front of him. His fishing line ran taut as a piano wire down into the water.

Jenny unlocked the door and opened it. Inside, it was little more than a kind of carport for a boat, no floor, just open water, with a pair of skids hooked up to an electric wench for lifting the boat out of the water. A couple of old orange life jackets hung from a nail beside the door, and a thicket of fishing rods stood in one corner, their reels a nest of tangled twines, rusty hooks, and bobbers. A single bulb swung from a wire dangling from the roof beam—the cherry on its teenage-slasher-movie cake. All it needed was a spear gun hanging over the door. "Beautiful, isn't it?" Jenny said. "Why did you want to see it?"

I thought up a lie and I thought it up quick. "I was just wondering if I could put a bed in here and get out from underfoot."

"Don't be ridiculous!" She closed the door and locked it. "You're not underfoot."

The old man reeled in his line. He pulled up a bare hook and set the pole aside, clucking his tongue. "Little babies keep stealing my bait."

"You and Sam used to catch some big ones here," Jenny said. She introduced me to Bert Quinn.

"Catfish as long as my arm," he said as he baited his hook. His knuckles were as big as walnuts and the veins stood out like worms across the backs of his hands.

"Bert was Sam's shop foreman at the plant before it closed. When Sam started the landscape business, he brought in Bert as his partner."

"I wasn't much of a partner," he said. "Sam did all the work. All I did was make sure we had people to work."

"You see that the job gets done, too. Sam would have been lost without you," Jenny said. "*I'd* be lost without you, Bert."

"Truth is, I ain't so sure I can do it without Sam." He stared at the bare planks between his feet. "I can't run the business by myself, Jenny. Sam always handled that end. I don't know what I'm doing and I'm too old to start over. I'm near seventy years old this October. I need to retire, but all I got is Social Security and my stake in the company."

"But you're doing fine. There's more business than ever, Bert," Jenny said.

"There's plenty of business, but there ain't no money in it. I haven't paid you the first check, nor me neither. I don't know how Sam did it. I guess I ain't got his head for figures."

Jenny rested her hand on his shoulder. "Neither do I, but we'll get through this. It will all balance out in the end."

"It pains me to say, Jenny, but I was hoping you might buy me out, so I can retire."

She stepped back as though he'd hit her. "I don't know, Bert. You and Sam built this business. I can't run it all by myself."

Bert cleared his throat and stood up. He looked at me, then back at Jenny with a pained expression, his old fingers working themselves into knots. "I'm just gonna . . . I need to use your facilities." Jenny nodded and Bert passed me, headed toward the house.

Jenny walked to the end of the pier and stood, gripping the rail and staring out across the lake. I'd been there before. Not at this particular rail, but one just like it, staring into a whole lot of empty while your life slowly fell apart behind you. Husband, job, everything gone. "I take it you don't have the money to buy him out," I said.

She shook her head and tried to tuck a strand of loose hair behind one ear. "I don't understand how Sam did it. He must have had some kind of magic with numbers because I can't get it to add up. The company is doing more work than ever. Bert has secured several new contracts since Sam died, but the money isn't there, so I haven't been drawing Sam's salary. The weird thing is, Sam didn't pay himself enough to cover our expenses. I haven't paid the mortgage in two months, Jackie. The bank is threatening to foreclose. I don't have the money to get the air-conditioning fixed. We've been living off the HELOC and the credit cards since Sam died, but the cards are maxed out. If it weren't for Eli and Cassie's survivor benefit checks from Social Security, I couldn't put food on the table at all."

Back in the day I would have suspected Sam of dealing, but that suitcase full of cash, combined with the photos of his daughter, made me think he was into something far worse than selling blow to his neighbors. It was too bad I couldn't just drop that suitcase full of money on Jenny's doorstep and disappear, but I knew she'd only turn it over to the cops and never see a dollar of it. The only thing I was sure about was that somebody had killed Sam Loftin.

Somebody might have had a damn good reason.

I looked back up at the house and the pool party. Three more neighbors had just arrived. Some of these people brought food and drinks, but most of them were mooching off Jenny, drinking her liquor and cleaning out her fridge. She had hidden all this from me, just like she hid it from the people at the party.

"Why don't you sell this place, move somewhere you can afford?"

"You've seen the For Sale signs on our street. In this market, I'll never be able to pay off what we still owe on the house. We're under water. Jesus, I don't know what I'm gonna do."

"What about Deacon? He could probably get the money from Mrs. Ruth. Enough to get you through, anyway."

"He has offered a hundred times. I won't take charity."

I knew how she felt. I'd lived off people's good will for the last seven years, doing everything short of hooking just to keep body and soul together. I'd sold myself in other ways, some of them worse than turning a trick.

And here I was still on the dole, living with Jenny. The rent I paid barely covered the food I ate. I didn't like it, but sometimes people don't have choices. Jenny didn't have many choices left. She just didn't realize it yet.

32

JENNY PUT BOTH KIDS IN HER bed with the fan blowing across them to keep them cool, then joined me outside.
We sat in a pair of teak deck chairs watching the light in the
pool play over the brick chimney. I wore a fleece pullover, my
hair wrapped in a big towel. Jenny borrowed one of my cigarettes and tried to smoke it and coughed a lot. The night was
as warm as bathwater, buzzing with cicadas, the single light
bulb above the back door swirling with bugs, but it felt better
outside than in the house.

"I think I'd rather sleep out here," I said.

"The mosquitoes would eat you alive."

Jenny had gone to the grocery store that morning but now
the fridge was empty. Her friends and neighbors had cleaned
her out. I only had a couple of dollars in my pocket, but I offered
to go to the store in the morning if she would lend me her
van. She didn't say no, but she didn't say yes, either. Instead, she
started talking about Sam again.

"We went through a rough patch about a decade ago, back
during the recession. Sam was a plant manager, he made good

money, enough to buy this house. I didn't have to work. I stayed home and took care of Reece and worked on my art."

She had never mentioned her art before. I never saw her working on anything. There were a few paintings around the house that weren't the usual hobby-shop or furniture-store stock pictures, but I hadn't paid enough attention to them to look at the signature. I supposed she had given it up.

"Then the plant closed. Nobody was hiring. Sam couldn't find a job, so I got a job as a teacher's assistant. Sam started cutting yards here in the neighborhood and before you know it he had built a landscaping company literally out of nothing at all. It was amazing. He got his first big contract doing the landscaping here in Stirling Estates. After that he always said we were doing OK and I never worried about money. He took care of everything."

So, Sam's first big contract was through the HOA where he was the treasurer. Jenny didn't seem to see anything unusual in that, and I guess there wasn't. That's just the way the world turns—for the wealthy. I didn't resent her for it. She had never known any other world. But if I didn't find a way to get Sam's life insurance money for her, she was going to find out. Soon.

It was getting late, but not too late for Deacon to pop by. We hadn't seen him all day. Jenny excused herself and went to bed. Deacon grabbed the last barely cool beer floating in a tub of melted ice. "Shouldn't you be practicing your sermon?" I asked. "Tomorrow is Sunday."

"I never prepare beforehand."

He had slipped off his usual black coat and undone his tie. "I just let the spirit move me." He sat on the edge of the deck chair Jenny had recently vacated, kicked out of his shoes, peeled the black socks off his enormous feet, rolled his pants up to his knees and walked down the steps into the water. "By God," he sighed.

"Busy day?"

"You could say that." He took a long swig of his beer. "I'm run off my feet. I had to make three trips into Memphis to pick up lumber just this afternoon, then Ruth asked me to stop by."

Malvern had a perfectly good building supply store of its own, but Deacon's people stopped shopping there after the third time they were accused of shoplifting. "How is Mrs. Ruth?"

"She's fading. These last six months, her age finally caught up to her. I hoped she would live long enough to see my church built, but with everything, all the setbacks, and going to the courthouse every other day . . ." He sighed and sat at the edge of the pool.

"Did you talk to her about Jenny?" He furrowed the old brow and pretended not to know what I meant. "Jenny told me about her financial problems. That's why you wanted me to move in, wasn't it? To help out, pay a little rent."

"That was one reason," he said.

"I just thought if Ruth has as much money as you say, she could help Jenny."

"If Ruth wants to help, she will."

"But how will she know if you don't tell her?"

"She knows. There's little that passes in this community that Ruth doesn't know about. Anyway, Jenny asked me not to speak to Ruth about her troubles." He downed the last of his beer and crumpled the can in his hand. "However, Ruth asked me to send you to her."

"Me? Why?"

"She didn't say. Ruth is a private person. If she wants to tell you something, she'll tell you. If she doesn't want you to know, she lies well enough to fool the Devil himself. I've learned not to ask too many questions. She wants you to visit Monday morning."

"Are you going to be there?"

"She asked to see you alone, and that you bring your camera. You can borrow my truck."

My natural inclination was to ignore Ruth's desires. People who expect their least wish to be fulfilled without question rouse the worst angels of my nature. But I knew Deacon would hound me all day if I didn't go. His truck was waiting in Jenny's driveway Monday morning, keys in the ignition, full tank of gas, half a pack of cigarettes on the dash. Sweet home Chicago.

Nurse Wretched met me at the front desk, all smiles and apologies. If only I'd told her I was a friend of Mrs. Ruth's, our previous unfortunate encounter might have been avoided. She hoped we could start over. I said we could. She nearly wept. Outside Ruth's door she admitted she'd nearly lost her job. "Pastor Falgoust convinced her not to fire me. He's such a good man."

"Convinced who?"

"Mrs. Ruth," she whispered.

"She tried to get you fired? Because of me?"

"No, she wanted to *fire* me. She owns this place."

Ruth was a regular jack-in-the-box. She had more surprises than Christmas morning. No wonder she lived in the penthouse of the old folks' home. I knocked on the door while Nurse Wretched retreated down the hall, banging her forehead on the carpeted floor. I hoped all this power wouldn't go to my head.

I entered without waiting for an answer and found Ruth sitting in her wheelchair at a desk of hand-carved, dark cherrywood that perfectly matched the shade of her lipstick. Her dress was white silk speckled with seed pearls, her earrings gold with black onyx or jet, her oxygen hose the very best medical-grade plastic. She was sitting perfectly upright with her head thoughtfully tilted to the side as though trying to remember the last line of a sonnet, but she was snoring.

On the desk lay a black-and-white photograph of Ruth wearing a 1950s-period white swimsuit over her svelte, unperiod-like body, dancing with a beach ball in the middle of a street that, judging from the stoops that lined it, might have been somewhere in Brooklyn. Three men wearing loose jackets and slouchy hats sat on one of the stoops, leering at her with cigarettes in their mouths. In the distance a milkman watched her through an empty milk bottle held up to his eye like a telescope.

"Arthur Fellig took that picture," Ruth said. She had woken soundlessly, without startling, like a person used to slipping out of bedrooms.

"Who?"

"Weegee," she said. "Arthur Fellig. They called him Weegee. They said he must have used a Ouija board, because he had a talent for arriving at crime scenes even before the cops got there. He sold his pictures to the newspapers. You didn't happen to bring any cigarettes?"

I shook one out of my pack into her hand. She laid it beside the photograph on the desk. "You remind me of Weegee," she said. "He was short like you. Same quirky eyes and quirky way of looking at things. He must have taken a thousand photos of me. Some of them would have got us both arrested, but this one is my favorite."

She backed her wheelchair away from the desk and turned to face me. "I asked you here to do something." She held out her hand. A bronze key lay across her narrow palm. She must have been holding it when she fell asleep, because I didn't see her go into her pocket. "This is the key to my deposit drawer at the bank. I want you to go there and get a box from it."

I took the key and turned it over. The number was 066. "What's in this box?"

"You'll see."

"But how will I know which one?"

"There's only one box. The bank manager is expecting you." She glanced at the clock on her desk. "Before lunch," she added, dismissing me.

33

I have two daughters who, as yet, have not known man; I will bring them out to you, and abuse you them as it shall please you . . .

—GENESIS 19:8

R uth's box was in the vault of the old Merchants and Farmers Bank in Malvern. It had somehow escaped the bank-consolidation fever of the previous decade and maintained its local ownership. No doubt the bank president lived in Sterling Estates. The Classical-styled building dominated the northeast corner of the town square, its double wooden doors facing the courthouse. It looked like the kind of respectable, small-change joint Machine Gun Kelly might have stuck up back in the day. Its marble floors were worn into grooves from the doors to the teller windows, where sat marble-faced tellers with blousing garters on their pinstriped sleeves. The manager posed like an undertaker, quietly rubbing his hands before taking my key.

Ruth had the biggest safe-deposit box in the vault, big enough to hide a body. Instead of a corpse, I found a cardboard box a little longer than a foot to each side, filled to the top with old photographs of Mrs. Ruth. Beneath it lay neatly stacked rows of bearer bonds and bundles of cash, all hundreds and twenties. There were also gold and silver coins, men's and women's watches, and a careless pile of jewelry, most of it antique. Just a rough guess said I was looking at a cool half million, maybe more, depending on the value of the bonds. I thought about how that money could help Jenny out of her difficulties. I thought about how much it could help me. I thought about how this was just the loose change Ruth had found under the cushions. All I had to do was dump the photographs back in the safe and fill the box with money and bonds, turn Deacon's truck south on I-55, drive until I hit water, then hop a shrimp boat until I reached a climate where it rained every day at four in the afternoon. I stared for a long time, until the bank manager cleared his throat just outside the vault door.

I locked up, returned to the nursing home and set the box of photographs on the desk beside Ruth. She held out her hand for another cigarette. "Did you see anything you liked?"

"One or two things." The cigarette I'd given her earlier was gone. I hadn't smelled smoke when I opened the door and she

wouldn't have smoked it in her room, not with the oxygen going. Maybe she'd bullied her nurse into turning off the gas or
rolling her outside.

She said, "I hope you took something for your trouble."

"Just the box you wanted."

She shook her head, quietly wheezing. "Jesus Christ. It's no
wonder you're poor, Jackie."

"I'm not in the habit of taking other people's stuff," I said.

"Why not?"

"I guess that's the way my mama raised me."

"Do you think I need it? I haven't set foot in that bank in
over ten years."

"If you wanted me to have it, you should have said something."

"Fortune favors the bold, my dear. If you took every penny,
no one would be the wiser, certainly not me. I wish you had.
When I die, Luther is bound to find out about it and the last
thing he needs is more money."

I offered to go back, but she declined. "No, it's too late. You
missed your chance. Let this be a lesson to you. Playing by the
rules is for chumps. My daddy Gus taught me that." That was
the second time I'd heard her call her father Gus.

"I wish you could have known him. When he inherited
Stirling Plantation, it was mortgaged up to the short hairs. The
land had gone wild because nobody was farming it. He used
the old house as a hunting cabin. He quartered his dogs on the
first floor and his whores upstairs. But after I was born, he determined to return the estate to the way he remembered it
when he was a boy, when it was the largest cotton plantation

between Memphis and Somerville. He wanted me to have something to be proud of when he died."

She opened the desk drawer and took out a small black-and-white photograph. It had been kept folded at one time, probably in a pocket, as the print had degraded along the fold leaving a line of white paper almost down the center. The photo was of a young woman, almost a girl, undoubtedly Ruth, standing with one laced-up boot resting on the running board of a Ford Victoria, a revolver nearly as long as her arm tucked into her belt. Beside her sat a striking Hollywood handsome whose face seemed familiar, though I didn't recognize him right away. I wondered if I'd seen him in a late movie. He held a black .45 automatic, one elbow propped on the butt of a double-barreled shotgun. A winking smile twisted his Clark Gable mustache. The Gladstone bag sitting on the fender was overflowing with loose cash.

"We fancied ourselves the Bonnie and Clyde of West Tennessee," Ruth said. Gus looked maybe five years older than Ruth, if that, but even by a generous estimate he couldn't have been younger than thirty and was possibly closer to forty. "Gus did whatever it took to buy back the farm. He moonshined, ran whorehouses and crooked dice games from here to Memphis. Robbed, stole, blackmailed and fenced. He never did a hard day's work in his life, because work is for chumps. A rich man gets the chumps to work for him. That's how he gets rich. Gus taught me that, too. He was a pirate and I was a pirate's daughter. We lived life to the balls, sucked the marrow out of every day. I wouldn't trade a minute of my life for a year of yours."

"How old were you in this picture?" I asked.

"Twelve or thirteen." She looked like a grown woman. And now I recognized where I'd seen the man before—in Nathan, only about thirty pounds lighter.

"These photographs are almost as valuable as anything else in that safe-deposit box," Ruth said. She opened the box and showed me her pictures. "These are all of me, my whole career. When I was younger, I dated all the best leading men in Hollywood, several politicians, a couple of generals, three colonels, an admiral, and a spy from the KGB. When I was your age, I was offered quite a shocking amount of money to pose in my altogether for a certain magazine; I think you know which one I mean—this would have been back in the sixties. Later I had the pleasure of entertaining a senator with a well-known preference for young Southern ladies."

I sat on the floor for hours going through the photos and listening to the stories of her many loves and affairs, none of whom she named outright. She dropped enough hints to fill a dump truck. The pictures on top were the most recent, taken when she was in her sixties. Some were glamour shots, some were nudes and some were candids, vacation photos and photos from events, weddings and cotillions and Coon Suppers past. I lifted out a photo of her naked and very pregnant, lying on a tiger-skin rug in front of a stark white backdrop. She leaned forward to look at the picture. "Oh, dear. How did that get in there?"

Even though there was nothing in the image to date it (and ageless as Ruth was, it was notoriously difficult to guess her age from any photograph without contextual clues), I guessed from the order of the photos in the box that she must have been in her late forties or early fifties. "And how old were you in this picture?" I asked.

"Oh, I don't remember." Smiling at me from under the oxygen hose, she took the photo and put it in the desk drawer. I didn't ask her what happened to the baby. The picture wasn't old enough for it to be Luther.

Digging deeper into the box was like going back in time. Down through the Hollywood years of the fifties and forties, through the Weegee years and the Irving Klaw period, then a stretch through the thirties when most of the photos bore Malvern and Memphis photo studio logos. The next group was of Ruth as a teen and preteen, some of them seminude or entirely unclothed, others in full flapper regalia or dressed for the cotillion at Twelve Oaks. "Little girl Alice age six," Ruth said, smiling. "I was locally famous, even then. A doctor from Germantown offered to buy me from my father after an all-night game of pinochle. I thought for a moment Gus was going to agree. He might have, had the doctor not already lost most of his money."

Beneath these were older photos of other little girls, going all the way back to Victorian times. "I found these among Gus's things when he died," she said. "I think some of them are his sisters, and his mother when she was a girl."

With a curator's delicate touch, I lifted out crumbling sepia daguerreotypes of more women and children. And beneath those lay charcoal sketches of naked slaves. "These were drawn by Josiah Overton Stirling, my great-grandfather."

What I had in front of me was two centuries' worth of erotica, much of it questionable and possibly illegal. Back when I

was a vice cop for the Memphis Police Department, I had arrested men for less than this. I had to assume Ruth knew this
much about my past, and possibly quite a bit more. "Why are
you showing this to me?"

"I'm not *showing* it to you, dear. I'm *giving* it to you," she
said. "I want you to keep these photos so Luther doesn't get
his paws on them. My son is waiting for me to die so he can sell
these to a bunch of dirty old billionaires. To be sure, he will
hold out the best ones for himself."

They reminded me too much of the photos of Reece I'd
found in Sam's suitcase. Why hadn't I destroyed them? Because
they were evidence. Evidence of a crime I had plotted with a
preacher to conceal.

"These are a historical record. I know you will take care of
them." I almost laughed. For the last five years I'd been ten
bucks away from homelessness more times than I could count.
I never owned more than I could carry in a shopping basket.
When this job for Deacon was finished, if it ever would be
finished, I didn't see my situation changing that drastically. I
couldn't take care of her pictures of naked children any more
than I could take care of actual children.

Ruth took my hand. Hers felt cold and dry and nearly life-
less, as though the length of her arm was too great a distance
from her heart to warm it. "You gave me something the other
day that I can never repay. You gave me my memories," she said.
"Memories of my life before all this, when I was still a simple
farm girl who loved a simple farmer."

Deacon had said Ruth could lie well enough to fool the
Devil, but she wasn't fooling me. At twelve or thirteen she was

helling around the country robbing banks with her movie star father, but at fifteen she was just an innocent farm girl? Not that it mattered. Maybe she believed the lies. Maybe the lies were all she had. Lies and a box of dirty pictures.

"The money and the photos and the land isn't all there is to my legacy, Jackie. Some of it I can never give away, no matter how much I try. Me and my daddy Gus, we robbed and stole, to be sure, sometimes just for the fun of it. But I have done far more terrible things than robbing banks."

"I'm no saint myself, Mrs. Ruth."

"That's why I know I can trust you. And Deacon has told me about your gift."

Had he betrayed me? I wondered as I asked, "What gift is that?"

"For finding out the truth," she said.

34

I STOPPED AT THE GUARD SHACK on my way home to file a claim on the HOA insurance for the theft of my car. Where it said to list witnesses who had seen my car on the property, I put Doris Dye. I also noted that the guard company's surveillance video showed my car enter the property but never leave it.

The guard was a young kid. He looked about fifteen, but he told me this was just his summer job. He was a tight end at the University of Tennessee and even though he was a sophomore this year, he was already talking to pro scouts. His dad was a UT alum and he lived in Stirling Estates, next door to a lineman for the NFL team in Nashville. "I can get you tickets to any game," he said.

"So why are you working the guard shack?" I asked as I handed him my insurance claim.

He muttered something about community service for a DUI and tossed my papers in an outbox on his desk. He was a cute kid, though. He filled out his rent-a-cop uniform in all the right places. I called him a kid, but he was six foot eight and every bit a man except the space between his ears.

"So you're, what, about nineteen?"

"Yeah," he grunted.

"Don't worry about it," I said. "When I was nineteen, I could drink a lake of beer."

A little understanding helped mollify his pride. "I know, right?" he said. "Everybody makes such a big deal out of it. I wasn't even that drunk. And it was on campus."

"Cops are assholes."

He grinned and flexed, his pecs fluttering like small trapped birds under his shirt. "Especially campus cops."

I leaned across the top of the desk to drop my pen in his cup. "So you probably went to school with my friend's daughter, Reece Loftin."

"Yeah," he said, shifting back in his seat and shooting me the old side-eye. "I didn't really know her. Just saw her around school."

"It's a shame what happened."

"I guess. I didn't really know her. I heard she was into cutting, listening to Slipknot and Rob Zombie, Nine Inch Nails, all that stupid goth shit."

"But I thought she played softball and was on the swim team."

"That was before. She went totally goth in like eighth grade."

"What about her boyfriend. Did you know him?" I asked.

He laughed once, explosively, derisively. "She didn't have a boyfriend. Not that anybody knew, anyway."

"But I thought she liked that boy . . . what's his name . . . ?"
I was fishing with the only bait I had—the universal banality
of teenage relationships. I'd been a teenager myself, once upon
a time. Also, nothing stays a secret in middle school. Somebody always knows what really happened. Secrets are the cur-
rency of the eighth grade hall.

He bit hard. "Look," he said, leaning toward me. "She told
everybody her boyfriend was this older guy who was supposed
to be this total badass. Anytime a guy asked her out, she'd say
my boyfriend would kill me."

"You asked her out?"

"Everybody did. She was really cute in seventh grade, but
she wouldn't go out with anybody because she was 'in a relationship,'" he said, with quote fingers and a roll of his eyes. "But
nobody believed her. Nobody ever saw this guy."

"How much older? Like in high school?" I asked.

"Way older. An adult. Had his own business and everything."

"That's weird."

"Seriously. But it was bullshit. I think she was just into girls
and didn't want anybody to know."

"What's your name?" I asked.

"Josh."

"If you think of anything else, you know, like a name for
this mysterious boyfriend, or somebody who might know something, will you call me, Josh?" I wrote my name and number
with a Sharpie on his hand.

"What are you, a cop?"

"Why, did somebody commit a crime?"

His face went red all the way up to his buzz cut.

"Because if they did, I'd advise them to call the police and tell them everything they know. I'm just a friend of the family. And if you just want to call me, that's OK, too."

"Seriously?"

"Seriously."

I knew he wouldn't actually call, but I wanted to give him a way to explain the cougar scars I'd left on his hand.

Before I went home, I took a driving tour around Stirling Estates. I hoped I'd spot the old jalopy parked behind somebody's house, but most of the houses were sprawling, towering piles of Federalist and mock Tudor, crouched like cats at the end of drives long enough to land a private jet. Everything I passed was beautifully manicured, expensively watered, meticulously groomed, hollow, empty, bereft of soul and meaning beyond the merely decorative, like sofa paintings in which people actually lived. I saw no one outside, not even the ghost of a gardener.

That might have had something to do with the heat. The man on the radio said it was a hundred and two and still rising. The Memphis city council was talking about restricting water usage for lawns and swimming pools. Shelby and surrounding counties had passed a No Burn ordinance. The weatherman had a special graphic counting the days since the last rain. Farmers were predicting disaster.

Jenny's house was a welcome respite, even though Jenny wasn't there. I found the kids in the pool with Holly and Nathan.

Nathan left soon after I arrived. I got the feeling he was start-ing not to like me, which broke my heart in the worst way. I took the box of pictures up to Reece's room and found the softball team photo lying on the floor again. I set it on the com-puter desk and changed into her bathing suit.

Jenny still wasn't around when I got down to the pool. Holly was smearing sunscreen on Eli's back. "She had a doctor ap-pointment," Holly explained. Jenny hadn't mentioned a doc-tor's appointment that morning.

I sat on the edge of the pool and shoved off, sank until my toes touched bottom. The water was so warm, it was like not being submerged at all. Turn off the lights and a person could almost go to sleep in this. I kicked off the bottom and broke the surface, shook wet hair out of my eyes. Holly said, "Dea-con's man stopped by. Definitely need a new compressor." Even if Deacon could get the work done at cost, there was no way Jenny could afford it.

I floated on my back for a while, wishing I had worn sun-glasses, until the sun had dried my face and was starting to burn out the backs of my eyeballs. I rolled over and looked at my shadow wavering on the bottom of the pool. A second shadow floated just to the right of mine. It reached out and touched my shadow's hand and I was out of the pool, scalding the soles of my feet on the hot concrete and shivering to my bones.

Still busy with Eli's sunscreen, Holly hadn't noticed my hasty exodus from the water, but Cassie was backed into one corner of the pool, owl-eyed, her fingers white-knuckled to the sides. I lifted her out by the arms and walked her to a chair, wrapped a towel around both of us and took her inside the house. I sat her on the hearth. Her eyes were still frozen into that thousand-yard stare.

"Cassie." She didn't respond. I turned her face to mine but I couldn't move her eyes. "I know why you won't go in the deep end."

Her voice wasn't even a whisper, just a movement of the lips. "No you don't."

"There's a dead girl down there."

Her eyes slowly focused on me, as though waking from a dream.

"I don't believe you."

"But I believe you," I said. Suddenly she was in my arms, squeezing so tight I thought I was going to pass out. "You're not crazy. If you are, then I'm crazy, too."

"You can really see them?"

"When I was a girl, sometimes I'd wake up in the night and hear my grandfather standing beside my bed."

"Weren't you scared?"

"Sometimes they're scary, but most of the time they don't even notice us. I think my grandfather just wanted to be with me." She pulled back, wiping away the tears with the back of her wrist. "The girl in the pool—is she your sister?" I asked.

She shook her head no. I felt strangely relieved. They are bad enough when they are strangers. To think she had to look at her drowned sister was just too much.

"Who is she?"

"Somebody bad," she said. "Very bad."

"Do you ever see Reece?"

She shook her head no. "I wish I could."

"Me, too. My brother died when I was in high school. I wanted to see him again so bad, but he never appeared. What about your dad? Do you ever see him?"

Fresh tears started down her face. "Why can't he see me?"

It broke my heart to think what she'd been going through, probably all her life, without anyone to talk to. At least I'd had my brother Sean. He couldn't see them the way I could, but he'd heard my grandfather's footsteps in the attic and his pocket watch ticking in the night. "I've seen your daddy, too. Somehow, it's like a movie recorded on the environment. It plays over and over, but it's not really him. I don't know why it happens, or how."

"Maybe God puts it there, so we won't forget him."

"Maybe so. The preacher told me that what I see is a gift from God. What do you think?"

"I just wish I could be like everybody else."

"So do I. But we can't help the way we are, can we? We just have to learn how to live with it. It's scary and strange, but you get used to them. It took me a long time."

She crawled into my lap. I wrapped the towel around her. Despite the heat of the house, we were both still shivering. My body started to rock of its own accord—I don't know how long I was doing it before I noticed. I'd never held a child to comfort it, never even been this close to one, not since I was a kid myself.

She fell asleep in my arms and I was halfway there myself when Holly brought Eli inside to get his bath. She passed us, a curiously annoyed look on her face. She and Cassie were besties. I got the feeling Holly didn't like me holding her, like she was jealous.

"Cassie shouldn't be sleeping. If she takes a nap now, she'll never go to sleep tonight." I watched her legs disappear up the stairs. She had the kind of legs that took a long time to do that. Maybe I was a little jealous, too.

35

CASSIE WAS IN THE SHOWER when Jenny got home. The baths and showers were a mere formality, an act of habit or tradition that in these circumstances did nothing to alleviate our stank.

We ate our supper of peanut butter sandwiches by the pool. It was just my luck to find a rich friend just when she'd run out of money. Jenny took the kids inside to change into their pajamas. Holly waited around until dark for Deacon to appear, but he never did. "Tell him to call me," she said as she stalked away.

"She's so strange," Jenny said after Holly had gone. "She's nothing like Luther and Virginia. They are good, solid, dependable people. Nathan, and especially Holly are . . ." Her voice trailed off.

"Adopted," Deacon finished for her. It was like he'd been waiting for Holly to leave. He sank into a chair. He'd spent the whole day installing the stained-glass windows from New Orleans. Even his sunburn had a sunburn.

"But they look like Ruth," I said. "Both of them."

"Luther used to operate an orphanage, back when he was

more interested in doing the Lord's work than counting tithes," Deacon said. "At some point he turned the orphanage into a nursing home."

"Ruth's nursing home?" I asked.

He confirmed this with a nod. "Luther and Virginia adopted four children—Nathan, Holly and Korean twin sisters whose names Ruth couldn't remember."

"Luther and Virginia don't have twins," Jenny said. "If they had grown twin daughters, why haven't we ever heard about them?"

Deacon picked a bit of old paint from his lip. "Ever noticed how Luther's house is newer than the other houses on his street?"

"Yes," she said.

"They used to live in Winchester House—the place Overton Stirling built for his second wife and abandoned after she died. Luther restored it and moved in with his family. Holly was maybe eleven or twelve at the time. One night, Luther and Virginia were at a party. Nathan and Holly were supposed to be babysitting the twins, who were not even a year old at the time. Nathan ran off with his friends and left Holly alone with the babies. Somehow a fire got started, they never said how, and the old house went up like a match. By the time the fire department arrived, it was completely gone. They thought they had lost all three kids, but the next morning here comes Holly up out of the woods half dead, without a stitch of clothes and most of her hair burnt off. She was in shock and to this day can't remember what happened or pretty much anything about her life before that moment. They don't know how she got out of the house or how she made it to the woods without anybody seeing her. By the state of her clothes and her hair, she must have been on fire at the time. She hasn't been right in the head since."

"I know she's a little odd," Jenny said.

"She's more than a little odd. Holly is what people used to call a nymphomaniac. I don't know what they call it today. She craves sex, but she derives no pleasure from the act. Instead, sex is how she obtains the approval and acceptance of others that she so desperately needs. Sex is the only kind of intimacy she understands, or wants. She also uses sex to manipulate others."

"Are you revealing secrets of confession?" I asked, half joking. I tried to laugh but it didn't sound very sincere. Jenny gave me a pained look.

Deacon pretended to ignore the lameness of my question. "I'm no priest. Besides, she confessed nothing."

"One time she hinted that the two of you were . . ." Jenny started to say.

"Her relationship with me is entirely one-sided." As a preacher, Deacon knew how to spout beautiful, believable lies to people who aren't ready to hear the truth. I prided myself on the micron-level sensitivity of my bullshit detector, but I couldn't smell what he was shoveling. He seemed perfectly sincere in his pity for Holly, even as he carefully avoided anything resembling an answer. He sat back in the chair and closed his eyes. "She has, of course, poured out her heart to me, confessed her undying love and her desire to settle down and be a faithful minister's wife. I didn't believe half of what she said, and I have my doubts about the rest. She doesn't need a ring, all she needs is to find Jesus. I tried to minister to her, but it is difficult to help someone who doesn't want your help."

Now I knew he was speaking to me, even though his eyes were still closed. Rosettes of pool light played across his smug, smiling face, while I resisted the impulse to dapple his forehead with my heel.

Jenny went inside to put Cassie to bed. Or maybe she left to give us a chance to be alone together. I saw her watching through the kitchen window.

"Remember when I told you about my dream of finding you dying in a desert, and my call to heal you?" Deacon asked.

"I don't know that I need healing," I said. "My demons are a part of me. If you take them away, I will no longer be me."

"I'd like you to come to my church this Sunday and hear me preach."

I decided to change the subject. "Earlier you mentioned Overton Stirling. Did you know he's buried in the crypt in the woods?"

"That's right," he said.

"You said he abandoned the house he built for his second wife after she died in childbirth. What happened to his first wife?"

"She and all their children died in the yellow fever epidemic of 1873. Overton had the tunnel dug so he could visit his dead wife and children without being seen. Ruth remembers seeing *memento mori* of the kids—photos taken after their death. Her father showed them to her when she was a little girl."

"Gus?"

"Caesar Augustus Stirling was Overton's last child. In 1893, he remarried and built Winchester House for his new young wife. Barely a year later, she died in childbirth and he moved back into the plantation house, so as to be nearer the family vault. He remained crippled by grief the rest of his days, obsessed with the dead and so unaware of the living world that he failed even to name his infant son.

"Gus was christened by his Negro wet nurse, who raised him. He lived a sort of Tom Sawyer life, while the plantation fell into disrepair and was heavily mortgaged. Gus seemed normal enough in the beginning, even to his nurse, who loved him to her own destruction. She described him to Ruth as a beautiful little baby with fat thighs and cherubic smile bouncing on her knee. She also told Ruth that the Stirlings had been cursed by Albert Stirling's Chickasaw wife, whom he had stolen from her tribe when she was only thirteen. The nurse blamed all their troubles, as well as her own, on that curse.

"By the time he was fourteen, Gus was running a moonshine operation out of the house. By twenty, he owned three whorehouses in Memphis, as well as the infamous Hitching Post tavern on the highway outside of Malvern. Under Gus, it not only provided prostitutes to any man, white or black, who could afford them, but many of his girls were barely of age, and in some cases several years shy of age. Ruth hinted that at one point he robbed the Malvern Bank, which held the mortgage on the plantation, and used the proceeds to pay off that same mortgage. After that Gus became quite wealthy, recovering much of his father's lost fortune by renting out the land for sharecropping. He restored the plantation to a semblance of its former glory. Somewhere along the way, he begat himself a beautiful young daughter named Ruth, some say by one of the Hitching Post girls. He never produced Ruth's mother, nor did he marry, remaining a bachelor until the end of his days."

As though talking about her had conjured up her ghost, Jenny appeared at the door with a phone in her hand. "Deacon," she said, her voice trembling. "Luther has been trying to reach you. Ruth passed away this afternoon."

36

I CALLED MY FATHER first thing the next morning and asked him to overnight express the dress I'd worn to Mom's funeral. I gave him Jenny's address and he said he would send it right over.

Deacon's HVAC repairman had promised to be at the house by eight with a new five-ton condenser, so while Jenny waited for him to arrive, I grabbed my camera and headed over to Ruth's. The job site was deserted and silent. I expected Deacon to be away handling the funeral arrangements, but I found him installing stained glass in the upper windows, just him and one other guy. No longer covered with blank plywood, the windows were filled with a glory of reflected color.

"How are the funeral arrangements going?" I asked.

"I've been cut out," Deacon said. "I guess I should count myself lucky. Luther respects his mother's wishes enough to let me deliver the eulogy." No doubt he was being cut out of a good many other things as well.

He noticed me looking at the bulldozers and graders parked

in the shade of the trees. "We were supposed to start running the main water and sewer lines tomorrow, but the county engineer wants more time to review our proposal."

"I thought everything was ready to go."

Deacon indicated by his frown that he was not unaware of the implications of the engineer's need to review something he had already approved. "Somebody's interfering," he shrugged. "Happens all the time with this kind of project."

"Somebody named Eugene Kitchen?"

"Eugene doesn't have enough influence to change his socks," Deacon said.

"But he does whatever Luther tells him to do."

"Luther's been waiting for Ruth to die so he can get his hands on the last bit of her land."

"But it belongs to you now."

He smiled hard, his teeth pressed together so hard I could almost hear them crack. "Only as long as I can keep it."

There wasn't a speck of dust in the air, and the old house was twenty degrees cooler than Jenny's place. It felt weird being here, now that Ruth was gone, though she had moved out a year before I set foot in the place. It was still Ruth's house. I wondered if I would run into her here, if she would still be walking, the way the old folks used to say. A century ago, people thought the spirits of the dead would walk awhile after they died, returning to their houses and visiting their loved ones before moving on. The loved ones would abandon the house until they were buried, so as to avoid that final parting. It would be just like Ruth to haunt her old house, if she could find it. So much had changed since Deacon got his hands on it.

I started upstairs, photographing the balcony area. As I set my tripod in the hall, I noticed a mattress in one of the bedrooms, its tangle of sheets pushed against one wall, and pillows scattered across the floor as though the bed had exploded. All those pillows bothered me, for some reason. They seemed like more than one person would need. Then again, some people slept with lots of pillows. And some people slept with lots of people. But who was I to judge, or be jealous?

I took pictures until my battery died, my best day of work since I started the project, and covered almost the entire second floor. Before I left, I sat on the porch smoking a cigarette and listening to the silence of the construction site. Not only was no one working, two-thirds of Deacon's followers had unplugged their trailers, folded up their tents, and decamped, leaving behind drifts of empty water bottles, dirty diapers, and hamburger wrappers. Those that remained hid away from the sun inside their campers, their air conditioners humming like a hive of drowsy bees.

When I got back to Jenny's, the man was still working on the air conditioner. He was a big Hispanic guy, enormous, with a head like a brown pumpkin, close-shaved, tats running down his neck into his shirt. He twiddled with his gauges and side-eyed me while I watched him fill the condenser with freon. I was making him nervous, but for no obvious reason. People usually have a reason for everything they do, even if they don't know it themselves. "When I was a vice cop," I said and watched his neck muscles bunch into knots, "I busted this guy for selling hits off his freon bottle to a bunch of middle school kids."

Without taking his eyes off his gauges, he said, without a trace of accent, "I have to account for every ounce I sell."

"That can't be easy."

He shrugged. "Stuff's expensive."

"I bet." I walked around to the other side of the condenser unit and leaned against the house. The bricks were warm enough to bake a pizza. "You do a lot of work for Deacon?"

"Sometimes." He unscrewed a hose, loosing a cold jet of frost across his fingers. He didn't even flinch. "I do the air and plumbing on his church."

"It isn't built yet."

"His other one." He unscrewed another hose. "In the strip mall off the highway."

"Oh," I said.

"I don't usually do residential work."

"What's going on over there?"

He looked up to see where I was looking. I was looking at him. "Over where?"

"At Deacon's church."

"I don't know." I let him think about his answer long enough to light a cigarette. I didn't really want it. I just wanted to give him time to think. "I heard they pulled his permit," he said after a while.

"The county?" He nodded. "When?"

"This morning. Served papers on him, too."

"What kind of papers?"

"Stop work. Cease and desist. Something like that."

"Is that why all his people left?"

He shrugged and finished unhooking his gauges. He stood up, picked up his freon bottle, slung the hoses over his shoulder, started to walk away, then stopped. "They said something about INS."

"I'm not INS."

He let out a long woosh of air and smiled. "Damn, I thought I was *atrapados*. I made you for a cop the minute I saw you."

I didn't know whether I should take that as a compliment. It had been years since anyone made me for anything but a junkie, but I still disliked cops. "That was a long time ago," I said as I grabbed his tool bucket and walked him to his van.

"Listen." He paused in putting his stuff away. "Deacon's people started moving out a couple of weeks ago. I talked to one guy. They were scared."

"Of what?"

"That old house. Have you been in it?"

"Once or twice."

"Deacon wanted me to put in central air and plumbing, but I turned him down. Like I said, I usually don't do residential work."

"Why not?"

"There's no money in it, unless you're doing a full install."

So naturally he turned down a full install. I wondered what had them so spooked. I'd never seen the first spirit inside the house itself. Maybe it was the woods that got to them. "Have they abandoned Deacon?" I asked.

"No. They still go to church. And they'll come back when he starts building. They just don't want to work in that house."

He picked up a couple of fuses and a roll of solder that had spilled out, tossed them inside and slammed the door before anything could escape. "I'll just get the power switched on," he said.

By suppertime, we had cold air again. At the time it seemed to be the only thing that mattered.

37

Behold, this dreamer cometh.
Come now therefore, and let us
slay him, and cast him into some
pit, and we will say, Some evil
beast hath devoured him: and
we shall see what will become of
his dreams.
—GENESIS 37: 19–20

I PUT ON THE DRESS DAD sent from home, the one I'd worn only once before—to my mother's funeral—and looked at myself in the mirror: ankle-length black dress with a small white flower print, white leather purse, belt, and shoes, black gloves, small white Doris Day hat with a gauzy black veil. I looked like a Mennonite.

Stirling Baptist Church was the sort of place you had to experience to truly believe. The complex of buildings, including a fitness facility with Olympic swimming pool, tennis courts and bowling lanes, a pre-K-through-eighth-grade private school, a private Baptist seminary, and a sanctuary larger than most college basketball arenas, stood in the middle of a vast gated compound that, with its layered embankments and ditches and overlapping fields of enfilading fire, seemed designed to hold off the entire Red Army, or more likely, hordes of left behind heathens at the Final Judgment. Deacon called it Fort God.

We were let into the sanctuary by one of Stegall's paramilitary goons. He was dressed in black suit, tie and combat boots, the chip on his shoulder bigger than the SIG Sauer holstered on his hip. I guessed by his presence that Senator Mickelson would grace the proceedings and was not disappointed. We found him bending over the open casket. For a second I thought he was biting Ruth on the neck.

He shook Deacon's hand and ignored me, embraced Jenny, picked up Eli and carried him around like a doll while he greeted his constituency filing into the church. I spotted Nathan and the *Elle* model, Mercedes LaGrance, sitting close together in a pew, playfully holding hands. I pointed them out to Jenny.

"Nathan and her mother, Annette, have had this on-again off-again thing for several years." As though to illustrate her point, the woman appeared with her other two daughters, one older than Mercedes and one younger, and kissed Nathan on the cheek as she slid in beside him. "The girls' names are Bentley and Porsche," Jenny said with a roll of her eyes. Deacon left to make final arrangements behind a curtain, while somewhere an organ droned mournfully through endless repetitions of "How Great Thou Art."

Banks of flowers spread out to either side of Ruth's coffin, which rested on a draped table, lid open, recessed lights in the ceiling shining down on her face. I barely recognized her. She didn't look like the same woman. I'd only known her in her final days, but even then her tremendous vitality lent the illusion of youth to her decrepit frame. The woman in this expensive box was old, shriveled like one of those apple-headed dolls you'd find in the hillbilly tourist shops of my childhood vacations. The mortician had powered her face almost white, erasing the deep, earthy coloration of her skin. Her hair, once so luxuriously sable, had turned dull gray in death. They put prosthetics in her cheeks and under her eyelids and lips to keep them from sinking and only succeeded in making her look fat and soft. She had been neither. People don't want to see what death really looks like. They pay a lot of money not to see it.

The woman in the coffin wasn't Ruth Vardry. That woman had gone elsewhere and left this cheap copy for her son to bury.

The last chord of the organ music faded into silence. Jenny and I sat together in the second pew with the kids between us. In the front pew, Virginia Vardry disappeared between her husband and Senator Mickelson. Nathan and Holly had instinctively left an empty space between themselves and their father, where Deacon's headless Iraqi soldier now sat. Holly turned around and whispered, "I'm freezing! There's a cold draft blowing right here." If she her dress were longer than a handkerchief, maybe she wouldn't be so cold. "And the smell! Ugh!" She rolled her eyes at the back of the church, where Deacon's saints filled the last six rows.

The remaining pews were elbow to elbow with old money and older politicians and their third and fourth wives, stuffed together for one final fleeting grasp at Ruth's patronage. Most had made sure they were seen by Luther and the senator before the service began, posing in front of Ruth's coffin like the junior high prom.

Deacon stood up before the congregation, arms upraised so that his hot pink shirt cuffs and glittering ruby-studded Blood of Christ cuff links dangled a good two inches from the sleeves of his jacket. He looked at me and then at the soldier in the front row. I nodded that I could see him.

Catching his breath, he started into the story of Sodom and Gomorrah, reading the verses from his old, worn Bible—the angels with mysterious powers and Lot's offer to give his daughters to the people of Sodom, so that they might know them, and the final destruction of the city by fire and brimstone, metaphors for the sermon he was about to give.

"On this day, let us remember the lesson of Lot's wife, who looked back to see the destruction of her city. Did she do so out of fascination? Curiosity? Grief for the loss of everything she knew? The Bible doesn't say. All we know is that she violated God's commandment to keep going forward, away from the old life of sin and corruption into a new day of perfection. What has passed is past. We mustn't look behind, lest our eyes be blasted by what we see. Lot's wife looked back, and for her sin was turned into a pillar of salt.

"Today we come together to mourn friend and mother, Ruth Stirling Vardry. Let this not be a time of mourning. Ruth has joined our Lord and Savior in heaven. This I know because the Gospel tells me so. Not the Gospel you have been taught. The true Gospel, the Gospel hidden by the early church, the Gospel that I will reveal to you today.

"Ruth Vardry was a sinner. To hear her tell, she was the worst sinner among us. Yet she died without fear of the grave, because of the Gospel I am about to reveal. She did not fear eternal torment, because of the Gospel I brought to her.

"Jesus Christ was crucified and died for our sins. We all know this. We've heard it all our lives and some of us have accepted Jesus Christ as our Lord and Savior and been washed in the Blood of the Lamb."

"Amen!" Luther cried fervently. His wife began to clap from between the senator's lapels.

"Amen!" Deacon echoed. "But that's only part of the Gospel. The part they kept. The rest they hid from us, until today. Jesus died for our sins, but not just our old sins. All our sins. The sins we have committed and the sins we have yet to commit. The price has been paid. Forever. For everyone. You. Me. Catholics. Baptists. Muslims. Jews. Everybody. You don't even have to want it. It's done. Nothing more is required of you and me, for as it says in the book of Micah, chapter 6, verse 8, 'What does the Lord require of you but to do justice, and to love kindness, and to walk humbly with your God?' Why would Jesus die for our sins, but only save us if we beg for forgiveness? If your children were drowning, would you only save the ones who asked for help? How is this any different than the old pagan religions and their demand for sacrifices and donations?"

Luther wasn't amening anymore. He sat with his chubby hand on the back of the pew, quietly knocking a three-carat diamond ring into the soft pinewood.

"I'm telling you this is not the Gospel of Jesus. Men made these laws, the early church fathers, to secure their power, and then they hid Jesus' true Gospel, the lost Gospel of the Good News, so you would keep giving them money and coming to their churches and begging for forgiveness over and over again. But what did Jesus say to the adulterous woman? Your sins are forgiven. Go and sin no more."

Luther stood up, furious, and stalked out. At the end of his pew he paused and looked back at his wife, but she hadn't moved. She didn't even look at him. Her eyes were closed, streaming with tears, her lips quivering in whispered prayer. He impatiently snapped his fingers a few times, then started up the aisle toward the back of the church. I noticed a few others rise to join him, but probably nowhere near as many as he hoped.

Deacon thundered onward as though he hadn't noticed. "This is the Good News, friends. You are forgiven. You are going to heaven. So is the person sitting next to you, and behind you, at the back of this church, down the highway, even those plying their trade in the whorehouses and crack houses of Memphis. You don't need to be afraid anymore. Not of your fellow man. Not of your vengeful and jealous god. You are free. Free to leave this church and never return."

The doors closed behind Luther and his handful of acolytes. Eugene Kitchen remained at the door, his face nearly black with rage.

"You don't need me anymore, not to save your soul. I can't save your soul. You can't save your soul. The Church can't save your soul. Only Jesus can do that, and He has done it. The price has been paid. Go and live a life of goodness and obey his Law, not because you're afraid of dying and going to hell, but because you love the Lord and His Law and the world and the people He made.

"That's not to say there's nothing left to do. Jesus said, go and sin no more. Death was defeated in the tomb. The sin of Adam was forgiven on the cross. But evil is real. There are demons among us, possessing us, trying to destroy all that is good and beautiful in this world. I know some of you have been possessed by the demons of lust, of greed, of addiction, of pride. You and I know these demons are real. Some of you have seen demons face to face, have wrestled with them in the dark places. You know what I'm talking about. I see the scars you bear. I bear those scars myself."

He grasped the microphone and ripped it from its stand, flung the cord back and strode forward, swinging his open Bible like a sword.

"We have a job to do. We have battles to fight. Wherever there are people suffering, there are demons causing that suffering. Wherever some company is pouring their industrial filth into a river or fouling a beach, polluting our earth, our one and only earth, with the poisonous by-products of their profits, we will take our stand against evil."

"Amen," several in the congregation said, Jenny among them.

Deacon's voice rose a notch in volume and intensity, so that I could feel it moving through me, like the thrumming of an engine deep below decks. "Wherever a man or woman sits in prison, wrongly accused or unjustly punished, so that some other man may profit by his suffering, we will fight the demons that torment him." He pounded the rostrum and the crowd shouted *Amen!*

"Wherever a child is beaten or starved or raped, or a woman lives in fear of her husband, or a man contemplates taking his own life so his family can collect his life insurance, we will succor them."

Amen! Now they were standing, lifting their hands into the air. Jenny's face was wet with tears.

"Wherever a grandmother rots in her own filth, or a grandfather dies alone in his bed, trapped in the corporate medical prisons that are our nursing homes, we will bring them peace."

Amen! They moved out into the aisles. Virginia Vardry staggered forward and slumped to her knees at the altar rail.

"Evil surrounds us. Every day it grows stronger while the good do nothing. Will we do nothing?"

No!

"What will we do?"

Fight!

I didn't know whether this was a funeral, a revival, a political rally, or a rock concert. Some of those women looked ready to fling their underwear on the altar. All I knew was that Luther had lost them forever. If Deacon had rolled out the

Kool-Aid carts right then and there, they would have drank it and lain down, arm in arm in the jungle with him.

He beamed across the shouting masses, his arms raised in victory until his eyes fell upon me, still sitting in the pew, and the headless Iraqi soldier sitting just in front of me. Neither of us had been moved by his words. He took a few long breaths and looked around him like a man bewildered by what he saw.

"No," he said, stepping back, distancing himself from the adoration. He laid his Bible on top of the lectern and returned the microphone to its stand. "No, my friends, Ruth Vardry was a good woman. She lived a long, full life. In her last days upon this earth, she tried to do some good with the riches God placed in her hands. Should we weep at her passing, or should we not make a joyful noise unto the Lord? Lift up your voices in praise. Serve the Lord with great gladness, and come before Him with song."

As he spoke these last words, the curtain behind the pulpit parted, revealing a seven-piece rock band. An electric hum of amplifiers preceded the first thundering power chord as they ripped into a metal version of the *"Dies Irae"* from Mozart's Requiem in D Minor. They followed with an assortment of traditional hymns, modern Christian Rock horrors, spirituals, and old-timey country songs of praise, to which Deacon's unwashed saints and Luther's lost converts danced in the aisles together, clapping, shaking tambourines, and singing in half a dozen languages. It looked like a Hare Krishna convention. Eugene finally fled, lest the unholy sight blast his eyes.

Finally the music died down. Deacon wiped the sweat from

his face with a towel and lifted up his trembling hands. "Jackie Lyons!" he cried. I groaned and tried to slide down in the pew. Jenny pulled me up by the elbow. "Jackie Lyons, you only knew Ruth a few weeks, but in that time she opened her heart to you. Those of us who knew her well know that she didn't give her friendship easily."

"Amen," Jenny intoned.

"Ruth Vardry admired you. She admired your spirit. She admired your independence."

He descended two or three steps, walking toward me with his hand outstretched. "We spoke quite often about the arrangements for her funeral. She knew her days were numbered, so she chose every song we have sung today, and she asked me to personally sing the benediction. Unfortunately, she passed before she made up her mind what song I should sing. So I'm going to ask you to pick something to close out her service."

"Help me out here," I whispered to Jenny. She shrugged. I groped around for the name of a hymn, something I had heard in church when I was a kid, anything. The only one I could remember was something my mother used to sing. "What about 'Peace in the Valley'?"

"The old Thomas Dorsey standard, that's a good one," Deacon smiled.

He nodded to the band, they tuned up and started to play, softly now, just the keyboard, bass, leading with an acoustic guitar. Deacon had a tremendous singing voice, powerful and deep, and the words, so simple and traditional, moved him to a depth of emotion I'd never seen in him. His tears began to flow as he sang, his face lifted heavenward. And not just his tears.

As he launched into the chorus, peace in the valley, I was lifted on a wave of grief so near to joy it left me shaking and sobbing. Jenny pulled me into her arms and I lost my soul to that sanctimonious bastard.

38

I DIDN'T KNOW I COULD still feel. I thought I had been broken of all sentimentality by the dead I witnessed on an almost daily basis. I thought my heart a callus, a calcified scar that barely beat enough to keep me alive. That stupid little gospel tune completely broke me down. Maybe it was the magic, the magnetism of Deacon's voice, or the moblike intensity of the congregation that swept me up.

Or maybe it was because now I knew why my mother's funeral had seemed unfinished. She had loved that song like no other. She had a collection of covers sung by Elvis, Johnny Cash, Randy Travis and a dozen other people I couldn't remember. She had cross-stitched its lyrics and hung them in a gilt frame beside her bed. *There'll be no sadness, no sorrow, no trouble, trouble I see. There'll be peace in the valley for me.* When I was a kid, growing up and hating everything about my mother, that song was just another reason to treat her as a stupid bumpkin blindly chasing a cartoon Jesus to church every Sunday in the misplaced hope of reforming me. It never occurred to me before that maybe her hopes and fears didn't involve me at all. Maybe she was just as scared, alone and tired of it all as I was.

But my father hadn't played this song, her song, at her own funeral. It had escaped his memory as easily as it did mine.

While we waited outside for them to put the coffin in the hearse, Deacon took me aside and pulled me close, his fingers laced behind my back, his chin resting on top of my head. His hair was still damp from his exertions on stage, but he had recovered nicely enough from his tears. My eyes were still swollen, my nose dripping into the tissue I held to it. He kissed my hair and whispered, "Jackie, do you long for death?"

The way he said it almost sounded like an invitation. I pulled back, momentarily alarmed, all my original Jim Jones suspicions reawakened. One of the religious charlatan's most powerful tools was his ability to seduce women and make them his staunchest defenders. "Not particularly. Why do you ask?"

"'*Peace in the Valley*' is about laying down your burdens and going to your reward. Are you tired of this life?"

"Are you offering me your Kool-Aid?" I asked, and immediately regretted it. He slid his sunglasses onto his nose and stepped out into the sun, away from me. I tried to apologize, but his thoughts were already elsewhere. He had already shaken my dust from his feet. I wondered if I had lost him, reminded myself that I had never had him.

Eugene approached, a smirk on his face below his still-swollen nose. Most of the bruising had faded to a dull yellow, like an old mustard stain around his eyes. I longed to crease his smug face with the knuckles of my right hand. "Is this the kind of church you're planning to build, preacher?" he asked.

Deacon folded a stick of gum into his mouth and balled up the foil wrapper before answering. "No, I plan to build a much louder one."

"I've never heard anybody preach a sermon at a funeral."

Deacon smacked his gum and smiled. "That's what Mrs. Ruth wanted. She says to me, preacher, I want you to preach the bastards a sermon. What about, Mrs. Ruth? I says. I don't want to hear any that resurrection shit, she says. I want some God-damn fire and brimstone. Preach them the story of Lot, she says. She picked it out in particular. Lot, all the way through, from the angels in the city to Lot's daughters fucking their drunk daddy in the cave. Let it be a lesson to them all, she says to me." He laughed derisively and stuck his hands in his pockets, and I wondered if some of his words hadn't been meant for me.

Scowling, Eugene pulled a folded piece of paper from his jacket and handed it to Deacon. "Here's a little something to remember her by," he said, then strolled away.

I rode with Deacon in his pickup. He listened to the country music radio station. The concrete highway under the wheels went *ku-chuk ku-chuk ku-chuk* in time with the music. The wind whistled through the side window, which I had lowered to let out the smoke from my cigarette.

Luther had originally planned to bury Ruth at Memorial Park in Memphis, but at Deacon's urging, he agreed to put her in the cemetery in the woods. We turned off the highway into the church construction area, drove over the gravel track past the half-empty camp of Deacon's saints and parked under the trees between two bulldozers.

We walked in single file across a meadow at the edge of the woods where the bulldozers and graders hadn't gone. The sun was really up now and the heat was like a breath of hell. Grasshoppers as big as your finger sailed out ahead of us as we pushed through the tall sunburned grass, the coffin held aloft on the shoulders of six strong men. Deacon led us to an old wooden bridge over the creek that ran out of the lake. It was as dry as the creek in the woods.

Deacon's workers had used cutting torches to remove the old rusted gate from the crypt and replaced it with a new one. They carried her inside. Luther stood at the entrance and read the funeral service like he was reading a menu, ashes to ashes, dust to dust, cuppa joe ninety-nine cents for seniors on Sundays. He closed the gate, locked it, dropped the key into his inside jacket pocket and patted it like a man whose ship had finally come in.

39

J ENNY AND I WALKED HOME through the woods well before dark, well before the children began to play their reindeer games. She opened a bottle of wine and we sat on the couch. There was nothing to watch on television. Eli sat on the floor in front of the fireplace and banged toys together. Cassie was upstairs reading a book.

Jenny crossed her legs into a lotus posture, her glass of wine resting on her knee. "Sam used to send Reece emails," she said out of the blue.

"What kind of emails?"

"After she was gone, you know? He'd send her emails. He said he could almost pretend she was away at camp and too busy to respond. But he sent them anyway."

"What did they say?"

"I don't know."

"You never read them?"

She took a sip of wine and held it in her mouth for a while. "I couldn't. He loved her that much."

Eli toddled over and showed her one of his toys, ran it up

and down her leg making *brumm!* noises, and she smiled and said *Wow!* until he was satisfied that she was thoroughly entertained. I stared at the fireplace, waiting for a girl to appear. She never did, but Jenny followed my gaze and seemed to read my mind.

"One winter night—this was a few years after Reece died and I think I had just found out I was pregnant with Eli. Sam and I were sitting here reading. We had a fire going because it was the coldest night of the year. For some reason, we both looked up at the same time. A black butterfly suddenly appeared from the flames and clung to the fire screen, fluttering, and we looked at each other, like, to make sure we weren't crazy. I was like, *Am I seeing this?* Sam got up and opened the screen. The butterfly flew across and landed on this lampshade." She indicated the lamp on the table beside her. "Sam said, look, it's Reece. She's come home."

People are very good at lying to themselves. I was living proof of that.

"Reece always loved butterflies. And pigs. Sam took it outside and let it go, but it was so cold I doubt it survived." She finished off her wine and stood up, took my empty glass. "I don't think it was real, anyway."

While she was refilling our glasses in the kitchen, I asked, "Did Sam have a camera?"

"Sure. It's upstairs. Do you need to borrow it?"

"No. Is that the only one?"

"He had another one at the office that he used for his landscaping business." She returned, handed me a full glass, folded her legs up like a fawn and settled on the couch. "I'll see if Bert can bring it by."

———

Jenny went to bed. With the house mostly asleep, I took my glass of wine and sat outside by the pool. Bats dipped in and out of the light over the boat dock, feeding in the halo of bugs. I needed a quiet moment to cogitate, try to put everything together. What I knew wouldn't fill an empty wineglass. Somebody had killed Sam. That person had then cleaned up after themselves quite nicely, probably burning every diary and journal, deleting every photo and email that might have pointed to a motive in his murder. The only thing they missed was that suitcase in the attic.

I didn't like where this line of thought was taking me. My cigarette burned down almost to the filter. I thumped it straight up into the air, as high and hard as I could. The glowing red cherry hung for a moment at the top of its flight, then sailed off across the lake as if by magic, scribbling a dizzy red trail across the stars. The bat finally dropped the butt and it vanished into the water.

Jenny wasn't the only person who had access to the house. That day when her air conditioner broke, dozens of people were in and out of the place, upstairs and down. Her doors were open to practically anybody who happened to wander by. She had invited me to live with her even though she barely knew me. Her social circle was enormous. For all I knew, it could have been Officer Lorio, Doris Dye, or Sheriff Stegall. For that matter, it could have been Deacon.

I watched a boat slowly drifting across the flat surface of the lake. The children in the woods had turned up and were having a regular pep rally. I walked out on the levee, hoping for another look at Sam, hoping he would appear, like the ghost of the king of Tyre or Denmark, to tell his astonished audience of his murder by a brother's hand.

And if Virgil and Shakespeare offered no clues, why not seek the services of Marlowe and Holmes, private consulting detectives? Maybe I would see something I hadn't seen before, some bloody thumbprint or claim check from a camera shop.

The levee was empty, but I spotted a dark shape crouched where Sam had fallen into the water. For a moment I thought it was the same doglike shadow that had led me to the graveyard in the woods. Then Officer Lorio stood up and shined his flashlight in my face.

"What are you doing here?" I asked.

"Just going over things, one more time," he said as he climbed the limestone boulders. Apparently, I wasn't the only one entertaining fanciful thoughts.

I noticed he had something in his hand. "What's that? A potato?"

"Just a rock." He showed me a smooth cobble of river stone about the size of a grapefruit. "Found it down there." He tossed it and shone his flashlight where it splashed at the water's edge. "The lake is at least five feet low. I was just thinking, there's probably some good noodling along this levee."

"Noodling?"

"Hand fishing for catfish. You swim along the bank and feel for holes. When you find one, you stick your hand in and wait for a catfish to bite."

"Bite what?"

"Your hand."

I could think of more entertaining ways of catching dinner. "Then what?"

"You pull it out."

The kids in the woods began to call to one another like coyotes. They were all over the woods, crying *Ollie Ollie oxen free.* There had to be fifty of them, and knowing that they were all ghosts made me wonder if they all died here. The history of the Stirling family went back almost two hundred years. This land had once been a plantation with dozens of slaves, and before that Chickasaw tribes lived and hunted here. But it had been my experience that the spirits of the dead rarely lingered more than a few decades, otherwise the world would be full of them. I'd often wondered what happened to the ancient dead— did they move on, in the Christian sense, to a better place? Maybe they just faded, like old Zuber wallpaper? If so, what had held these kids in this place for such a long time?

Lorio brought me back to the land of the living. "Sam and I used to noodle along here when the water was low. I've seen him pull forty-pound catfish out of the water with his bare hands. He was the best swimmer I knew. Sam and Jenny met in college at a swim meet. Sam coached Reece's swim and softball team. Reece was captain of her school's swim team, too. I watched that girl grow up. I loved her like she was my own daughter." His voice broke at the end. Did he love her enough to kill his best friend?

But if he killed Sam, he wouldn't be out here in the dark for the twentieth time looking for evidence. Unless he was looking for evidence of his own crime.

"What was Sam like after Reece died?"

"You can imagine. It nearly destroyed him."

Lorio told me how he and Sam grew up together. Their daddies had been best friends, used to hunt deer and quail and go noodling for catfish all the time. When they grew up, he and Sam followed in their father's footsteps. "Sam's the only real friend I ever had," he said as his eyes strayed once more to the noisy woods below. "I got friends, you know, but nobody was ever like Sam."

Lorio shined his flashlight on his watch. "It's kinda late for these kids to be out, don't you think?"

I shrugged.

"I wonder who their parents are."

"I don't think they have parents."

He laughed. "I know what you mean."

But he didn't.

"Sam stopped fishing after Reece drowned. When they found her clothes on the levee here, he searched and searched the bank for hours, but a body will do strange things underwater, drift away from where it went in. They found her the next day on the other side of the lake. Me and Sam went noodling one time after that, but he couldn't do it anymore. He said he couldn't put his hand in the hole. He was afraid of what he might find."

The kids were really getting rowdy. I'd never heard them this noisy before. Lorio looked at his watch again and continued, "But he wasn't suicidal. I'd bet you a hundred dollars he didn't kill himself. And I know Sam couldn't have fallen in and drowned. He was like Tarzan in the water."

"I have my own reasons for believing you," I said. "But a hundred bucks and your hunch won't buy us lunch. We need more to go on if we're going to question the local coroner."

"Jenny can request an independent investigation by an outside party. She can authorize an exhumation."

"If you can get her to agree to that, I have a friend who might do the exam." I was thinking of Wiley, who wasn't my friend at all. "But I'll need your help."

Out of the woods came a jerking, rusty-edged scream, as though some child were being torn apart in a hay baler. Lorio drew his piece and started down the hill. I caught his arm and said, "Don't."

"That kid is in trouble."

"You won't find anything."

"How do you know?"

"Because they're not real."

He didn't say anything for a long time, just stood with the beam of his light shining into the woods, too weak and too far away to illuminate anything. Finally he said, "Seriously?"

"They're not there. I know. I've tried to find them. They're just voices, left over from another time."

Hilarious laughter erupted all along the edge of the woods, then gradually receded into silence. After a while, the crickets and frogs started up. Until that moment, I hadn't noticed their absence.

"Well," Lorio sighed shakily. He holstered his weapon. "It's getting late."

As we turned to leave, a girl's voice cried out, "Mama, don't leave me here!"

Lorio dropped his flashlight. It rolled down the levee, gathering momentum until its beam was thrashing and flailing like a living thing. Finally it struck a rock and the bulb broke.

I could see his face in the moonlight, pale and drawn, haunted. Terrified. His fingers dug painfully into my arm. "Jackie," he hissed. "That was Reece."

40

L ORIO ARRIVED DURING BREAKFAST and of course
Jenny made a plate for him, even though he had already
eaten. He was a big guy. He always had room for more, especially home cooking, which he didn't often get, being a bachelor. It was his day off, but he wore his uniform because if Jenny
went along with our little scheme, we would need the access
and cooperation his uniform would buy.

He had also brought an exhumation order. It was already
filled out. All it needed was Jenny's signature. She sat at the
kitchen table with her face in her hands while Lorio told her
why we wanted to dig up her husband. "Nothing else makes
sense. The coroner said he didn't have a heart attack or a stroke.
He hit his head and drowned. And I know he didn't jump in
the water."

"Because Jackie saw him fall." Her bottom lip had begun
to tremble and no matter how hard she tugged, it wouldn't
stop.

"That's right," I said.

"Do I have to be there?" she asked.

"Absolutely not," Lorio said.

She pushed herself to her feet, slid the chair back, wiped a stray hair from her face. I thought she was going to leave without giving an answer. She crossed the kitchen and opened a drawer, rummaged, pulled out an envelope of coupons and a roll of tape and set them aside and grabbed the ballpoint pen she'd been searching for.

"Where do I sign?"

Brilliant white marble statues of Truth and Justice presided in the sun on opposite sides of the grand Adams Street staircases to the Shelby County Courthouse in Memphis. We button-holed Wiley on the Washington Street side slipping out a small side door, where cops waited in the shade, smoking cigarettes and shooting the shit between courtroom appearances. The old bastard spotted me and tried to pretend he hadn't seen me as he hurried to the car parked at the curb. His office had told us he was in court.

"Dr. Wiley!" Lorio shouted, loud enough to hear him two streets away. Every cop and lawyer from Second to Third Street stopped to look.

Wiley's shoulders fell and he turned slowly, glowering at me for a moment before turning his eyes on to Lorio. "Yes, Officer . . . Lorio, is it? Aren't you outside your jurisdiction?"

"Dr. Wiley, I need your help. I was wondering if we could have a moment of your time."

Wiley opened the door of his car, tossed his briefcase on the front seat, leaned back against the car with his elbows on the roof. He was a tall, ungainly bird of a man, with a thin wattle of skin dangling below his jutting chin. A few strands of long, unkempt gray hair floated in the heat rising off the asphalt. He shook his watch down to the end of his bony wrist and checked the time. "You can have five minutes of my lunch. I'm due back in court at two."

It was only a little past twelve. I'd forgotten about the long, difficult hours put in by our dedicated public servants. Lorio explained the case to him in less than a minute, which just goes to show how little we had.

Wiley didn't even work up a sweat. "I've already told Mrs. Lyons to contact the Fayette County coroner regarding this."

"I have reason to believe the coroner's report may be in error," Lorio stated politically. Not that the coroner had lied. Not that he was covering up a crime. Just an error.

"That's a pretty serious allegation, Officer . . ." Wiley ogled his badge again. ". . . Lorio. No doubt when I contact your supervisor, he will state you've already brought this matter to his attention."

"*Her*, sir," Lorio said, "and, no, *she* knows nothing about it. I'm here on behalf of Sam Loftin's widow."

"If this is a private matter and not an official investigation, then you shouldn't be in uniform," Wiley said. He stepped to the side and put his hand on top of the car door. "You should have handed this off to an unlicensed private investigator. I would have then told her, as I told her before, to take her suspicions to the Fayette County coroner." I stepped off the curb and blocked Wiley from closing the door.

"Sir, I'm asking you, as a favor . . ." Lorio began.

"Son, I don't know you from Adam's off ox." He gestured that I should move out of the way so he could close the door.

I pretended not to understand, dug out a cigarette and stuck it in my mouth. "Got a light?" Nothing had changed since the days when I was a vice cop for the Memphis Police Department. Sometimes the facts of a case were only useful insofar as they agreed with the story some powerful person wanted told. Anything that didn't fit the narrative would be quietly gathered up, weighed down with a brick, and tossed like a bag of cats in a creek. Doctors, lawyers, judges, cops—they always protected each other. Wiley didn't want to stick his nose into Fayette County business because he didn't want Fayette County questioning his own findings.

Lorio thrust a piece of paper at Wiley. "What's this?"

"It's an exhumation order," Lorio said. "Signed by the widow, Jennifer Loftin."

Wiley shook his head and laughed at our hapless attempts to circumvent the law. "You know I can't order an exhumation in Fayette County without the approval of a Fayette County judge."

"If you please, sir," Lorio patiently explained, "Sam Loftin is buried in Eads. That's Shelby County."

Wiley's eyes darted to the paper in his hands. He scanned it and, after a minute or so, furrowed his liver-spotted brow. "Tell me again what happened."

Lorio went through it one more time. "As you can see, we don't have any proof, but Jackie and I both believe Sam Loftin was murdered. You can't lightly dismiss the informed opinion of two police officers."

"One," Wiley reminded him, without neglecting to give me a vicious sneer.

"Unfortunately, any evidence of the crime was buried with Sam and, quite frankly, sir, you're the only person we can go to about this. I've lived and worked in Malvern all my life and it's a close, tight-knit community, if you know what I mean."

"I believe I understand your meaning," Wiley muttered.

"Sir, I know you don't owe me anything. But I hope, if nothing else, you will want to see the truth revealed as much as we do. Sam Loftin was my friend."

Wiley reached into his car, took out his briefcase, and opened it on the roof of the car. He slipped the exhumation order into one of the pockets. "I'm a very busy man, I hope you understand," he said as he clicked it shut. I moved back to the sidewalk, nudged Lorio with an elbow and shot him a wink. "As soon as I have a free moment, I'll forward this to the funeral director listed on the order and have the remains delivered to my office."

"Thank you, sir." Lorio reached out to shake the good doctor's hand. Wiley stared at it for a moment without touching it, then walked around to the other side of his car and opened the door.

Before he ducked in, he said with a nod in my direction, "One more thing, son. You'd do well to find better company."

He started the engine and pulled away from the curb with a
screech of tires, forcing a MATA bus to slam on its brakes.

When he was gone, Lorio turned to me. "I thought you said
Wiley was your friend."

I flicked my butt under the wheels of the bus as it rumbled
by. "We had a falling-out. It's a long story."

41

I T HAD BEEN OVER A WEEK since I shot any of Deacon's
photos, so after Lorio dropped me off at the house, I grabbed
my camera and headed out. If the sun was murder, the humid-
ity was a mother drowning her children in a bathtub. I was glad
to get under the trees, but even there the air was almost thick
enough to swim through.

Deacon wasn't at the house and the door was locked. I
knocked on the door but no one answered. His truck was
parked next to the scuppernong arbor. I circled the house once,
shooting photos of the stained glass in the upstairs windows,
then walked home through the silent, empty woods.

Something had changed. I could feel it in my bones. Day
or night, I usually heard, at the very least, a titter of childish
laughter whenever I walked that path. Now there was nothing,
neither living nor dead. I wondered if, somehow, the trees and
the weeds, the brambles and briars, had died with Mrs. Ruth.
It was just a place now, not a forest or a woods; it was just a
collection of sticks and ashes waiting for a bulldozer to push
them down.

I opened the door of Jenny's house to a sound I'd never heard before—Jenny shouting. "Your brother wants to go swimming!"

And Cassie. "I don't want to!"

"Put on your bathing suit and get in the damn water with your brother!"

"No!"

"You'll do as I say or I'll . . ."

Cassie pounded up the stairs, shrieking "NO! NO! NO!" with her hands clapped over her ears. Then down the hall, footsteps thumping, rattling the pictures on the walls, and finally the slamming door.

I found Jenny in a chair by the window, staring out at the lake. Eli was sitting at the kitchen table, dressed in his Thomas the Tank Engine swimming trunks, pounding down Cheetos out of a family-sized bag. I looked out the window at the pool and saw a dead girl in a red one-piece bathing suit floating in the deep end. I grabbed a beer from the fridge and another one for Jenny.

I popped the top and handed it to her. She glanced at the clock as she took the beer. "It's not even three."

"Jenny, don't make her go in."

"It's just a swimming pool. She's been in it a thousand times. She's a great swimmer. First she won't go in the deep end, then she won't go underwater. Now she won't even get in."

"Trust me on this. When Cassie doesn't want to get in the pool, don't force her."

She took a long, angry, savage pull at the beer, trying to kill it before the carbonated burn kicked in. She failed and set it down with a pained gasp. "Why the hell not?"

"She's scared."

"Of what?"

I didn't say. I didn't have to. She didn't need to see the dead girl in the pool to know she was being unreasonable. She just needed a minute to get her head together.

It didn't even take that long. "I know. I'm sorry. It's just . . . all this about Sam . . ." She turned and rested her forehead against the window pane. "What happened?"

"Wiley will do it."

She was neither relieved nor grieved by this news. Her response was mechanical. "And you're certain I don't have to be there?" I told her the funeral home would handle everything. "And where will they put him . . . after they . . ."

"He'll be returned to the funeral home."

She sighed, her can of beer sweating, forgotten, on the arm of the chair. I finished mine and dropped the empty in the recycle bin. His fingers orange up to the second knuckle, Eli was finishing off the last of the Cheetos. "Did you eat that whole bag?" I asked.

"Un-uh," he lied.

When I returned to the den, Jenny said, "Will you talk to Cassie?"

I suddenly felt ashamed for thinking Jenny might have killed Sam. If she had, she wouldn't have agreed to his exhumation. She could have played the hysterical grieving widow, begged us not to defile his remains. Her grief was as real, and still as raw, as the day Sam died. She didn't want him dug up, but she would have dug him up herself if she had to.

"Of course," I said, and headed upstairs. Of course, I didn't know anyone else who might have had a motive to kill Sam. Jenny was the only good suspect I had, but I was happy to mark her off the list. I'd sleep better, anyway.

I found Cassie in her bedroom, under the bed with her feet sticking out, waiting for somebody to see her. I sat on the edge of the bed, picked up the Disney princess pillow and laid it across my lap. She didn't move from under the bed.

I didn't know what to say, so I said, "What's up?"

She didn't answer. I didn't expect her to. "She's in the pool right now." I walked over to the window, which overlooked the pool. The girl in the red one-piece was still there, but she had sunk to the bottom. Jenny sat at the pool's edge, her feet in the water, watching Eli try to climb into an inflatable lifesaver. "I talked to your mom. She's sorry she yelled at you."

Cassie's little blond head rose up in the space between the bed and the wall. Her eyes were as big as the knobs on her bedposts.

"I didn't tell her about this, or about us, what we see." I sat on the bed, and Cassie climbed up beside me, curled up in my lap like a dog and stuck her thumb in her mouth.

"I won't tell her unless you want me to. But she won't make you go swimming now."

She pulled out her thumb and whispered, "Thanks."

"You don't have to be scared of them," I said. I clumsily stroked her head, streaming her fine hair through my fingers.

"Aunt Jackie?"

I cringed. "Just Jackie."

"Mama said to call you . . ."

"We don't always have to do what Mama says." I cringed

again. This is why I disliked children. It wasn't so much the kids as what I turned into around them.

"Can I tell you something?" I nodded that she could. "Reece made me promise never to tell."

My heart climbed up my throat and tried to push past my tongue. I swallowed it down before saying, "I think maybe you can tell me. I won't tell anyone else."

She thought about that for a bit, nervously gnawing on her thumb, while my shaking fingers continued to brush through her hair. Finally, it came out. "Reece had a boyfriend."

"Oh?" I pulled a strand of hair from the corner of her mouth, gently, so as not to floss her teeth with it. "Did she tell you his name?"

"No."

The anchor chain of my heart rattled through its hawse and sank, sixteen fathoms deep.

"She was meeting him," she continued, "that night. She snuck out through her window. She made me promise not to tell."

Back went the thumb into her mouth, a plug to stop her sobs, and I wondered how many nights she had lain in this bed, gnawing it raw to keep anyone from hearing her tears. How many times had she blamed herself for keeping Reece's secret, when doing the wrong thing and being a tattletale might have saved her sister's life? I had slept in Cassie's bed more nights, walked more miles in her shoes that she had logged herself, blamed myself a million times for my own little brother's death. We shared more than a talent for seeing the dead. We carried them on our backs, too.

Grown-ups aren't allowed to suck their thumbs. All we had were words, but at times like this, words were hollow noises, empty as a junkie's promises. I couldn't tell her she did the right thing. She would know I was lying. That's why she hadn't told anyone until now. She'd never met another person who could keep her secrets.

42

I FOUND REECE'S SOFTBALL TEAM photo lying on top of the computer. This time, the nail had been ripped out of the wall, the glass shattered in the frame and the photo slipped part of the way out. I stood at the door for a moment, my fingers clamped to the knob, then stepped inside and quietly closed and locked it. In the kitchen below I could hear Jenny banging supper pots on the stove, Holly laughing at something on television. Nathan had taken Cassie for a ride in his boat to cheer her up.

I picked up the broken frame and slid the photo out, careful not to rip it on the shards of glass. On the back Reece had written in round, girlish script her entire team roster by name and number. Next to her own number, 59, she had written, instead of her own name, the word *Piglet*.

Piglet59 was Reece's username. I turned on the computer and pulled up her email account. On a hunch, I typed DLGOXOXOX into the password box and waited.

The first dozen pages of emails had never been opened. Most were spam, but about fifty or so were from her father—the emails Jenny said he wrote to Reece after she died. Page after page of the most tedious descriptions of family life mixed with heartrending apologies for failing her, for letting her down, for not being there when she needed him most. How he could have done more, should have done more. How he couldn't live without her. Promises to kill himself and apologies for failing at that, too.

I knew now why Jenny never wanted to read these. I also knew that if the insurance company ever saw them, Jenny would need a signed confession from Sam's murderer before she saw the first penny of life insurance money. There was no doubt Sam loved his daughter, loved her beyond the point of obsession, but I detected nothing sexual in any of his epistles.

I kept going, plodding through hundreds of emails from Reece's friends, dating back years before her death. Reading about the horrors of middle school and the wonders of boys. About eight months before she died, during her goth period, Reece had also got herself mixed up in a cutting clique.

When I was growing up and couldn't deal with life, I'd smoke a joint or drink a beer. We take that away from kids and now they cut themselves.

She stopped using email not long after she started cutting. I reached the end of the inbox without finding a single email from a boy or man, other than the ones from her father, and there was nothing in any of the other folders, including the sent folders and trash can. That made sense. Whoever had raped her had covered his tracks too well to leave something as traceable as an email lying around where he couldn't delete it.

Next I tried the social networking site and found that, like most people, Reece used the same password for everything. When it opened, I was met with a black page covered with pictures of corpses and screenshots of B-movie horror flicks, backed by the quiet strains of Rob Zombie's *"Living Dead Girl."* In her profile, Reece listed it as her favorite song. Cute.

This is where she moved when she stopped using email. I was able to pick up the unbroken narrative of her tragic life, but now in her messages she began to mention this mysterious older boyfriend. My young buddy at the guard shack had said that most of the kids in school believed this boyfriend to be a fiction to hide her lesbianism.

The boyfriend was real, only he wasn't a boy. I found the first photo in her private photo album—a selfie taken in a bathroom mirror. Shot from the neck down, there was nothing in the photo to identify the bastard. The bathroom looked tiny, perhaps a half bath, with blue wallpaper and a fuzzy orange-or-peach-colored cover on the toilet seat, not unlike the half bath under Jenny's stairs except the colors were all wrong. Still, it looked vaguely familiar, but I could have seen it anywhere. He had shaved his pubes, but still sported plenty of belly hair. It formed a curious curl, like a question mark, around his navel. I didn't need to see his driver's license to know he was at least twice Reece's age, and probably a lot older, maybe old enough to be her daddy. His username was Nastyb01. *Hey Piglet,* his message said, *I can't wait to be with you again. And neither can my little friend. Look how happy he is.*

I went through all the Nastyboy messages, one by one. In some of them, he sent her thumbnails of the photos he'd taken of her, photos I'd found in the suitcase in the attic. I saw the same phrase, over and over, sometimes from him, sometimes from her—*What are you thinking about?* It was like some pass-phrase or inside joke, the kind of insipid code that secret lovers use when people are around.

In the later messages, he began asking for her password, saying that if she loved him she would trust him. When she refused, he demanded it, then said she couldn't see him again until she learned to trust him. They went through a rough period, maybe a month or two in which they barely wrote, before she finally caved and crawled back to his lordship. Only the password she sent wasn't DLGOXOXOX.

In one of his last messages before she killed herself, he promised he'd love her forever and sent the picture of her crying in the rain. *This is my favorite,* he said. *I love it so much, I sleep with it every night, if you know what I mean. I'm running out of photo paper! LOL.*

Jenny called upstairs that supper was ready. I shouted that I'd be down in a minute, then scrolled back through, reading the messages again, looking for anything that might identify him. The only one that provided a hint said, *I'm the luckiest man in the world. No man alive ever had a woman who loved him the way you love me.* I recognized these words. I'd seen them or heard them somewhere, maybe a love song or something from a movie. I was sure it was a direct quote, word for word. In my mind I could even hear a man's voice whispering them, as if he were saying them directly to me.

I wanted to vomit.

The worst part was reading Reece's responses. She loved this creep with the sort of desperation that only a thirteen-year-old girl can know or understand. When he ignored her, she cut herself. When she was going to meet him, she couldn't sleep the night before. She hated her mother because she kept getting in the way. She hated summer because Jenny was home all day and her boyfriend had to work all the time. She preferred winter, when they could be together whenever they wanted. Then the school year started and she was going to stay home sick and this time she promised she wouldn't make him stop, she would go all the way and she loved him forever. Then she did it. Then he acted like he didn't want to see her anymore. He demanded her password. He was just using her, and she started cutting again and she hated herself and him and the world. Then, finally, she gave him her password and they were going to meet again and he was so sorry he had let her down. He couldn't live without her anymore. He promised he would make it up to her, if he could just see her one more time.

And that was it. The last message. It was April and Reece Loftin was dead.

I could imagine him, after she died, going mad as he tried to gain access to her account to delete all his photos and messages, realizing she had changed her password before that last meeting. Living in constant fear, waiting for a knock on the door.

A knock that never came.

Had she changed her password when she was planning to kill herself? Had she planned to kill herself, or was it a sudden reaction, perhaps to some rejection or betrayal on his part? If

so, why had she hidden those photos in the attic? And where
had she gotten the money she hid with the photos?

I didn't know. I couldn't wrap my head around the enormity of it. She hadn't hated her abuser. If she was afraid of anything, it was getting caught or losing his attention. She loved
the guy. She cut herself when she couldn't be with him.

Absolutely no doubt he was manipulating her, playing with
her tender emotions. But there was nothing unusual about that.
I'd been through that game myself, a half-dozen times at least,
since I turned eighteen. Once with the man I married, another
with a man I almost married. Before that, with a boyfriend who
killed my own brother and kept dating me until I finally un-
covered his crime.

I kidded myself that I couldn't have been trapped by the
same guy, or someone just like him. I kidded myself that I
would know him when I saw him because he was a monster,
that the enormity of his sin must leave a mark for everyone to
see. But the sheer adolescent banality of it appalled me. When
I tried to access Reece's accounts, I had expected to read heartrending stories about how he raped her, abused her, tortured
her. Instead, he was just a jerk, a jerk like the million other jerks
who ever mind-fucked the girl he pretended to love.

The only difference was this girl died. This one died, out of
how many?

I needed to talk to Deacon. He had been right all along.
The man who had molested Reece and photographed her hadn't
been her father. If Sam wasn't a child molester, why kill him?
Who had a motive?

Nastyboy.

Maybe Sam figured out who Nastyboy was. Maybe he saw the same messages on his daughter's computer and recognized the guy.

Deacon knew the people in this community better than almost anyone. If I showed him the pictures of Nastyboy, maybe he'd be able to identify the bastard. He was the only person I knew, other than Jenny, who might, and I couldn't show her the photos without revealing everything I knew about Reece. Things she didn't need to know.

Sometimes people aren't what they seem. Sam and Jenny didn't know their own daughter. But in this case, it was better that they didn't.

My phone rang while I was shutting down the computer. It was Deacon, as though in answer to my prayer. I glanced at the window. It was getting dark outside. I'd been at it for hours.

"Were you just over here?" he asked.

"I stopped by earlier. You weren't home."

"I've been home all day. I thought I heard someone knocking just now. I looked out the window and saw you leaving."

"That was hours ago."

"I could have sworn it was you." He sounded uneasy, confused and tired. "You can't see anything through this stained glass. I don't know what I was thinking, putting these windows in a house. They belong in a church."

A tremendous bang, like someone dropping a bathtub through the floor, drowned out his next few words. All I heard was ". . . can you be here?"

"Are you working?" I asked.

"No. I sent everyone away. That's why I need to see you."

He hadn't heard the bang I heard. He had seen me when I wasn't there, and not seen me when I was. Something was wrong. "Let me put some shoes on."

"Be careful," he said before hanging up.

Careful? Of what? He didn't sound like the Deacon I knew. I sat on the edge of the bed for a moment, staring out the window at the empty levee and the dark eaves of the forest in the distance. I saw a flash of white in the underbrush, like a torn piece of cloth blown by the wind. Only there wasn't any wind.

As I stood, I heard a girlish whisper on the bed behind me. *What are you thinking about?*

What wasn't I thinking about?

I ran into Holly coming out of the bathroom under the stairs. She was dressed to the hilt in a little red sleeveless thing stretched thin as a stocking over her curves. She towered over me in her heels. "Excuse me," she said, ducking through the doorway. She saw the laptop in my hand and the camera around my neck. "You're not working this late, are you?"

"No. Are you?" I don't know why I said it. She was in my way and it just popped out. I tried not to look at her as I slipped by and headed for the door.

Jenny called from the kitchen, "Aren't you eating supper?"

"I need to see Deacon."

"Then take him some supper."

I waited in the kitchen while she made a couple of plates—

pork chops, fried rice, steamed asparagus; all of it cold but still edible. I heard the front door slam. I don't know if Jenny had heard my comment to Holly, but she said, "Going out with one of her gentlemen friends, I suppose."

I didn't particularly care. I just wanted to go, but I made the small talk. "Does she have many?"

"A few." She wrapped both plates in plastic wrap and put them in a picnic basket with a bottle of wine and two plastic cups. "Though one rarely sees any of them," she grinned. She had an infectious grin, full of mischief. She suppressed it as best she could, which was barely at all.

"One doesn't, does one?" I snorted.

"We shouldn't make fun. The poor thing has nothing to do," she chastised herself. "No job, no life except lying around the pool all day. I don't think she even graduated high school. She must be bored to tears."

She handed me the picnic basket and I headed for the door, remembered my manners and said, "Thanks. I'll be back before you go to bed."

She grinned and winked. "No, you won't."

43

A S I APPROACHED THE HOUSE, Deacon's bedroom
window was a square of colored light though the trees.
The front door stood open and he was waiting in the doorway,
a shotgun resting in the crook of his arm. I had never seen him
with a gun before. I shouted his name. He turned without ac-
knowledging me and entered the house. I climbed the steps
and followed him inside, only to find the front hall empty. I
heard him upstairs banging around before he appeared at the
top of the stairs. He had no shotgun, and there was no way he
could have got upstairs that quick.

I dropped the picnic basket and scanned the room for an
intruder, stepped behind the door to my right and peered through
the hinge crack into the next room. I watched a frail, emaci-
ated old man lower himself into a rocking chair. His tiny body
was nearly swallowed by a Kentucky colonel suit of immacu-
late seersucker. He rested the butt of the shotgun on the floor
between his boots.

"Did you just get here?" Deacon asked as he descended the

stairs. I said that I had. He gave me an odd look to match my odd behavior.

"Thought I saw a rat," I explained, pointing. The old man's skull-like face drawn into a mask of grief, he turned in his chair and set an ambrotype photo on a table by the wall. Before table and photo disappeared, I saw a woman and three children in the oval brass frame. Grinning furiously with toothless gums, he leaned his nodding chin onto the barrel of the shotgun and pulled the trigger. I jumped as his head dissolved, but there was no sound of the gunshot. He left the chair rocking silent and empty in the corner.

Deacon followed my gaze into the room. "Are you sure it wasn't the Opposum Paul? Sometimes he wanders the house at night."

"Pretty sure." I was surprised by the steadiness of my voice. You never really get used to seeing them. Until this moment, I hadn't seen a ghost in Ruth's house. I had felt them, felt sure they were there, but they had kept themselves hidden. Until tonight. I worried what that portended. I knew it couldn't be good, and I knew it was connected to the strange phone call that had summoned me here.

The chair rocked itself to a stop. Deacon stared at it for a moment. "Sometimes it does that when I leave the door open." He tried to laugh. "Must be a draft." There was no draft. His eyes nervously searched my face for some indication of what I had seen. I didn't give it to him, not yet anyway. Not until I knew what was bothering him.

He pointed at the picnic basket. "What's that?"

"Dinner."

———

While we ate I told Deacon what I had found on Reece's computer. We sat on paint buckets in the dining room, a suitcase propped on dusty boxes of plaster for a table. A couple of altar candles burned in golden candlesticks on the mantel. Deacon picked at his food without tasting it. He hardly seemed to be paying attention to what I said.

When I finished, he asked, "Do you remember that scene at the end of *Out of Africa*, when Karen is sitting in her empty house just like we are sitting here, all her things sold off, just a few trunks remaining?"

I poured some wine into his glass. "Never saw it."

"Really? Never?" He picked up a limp piece of asparagus and bent it across one finger. "Well, her house is empty and she's about to leave Africa and everything she loves. She says to Denys Finch-Hatton, *'We should have had it this way all the time.'*"

He was trying to be casual, but his eyes were jumping all over the place. He laughed nervously and dropped the asparagus spear onto his plate. "I don't know what I was thinking."

He stood suddenly and walked to the window, rested his hand against the brick that filled it. "You probably noticed most of my saints have abandoned me. They are too afraid to come here. They believe this house is cursed, haunted. About a month ago, something happened in the cellar. I don't know what. Several men were working on the plumbing when they saw . . . *something*. They couldn't describe it."

"What do you mean, they couldn't describe it?"

"They didn't know the English words for what they saw and I didn't understand their Spanish, but it scared them so bad they refused to return. The others heard about it. They started leaving during the night, one or two at a time, sometimes a whole family."

He turned and set his back against the bricks. "I want to be honest with you, Jackie. When I hired you, I had two purposes. The first was to capture details of the house. But I also hoped you would capture an image of the evil that dwells here, so that I would know what I'm fighting. Or that perhaps you could see what I could not, and help direct me. But whatever it is, it hides itself from you and your camera." He took a large envelope from the mantel and gave it to me.

"What's this?" I asked as I opened it.

"That is why I called you. I took the best pictures you have given me so far and had them developed," he said. "Look what came back today."

The envelope contained two dozen 8 × 10 glossy photos of the interiors, mostly shot in the first days before the dust really started ruining my work. I had given him good image files, but all of these were obscured by orbs. "Are you sure you sent the right files?" I asked, even though I already knew the answer.

I set the plates on the floor and opened Reece's laptop, pulled up the files where I had stored all the usable images I had taken. They were ruined, every single one. Next I checked the files I hadn't transferred from the camera. Same result. As a final test, I shot a picture of Deacon standing in front of the fireplace. Deiter had told me orbs were caused by specks of dust reflected in the camera's flash. Because of the candlelight, I set the ISO to 400, f-stop to 2.0, shutter speed to one-quarter.

Deacon's face was completely obscured by orbs, even though I hadn't used a flash at all. He stood behind me, looking at the image of himself on the camera's LCD display. "I feel evil all around me, trying to get inside, infect my soul. I have blessed this house a dozen times and it does no good at all. Only the power of my faith has kept me safe. Ruth fed me visions of a grand temple filled with song and joy and overflowing collection plates. My pride watered and fed this evil, gave it fertile ground in which to grow."

His Bible appeared in his hand as if by magic and he began to pace the room and speak in his booming, preacher voice. The old dry wood of the empty house resonated and amplified it, until it seemed to come from everywhere, as though the house itself were speaking Deacon's words. "My place was among the poor and hungry and the sins they commit out of fear and want and desperate need, not these wretched millionaires and their greed, their pride, their all-consuming lusts, sins for which they want no forgiveness, no redemption. They feel no shame or remorse. The Gospel is wasted upon them, like pearls before swine. The Church, to them, is just another market—in this shop I buy insurance for my investments, here I buy insurance for my properties, and here I buy insurance for my soul."

Spirits began to appear all around the room, stepping out of corners and shadows, old men and young girls, slaves in rags, slaves with white gloves and black ties with tails, gangsters doffing Al Capone hats with their molls dressed in flapper gowns, fat white planters with bulging bracers, shirtless sharecroppers with their overalls dangling, Army-green soldiers and soldiers of a more sordid kind dressed all in white. Deacon's headless Republican Guardsman stepped out of the corner wreathed in flames of hell. They came from Purgatory to hear him preach and maybe find redemption or escape from their soul's plight.

Deacon flipped open his Bible and held it spread upon his palm. "I did not listen to Paul's clear warning in his letter to the Galatians, chapter five. I sought to minister to debauchers, idolators, selfish people full of envy and ambition and petty jealousies. I strayed from my true path. I traded my mission for empty robes of gold."

He turned and faced me, arms outspread, not in a gesture of victory but of surrender. "Like the early Church fathers in their pride and their greed, I also lost the Gospel. But the Gospel of Jesus wasn't lost. It was suppressed. The early Church fathers saw the danger of Jesus' message. So they took into their greedy hands the keys to heaven and locked the doors and set up a ticket booth outside. *Join our church and receive the one true truth and heaven will open its gates for you and you alone. Those who do not join will burn in lakes of fire for all eternity. God will punish them, but you will be loved. You will be anointed. You will be given secret knowledge and true understanding and a crown in heaven.* But I ask you this, what do you want with a crown? Why do you want Jesus to anoint your head with oil? Why do you want to see your fellow man burn in lakes of fire for all eternity?"

"I don't," I said, but he didn't hear me. I wasn't even there. He was preaching to the lost souls of that house and the shades

of the children in the woods. I could hear them outside, singing that *wire–briar–limber–lock* song, and I wondered if Deacon heard them, too. If he did, he didn't show it.

He dropped to his knees and gripped his Bible to his chest,
wrapped his arms around it as though it were the only thing
keeping him from sinking into the earth. "That's when the
Gospel lost its power. That's when they started spreading the
Good News at the point of a sword. Their followers lost the ability to do miracles and speak in tongues. Speaking in tongues isn't
nonsense, it isn't yabbadabbado television-preacher jibberish.
We learn in the book of Romans that at that time, it was Pen-
tecost and people were gathered in Jerusalem from all over the
world. So that each and every one of them should have the
opportunity to hear the Good News, the Holy Spirit possessed
the apostles and spoke through them in the tongues of those
who had gathered. The apostles spoke the known languages of
the world—Aramaic, Syriac, Latin, Egyptian, Greek. But
when the Good News was lost, so were the gifts of the Spirit.
God does not bless those who lie. His bestows His gifts upon
they who carry his Gospel in their hearts. People like Jackie
Lyons, who can discern the spirits of the dead."

He slumped forward, his head to the floor, the Bible clutched
beneath his chin. I knelt beside him and heard him whispering. "The debt of sin has been paid. Our souls are assured a
place in heaven."

"Come on," I said as I pulled him up by the arm. He left
behind a puddle of sweat soaking into the floor. "Let's get you
to bed."

44

I LOWERED DEACON to the mattress. He rolled over and curled up into a ball with his Bible to his lips. I gathered up the scattered sheets and blankets and spread them over his body. He seemed to already be asleep. I started to leave, then he said, "Jackie, will you stay with me while I pray?"

He hadn't moved except to lift his head a little from the pillow. I said that I would stay.

Deacon's breathing was regular and deep. When I was sure he was asleep, I got up to leave, but paused at the doorway. I couldn't leave him alone, and there was no one else to watch him. I thought about calling Jenny, but remembered she had the kids and couldn't leave them. I sat on the floor beside the mattress and watched his chest rise and fall.

He sat up suddenly and stared hard at the dark doorway. A slave woman stood there, holding a dead slave girl in her arms. Her face was streaked with cuts or welts, as from a razor or whip.

"What's wrong?" I asked.

"I thought . . ." He paused. The woman turned and walked

into the darkness. He lay back down and pulled the sheets up
to his chin. "I thought you had left me," he said.

"I'm not going anywhere."

"I'm glad." He reached his hand out of the blankets and I
took it. "This is my Garden of Gethsemane."

"Are you OK?"

"I am now. You are here. I'm at peace." He rolled up onto
his elbow. "And hungry."

I went downstairs and brought up his cold dinner and the
bottle of wine. We sat on the mattress and I watched him eat.
Deacon asked me to honestly tell him what I had seen tonight. "All day long I have seen you wandering this house," he
said. "I knew it wasn't you. I knew it was Satan taunting me
with what I most desire. I also know that you have seen things
tonight you have never seen in this house before. Don't deny
it, Jackie Lyons. The first battle, the battle within my soul, is over.
But the Romans are waiting at the gate."

Even though his continuing Messianic allusions didn't fill
me with confidence that he wasn't about to nail himself to some
cross, I decided to tell him what I had seen. Of the old man in
the rocking chair, he said, "Overton Stirling. Ruth said he
killed himself. She didn't mention how. " He seemed especially
interested in the congregation of the dead, asking had they
looked redeemed by his Gospel message.

"I'm not sure what you mean," I said.

"Did they walk off into a heavenly light?"

"Not that I noticed. I was trying to get you upstairs. You're
not an easy man to shift." In truth, they had faded back into
the woodwork much the way they had come.

He seemed disappointed, not in them but in me for ignoring the things most important to him. I suppose I should have left him lying on the floor to chase ghosts through the house.

I collected our plates and returned them to the picnic basket while he poured the last of the wine. "What did you mean about the Romans at the gates just now?" I asked.

He reached across the mattress and picked up a piece of paper from the floor. "Not all my enemies are supernatural, nor have all my saints abandoned me in fear of the dead. Many have been arrested by Roy Stegall for immigration violations. Others have been harassed and attacked. I have received threatening letters in the mail. And then there was this." He tossed the paper into my lap. "Luther Vardry's restraining order, stopping all work on the house while he challenges Ruth's will in court."

"What's he challenging?"

"Everything. Ruth didn't just give me this land and the money to build my church. She left me everything, her entire estate, donated to the church. Luther got nothing."

"Did you know?"

He shook his head. "I don't understand why she has done this, but I have to stop work until it gets out of probate." He sounded defeated already.

"Ruth wouldn't have signed that will unless it was bulletproof. Luther can challenge it, but he can't win."

"Even if he doesn't win, he can bury it in court for years."

"Let him. You're younger than he is. He won't live forever."

"He's Ruth's son, a Stirling. He could live another twenty years, easy."

"But aren't you going to fight? You've got the money."

He tossed his wine back with one smooth swallow and set the plastic cup carefully on the floor beside the bed. "Money, yes, I have money, but even in Malvern money isn't everything. This is Luther Vardry's county. He's got the biggest, wealthiest church around and all the power, influence and money that position brings. He's pastor to all the judges. He owns a United States senator. He doesn't want the True Gospel cutting into his take."

I couldn't believe what I was hearing from this brave, strong, fearless Christian warrior, this man who had battled demons and spent his lonely vigil in the Gethsemane Garden of his soul. Luther Vardry's unassailable power was the best reason to fight, not give up and blow away.

Deacon continued despondently, "I offered to give Luther everything else, if he would let me keep the property, plus enough money to restore the house and build the church. He refused. I don't blame him. I don't know what got into me, preaching that way in his church at Ruth's funeral. Pride, I suppose, that old demon. I get so high on it, I can't stop myself. I didn't even follow Ruth's wishes. She wanted me to preach the story of Lot, but I barely touched on it. All I wanted to do was jab a shiv in that old preacher. I guess I succeeded. He won't even talk to me now except through his lawyer."

"Screw him then. You'll own him in court. I know a lawyer who would take your case just for the pleasure of sticking it to a guy like Luther Vardry."

He took my hands and pressed them between his, trying to get me to understand. "I can't beat him, Jackie. Ruth died before our church was built. She was the only thing standing between me and Luther. You, of all people, should know you can't go against the government in a small town, not unless you've got a bigger government on your side."

"But you can't give up."

"I'm glad to hear you say that." His demeanor was so disgustingly Christlike, I could almost see the bloody holes in his hands. "I hope you never give up, never stop fighting." He leaned forward and kissed me, once, on each cheek.

We lay together, sharing a cigarette, which was my second favorite thing to do in bed. I blew a couple of weak smoke rings, which made me cough. Deacon took the cigarette from my fingers and flicked the ash onto the floor. "Even if Ruth had lived, I wonder if the church would ever have been built. Very little was getting done."

"It's a wonder Mrs. Ruth could stay here alone all those years," I said.

I rolled over on top of him and took the cigarette, inhaled one last drag, and dropped it into the empty wine bottle. He reached up to me, cupping my head with one hand while I leaned down and forward, my hair falling down around my face and framing his.

Deacon closed his eyes. I paused, hearing a scream outside. The stained-glass window at the far end of the room shattered and suddenly the room was full of fire. Flames leapt up over the mattress and ignited the blankets. We threw them off and rolled into the hall. The window behind us shattered and fire surrounded us again.

We made it to the front door but the front porch was an inferno. The dining room boiled with smoke and hellish light, its exit the mouth of hell. Flames came tumbling down the stairs like children on Christmas morning. Two-hundred-year-old Zuber wallpaper curled and turned to ash just from the heat. Every doorway was a sheet of fire, and black smoke drew down around us like a curtain. "The tunnel!" Deacon shouted over the roar of the fire. I don't know where he got the air to breathe.

We headed for the basement, slipped and fell halfway down the steps, ended in a heap against one wall. The bricks were cool and the air breathable, but there were already gaps of flickering light showing through the boards above our heads. Deacon grabbed a flashlight one of the plumbers had left behind and we dove through the jagged entrance he had knocked through the cellar wall.

I snatched the flashlight from his hand and clicked it on, grabbed his arm and started to pull him down the passage. He jerked free and said, "Wait."

Someone was upstairs, inside the burning house. She was screaming Deacon's name.

"That sounds like Holly."

Deacon? Deacon, where are you?

"What's she doing here?"

"She must have seen the flames." He hurried back to the cellar and shouted up the stairs, "Holly! Down here!"

Deacon! Oh my God! Deacon help me!

"How did she get in the house?" I asked.

He started up the steps. I remembered the voice of Reece

Loftin calling out to me and Lorio, that night on the levee. I remembered her voice behind me on the bed. I remembered the little girl and the dark shape that tricked me into the dusty tomb at the other end of this tunnel and locked me in. I grabbed his arm. "Deacon, don't go. It's not her."

"I have to go."

"It's them. The voices in the forest."

Deacon! Please, where are you?

"Jackie, I have to go," he said.

"But it's not Holly!"

"If there's even a chance." Glowing cinders drifted down the stairs as the house groaned and cracked. The upper floors were collapsing. "I can't just let her die."

"I'll go with you." I looked around for a fire extinguisher but the place had been stripped bare.

"I have to go back and try to save her. You owe nothing to Holly."

"What about me, Deacon? If you go back, who is going to save me?"

He looked down at me, his face shining like Moses on the mountain, but it was only the glow of the fire surrounding his head. "You have already saved yourself, Jackie Lyons. Now go." He shook loose of my grasp and disappeared up the stairs.

I waited for him until burning timbers were falling into the cellar. I couldn't see for the smoke, couldn't hear for the dying shrieks of the house as it was consumed in flame. Deacon had made his decision. I had made mine. He was the only thing that mattered to me, the only reason I had to be there. Not the work, not the job or the camera or the pictures, not even justice for a murdered man. Just him, and without him, there was nothing. I closed my eyes against the stinging smoke and waited.

Then I felt his strong hand in mine, dragging me away into darkness and into air I could breathe. I didn't know how he made it out. "Did you find her?" I gasped. He didn't answer, just pulled me along. A hot wind choked with ash and cinders carried us down the tunnel and we emerged into the crypt as though spat out of hell itself. As I collapsed against the wall, I felt his hand slip from mine. It was a few minutes before I could even see, but I knew he was gone. I'd felt his hand, felt his strength drag me forward when I would have lain down and died, and I knew he'd never been there. He was still in the house, looking for someone or something he would never find.

The gate of the crypt was locked. I sat with my face against the bars, swallowing sips of air while smoke poured out around me, watching the house burn in the night and collapse and then transform into a whirlwind of fire that lifted up and up, covering the sky, while in the distance futile sirens screamed their aching slow progress through wood and field only to watch it burn from a safe distance, helpless to stop it, miles from the nearest hydrant.

It reminded me of something I had forgotten, buried most of my life, only now to recall in stupefying clarity. I remembered the first time I saw a ghost. I must have been four or five years old. The terror of that vision was my earliest clear memory of anything.

It was Christmas and we were staying with my mother's sister, who lived in Mountain Home, Arkansas. I was looking out an upstairs window when I saw a man standing next to the mailbox by the road. Somehow I knew he was dead. I screamed and screamed, but when they pulled me away from the window, they couldn't see him. They thought I was having a fit (later they would take me to the doctor, but this was an ill that had no cure).

They put me to bed in my aunt's bedroom and later that night she came in to talk to me. She asked me about the man and I described him—short, thin and dark, wearing a hospital gown. She nodded and said, *Yes, that's him,* without ever explaining what she meant. She lay down beside me in the dark and fell asleep holding my hand, and during the night she woke me up, pulling me out of bed because the house was on fire. I watched my father and uncle carry the furniture out of the house while the upper story burned, ashes and cinders falling like snowflakes all around and setting little fires in the dry grass. We made a game of stomping them out.

There was nobody to carry furniture out of Deacon's house. There was no furniture to carry, nothing worth saving. Priceless, two-hundred-year-old chestnut beams and planks and molding, dry as snake's breath, burned like fireworks.

During the night, the Opossum Paul crawled through the bars and curled up in my lap. As dry as the summer had been and as hot as the fire had burned, somehow it didn't spread into the woods, probably because Deacon had cleared all the underbrush from around the house. Otherwise the whole forest might have gone up and saved Luther the trouble of bulldozing it. Otherwise, Paul and I would have been baked like blackbirds in a crypt with the bones of Luther's forgotten ancestors.

45

*A dream, all a dream, that ends
in nothing, and leaves the
sleeper where he lay down.*
—CHARLES DICKENS, A TALE
OF TWO CITIES

HOLLY DISCOVERED ME AROUND nine o'clock the
next morning. I don't know how. She was clutching a
blanket as though she knew just where to find me. "Oh Jacqueline," she cried when she saw me, speaking with that soft
French "J" that sounded so beautiful and yet so full of despair.
She passed the blanket through the bars of the gate.

They couldn't get fire trucks close enough to the house to
put out the fire. They didn't have hoses long enough to reach
the hydrants on the highway. Senator Mickelson had funneled
ten million dollars through Congress to build a paramilitary

force to guard his gated mansion, while the county was still re-lying on volunteer firefighters driving thirty-year-old second-hand trucks. Rescuing me from the crypt finally gave them something to do. Holly led them to me. I recognized some of the firemen from last April, when they came to fish Sam Loftin's body from the lake. They recognized me, too, but we didn't hug.

Luther brought the key, unlocked the gate and rolled back the stone. Holly helped me through the woods back to Jenny's house. She hugged me close, her arm tight around my shoulders. "Now you and me are just alike," she said. "We have both gone through fire and been resurrected."

It wasn't even August yet. The grass was dead and brown, but the lawn services were out mowing the levee anyway, throwing up clouds of choking red dust. Jenny met us at the door of her house, folded me into her arms and held on, rocking and moaning. Holly guided us inside and into the kitchen, where she attempted to prepare breakfast as though nothing in the world was wrong. She poured me a cup of coffee and put the cup in the refrigerator and set the hot coffee carafe on the table. Then she cracked three eggs into the sink before she knew what she was doing. She stood there looking at the eggs in the sink. "Oh Lord. Look what I done." She tried to laugh, but it was more of a whimper. She washed the eggs down the drain, then picked the shells out and tossed them in the garbage. Cassie sat by the fireplace and cried.

Everybody was a wreck except me.

Later in the day the fire marshal stopped by with Sheriff Stegall to interview me. It was just a routine procedure, he assured me, but an investigation was required since the fire had resulted in a fatality. According to me, anyway. They hadn't found a body yet. "We're still looking," he said as he patted my hand.

I didn't know men still looked like Fred Mertz. He wore his fireman's coveralls with big strapping suspenders stretched crosswise over his belly, a smear of soot across the bridge of his nose and up the outside of his right forearm to his elbow.

Jenny and I hadn't talked yet. I hadn't told her what happened. It was too soon. She asked the fire marshal if he had any idea how the fire started. "Well," he growled in a friendly way, "that old house, it just went up like a box of matches. But it's been my experience, thirty years putting out fires in this county, that when you have a fire starting late at night upstairs, it's usually somebody smoking in bed." He shot me a quick side-eye that said, *Ain't that right, Ethel?*

I hated to disappoint his thirty years of experience. "We were firebombed."

Stegall stepped from the kitchen, half a chocolate cake falling out of his mouth. Fred did his famous double take. Jenny gripped my hand.

"Molotov cocktail through the bedroom window." I made a sound like breaking glass. "Another one in the hall. Woosh. Downstairs, too. Front porch. Back door." Thinking about the fire seemed to rekindle it in my flesh. My skin felt tight and dry, like an old glove left out in the sun.

Sheriff and marshal exchanged a worried glance. Malvern was a small town and its officers liked nice easy investigations where they didn't have to wait for the ruins or the bodies to get cold. They liked going home to supper at six o'clock Monday through Friday. They liked suicides and people smoking in bed and events that could be explained from a nice safe distance.

Fred took his notepad from his shirt pocket and licked a pencil. "What time was that?"

I didn't know the time. I wasn't wearing a watch. It was late. He put his notebook in his shirt pocket and leaned back in the chair, creaking the wood with his weight. "Renovating these old houses," he said, thumbing his bracers, "I've seen it a hundred times. All kinds of accelerants laying around, paint thinner, mineral oil, piles of rags. Add some old wiring and a little carelessness . . ." He shrugged.

"There wasn't any electricity in the house."

"A house will go up so fast, it's easy to think it's been fire-bombed."

I sighed and pressed my fists between the cushions of the couch. "I saw the bottle come through the window and break on the floor."

"Fire gets so hot, it blows out the windows," Stegall added helpfully.

"I've heard houses groan and scream, just like somebody was dying inside it," the fat old man said. "It's downright creepy. It's just hot gases escaping, but it makes you wonder sometimes. You never really know until you find the bones."

I wondered if they would ever find Deacon's bones. There was nothing left of the house, nothing but a smoking white moonscape between two crooked, blackened brick chimneys rising impossibly slender from the ash. It had burned up even the largest beams.

"There's just one more thing," Fred said, leaning forward and putting his fat, sooty hand on my knee. "Why didn't Mr. Falgoust escape with you?"

The next night, Jenny and the kids were all safely ensconced in their beds, already able to sleep again, already getting on with their lives. I returned to the scene of my resurrection, walked between the headstones white in the moonlight, and the shaggy cedar trees blacker than the night itself, my feet shuffling through drifts of brown needles dry as the still-smoking ash of Deacon's pyre. All the normal human superstitions had been burned out of me over the years, like an overexposed photograph. I had seen too much human meat, photographed too many murders and accidents and suicides, gone home too many times with the smell of them lingering in my clothes and woke up too many mornings with their blood dried to the soles of my Buster Brown shoes. A person can grow accustomed to any-thing. I found it far too easy to imagine Deacon's disarticu-lated bones sprawled six feet below my toes, too easy to visualize the ultimate ruination of a man. I tried not to think about it. I tried not to think about him coughing out the last breath of life as the black smoke lowered and the flames crept up his legs, nobody there to hear and remember his last words, nobody to deliver a last message to his flock of saints or even the woman or women he loved.

None of it mattered. Look at John Vardry, dead these sev-enty years in his dead wife's crypt. Lying among his bones the bits of shrapnel and German lead that put a swift end to his life. John Vardry, one of seventy-two million people killed in that war. Seventy-two million—a number too enormous to comprehend. Think of that many bodies stacked up. It beggars belief. Their bones would fill a hundred Superdomes. But was the world diminished one jot, one tittle by their loss? John Vardry had sired Luther Vardry and by extension this whole land and this whole situation, even me, standing here in a graveyard with nothing and no one to mourn.

That's all that mattered. The world would go on, but for me, it had stopped when I looked between the bars of the crypt gate and watched the burning house collapse upon itself and the fire go up like a whirlwind from hell. The world had not turned for me since that moment. I was frozen in that instant, like a phantasm endlessly repeating. A hundred years from now I'll still be sitting in that crypt, staring through the bars, and maybe the people living here might feel a cold spot in the air where my heart once hung, or maybe they would hear the hollow keening of my voice and tell themselves *It's the wind, only the wind, my dear, go back to sleep.*

Grief itself must leave a ghost. I was already that ghost, blind to the world's continuing revolutions. Two solid days of bone-deep grief had done that to me, worn me down like an old tooth. I hardly felt alive. My heart was an empty sack, still beating.

I didn't know what else to do. I looked up at the weak, hazy stars. *If only it would rain,* I thought. *Everything is dying. If only it would rain and wash it all away.*

I crawled back to Jenny's house in the dark and out to the end of the boat dock beneath the bug-swirled lamp. I stood there for I don't know how long, standing until I could stand no more, until I sank to the deck and sat with my feet dangling over the water, rubbing the crusty edges of hunger and exhaustion against the file of my grief until the file was dull and smooth, and I fell asleep and slept nearly six hours and woke with the sun baking my already baked face red as a beret.

I entered the kitchen and found Jenny standing at the stove watching a pot boil. Her hair was pulled up in a banana clip with a few wet strands of blond hair dangling in her face. "Have you eaten?" she asked over her shoulder.

"No."

"Sit down and let me fix you something."

"I'm not hungry," I said. "What are you doing?"

She turned back to the stove and adjusted the flame under the pot. "Parboiling peas so I can freeze them." She had been to the farmers' market.

"That's not what I meant," I said.

"I know what you mean, Jackie." She moved things around on the counter—a ladle, the lid of the pot, a shaker of salt, nervously rearranging them. "I'm doing the only thing I know how to do. I've been through this twice already. The only thing to do is to keep going. Try to keep busy." She seemed to have grown smaller somehow, older. She looked frail, with her face sweaty from the steam. She wasn't wearing any makeup, and I couldn't recall a time when Jenny wasn't wearing her face after nine in the morning.

She rested her elbows on the edge of the sink and stared

out the window at the sunburned grass of the back lawn. "Go upstairs, take a shower and get some sleep. We're going to church tonight."

"Church!" I said, incredulous. "Why tonight?" She knew what I was thinking. More and more, she seemed to always know.

"We can't have a funeral, so Luther is doing a memorial service for Deacon."

I dragged myself upstairs, but I knew I'd never be able to sleep. I sat in a chair by the window and watched Sam do his familiar old dance on the levee, over and over. *What the hell are you trying to tell me?*

He wasn't trying to tell me anything. He really was just a broken record, worse than useless because all it did was remind me of what I could no longer hear. Like the photos full of orbs, reflections of light off dust motes. All destroyed in the fire.

Downstairs Jenny was making lunch for her kids. Holly was swimming laps in the pool, Nathan sitting on the edge of the pool with a stopwatch. Sometimes I knew what it felt like to be a ghost, to sit on the edge of other people's lives, unheard and unseen, often unsuspected, watching people come and go, unable to participate in the simplest human interaction—a touch, a kind word—never again belonging anywhere or with anyone. I still didn't believe in Deacon's idea of Jesus or redemption, heaven or hell, but if there was a hell, this was it. It must grieve the dead most to know how swiftly we forget them.

I couldn't stay with Jenny any longer. My reason for being

there had burned to the ground. I couldn't go with them to Deacon's memorial and listen to that old man tell his lies. I had attended too many funerals already.

I slipped out of the house while they were eating lunch by the pool. The grass in the yard was brittle beneath my naked soles, the cedar boughs turning brown as though sprayed with herbicide by a leaky crop duster. The heat off the street was swollen and vampiric, baking the last life from the weeds growing along the verge and from anything that dared cross. I crossed, oblivious to the heat, worn out to my bones, aching in body and soul.

I went back to take a last look at the ruin in the light of day. The chimneys had fallen, one across the other. Crime scene tape was strung through the silent woods like confetti after a New Year's Eve party. Deacon's saints were gone, their camp as empty as if it had never been.

I went home to pack. They had gone to church, the house was empty, supper sitting on the stove. Even though I wasn't hungry, I picked up the plate and took it into the den, turned on the television and sat down with the plate in my lap—baked chicken in some kind of cold white sauce, cold steamed broccoli, glutinous beans with onions and peppers. I tasted nothing while I clicked through the channels, finding nothing, until there was nothing, just darkness and silence and at long last sleep.

46

I WOKE WITH THE FEELING THAT someone had touched my face. I sat up in the dark. My supper plate had been put away and a blanket spread over me while I lay unconscious on the couch. The grandfather clock in the hall chimed twice.

It was agony to move, a trial of will just to lift an arm, every breath a deliberate act. Yet somehow I managed to stand and stagger to the kitchen, where I found the keys to Jenny's van. I had just one thought, one desire—somewhere out there on the streets of Memphis was a score to end all scores. I knew how I would do it. Not by drowning or hanging and certainly not by way of a bullet. My old friend, Mr. Brownstone. We'd been apart too long and that was no way to treat such a dear friend.

I dragged myself up the stairs, hand over hand, to gather what little money I had from pockets and drawers, enough to buy enough smack to stop my heart one last time. At the top I stumbled over Jenny sitting on the top step in her lavender housecoat, silent and still as a cat, her arms wrapped around her knees, long blond hair spread over her shoulders and back.

"I know you hurt," she said. "Trust me, I know. But when the people we love die, we don't have the luxury of falling apart. Not when others are depending on us."

"I can't, Jenny."

"You have to."

"*You* have to. I don't have to."

"Dammit Jackie, you were a detective."

The strangeness of her declaration was like a dash of cold water down my back. It made me stand up straight, asshole puckered. "So?"

"So . . . go detect something. Investigate. Find out who did this." She meant Deacon. She didn't know I'd spent the last two months trying to prove her husband had been molesting her daughter. I was glad I never shared my suspicions with her, because I'd been as wrong as a person could be. I'd been wrong about everything.

I said, "I don't know anything about fire investigations."

"All you need to know is who wanted Deacon dead." She got up and walked down the hall, stopped at her bedroom door and turned on the light. "That's why you're here, Jackie. That's why you have to go on. You owe it to Deacon."

Let the dead bury the dead, I thought, but I mustered enough genuine sincerity to say, "Good night."

"I'll see you in the morning." She entered her bedroom and closed the door. I heard the click of the light switch as the light under her door winked out.

Sleep had left me again, maybe never to return. I stood at Reece's door, paused in the act of opening it because just as I touched the knob I heard a thump on the other side. I stood at the door with my hand on the knob, afraid to open it, afraid for the first time in my life of what I might find looking back at me from the other side. Not Reece. I was afraid I'd open the door and find Deacon waiting there. He'd want to know what I was waiting for. *I owed it to him,* Jenny said.

I walked back downstairs and sat on the couch until dawn slid up the sky, my mind crawling through every fact I knew, every guess, every theory, trying to find something that tied it all together. Two men were dead—Sam and Deacon. How were their murders connected?

Sam's murder seemed obvious enough. He had found out something he wasn't supposed to know. Maybe he was killed by the guy who molested his daughter and drove her to suicide. But if that were true, why kill Deacon? If Sam had told Deacon before he died, Deacon would have settled that bill long before I arrived on the scene.

Maybe it had something to do with the finances for the homeowners' association. I remembered the question Deacon had asked that night at the meeting. *How did they spend all those HOA fees? A little landscaping? The senator's Coon Supper?* What if Sam found out the money was going somewhere else?

Then there were Sam's finances. Spending cash that had no source. Was Sam the one skimming HOA fees? Or was he part of a team of grifters? Did he grow a conscience and threaten to expose his accomplices?

What did Deacon know? Far more than he ever told me. I'd never know what Sam told Deacon before he died, whether he confessed to stealing or exposed those who were. What I did know was this—with Deacon dead, there was no one to contest Ruth's will. All her money and all her land would go to Luther Vardry.

Luther Vardry was the president of the HOA.

Luther Vardry grew up here and knew the area, including the woods, as well as anybody.

Luther Vardry, seventy-odd years old, couldn't have killed Sam Loftin. He couldn't have hurled Molotov cocktails through the second-floor windows of Ruth's plantation house. He was physically incapable of the murders of either man.

It had to be somebody else. Someone with the same motive and the same opportunity, plus the means to accomplish the deeds. Someone with a good throwing arm and huge chip on his shoulder, someone who already hated Deacon enough to kill him, even if Luther didn't personally order his murder. The kind of man who could interpret the cries of the king and take a baseball bat to the head of a meddlesome priest.

Too easy, but it was the only thing that fit the facts.

But as the sun crept in through the windows, one fact threw a shadow over the whole thing. The fact was, I had no facts. Just a bunch of theories linking together a trail of coincidences. Theorizing on coincidences had nearly led me to accuse Sam Loftin of abusing his daughter. Luther Vardry had the money and the local power to take Ruth's property, no matter what her will said. He didn't need to kill Deacon to destroy him. All he needed were his lawyers and his connections.

I lowered the shades and clicked on the television, flipped through the early-morning news programs looking for something to dull my mind and maybe send me back to sleep. Instead, I found a movie, a movie I hadn't seen in years—*Taxi Driver.* The scene was where twelve-year-old Jodie Foster and her pimp are dancing alone in her apartment. The pimp's talking to her, whispering vomit-inducing sweet nothings into her hair as he holds her close, rocking side to side. *I'm the luckiest man in the world.* I had to turn up the volume to hear the rest of it. *No man alive ever had a woman who loved him the way you love me.* These were Nastyboy's words, word for word, written to Reece.

I watched the whole movie, looking for anything that might help me find him. All I found was a fresh desire to hunt down the bastard who raped that little girl and go all Travis Bickle on him. I'd have given anything for that kind of catharsis, that kind of purity of purpose.

But life isn't like the movies. Not even the ones that are more lifelike than anybody wants to know.

47

I VEGETATED IN FRONT OF THE television half the day, ignoring every good-morning, every offer of diversion and conversation, every call to breakfast and then to lunch. Holly wandered through at midmorning and I rebuffed her attempts to become soul sisters of the vestal fire. Nathan sat beside me for a while and tried to interest me in buying his camera and taking off my clothes. I watched the clock count down on the floor-mop deal of a lifetime.

The noon news came on. There was a report about the fire in which a local preacher was believed to have died. "Fire investigators have stated," the reporter repeated, "the blaze began in an upstairs bedroom and that smoking was involved."

They cut to Fred the Fire Marshal in his dress uniform. I didn't know volunteer firefighters had dress uniforms. "We believe the fire is the result of someone, perhaps the victim, smoking in bed." The body of the victim, whose name had not yet been released, had not been found at the time of the report.

My phone, like everything else, had burned up in that blaze, so I used Jenny's to call Lorio. He apologized for not stopping

by. He'd been very busy. His superiors had him directing traffic at road-construction sites. I bet him I knew why, but he
didn't bite. "I haven't heard from Wiley, but they only exhumed
Sam yesterday."

"Give him a call, just the same," I said.

He promised he would.

They had covered up Sam's cause of death. Now they were
covering up Deacon's. The two were connected somehow. I
hoped, once Wiley did his job, I'd have more than theories and
coincidences. Until then, there was nothing to do but wait.

I was prepared to wait. I had nothing else in the world but
time.

I found an egg salad sandwich on a plate in the fridge and
heard water rushing in the pipes from Jenny filling the bathtub upstairs. I stood at the sink eating the sandwich, looking out
the window at the pool. Cassie stood in the pool near the steps,
Holly sunned herself on a towel behind her. Nathan floated on
his back with his package breaking the water like a half-
submerged bicycle tire. I went upstairs and put on a swimsuit.

Nathan was swimming laps by the time I stepped outside.
Holly had rolled over on her belly. "Hey, Aunt Jackie," Cassie
said. I dove into the deep end and let my momentum carry me to
the shallow, where I glided up beside her. Her brown legs
looked pale because of the greenness of the water. Her pink bikini bottom was little more than two triangles held together
by shoestrings, her feet flat and dainty and wrinkled, with their
wrinkled white soles turned out slightly.

Nathan turned and pushed off the wall. I saw him coming
up from the deeper green haze of the deep end, like some hairy

leviathan, shafts of light playing over his back. He rose to the surface as he reached the shallows and found the bottom with his feet. Cassie climbed the stair and got out of the water. Water dripped from her body and from the ends of her hair. Her bare feet slapped across the hot concrete. She snatched a towel from the brick wall and began to dry herself, her legs, her hair, tilting her head to shake the water from her ear.

Nathan followed her out of the pool. He toweled off, then got his camera from the bag under the window. Holly moved to a deck chair and Cassie sat down between her long legs. Nathan sat in the chair beside them and dried his hair.

I sank to the bottom for a while, holding my breath, waiting for something, I didn't know what. Then I knew. I turned around and the girl in the red bikini was lying on the bottom in the deep end. Cassie must have already seen her.

When I came up again, Nathan was telling them how pretty they were and shooting close-ups of Holly. She turned her head this way and that, flipped her hair over her shoulder, shifted her sunglasses down her nose, pouted. "Don't you think Holly is pretty?" he asked.

Cassie said she was. He asked if he could take their picture together.

She glanced at me. He took a step back and shot a couple of pictures, then lowered his camera. "What about that smile?"

She pulled her feet up and wrapped her arms around her knees. I was shocked by how much she looked like her sister. Cassie was about the same age as Reece had been in the youngest photos. "I don't feel like smiling," she said.

"Why not?"

"Because Aunt Jackie is leaving."

He turned to me. "Are you leaving?"

How had she known? Maybe her friend from the fireplace told her. "I'm not going anywhere," I said. "I'm having too much fun."

He moved around to Cassie's side of the deck chair. "Come on, smile for me sweetheart. Smile like Holly. Don't you want to be pretty like Holly?"

I climbed out of the pool, picked up my towel and sat in Nathan's chair. Cassie switched chairs and sat beside me holding my hand. Hers was trembling. "I wish you wouldn't go," she said.

"Now I've got three beautiful girls." Nathan moved over to photograph us. Cassie turned her head away from him. As he knelt at the end of the deck chair to photograph her, I could see his tight black Speedo tightening across the hardening swell between his tanned, muscular legs. And just above that, the hair on his belly rising like a curl of gray smoke from the waistband, a curl in the shape of a question mark. He blew a kiss at Cassie and said, "You're so much prettier when you smile, little pig."

It was like a curtain parted, not just revealing the screen behind the curtain, but also the fact that I was sitting alone in a dark, empty theater. I held on to the arms of the chair to keep from falling out. Nathan had destroyed Reece, and now he was hunting Cassie. I thought of how many times over the last three months we had left him alone with her in the pool. How many times he had taken her for joy rides on his boat, or tucked her into bed at night.

"Smile, Aunt Jackie," Nathan said.

I pulled back my lips. I'm sure I looked like the mother of death, but Nathan liked it enough to reach down and give himself a little squeeze so I could see him do it.

"How about I stand up?" I said.

"OK."

I stood and turned slightly, rising up on my toes, showing him my back and the curve of my ass. He groaned happily and brushed himself against my leg while moving to get a better angle to shoot. When his face was behind the camera snapping away, I grabbed him by the elbows and shoved him into the pool, camera and all.

Holly jumped out of her chair. "What the hell!"

I grabbed an empty beer bottle and got ready to bean him the next time he came up for air, but he didn't come up. He was sinking toward the bottom, slowly flailing his arms. His camera floated free of his hand and drifted away.

I dove in and found Nathan pinned to the bottom of the pool by the girl in the red one-piece. Her arms and legs were wrapped lovingly around him, her chin on his shoulder as she stuck the black worm of her rotting tongue in his ear.

As I swam down to them, she frowned at me and released Nathan, but his eyes were starting to glaze over. I grabbed him by the back of the Speedos, kicked off the bottom and dragged him to the shallow end. He was a big guy, but I managed it.

I flipped him over. Thankfully I didn't have to give him mouth-to-mouth, because as soon as the air touched his face, he vomited out a lung full of water and struggled to his feet, coughing, spluttering and livid.

"Cassie, go inside right now," I shouted. Holly grabbed her hand and they both hurried into the house.

Still coughing, Nathan said, "What the fuck! You were trying to kill me!"

"I think I was saving your worthless life. Prick."

"After you shoved me in the pool!" He looked back at the dark spot resting on the bottom at the deep end. "My camera!"

"Sorry about that." I truly was. Any incriminating pictures that might have been on the camera were lost.

"It cost over seven thousand dollars!" Mad as he was, he didn't go diving for it. He stood looking at it, shivering slightly even though it was hot enough outside to melt the lead from your fillings. "I thought for a second somebody was holding me down."

"You shouldn't go swimming by yourself." I climbed out of the pool. He followed me to the ladder. I stopped with my hands on the rails, blocking him. "You took those pictures of Reece, you sick fuck."

He paused, halfway up, and brushed the wet hair out of his eyes. "What are you talking about?"

"I've seen them, Nathan." He got quiet, staring up at me with enough ice in his eyes to freeze the pool solid. "Reece printed them out, left them for somebody to find. You seduced that little girl and broke her heart so bad she killed herself."

He grinned and pulled himself up the ladder. "Fucking cunt. You don't know jack shit about anything."

"I've also read your messages. You never should have sent her that picture of your willy. It's all I need to get a search warrant . . . Nastyboy."

"Crazy fucking bitch," he laughed as he wrapped a towel around his waist.

"Why don't you show it to me now, Nastyboy, and save us both the trouble?"

"You'd like that, whore. But you'll pay for that camera, one way or another."

"Why don't you call the cops on me. Go ahead. Assault. Felony criminal mischief. If you hang around a bit, I'm sure I can think of something else to do to you."

After exchanging several more empty promises, he headed for the boat dock. Tossing the towel into a seat, he started the engine and gunned it, lurching the boat away from the dock, then turned far out on the lake and came roaring back, spraying a rooster tail forty feet long and flipping me the bird, his last great act of defiance.

I was completely crushed.

I went inside to dry off and put on some clothes. Jenny met me outside Cassie's door. "What happened?" I could hear Cassie inside, bawling her eyes out. I wondered if she was already in love with Nathan, if it was already too late for her. "Holly was furious. She couldn't even talk. She left."

I couldn't tell Jenny yet, not until I got my head wrapped around this and sorted it out. Things were starting to fall into place like a good game of solitaire, but I still had a jack or two that needed revealing. "I got a little mad at Nathan and shoved him in the pool."

"Oh," she said, grinning. She didn't bother asking and for the moment I let her fill in the details herself. She knew Nathan well enough to know he probably deserved it.

But she didn't really know him at all, and I was only beginning to find out.

48

AN HONEST-TO-GOD BUTLER LET ME in Luther's front door, not some personal assistant, not a house-keeper—a real Jeeves type, black tie, white gloves, long nose for looking down at people, only he was about twenty-three years old and looked like he'd just stepped down from an Elgin Marble. I hadn't seen him at the Coon Supper, but maybe he had the day off. I wiped my shoes on the rug and stepped inside, wishing I had found a dog turd to step in before I got there. I would have to remember next time.

I handed young Jeevesy a plain brown envelope. "What's this?" he asked.

"My card. Tell Luther I wish to see him."

"The reverend is a very busy man."

"Tell His Reverence to pull his little pastor out of Eugene's pulpit and come down here. It's about his son, Nathan."

He took the envelope and glided away, the starch in his slacks whispering like a confessional. I wandered into Luther's library, cracked open a few cabinets until I found his secret bottle and poured myself four fingers of giant killer into the jelly jar he kept with his stash. Luther seemed to be in no hurry. I lit a cigarette, took a couple of puffs and breathed smoke into the four corners of the room. His window had a fine view of the sun setting over the lake, and the woods dark as a storm cloud over the horizon. From here Luther might have witnessed Sam's murder. From here, he could have watched the fire that burned down his mother's home and freed him from a lengthy and expensive court battle with a meddlesome priest.

I glanced at a passage Luther had marked in the Bible that lay open on his desk. This must have been his private Bible, because he had underlined all the naughty parts in Genesis, Judges, Song of Solomon.

Yet she became more and more promiscuous as she recalled the days of her youth, when she was a prostitute in Egypt. There she lusted after her lovers, whose genitals were like those of donkeys and whose emission was like that of horses. So you longed for the lewdness of your youth, when in Egypt your bosom was caressed and your young breasts fondled.

"I wonder if you noticed that there are no ashtrays in my house?" Luther said as he entered the library. He batted faintly at my smoke. Dear old Jeevesy closed the doors behind him. "Ezekiel, chapter twenty-three. I was planning to read it at Mother's funeral, until Deacon hogged the show."

She would have liked that. She would have liked Luther's whiskey, too. "Nice hooch. Expensive stuff. Who buys it for you?"

Frowning primly, he dusted off his good book and closed it, tucked it away in the same drawer where I found his whiskey. When he turned back around, he had my calling card in his pudgy hand. I could tell by the torn flap of the envelope that he had opened it.

"You wanted to see me about something?" A normal man would have feigned outrage and revulsion, demanding I explain myself. He knew what those photos meant. All that remained was to determine how much I knew. I already knew how much he knew. He was up to his stiff neck in it.

I took a deep puff and blew the smoke his way. "You saw those pictures?"

He coughed slightly and turned his head to one side. "What have they to do with me?"

"Your son was the photographer."

"You can't prove that." He waved the envelope at the smoke. "Just a bunch of cheap printouts. Anybody could have taken them. Sam . . ."

"Ah, yes, Sam," I interrupted. "Well, I thought of that already. Then, I thought to myself, people would pay a lot of money for pictures like this." I knocked back another swallow of his whiskey. I'd tasted its kind once before, out of Mrs. Ruth's flask.

"Dirty old men, for instance. And dirty young men. This afternoon I did a little digging around. Google's a wonderful thing, you know. It didn't take me long to find those same photographs for sale on a website. A dirty little website that charges twenty bucks a month to join and obtain access to all the photographs of the underage models."

"I fail to see what any of this has to do with me," he said. He opened the top drawer of a Louis XVI semainier and dropped the envelope inside, closed the drawer and crossed to the window. It was mostly dark outside by now, just the lights at the end of Luther's pier shining on the lake.

"This website sells photographs of nubile young models like Reece Loftin, Mercedes LaGrance and her sisters, even your own daughter Holly. Plus a lot of other girls whose names I don't know. But I bet you know their names."

Still staring out the window, fingers laced behind his back. "Baptists don't gamble."

"You don't drink either," I said as I topped off my glass from his bottle. "The owner of this website is one Nathan Vardry. I believe you are familiar with *him*?"

"What do you want?" Luther asked.

"Your son seduced one or more of these girls. I know because I've seen his messages to Reece Loftin. I've seen how he played her. He abused her at some point. Eventually she killed herself."

"You have not explained yet how Nathan broke any laws. You say he abused this girl . . ." This girl, daughter of his neighbor and supposed friend, whose name he now would not pronounce. This nameless girl, an object to be ridden and thrown away like an old broom.

". . . but you have no proof, no photographs or videos of the act, just messages on a computer."

And the only witness conveniently dead these five years. I was beginning to wonder if her death had been a suicide after all.

"Nor have you explained, despite my repeated requests, how any of this concerns me." Luther turned and leaned against the windowsill. "This is your last opportunity to do so before I have you thrown out."

"Even if none of the pictures are technically pornographic, these are underaged girls we're talking about. Nathan can't sell their photos without the signed consent of their parents."

He pulled out his desk chair and sat, leaned back into the fat, creaking leather, steepled his fingers across his belly, smiled. "Oh dear. Publishing photos without the consent of their parents. With such a Sword of Damocles hanging over his head, how will Nathan go on? Why, if it were brought to trial, and I can assure you he'll never see the inside of a courtroom concerning this, he might get ninety days playing tennis in a minimum-security prison. Are you prepared to risk everything in a futile effort to accomplish his doom?"

"Accomplish his doom?" I said, more in shock than wonder. Who talked like that?

He chuckled and shook his head in bemusement. "Surely you know what I mean."

I did, only too well. But I wanted him to spell it out.

"You do this and I'll destroy both of you. Jenny will lose her house and everything she owns. Sam was swindling the HOA, stealing hundreds of thousands of dollars, and I can prove it. I offered him the opportunity to pay it back. He chose to kill himself instead. The HOA will sue Jenny to recover those funds. She'll lose everything."

Tiny beads of sweat lined themselves up along the top of his pencil-thin mustache. It was hot outside, but the library was deliciously cool. I swallowed a gulp of his whiskey and asked, "And how will you *accomplish my doom,* Luther?"

"If the police were to search your belongings, might they not find illegal drugs?"

"No doubt Stegall could plant something incriminating. Proving it would be another matter. I used to be a cop, you know."

"Used to be," he reminded me. "Your past is against you, my dear. So you see, calling the police in this matter would be detrimental to us all. I'd much rather we settled it personally, so that we may part as friends."

"Friends?" I didn't know we were friends. Maybe he wanted to make friends, but I didn't think his door swung that direction.

"The Bible tells us in Paul's first letter to the Corinthians, *'If any of you has a dispute with another, dare he take it before the ungodly for judgment instead of before the saints?'* I said that I could destroy you. I could also make you."

He opened a desk drawer and took out a large checkbook and a bejeweled silver pen in the shape of a large cross. "This discussion doesn't have to go beyond my door. Do you understand?" He began to write.

"I think I do." I finished off the glass of whiskey and dropped my cigarette into the dregs. "What about Jenny?"

He spoke slowly as he carefully spelled out my name on the check. "Jenny Loftin will be taken care of. She will find a new business partner, a competent partner who will make the business prosper. They will never want for customers, customers who will pay premium prices. Her children will go to the best schools and colleges. Senator Mickelson is a friend of mine and a Harvard man. If Eli or Cass want to go to Harvard, West Point, Annapolis, we can make that happen." He signed his name and carefully tore the check out of the book, folded it once and slid it with his fingertips across the desk.

Annapolis. I wondered if that's how Roy Stegall got his commission. All these bastards were attached at the hip. I picked up the check. "What about Nathan?"

"I'll see he gets the treatment he needs. He'll spend a long time in the hospital. You can be sure of that."

"Is that what you promised Sam?"

He cleared his throat and tapped his fingers on the desk two or three times. "I don't know what you mean."

"When Sam discovered Nathan had *known* his daughter." The check was blank. I could fill in any amount I wanted. I pulled out my pack of smokes, shook the last one out and stuck it in my mouth. "*Known* her in the Biblical sense. Did you promise him Nathan would go to a hospital?"

He coughed in anticipation. "I wish you wouldn't smoke in here."

I patted my pockets, looking for a lighter.

"Yes, to answer your question, Nathan did go to the hospital and he did receive treatment. Sam was wise enough to accept my gifts and the business I sent his way. Perhaps you've noticed that Sam's company does all the groundskeeping and landscaping here at Stirling? That's no accident."

So Sam must have figured the damage to his daughter was already done. Maybe he wanted to save her from the further humiliation of a trial. Or maybe he wanted to cash in. Jenny told me Sam had been out of work for a year when he started his landscaping business. Luther made sure the business was successful, probably gave him the capital to get it off the ground. Sam might even have been blackmailing him.

Even so, Reece had to know her father had found out about Nathan, and that he'd made a deal with the devil in exchange for their silence. Reece had to know because Sam had to make sure she never told anyone. Once word got out, that would violate the terms of their covenant.

I lit the cigarette dangling from my lip, then touched Luther's check to the lighter's flame. I dropped it into the empty jelly glass. The residual alcohol ignited and the check vanished in a hot blue incandescence.

49

LIGHTNING BLOOMED AND DIED all along the western horizon, dimly flickering orange and pink mushrooms feathered by broken veins of brighter light, as though I had landed on some alien planet. If it didn't rain, there'd be fires for sure.

As I crossed the levee, I thought about the lives I'd ruined. I couldn't even go home and tell Jenny why she was about to lose everything, not without revealing the truth about Sam and Reece. Not the horrible truth I'd previously suspected, but horrible all the same.

Her house had become a home to me, a refuge I had not known since the day I left my mother's house. Maybe even before that. I'd never had a haven in my marriage—my house, even then, had been nothing more than a space I occupied during my off hours. Seeing Jenny's house rising at the far end of the levee with its windows aglow with warm yellow light, the steep angles of its dark roof rising against the storm-flecked sky, I wanted to run to it, embrace it, crawl inside it and never leave again. I wanted to make its children my children, its life my life, its ghosts my ghosts; to leave behind the endless scraping and scrabbling uncertainty of a drug-addicted part-time photographer of the dead and dying and become something approaching a normal human being, with a life and a reason to wake up in the morning. But just when I'd found this life and started to learn to love it, I had lost it. I had lost Deacon. I was about to lose the only real home I'd ever known. I could have had it all, just by taking Luther's check.

Instead, I'd burned it, and with it my future and Jenny's future and the future of her kids. Burning bridges was my speciality. Too bad I wasn't born fifty years earlier; I might have had a promising career as a saboteur in some leftist uprising. I hadn't even stopped to ask Jenny what she wanted. She might have taken Luther's check. She couldn't feed her children with moral outrage. Sam had made his choice, and I was beginning to wonder if maybe he hadn't made the right choice after all. He couldn't turn back the clock, but he could take compensation. And protection.

My footsteps slowed as I reached the place where Sam died. How many times had he stood here, looking down into the dark water that took his daughter, grief eating away at him, rotting him from the inside, like mold behind the wainscoting? How many times had he walked this path, coming home with Luther's filthy money padding his pockets? No wonder he hid it in the attic. He probably couldn't bear to look at it. Maybe Sam stashed Luther's money with the pictures of his daughter so that every time he made a withdrawal, he had to look at what it bought. Probably he blamed himself for her suicide.

He should have.

The day I found him in the water, his pockets hadn't been weighed down with thirty pieces of silver. He'd been coming home across the levee. From where? I looked back at Luther's house, and if I squinted hard enough I could almost see the old murderer standing at his library window. What happened that morning? Had Luther shut off the spigot? Did Sam threaten to expose their embezzlement of the HOA fees?

Or had he discovered something new? Had he discovered Nastyboy's young-models website and seen that Nathan was now posting and selling photos of his youngest daughter, Cassie?

A gust of wind came up and blew hard and strong for almost a minute, pinning my slacks against my legs. As it died down, a voice behind me said, "Looks like it's about to blow up a salcoon."

"Heard from Wiley?" I asked Lorio.

"Yeah."

Another gust ripped across the lake, bringing a smell of fishy rot.

"Give me your flashlight," I said. He handed it over and I climbed down the rocks to the water's edge.

"Sam was struck on the head by a smooth, blunt instrument," he said. "Care to take a guess what it was?"

"I'd say a rock."

"He fell on some rocks before he went in the water."

I shined the flashlight at the rough limestone boulders. "These aren't smooth. They're jagged." I turned the beam on a smooth round river pebble, about the size of a grapefruit or softball, still lying where Lorio had pitched it several days ago.

The lake level had dropped another six inches, exposing a second cobble that was the twin of the first.

I dug both out of the mud and climbed the bank. Lorio took one in his hand and turned it over, then looked at me and shrugged his eyebrows. "I've seen rocks like this before." I hefted its weight and guessed about three pounds. "The murderer must have brought it with him."

"It doesn't make sense. A rock is a weapon of opportunity. Heat of the moment."

"Not if it's your weapon of choice. The one weapon you know you can kill somebody with."

"But there's two rocks," Lorio said. "Why take two rocks to bash somebody over the head?"

"In case the first one misses."

He didn't get it, and I never got a chance to explain it to him.

Neither one of us spotted Nathan coming across the levee. Lorio's back was to him and I was too busy congratulating myself on the brilliance of my deduction. By the time I saw Nathan, he was already lifting the shotgun to his shoulder. I tried to shove Lorio to the side, but he was a heavy guy, mostly muscle, and I just bounced off him. He took most of the charge in his back while I tumbled helplessly down the levee, like a doll thrown out of a car window.

I ended up on my feet at the bottom just as Nathan was swinging the gun toward me. A flash of lightning lit me up bright as day as he let loose. The elevation, or the darkness, or the sudden light, or maybe Divine Providence threw him off, because all I received was a single pellet in my left cheek.

One was more than enough. I lit out for the trees. Nathan chambered another round and blasted at me. I felt a swarm of wasps sting my backside but none of them broke skin—I was already too far away, running serpentine through the tall grass.

I had lost a shoe by the time I entered the woods, but I kept running. Sticks and stumps murdered my bare foot and wild rose vines snatched and jerked at my skin and hair and ripped my legs like whiplashes, but I kept running. I heard Nathan crashing through the woods behind me. He knew this place better than I did. He'd grown up here. I was blind in the dark. I couldn't even see the trees I was blundering into, but I kept running.

Then I remembered Lorio's flashlight. By some miracle, it was still in my hand. I clicked it on and found myself standing in a gully in the woods with trees arching completely overhead, like the roof of a church. Part of the roof had been broken through and my car hung through the hole, its tires wrapped in vines, headlights smashed, windows empty with broken glass, like small piles of diamonds, lying beneath the wheels.

My face felt swollen to twice its normal size. I touched my cheek and held my bloody fingers up to the light. The collar of my shirt was dark with blood. I heard a crunch of gravel and dove to the side but the blast hit me in the legs and spun me in the air, flinging the flashlight spinning, its beam slicing through the woods until it hit a tree and the bulb shattered into darkness. I lay on the ground beneath my car amid the broken window glass and saw a violent orange flower erupt from the barrel of the gun and light up Nathan's face.

Then I was running again, through the pain and the darkness, without even a moon to steer by, just the occasional whip of buckshot to guide and goad, until I tripped and fetched up headfirst against the trunk of a bald cypress as black and hard as the gates of hell. I rolled over and the woods were no longer dark. They were flashing with lights that illuminated nothing, ghost lights moving in and out of the ghosts of trees. I lay in a shallow muddy pool at the bottom of a crown of cypress knees, while Nathan roamed the witch fields behind me, bellowing like a castrated bull, the *blast* of his shotgun cutting through the underbrush like a million angry bees.

I closed my eyes and lay rabbit-still, hoping he would miss me in the dark, maybe give up, go home, wash the blood off his hands and pretend it never happened. I knew better but in my pain I preferred the safe fantasy this notch afforded, this moment of rest with the muddy cold against the blistering stings of buckshot peppering my legs. I knew Nathan couldn't give me up now. If he couldn't find me here, he'd look for me at Jenny's. I couldn't call her because my phone had burned up in the fire. Before long I realized something was sharing my mud pool. It felt like a snake trying to crawl up my leg, but I didn't move. If I moved, he'd find me. He was still out there, somewhere close by, stuffing fresh shells into his shotgun.

I wondered how I was still alive. He'd hit me twice, once from close range, but I knew from the intensity of the pain that he hadn't done much damage. I tried to brush the snake off my leg and felt a hard lump of buckshot with my fingers, just below the skin behind my knee. I was lucky he didn't blow my leg clean off.

Then I wondered *if* I was still alive. I opened my eyes and couldn't tell if my eyes were open at all. The ghost lights were gone, the woods dark again, dark and lovely deep and miles to go before I sleep. I reached out my hand and groped blindly for the tree under which I lay and instead my fingers closed around a cool, strong hand.

"Get up, Jackie," a familiar voice whispered. His fingers tightened around mine and he pulled me to my feet. He guided me past trees I couldn't see but could feel with my outstretched hand, then past trees I thought I could see, dark vertical stripes against the greater darkness, and then there was the moon shining down through the branches well enough to see by, and at last the silver of the lake in the woods spreading out before me. He turned at the shore.

I stepped into the circle of his arms and nestled my cheek against his chest. I thought about Holly and how as a child she had run from the fire and hidden in these woods, maybe even by this same lake. "How did you escape the fire?" I said into his chest. "I waited for you. Where have you been?"

I felt him stiffen. "I didn't escape . . ." But it wasn't Deacon's voice that spoke. It was deeper voice, with a drawl slow and thick as cold molasses, uneducated but not ignorant. He felt thinner and taller, the muscles of his arms leaner, harder, strong enough to lift an eight-pound maul with just one hand and split a stick of green sweetgum with a single stroke.

". . . that far," he finished.

I pushed him away.

He leaned over me, tall, taller even than Deacon, black and featureless and two-dimensional, like a silhouette. "Roof sent me."

"You saved me from the fire."

"Yessum."

"You stole my car."

"Yessum."

"Why?"

"Roof sent me," he repeated, but his voice had grown distant, not in space but in time. A memory of a voice. A memory of hands on my body, of flesh against flesh and the memory of a moment of purity that consumed its fuel in one incandescent flash and was gone. Not even my memory. His memory and Ruth's memory.

I saw him move across the water with the trees limned like clouds in the moonlight behind him. Then he was no longer there. He didn't disappear. He was just gone, as though he had never been.

But Nathan was still out there.

50

I COULDN'T WALK ON water. I was still too tied to the world to let go entirely. So I swam, gliding out quietly on my back so I could watch the shore behind me. The water was arctic-cold. A summer of unseasonable heat had done nothing to warm it. My muscles stiffened around my bones and threatened to cramp from exhaustion, but the lake wasn't deeper than my shoulders at its deepest point.

Nathan appeared under the trees. I stopped and felt the sandy bottom under my feet, sank down until the water was just under my nose, then submerged as he lifted the shotgun to his shoulder. The report was like distant thunder heard under the covers. Pellets sleeted across the water above my head like a handful of gravel thrown by a sissy.

I kicked off and glided along the moon-striped bottom, a curious, nightmarish feeling of heavy flight through water clear as air or air thick as water, while load after impotent load of steel buckshot pocketed the surface and sank bubbling around me. I swam until it was too shallow to swim, then stood up and climbed out onto the bank, hidden by the shadow of the trees.

I lay in the leaves looking up at the dim stars, listening to Nathan thrash through the woods rather than make that swim. What had sounded before like incoherent roars of rage I now recognized as screams of frustration. "Go away! Leave me alone!" Every time he spoke, a ripple of taunting childish laughter spread through the woods. *Wire, briar, limber, lock.* He fired his shotgun into the darkened woods, but they continued to sing. *Three old geese in a flock. One flew east, one flew west, one flew over the cuckoo's nest.*

It would take him a while to circumnavigate the lake, time I badly needed to rest and ease my legs. I'd never felt so tired in my life. I shivered uncontrollably, my breath painfully cold in my nose, heart kicking like a mule so that my pulse shook the leaves. The cold spring water helped slow the flow of blood from my wounds. Slow, but not stop entirely. Even an idiot like Nathan could follow my trail, and in these woods he was no idiot.

I had to go on. I followed the bed of the dry creek, leading him away from the lake. I passed the stone where the slaves used to wash Marse Stirling's linens. My sopping clothes dripped where their sweat had fallen, my blood spattered the gravel where they had walked. I couldn't go home. Nathan would have to kill Jenny, too. He couldn't take any chances now. I'd have to stop him, or at the very least keep him busy until help arrived. If help arrived. I hoped someone would hear the shots and call the police, but out here in East Bumfuck, a few shots even in the dark of night might not rouse any interest.

I hoped Doris Dye was wearing her hearing aids.

I crossed under the log footbridge and continued down the creek another twenty yards, then climbed up the steep bank and doubled back. I crouched down at the end of the log among blackberry brambles and waited. I didn't think about dying. I was past dying. I just wanted one shot at him, the shot I was owed.

Nathan moved tactical-fashion up the creek bed, his Benelli M1014 combat 12-gauge in a constant state of readiness, the flashlight mounted under the barrel scanning every bush and twig. He'd spent some of his considerable money on some kind of urban-warfare course, probably in preparation for the race war he and his ilk asked Santa for Christmas every year. He was dressed in full camo with a black ski mask and black gloves, black combat boots crunching the gravel. Enough buck-shot slung on his bandolier to fight a small war in a third-world country. It must have been hot as Texas Dick's balls in that ski mask, but it probably kept the mosquitoes from suck-ing him dry.

He stopped just below the bridge and pointed the beam of his flash down at a splatter of my blood decorating a rock be-side his boot. "Cunt," he whispered, switched instantly back to ready position. "Got that cunt. Got her," he reassured himself nervously. He was so scared he could barely move, but one sound out of me and he'd swap my face for a fistful of steel. I was close enough to piss on his head, too close for him to miss this time.

A girl's voice said behind him, "What are you thinking

about?" He spun and I jumped. He must have heard the crack of wood as my weight left the log because he dropped the gun to his hip and let off a charge that smashed the log to splinters.

My knee snapped his collarbone as I rode him to the ground. He broke my fall nicely, soft as a pile of mattresses, but God must have been looking out for him because I'd been aiming to break his neck. I snatched his gun away and caved in his face with the butt. "Hello, sport," I said as I staggered to my feet. "How's it feel?"

"I'm sorry," he said through bloody teeth. "I'm sorry."

"You're sorry?"

"I'm so sorry."

The wail of sirens sounded through the trees and I heard the distant *thump-thump-thump* of an approaching helicopter. Sorry bastards, just when I didn't need their help. Now, I only had a couple of minutes to work. "You think you can say you're sorry and everything will be OK? Did you kill Sam?"

He dragged the ski mask off his head, screaming in agony as the splintered ends of his collarbone ground together. "I didn't! I swear, I never killed anybody in my life."

"Until now." His lips looked like hamburger, but his nose was still as straight as a catalogue model's. I bent it for him. He fell back in the gravel with a groan, his eyes rolling in his head. "Pal, you just killed a cop. I could dust you right here and Sheriff Stegall would shake my hand. Senator Mickelson himself would pin a medal to my tit."

"Please don't kill me," he sobbed. "I'm so sorry." He lay on his back, hands waving weakly in front of his face, waiting for the next blow.

I kicked his arms out of the way and ground my bare foot into his broken collarbone. When he screamed, I shoved the barrel past his last good tooth and said, "Suck on this." I pulled the trigger but the action was fouled with sand. I squeezed with everything I had left, but it wouldn't budge.

I flung the gun away. A spotlight hit the lake from above and began a grid-pattern search up the creek toward us, the bright beam shining weirdly through the trees. The wash from the chopper blades began to swirl up dust and leaves. Nathan blinked up at it, his mouth a gaping bloody hole in his face.

I said, "God's looking out for you, sport. A good-looking short-eyes like you, they'll love your cherry ass down on the farm. You'll be their favorite."

"Thank you," he wept. He grabbed my ankle and tried to kiss it. You'd have thought I just saved his life.

51

JENNY PICKED ME UP AT THE hospital. I didn't have
insurance so they didn't give me a room, just picked the
buckshot out of my ass and stitched up the holes that would
give my butt that desirable cellulite look despite my heroin
junkie body, and pushed me out the emergency room door.

As we pulled into the driveway, she noted with a sharp, dis-
gusted suck of her teeth the promiscuous ruin of her stately
home. "God, look at this place." The hedges surrounding the
property had grown huge and shaggy over the summer, some of
the ancient pecan trees were entirely barren of leaves, the flow-
erbeds hip-deep in weeds.

The June bugs were already up and whirring in the trees,
their noise the very voice of August itself, as though August
were a living thing composed of biscuit-colored dust and rain-
less moist heat and the mirage shimmering above the road. It
was not yet eight in the morning. She helped me to the door
even though I didn't need help, ducking under a rosebush gone
wild and running up the porch trellis almost to the second-
story windows.

She made me breakfast and I told her about Sam and Reece and Nathan, how Sam had hidden what Nathan had done to Reece, how he had taken Luther's money. I told her how Sam broke it off when he found out Nathan was sniffing around Cassie. I told her how I'd discovered the whole thing, from the photos in the suitcase to the website where Nathan sold patty-cake pictures of her daughters. I told her how Luther had tried to buy me off, and how I had refused, and what Luther had promised to do her, to us both.

Nathan's lawyer was already denying the whole thing. He claimed he'd shot Lorio by accident. Lorio had just got off work when he met me on the levee and he was still wearing his vest. It saved his life, and Nathan's, too, because if he had killed a cop, the State of Tennessee would have strapped him to a gurney no matter how many senators his daddy owned. I was happy Lorio survived. He held my hand in the emergency room, even though he looked like a mummy with his head wrapped in a couple hundred feet of bandages. He was a good Joe. Having him survive was the first really lucky thing that had happened to me in a long time. He'd woke up on the levee with his scalp hanging over his face like a bad wig, heard the shots in the woods, and radioed it in.

Nathan claimed that after he'd accidentally shot Lorio, I'd gone berserk and attacked him, and he'd only shot me in self-defense. If you ignored the fact that all my wounds were in my backside, it made perfect sense. A guy like Luther could probably find a lawyer and a judge who would rule my injuries inadmissible while using Nathan's to prove the savagery of my attack.

Stegall hadn't arrested me yet, but I knew it was only a matter of time before I was staring down the barrel of an attempted murder charge.

I honestly didn't give a flying fuck-all what they did to me. I was glad to be alive. Nathan was still lying in a hospital bed with his shoulder in a cast and eating his breakfast through a straw, while I was sitting by a pool dining on poached eggs and margaritas at nine o'clock in the morning. Best of all, Nathan's days of seducing teenage girls were over. I'd dropped his male-model looks into a wood chipper. His face was a bowl of moldy prunes. Maybe one day the doctors would be able to put it back together well enough to recognize him by his driver's license picture. If only that gun hadn't fouled, I could have solved both our troubles. Like they used to say in the old days, I'd have swung for it, and gladly.

Jenny listened to my tale to its unsatisfactory conclusion without saying a word. Then she got up and went inside and I didn't see her until three in the afternoon. I found her in the den, pulling on her stockings. A warm, moist wind billowed the curtains in the open window. Her white dress was border-line conservative—just a little high at the thigh, just a bit low and open at the breast, trimmed in black, with a fat double strand of pearls hanging around her neck.

"Where are you headed?" I asked. I was just going to make another pitcher of margaritas.

"I'm going to see Luther," she said.

I knew she was doing the right thing, but I still felt a little let down. She still had two kids to provide for. She knew that in this town, our chances of obtaining justice were in the house's favor. Nobody had died yet, and Luther's grasp upon the strings of power were as strong as ever.

I didn't want her to think I disapproved of her choice. "Do you want me to go with you?" I asked.

She smoothed the stocking on her leg. She had better legs than me, and she was going to need every inch of them. "I was hoping you would."

We found Luther propped up in bed, dressed in pale blue pajamas with half-dollar buttons, his foot wound in a huge white bandage, like a gout patient. Adonis the Butler let us in the room. Luther shooed his nurse out and invited us to sit. His bed had four posts wide enough to kick a football through, and a headboard like a library wall, shelves piled six deep with books, a couple of neat drawers in which to hide liquor bottles and porno magazines and whatever else an old retired preacher needed to keep him warm and safe on winter nights.

Jenny chose the love seat by the window, picked up a throw pillow and rested it in her lap, crossed her legs. I sat in a high-backed chair that was still warm from the nurse's ass.

"Nathan shot me," Luther explained, pointing at his bandaged foot, "when I tried to stop him from taking the gun. I'm so very sorry, Mrs. Lyons."

"Miss," I corrected habitually. "I'll survive. That's not why we're here."

"I see." He glanced at Jenny then back at me, his eyebrows a question mark. I nodded. "I see," he repeated.

"Jenny had a right to know," I said.

"Of course she does." He turned his patronizing smile upon her and repeated himself again. "Of course she does. She must make her own decisions regarding her family. As do we all."

"I just want to know one thing," Jenny said, forcing the words through the catch in her voice.

"Yes?"

She came up off the couch and flung the pillow at Luther. "How could you?" The pillow bounced off his foot, eliciting a choked sob of pain.

"Nathan is my son. I had to protect him."

"Reece was my daughter!" Jenny shrieked.

The nurse opened the door a crack and stuck her head through. "Everything OK, Brother Vardry?"

"I'm fine."

She closed the door. He mopped the sweat from his face with the sleeve of his blue pajamas. "Sam and I tried to take care of this delicate matter within our two families rather than draw in outsiders, people who wouldn't understand."

"*I* don't understand, Luther."

I picked up the pillow where it had fallen to the floor, in case Jenny got the crazy idea to murder him with it.

He eyed me nervously. "If there is a dispute between church members, the Bible tells us to settle it within the church. In his first letter to the Corinthians, the Apostle Paul says, 'If any of you has a dispute with another, dare he take it before the ungodly for judgment instead of before the saints?'"

That was his stock answer. I tossed the pillow in the air and caught it, but not before Luther had crawled halfway up the headboard. I pitched it to Jenny, then picked up his cell phone from where he'd left it on the covers. I'd noticed he was texting somebody when we came in the room. I thought maybe he'd been calling the police, but I noticed his last text was to Holly, telling her to stay in her room.

Jenny shouted, "This wasn't some theological dispute, Luther. Or a fight over parking spaces or loud parties or how often somebody mows their lawn. Nathan is a predator. He abuses little girls, my little girls!"

"If he were your son, wouldn't you try to protect him?"

"Not from this!"

"You can't understand," he said. "You're not one of us. You were never one of us, Jenny."

"Looks like you've raised yourself quite a pair of monsters, Mr. Vardry," I said. I'd heard the clatter of heels on the parquet outside his door. It opened. It wasn't the nurse this time.

"Daddy?"

"Holly!" Luther snapped. "I thought I told you . . ."

"Change of plans." I set his phone on the nightstand. "Come on in, Holly."

She slunk into the room and cringed up to his bed. I wondered if there were a time of day that she didn't wear heels. She probably even wore them to bed, but only for the right sort of people.

"Pair of monsters?" Jenny asked. She never missed a thing.

"Ask Luther," I said. He stared at me blankly, little dots of perspiration lined up like birds on the wire of his mustache. "If he won't tell you, ask Eugene Kitchen. Ask him who killed Sam."

"I thought . . ." She paused, looking from me to Luther to Holly. "Nathan?"

"Nathan's no killer." I turned so that only Holly could see my face, shot her a wink that made her ankles give under her. She wobbled on her heels and sank to Luther's bed, hugged one of the posts. "I shouldn't be standing here right now. As much as Nathan wanted me dead, he didn't have what it took to finish me off. I saw him, not five feet away, close his eyes when he pulled the trigger. He also shot low at Officer Lorio. And he hit you in the foot, Luther."

Luther began to laugh to hide his nerves. "You're not seriously suggesting that Eugene Kitchen killed Sam."

"Not at all. Just that he knows who did."

The man had no choice now but to brass it out. "And who, pray tell, is that?"

I walked to the window and looked out over the lake, at the roof of Jenny's house and the window of Reece's room, and the figure moving slowly across the levee, his hands in his jacket pockets, his head sunk to his chest. "The medical examiner in Memphis concluded that Sam was killed by two blows to the head from a blunt, rounded object."

"A rock." Luther reached across the bed and grabbed his phone from the nightstand. "That's exactly what our coroner ruled. I'm calling the police."

"Actually, two rocks," I said as he dialed. "And your local boy said Sam drowned. Memphis disagrees." The figure on the levee stopped and turned, waved to someone behind him and waited a moment.

"Two rocks, thrown from close range, by someone who

knew how to throw them." Luther stopped dialing, while the figure on the levee turned suddenly as though to run, but instead staggered forward. "Someone Sam knew closely and never suspected, someone he would wave to when she shouted his name, let her get close enough to kill him."

Jenny whispered, "Holly."

"What was it, Holly? What did you use? Maybe a couple of the river pebbles from Luther's Roman garden?" I watched Sam go headfirst into the lake and wondered if maybe he'd tried to escape to the safety of the water, like a man running from a swarm of bees.

Luther straightened the lapels of his pajamas and brushed the sweat from his lip. I was amazed by his effortless shift to a new strategy when his previous position became unviable. He was a man alone, an island unto himself, clinging to no one and nothing, not even his pride. He laid his phone on the bedspread.

"I'm glad you didn't call the police on my daughter. I'm sure you're aware that Holly is a bit unbalanced."

Holly groaned and bit the bedpost, scraped off twin gouges in the varnish with her teeth. She spit it out savagely. "If I am, it's because of you and Nathan and Gus and Meemaw. Y'all did this to me. Even Mama, because she never said anything. She just let Nathan do whatever he wanted. She wouldn't believe me when I told her, not after the fire."

"I think I can rely upon your discretion when I tell you that Holly set the fire that burned down my house and killed my two children." Luther spoke as though she wasn't even in the room. "It was an accident. She was burning herself with matches."

Holly slid off the bed to the floor and lay there, moaning and mewling.

"We'll have her committed, of course. Nathan will spend the rest of his life in prison, and the DA has decided not to charge Mrs. Lyons with attempted murder."

That was nice of him. I guess the DA was just waiting for Luther to make the call.

He continued coldly, "I can't make up for what my children have done, but I would like to try."

Jenny wasn't talking, wasn't moving. I couldn't even see her breathing. "How?" I asked.

He hid his smile behind a yawn, already writing the check in his mind. "The same deal as before, only better. I'll buy Sam's company for a substantial sum. Jenny will never have to work. I shouldn't have tried to cover for Nathan, but he was my son. What would you have done, Jenny, if it were your son?"

I answered for her. "That's just the thing, Luther. Nathan isn't your son. Holly isn't your daughter. They're adopted. Ruth told Deacon everything."

"I doubt she told him *everything*," Luther laughed. "Besides, they are my children even if they aren't my blood."

"They are your blood, Luther. You're Ruth's children, all three of you."

He slipped that punch with a shrug. "Son or brother, it doesn't matter. I had to protect Nathan."

"You've no idea the things they've done to me," Holly said

from the floor. She had dragged something out from under the bed—a long cardboard box. "And not just me. There are others. Dozens, hundreds. Gus and his girls. That hill is full of bones."

"Holly, be quiet. You're in enough trouble." Luther grabbed a pillow and rested it in his lap. "Don't make it worse."

"Worse! You son of a bitch. How could it possibly be worse?" She opened the box and pulled out another God-damn Benelli shotgun. This family had more money tied up in guns under the bed than I had in the world. I made a jump for her but she twisted aside and left me lying on my back at her feet. I glanced under the bed but I guess she'd taken the last ace.

"Sometimes I think I'm going crazy. Sometimes I have this corkscrew in my brain, turning around and around, getting tighter and tighter, so tight I can feel it pulling my hair, and I just want to take a gun and dig it out." She wedged the barrel under her chin.

"Holly no!" Jenny screamed. She was a better person than me. I'd just as soon Holly painted the ceiling as the floor.

"Don't worry, Jenny, I'm not going to do anything until I've made her pay for what she's done."

"What have I done, Holly?" I asked. There was nowhere to hide. I couldn't slide under the bed before she unloaded on me. She wouldn't pull her shot, like her brother.

"Nathan is in the hospital because of you, and he'll go to prison because of you, and Deacon is dead because of you." She noticed me gathering my feet and stepped back into a shooting stance, her cheek nestled against the stock, the bead nestled on my forehead. "I loved him, and he loved me, not you. Why did he want you? He wasn't supposed to die."

"Go on," I said. "You killed them all, didn't you? Every girl who got between you and Nathan. What about that one in the red one-piece, the girl in Jenny's pool? She stole him from you, didn't she, when Nathan owned that house? How old were you then? And that girl on the softball team, the one who disappeared."

"No," she whimpered.

"And Reece. What about her? Did you drown her in the pool, or was it in the lake?"

She lowered the shotgun a hair and glanced at Jenny, her lips trembling. "I'm so sorry." Sorry, again. This family.

"What did you do to Reece, Holly?" Jenny asked.

"Reece was my best friend in the whole world!" Holly burst out hysterically. "She used to sneak out at night and we'd go swimming in the lake. But that night, she was already in the water, her and Nathan, and they were naked and he said he loved her. I don't know what happened. It's like it wasn't even me doing it. But it was my hands on her ankles, pulling her down."

"Oh Holly."

"By the time I knew what I was doing, it was too late."

"Oh God." Jenny staggered as though hit by one of Holly's rocks. Holly dropped the gun and ran to catch her. An explosion close by my head stunned me. I thought the shotgun had gone off when she dropped it. Jenny was screaming and something heavy tumbled to the floor. The door burst open and I heard a noise like somebody stepping on a cat.

I stood up, ready for almost anything.

Almost.

Holly lay on the floor at the end of the bed, Luther's nurse stooped over her trying to hold in the blood and brains leaking from a grapefruit-sized hole in the side of her pretty head. Luther sat with a long-barreled .44 revolver smoking between his fat fists. He'd taken it from one of the drawers in his headboard. His eyes were as dark and empty as the end of that barrel. He laid it on the bedspread as casually as if it were a book he'd tired of reading.

"I thought she was going to kill Jenny," he said.

I scooped up the shotgun and gave Luther the old John Wayne treatment, right across the kisser. He snapped back into the pillows with a surprised look, then folded forward on the bed.

Like father, like son.

Or brother.

52

*There are many things in this
world that a child must not ask
about.*
— NATHANIEL HAWTHORNE,
THE SCARLET LETTER

THE NEXT WEEK I BOUGHT A LITTLE place on the
South Bluff in Memphis, barely enough room for me,
my ghosts and nine or ten guests, but it was home. All that
country air was starting to choke me, and I was getting a
bad habit of busting men named Vardry across the face. I
worried I might run out of them just when I was starting to
enjoy it.

There wasn't much left to do but dig up the bodies. I pieced
most of the story together by talking to Virginia Vardry. Freed

of her shrubbery, she was a remarkable conversationalist. She was neither dull nor stupid, just deathly afraid of the monster she'd married and the monstrous children he'd forced upon her.

Nathan's first conquest had been his sister Holly, age eleven. He'd gotten her pregnant when she was thirteen. "Jesus," Virginia said of my apparent shock at this news. "Don't look so surprised. Incest runs in the family." We met over Cosmos at Blue Fin and she had just ordered her third.

"I didn't think Ruth was Gus's true daughter."

She popped a maraschino cherry in her mouth and rolled it around her tongue. "No doubt Ruth told you she had no memory of her mother. That was one of her pretty little lies. She told me once about the day she first met Luther's grandfather. I use that term loosely. They don't have names for the kind of relationships they had in that family."

The waiter brought our drinks. Virginia ordered another before she'd taken the first sip of the new one. I suppose she was trying to make up for all those years she'd wasted being a good Baptist. "Ruth was maybe four years old—she would change the story every time she told it. Four or five or six or seven. The thing is, she was the prettiest little thing Grandpappy Gus— he hated it when Luther called him Grandpappy—had ever clapped eyes on. Maybe you've seen pictures of her?"

I didn't answer and she didn't wait for my response. "Her mama was one of Gus's working women, though I also use the term 'woman' loosely—she was just a child herself. She hoped that by convincing Gus that Ruth was his daughter, he would marry her. Instead, he took Ruth and left her mama to her work. Ruth saw her mother quite often—the old woman was still living around here somewhere when Luther and I got married. Ruth preferred living with Gus to sleeping on cases of whiskey in the back rooms of his joints, watching her mother service the poor tenant farmers and railroad workers and small-town hoodlums who blew through the door and emptied their pockets into the Stirling bank account."

She lifted her glass in toast. "To the Stirling bank account." I joined her. We were each in our own way still profiting off the nameless child whore who traded her daughter for a handful of magic beans. Virginia had served Luther with divorce papers in his hospital bed, right after a letter arrived from the Baptist leadership requesting that His Reverence take an extended sabbatical from his semiretirement. I found a key— the key to Ruth's safe-deposit box at the bank—while I was going through my stuff back at Jenny's house, getting ready to move out. I had forgotten to return it, and she hadn't asked for it back. She also said Luther didn't know about the safe-deposit box. And that I should take whatever I wanted. That's how I remembered it, anyway.

Virginia sucked her drink to the bottom and spit the lemon twist into the empty glass. "Gus Stirling raised Ruth up to be his lover, which she remained to the end of his days. Holly and Nathan are his children."

"What about Luther?"

"What do you know about John Vardry?"

"Nothing, really. Ruth barely mentioned him."

"Did you know that Augustus Stirling once lynched a black man named Lonnie Jackson? Hung him from a tree up on that hill in the woods."

Up on yonder gallows hill. That was a line from Holly's jump-rope song. *Where my father's bones do dwell.*

"Ruth's Lonnie?" I asked.

"That's him."

"Ruth said he was a sharecropper. She never mentioned he was black."

"It was a terrible scandal. Not the lynching, nor even the affair. Gus was, by that time, a respectable planter, even though he still had his hand in any number of illicit activities. But he was a Stirling, which meant he was respectable and could be forgiven for taking the law into his own hands, so long as he was discreet. This hanging was not discreet. It was downright appalling, even to people used to seeing men lynched. They strung him up by his hands and lit a fire under his feet."

"Jesus!"

"Even so, no white man had ever been arrested for lynching a black man in Fayette County, or to my knowledge anywhere. But there was a hot shot new sheriff in Fayette County, a man elected to clean out the juke joints and whorehouses and gambling halls. With this lynching, he saw an opportunity to bring down Boss Stirling, even if no jury in the state would convict him of murder. Gus was arrested, and that was the scandal."

"That sheriff," I said. "His name wouldn't be John Vardry, would it?"

She patted my hand and winked. "The Vardrys were a cadet branch of the Stirlings, descended from one of old Albert Stirling's daughters. To settle the case, Gus married, or more likely sold Ruth to Sheriff Vardry. There are some who believe she was carrying the black man's child on the day of her nuptials, but you've seen Luther, so you can decide for yourself whether that's true. I don't believe it is. Whatever the truth is, barely eight months later she gave birth to Luther. John Vardry turned in his badge and joined the army. He was killed in North Africa fighting Rommel."

Virginia was enjoying this, and not just the vodka. Like Holly, she was setting fire to the source of her pain and dancing around the flames. "Gus, he loved girls, the younger the better. You know what he used to say to me, when he'd sit there with Holly on his bony lap? He'd say, 'Seven is heaven, eight is great, nine is fine, ten ain't no sin, but eleven is heaven all over again.' But Ruth was *his girl*, the one he could never quit. And she couldn't quit him, not even after he was dead. Does that shock you?"

"Nothing about this family shocks me anymore," I said.

"Why do you suppose Luther forced her to move into the nursing home? It wasn't for her health. Ruth couldn't quit Gus. She went down to that crypt and I don't know how she did it but she pried the lid off and carried his bones back up to the house. Sam Loftin found her lying on the floor with them and called Luther."

I had liked Ruth. I couldn't imagine her doing anything of the sort. Maybe Virginia was inventing stories out of spite, but I didn't credit her with that much imagination. I changed the subject back to Nathan and Holly. She warmed to that, especially after the waiter brought her fourth Cosmo. "I think I've had enough of these," she said. "Bring me something different."

I had already found Nathan's website where he posted the photos of the girls. A monthly subscription cost $19.99, with over a thousand subscribers, giving him almost $20,000 a month in income, of which he paid out less than a tithe in maintenance and web hosting. No wonder he never had to drive one of his popsicle trucks. His internet operation had never been large enough to attract the attention of the feds, and even if it had, nothing on his site was illegal.

It was just vile. Monstrous, like everything else about this family, even Virginia Vardry, in her way. She was Luther's third cousin and fifteen years his junior (though she didn't look it), fiercely devout, and completely in awe of him when they first met. They'd agreed before the marriage to live a chaste life together, priest and nun, and to raise a family of adopted children. Back then she couldn't imagine a better life, in service of the Lord.

Nathan's private collection was another matter altogether. It didn't take Sheriff Stegall's techs long to crack Nastyboy's hard drives.

Like his sister Holly, Nathan was nothing if not damned good-looking. With his money and his connections—he was a youth pastor at Luther's church—it was easy for him to get close to these girls and their families. Pretty soon, he would convince their parents to let him meet up for private photo shoots, or failing that, take them on rides on his boat or in his truck, where he'd slowly talk them out of their clothes. A few girls, like Reece, had fallen hard for him, hard enough to give him everything he wanted.

But he'd perfected his techniques on his sister before setting his sights on fresh game. After Holly got pregnant, Nathan brought her to Memphis and paid a bankrupt dry cleaner of an abortionist fifteen dollars to pump her full of naphtha and fish the fetus out of her womb with a coat hanger and a pair of salad tongs. He couldn't take her to a real doctor, not at her age. She'd have blabbed everything.

"After that, Nathan wouldn't have anything to do with Holly," Virginia said.

"Then the fire . . ." I offered.

She played with the lemon twist in her glass for a moment. "Nathan was supposed to be home that night, but he'd gone out with his new girlfriend. Holly was jealous, burned herself with matches and accidentally set the fire. But instead of saving those babies, she watched the fire burn until it set her clothes on fire. Then she ran down to the woods and hid until she got hungry."

The day after Luther murdered his daughter to keep her from talking, Jenny brought in a brickmason to take the fireplace apart. In a compartment behind the firebox he found a red one-piece bathing suit, a skull and an old popsicle box full of small bones. They had cut off her hands and head, so that if her body ever surfaced, she couldn't be identified. Her body never did surface, but they were able to make an ID based on dental records. Turns out she was just one of a half-dozen neighborhood girls, ages eleven to fifteen, who had disappeared or died over the years. After he helped his sister cut up the body and bury the best parts in the fireplace, Nathan sold the house to Sam and Jenny and moved to a bigger estate across the lake.

As I bought Virginia Vardry her fifth martini, I thought how even six dead girls couldn't account for all the children haunting Ruth's woods.

. . . And One More Thing

I WAS BEGINNING TO WONDER if any of this really happened. I was beginning to wonder if Deacon had been a real man and not some revenant or avenging angel sent down to Shitkicker, Tennessee, to end the line of Stirling and Vardry both. They never found his remains, and not even Fire Marshal Mertz believed the house had burned hot enough to destroy bones, much less teeth. Sometimes at night I imagined him escaping, leaping through a door as the house came crashing down, running through the woods with his hair on fire, diving into Spring Lake to be rejuvenated by its healing waters. He might be lying there still, his body clad in glistening samite, waiting for some king to come and take his Lost Gospel and spread it at the point of a sword.

Nights were hardest for me.

Nights were when I thought about how Stegall never charged Luther in the death of his daughter. How Nathan pled out for the attempted murder of Officer Lorio and got a sentence of fifteen years in a minimum-security prison. He'd be out in five. There was no investigation into Sam's death, or

Reece's, or the deaths or disappearances of any of the other girls. They were all stamped *Closed,* Holly Vardry listed as the perp, and the files placed in storage for eventual loss or accidental destruction.

With Sam's death finally ruled a murder, Jenny was awarded his life insurance settlement. She sold the house and moved to Arlington. Eugene Kitchen bought her house at her asking price, which was twice what it was worth. I suspected, as did she, that the money came from Luther. He had paid her off anyway.

It was early September and it still hadn't rained but the weatherman was predicting showers any day now. It was cloudy when I woke up, overcast as I stood on my patio watching the river ooze between its sandy and shrunken banks. Thunder from a storm over Arkansas nearly drowned out Sheriff Stegall's voice when he called and asked me to stop by. I took it as a sign and agreed to see him.

I expected more questions. Instead, I got a ride in his paramilitary recreational vehicle.

We pulled up in the field where Deacon had planned to build his church. There was a road now, with fresh white curbs, and flagged stakes marking off the lots of the newest expansion of Stirling Plantation. Jenny's street had been extended and connected through, and they were already pouring concrete slabs for new houses. Ruth's woods were bulldozed, though there were still a few trees sticking up here and there, looking naked and raped. Spring Lake was just a mudhole at the bottom of the hill, and bulldozers were shoving more dirt into it as I stepped out of the RV.

There was nothing left of the house, not a single brick, not even a pile of ash and cinders, just a hole in the ground that used to be the cellar. If not for this, I wouldn't have known where the house stood at all. Stegall led me to the edge, where a large round stone hung by a strap from the bucket of a backhoe. "Workers were clearing this away when they found it."

"What is that?" It looked more dirt than stone.

"An old millstone."

An older man with a thin beard and a couple of rough-looking college girls were working in the cellar, peeling back the dirt with trowels and paintbrushes. "Archaeologists," he explained. "See, when they moved the millstone, they found a well."

I felt a cold finger touch the base of my spine. It wasn't Stegall. It was Goober Trey, the call-before-you-dig man, who had predicted, three months and a lifetime ago, that we would find a well in the cellar.

"The well was full of bones," Stegall said.